Clinton Smith has spent much of his life writing advertising material, documentaries and fiction. His commercials have won thirty Australian and international awards, his short stories and screenplays ten more. His shoots have taken him to many countries and people as diverse as Edward de Bono and Ronnie Barker have fronted his campaigns. For twenty years, he wrote the classic King Gee workwear campaign that featured the slogan 'If they were any tougher, they'd rust'. He became a partner in his own agency then retired to write thrillers. His books are extensively researched using his military contacts, and the first two have been optioned for film.

Also by Clinton Smith

THE FOURTH EYE

THE GODGAME

EXIT ALPHA

DEEP SIX

CLINTON SMITH

HarperCollinsPublishers

HarperCollins_Publishers_

First published in Australia in 2004
This edition published in 2005
by HarperCollins_Publishers_ Australia Pty Limited
ABN 36 009 913 517
www.harpercollins.com.au

Copyright © Clinton Smith 2004

The right of Clinton Smith to be identified as the author of this
work has been asserted by him under the _Copyright Amendment
(Moral Rights) Act 2000._

This work is copyright. Apart from any use as permitted under the
Copyright Act 1968, no part may be reproduced, copied, scanned, stored
in a retrieval system, recorded, or transmitted, in any form or by any
means, without the prior written permission of the publisher.

HarperCollins_Publishers_
25 Ryde Road, Pymble, Sydney, NSW 2073, Australia
31 View Road, Glenfield, Auckland 10, New Zealand
77–85 Fulham Palace Road, London W6 8JB, United Kingdom
2 Bloor Street East, 20th floor, Toronto, Ontario, M4W 1A8, Canada
10 East 53rd Street, New York NY 10022, USA

National Library of Australia Cataloguing-in-Publication data:

Smith, Clinton, 1938– .
   Deep six.
   ISBN 0 7322 8071 0.
   I. Title.
A823.2

Cover design by Anthony Vandenberg, Mayfly Graphics
Cover image (plane) courtesy Newspix; (fire) courtesy Corbis and
Australian Picture Library
Typeset in 10 on 12pt Sabon by Kirby Jones
Printed and bound in Australia by Griffin Press on 50gsm Bulky News

5 4 3 2 1   05 06 07 08

for Gerry Harris

Contents

1

INCURSION

It wasn't the regular flight from Katmandu. It wasn't the regular flight from anywhere.

Blake gazed through the aircraft's window at the vastness of the Himalayas — at Everest's death zone soaring from a sea of cloud. Its north face, he knew, was littered with ripped tents, bodies, rubbish. The human plague had contaminated even this.

He turned from the snow-glare to the man across the aisle — a hard-arse with tattooed hands. The five other men and the woman in the cabin wore expensive hiker's boots and clothes but had the nails-for-breakfast toughness of a special-forces squad.

Six combat-scarred vets disguised as tourists in a business jet stuffed with weapons — sub-machine-guns with snap-on grenade launchers, night-vision goggles, laser aimers, field radios, ammo boxes and the black-plastic cylinder holding the SAM.

In this cocoon above the roof of the world he felt suspended in time. Colin Blake, warrior's apprentice. How things had changed. He'd been Colin Blake, photographer — the wary man who never got involved, the smug successful trendoid who slept with models and drove expensive cars. But when Kate drew him into her crusade, that Blake had officially died. Six months later, she'd left on another mission. And would he ever see her again? Christ, she could be dead.

The runway at Paro neatly fitted the valley floor. The Astra SPX approached from the west, circled once, landed sweetly. The DEMI squad shrugged on parkas, exchanged the cabin's warmth for mountain air.

Bhutan looked a spectacular country. But what the hell were they doing? After two years with this outfit, all he knew about an assignment was that it could kill him.

2

BRADEN

Charles Braden, Colonel USAF (Rtd), chairman of Braden Aerospace, was sixty.

His secretary, Connie, the same age, managed without contrivance to resemble a woman twenty years younger who'd just stepped off a twelve-hour flight. She'd pleased him in bed for fifteen years, unflappably supported him at work, was used to handling powerful men, but her voice quavered as she buzzed him. 'I think it's a hoax, but it could be the President.'

'Soon tell you. Put him through.'

A click.

'Braden here.'

'Hello, bastard.'

'Dougie? Jeez, you gave my girl a stroke.'

'She wouldn't connect me. I get that a lot. Then the penny drops and it's God Bless America. See how people need something to believe in? Now listen. I need your butt over here.'

'Don't tell me the Commander in Chief's after some washed-up gunship pilot?'

'Affirmative. Your country calls. But I can't go into details on this line. I'll send someone to set it up. You owe me one, remember?'

He did.

He'd dragged President Douglas Jessop to the Spectre Association reunion, insisting that he postpone an important meeting in Mexico to attend. The retired air force men who'd come to relive their days in USAF C–130 gunships had no idea he'd conned the most famous of them along, although they possibly wondered why the street was half blocked off. What a night!

'And Chuck, forget the company jet. I'd like you to fly the bird here. My press secretary needs you high-profile. Media circus is part of the plot.'

'They'll say I'm angling for the ATGM contract.'

'I'll hose that down. So — look forward to it. Gotta go, good buddy. Bye.'

Braden replaced the handset slowly, dismayed to find he felt flattered. He'd thought he was past that crap. It was just Dougie after all.

His secretary burst in, red-faced. 'Was it . . . him?'

'Yup.'

She slumped against the doorframe, hand to the elegant slope of her breast. 'Oh-my-Godddd.'

'What on earth did you say to him, Connie?'

'Don't even go there.'

Braden watched her trim rear as she left, wondering what the call meant. He was at the top of the food chain, but this wasn't about campaign funds. An aerospace query? Unlikely. There were better sources of information.

What had Truman said? 'If you want a friend in Washington, get a dog.'

Jessop was in a bind. Needed a buddy.

For what?

3

BHUTAN

The traditional Dzong design of the terminal enhanced the wooded hills. It was the first airport Blake had seen that blended with its surroundings. He watched their dubious luggage being loaded on a trolley, asked Henri, the man beside him, 'How do we get the gear through customs?'

'Special weapons exemption.'

Their breath fogged the bitter air.

'They'll let the SAM through?'

'Like shit through a goose.' The Frenchman was hoarse with flu. 'Ko's Bhutanese.'

DEMI was a privately funded force that opposed the manipulation of information by power blocs. And Ko was not only its head but also had unusual abilities. If Ko were Bhutanese, he thought, Bhutan was their oyster.

They walked over glaring concrete to the arrival hall. Large space, ornate decorations — the aura of a medieval church. This sparsely populated kingdom saw perhaps two flights a day. Their fake passports were stamped, their luggage wheeled in.

Blake collected his share of baggage and trudged toward the waiting minivans. The few people outside the terminal were a contrast to the inquisitive crowds at Dacca. He noticed a European in a car near the end of the long building. He'd seen him before.

Where?

The Clare Valley, South Australia, the Tuesday morning he'd first met Kate. The scene replayed in detail. Not like a memory. Overwhelmingly. Sounds, gestures, expressions — a window on the living past: thickset men holding carbines. Menacing and droll.

As they drove past fertile fields at the base of cloud-backed hills, he searched his mind's archive for more. No. He hadn't seen the man again.

His eidetic memory, the reason why DEMI wanted him on missions, registered everything instantly, exactly. Faces, pictures, events, scenes, news articles, names, conversations . . . The photographic recall had proved more effective than a weapon. But there was a downside. He couldn't forget. An abundance of detritus was his bane.

THE HAPLESS NORFOLK VICAR OF STIFFKEY, DEFROCKED IN OCTOBER 1932 FOR ALLEGED SEXUAL MISCONDUCT, MADE A CAREER SWITCH TO LION-TAMING AND WAS PROMPTLY MAULED TO DEATH.

SPITFIRES, MASS PRODUCED DURING THE WAR, WERE MADE TO LAST ONLY 30 TO 50 HOURS IN THE AIR.

DIOGENES WAS A FORGER, PYTHAGORAS A WRESTLER.

CAMELS STORE FATTY ACIDS, NOT WATER, IN THEIR HUMPS.

They were crossing a pristine valley on a narrow empty road. Long prayer flags fluttered from poles.

He nudged Simpson, the squad leader. 'We could be sprung.'

'Come again?'

'There was a man at the airport. I've seen him before.'

The others glanced at him uneasily. They regarded him as a freak.

'What outfit?' Simpson grunted. 'I'm not getting the full signal here.'

'He was one of Doyle's men. Before the Blitz.'

'We retired that lot. Or uninstalled them.'

'He had the same face.'

'Bloody hell.' The squad leader, a scarred British giant with one ear, scratched his stubble with a spatulate hand.

'Do we know what we're doing here?' Blake asked.

'As of now, watching our bums.'

In ten minutes they reached Paro's quaint and spotless main street. Blake's cameraman's eye took it in, automatically framing shots. Strollers in traditional hitched-up tunics. People seated outside shop-fronts. Small succulent street plants. Saffron-robed monks. He'd read up on the country, could quote its primary exports, geology, educational policy, draw a perfect map with every name and feature.

Five children were playing in the street — two sober, three naughty. The open beauty in their faces told him he didn't know Bhutan at all.

Beyond the one-street town was a mosaic of subsistence holdings. The rural wood and rough stone houses had spaces beneath for animals, open lofts reached by ladders and shingles anchored by rocks.

The flatland changed to hills with terraced farms nestling on the slopes.

Henri nudged him, 'Hey, cobber.' He'd got the term from Simpson. Blake was the only Australian on the team. He pointed to vegetables spread on roofs to dry. 'What are those . . . ?'

'Chillies. A staple diet here. They're Buddhists. Can't kill animals so they import Muslims to butcher yaks.'

'And why rocks on the roofs?'

'Wind. Big venturi effect in these hills.'

They drove for half an hour, sometimes beside a swift-flowing river, and stopped at a stone building with painted woodwork and elevated roof.

A woman walked down steps from the wooden porch. Narrow hips, strong limbs and sleek muscles her skin barely seemed to cover. Strong cheekbones, delicate mouth, the eyes of a war-conditioned youth.

Oh, Christ! Oh, Christ!

His heart almost came through his ribs.

Surprise rippled through the squad.

Simpson grunted, 'Score one for Blake.'

Kate! Here?

He stumbled from the van almost in tears.

The squad leader went ahead to greet the striking woman who was also his commander. He snapped out a brisk, 'Morning, ma'am.'

'Simpson. Been a while.'

'Didn't expect to see *you* here. Must be a big deal op?'

'I've no idea. I was just ordered here, like you. Dump your gear beside the house. We're packing it on ponies.'

'Right.'

Then she was in front of him, outwardly impassive as always. The strange empty eyes. But he saw the tremble at her lip. And when he dropped the duffel bags she hugged him back and kissed him. The squad cheered — thrilled to find that the legendary woman had feelings.

He gasped, 'Didn't know if you were alive. God, I've missed you so much.'

She held him off gently to look at him. Her hand touched his cheek. 'Missed you, too.'

He hoped it was true. He never knew what she felt. It was hard loving someone you couldn't understand.

'Come on.' She hefted a bag. 'Reunions later. Business now.'

Stunned by the pain of separation the meeting had recalled, swamped by the release of being with her, of knowing she was safe, he tried to pick up his gear but fumbled like a dolt.

She looked back at him and smiled.

He followed her to the building in a daze.

4

WHITE HOUSE

Two hours after the call from the White House, Braden was visited by a major in civvies who explained arrangements. 'And we'd like you to stay in your flying suit. It's to do with media perception.'

'Front the White House in a green tuxedo?'

'Protocol's in meltdown but it's the President's specific request. Would you care for a VIP tour prior to the appointment?'

'I'm not into tours.'

He owned the ancient AC–130A Gunship 2, maintained it, paid its crew, provided it to air-shows gratis. That was what too much money was for. The thing was his hobby, his obsession, but he'd never flown it to Washington. He left it parked where the tower at Andrews Air Force Base directed and, as the ramp went down, was confronted by the welcoming committee — aides, security staff, government limo, camera crew . . .

He was joined in the car's plush interior by two plain-clothes men and a naval attaché in full dress gear. The joy of secure junkets like this was checking in your babysitters. Dropping the retinue of wealth was like shucking off a heavy coat.

Of course, his bodyguards, Buick and Stick, had wanted to see the West Wing. Buick had told him the White House grounds had multiple security devices, that the doorframes were metal detectors and the Oval Office windows had 3-inch-thick bulletproof glass. What was it about the presidency that created such slavish veneration? Connie having vapours . . . his own appalling reaction . . . even the emotionless Stick had sulked when told he couldn't go.

Hell! It was just Dougie after all.

They'd been scared, exhausted pilots clinging to bar girls for comfort in the humid oven of Cambodia. Now his flying-mate lived in the White House and flew in Air Force One . . . !

Credentials were checked at the northwest gate and they glided past intricate flowerbeds. After more rigmarole with duty agents and identity badges, there was an unexpected photographic session. Then he was escorted along a corridor swarming with aides.

Finally, the President's private secretary ushered him into the sanctum sanctorum of his country. A stage-set of course — the oval shape, the pediments over the doors, the flags, the desk, the man framed by the light from huge end windows . . .

A lump formed in his throat which he considered legitimate enough. 'Jeez, how can you sit in here and still feel you're human?'

'It's not easy.' Jessop rose. 'No wonder this fishbowl's seen so many dysfunctional families.' He stretched tiredly, fists near his neck. 'They say power corrupts. It also makes you stupid. It's too easy, in this building, to believe your press releases.' He came around the desk, a big man with unmanageable hair.

Hair was important in this job, Braden thought. Hair you could part. After they pumped hands he punched his friend gently. 'How come you still have hair and I don't?'

'How come a runt like you ends up a squillionaire who flies his personal gunship to Washington? And I'm stuck on a fixed salary, getting fed lies?'

'You did it to yourself, pushy bastard. And *you* ordered the bird.'

The President gripped him by the shoulders. 'You can't imagine how good it is to see a friendly face in here.'

Braden looked down, fighting his feelings. It wasn't a smart move. The brilliant-blue oval rug that dominated the room had gold stars around the perimeter and an American eagle in the centre. 'Christ, this room breaks me up.'

'Me too.' Jessop gently steered him to the couches near the fire where they sat grinning at each other like good-natured dogs.

Braden said, 'Some rug.'

'You bet. Nixon had it in here. Then it was stored for years — considered too over the top — but I got 'em to put it back. They call us rednecks, Chuck. Well, screw 'em is what I say.'

He agreed. They were hawks at heart, unsettled by the new way of the world. 'So, despite all this crap, you're still relatively sane?'

'My motto is: never hold the head too high or too low. And there's a prayer I like a lot. "Lord, grant me something only after I've ceased to care." Perspective implies distance, wouldn't you say?'

'Agree.'

'A moneybags like you?'

'Things are a pest. Got to dust 'em, insure 'em. Things just take you so far.'

The other slowly nodded. 'You're a good man, Chuck.'

Braden shrugged.

A ticking clock emphasised the silence.

'So how pushed is the boss of Braden Aerospace?' The President's friendly eyes probed.

'Got a great team. Leave it to them pretty much. I'm semi-retired, you could say.'

'That's good. Because I need you.'

'Stop mounting my leg. What's this about?'

'Wish I knew. Tell me, how cosy are you with the Department of Defense?'

'We make satellites. We have contacts.'

'Specifics . . . ?'

'I have people to brown-nose and hustle. I'm the public face now, smoother-groover.'

'But you still have buddies.'

'A few guys in NORAD, the NRO, the CIO.'

'I know NORAD. The others?'

'National Reconnaissance Office. The Central Imagery Office. NASA of course. NOAA. That's the oceanic and atmospheric side.'

'What about the intelligence community? All those spooks one-upping each other. The CIA, NSA, DIA . . .'

Jessop, Braden noted, knew his intelligence acronyms at least. 'We talk to some NSA scientists but the place is a clam. Got contacts in the DIA and the service intelligence directorates. I'm cosy with a senator or two in the Defense Appropriations Sub-committee and the Armed Services Committee. But you don't have to remember that.'

'So you're pretty much plugged in?'

'Get by.'

'Exactly what I need.' Jessop got up and walked the fair distance back to his desk. He picked up leather-bound folders, returned and handed them across. 'The *National Intelligence Daily*. The President's Daily Brief. Stuff from the State Department. It's what I get.'

Braden thumbed the documents.

'There's the Situation Room downstairs,' Jessop went on, 'and the Security Council with the various regional and functional directorates. There used to be a National Security Adviser who handled that CIA smart-arse, Stone. She discussed the PDB with him and brought it into me later. About all she did. I canned her.'

Some on the Hill, Braden knew, were surprised that the Director of the CIA hadn't gone with the change of administration. 'How come you kept Stone?'

'He does a good job as far as I know. And like and dislike are crap. But I don't want to see his dismal face straight after breakfast.'

'So what are you trying to tell me?'

'Right.' Jessop breathed out slowly. 'There are effectively two executives here. One handles mainstream politics. That's my thing. Do what you do best — subcontract the rest. The other shadier side handles dirty tricks. And most presidents don't have the time, interest or background to tackle that end. Which is what they count on.'

'Who's "they"? The Special Group?'

'They don't call it that now. And it's economical with the truth. Or there are things it's just not telling me. Some major security decisions don't come near this room. The NSC's mostly show. And I'm an inquisitive bastard. You read me?'

Braden nodded and scratched his belly.

'Now, I hear things from people. People with information but no clout. I guess you've read about an outfit called DEMI? They're a privately financed bunch — a kind of Greenpeace with guns. Multinational, efficient . . .'

'They exposed the oil cartel.'

'Right. Well, someone close to them recently told me that our top brass is condoning certain highly questionable projects that no decent country should touch.'

'What projects?'

'I don't know. But I want to. And that's where you come in.'

5

TREK

Barely an hour after reaching the house, the DEMI squad moved out. They were accompanied by five locals, an English-speaking guide and four men to tend the laden ponies, to set up camp and cook.

The track followed the valley then wound through wooded lower slopes. Kate, supremely fit, walked uphill as if strolling on the flat. Blake longed to hold her hand but resisted. She was commander here.

They passed a roofed stone shrine sheltering huge turning prayer wheels. They were powered by water-wheels in a covered stream below. As the wood gave way to pasture he constantly checked the terrain, comparing the matrix of each sweep against the last. His peculiar mind made it possible to spot an added shadow from a boulder or a suddenly appearing glint. But there was no sign of surveillance or pursuit.

The temperature fell. The track became pressed-down grass. Higher still, they crunched in single file on rubble. By nightfall they were in a saddle between precipitous lower mountain slopes. Their guide called a halt near an outcrop of stones by a stream.

Snow-clad mountains beyond made the place beautiful. And cold.

The donkey-sized Bhutanese ponies were unloaded near the windbreak, given nosebags and tethered to each other. The Dzongkha-speaking Bhutanese pitched two-man tents. They built a fire, placed folding chairs around a trestle table and cooked rice, potato and chilli into sweet-smelling curry.

He helped Kate lug her gear to their tent. 'Great view. But what are we doing here?'

'I honestly don't know.' She found some soap and a flannel and walked toward the stream.

He rubbed tired muscles that had stiffened his legs to stilts, crawled into the tent and spread self-inflating bed-rolls in it. He rezipped two sleeping bags into a double, went back to the squad and helped unpack.

Simpson lifted out an uncooled thermal viewer. 'First rule,' he grumbled, 'is remain inconspicuous, avoid trails and smells. So we march straight up the track, put up red tents and cook curry. Bloody hell. Might as well send up flares.'

'It works both ways,' the Frenchman said. 'All afternoon, we have total field-of-view. If they follow us, we see them.' He sneezed, turned his back to the snow-chilled wind, pointed down the way they had come. 'No road or cover. *Merde*. To attack here they need a Wiesel or Black Hawk.'

Simpson adjusted the viewer, grumbling. 'I'd feel safer with a Rasit 3109–B, UGS and tripflares. Can't secure this spot with what we got.'

Blake helped Conchita, the Brazilian woman, tape magazines together.

Kate came back. 'Problems?'

'We're sitting ducks here, ma'am,' Simpson said. 'Wide open to attack.'

'We're supposed to be tourists.'

'But if they're watching us?' He turned to Blake. 'You tell her?'

'I saw a face at the airport,' he explained. 'One of Doyle's men. So he could be CIA.'

'Is the CIA trying to nobble us,' Simpson asked, 'or what?'

She gazed at the bare hills near them as if debating whether to answer. 'As far as I know, we've knocked out the moles in the Company.'

One of the Ngalops walked within earshot. Simpson checked the goggles, waiting until he'd gone. 'Well, if we're up against the CIA, we've picked the wrong way to enter this country. Wrong approach, wrong methods, wrong equipment. Can we know our next objective?'

'To reconnoitre with others. A two-day march.'

'Ma'am, you know what Patton said?'

Kate raised a delicate brow.

'An average plan now is better than an excellent plan in a few hours.'

'What's wrong with an excellent plan now? That's what we have if the contact was neutral. As you say, there's no cover. So we go on being tourists.'

Unusually sober ones, Blake thought. With weapons.

The squad leader scratched his thick neck. 'Still don't like it.'

She shrugged. 'I know the rendezvous. But I'll leave getting there to you.'

Simpson barked to the others, 'Right. We do stand-to checks, establish arcs, put sentries on two-hour shifts.'

Kate stared at a darkening slope.

Simpson turned back to her, frowning, 'So you reckon this geezer Blake spotted could be a neutral observer?'

She shrugged. 'I don't know. Things have moved. Corporations run governments and we could have compromised a Pentagon sweetheart deal. If we have, we won't know till they hit us.'

'Jesus,' one man muttered. 'We're taking on Uncle Sam?'

6

WHITE HOUSE

Sun slanting through the windows shed lustre on the patriotic rug. But the President lowered his voice as if he distrusted the walls of his own office. 'Pentagon, NSA, CIA . . . they collude with each other. So I'm going to issue an executive order.'

Braden listened, frowning.

'This administration will have a security level higher than a directorate, run by an Executive Coordinator of Covert Initiatives. He'll monitor the Secretary of State, the Secretary of Defense and the Director of the CIA. A watching brief. And that panjandrum will be you.'

He was flabbergasted. 'Me?'

'You're it.'

'Jeez. You can't do that. They'll knock us off.'

'That's the risk. But I'm game if you are. I want you to dig. You report directly to me. You in?'

'How come Chuck gets the poison chalice? What's wrong with the Veep?'

'Yes, they'd love that.' Jessop's sour laugh. 'What's wrong with the Veep is you could take his pants off and he wouldn't notice. There are four reasons I need you. One: I can trust you. Two: you're the most vicious shit-kicker I know. Three: the media love you. You're a character — hard to ignore.'

'And that matters?'

'It's vital. Because you can't crack this from the inside. Each time a president tries, a leak hits him in the neck like a firehose. It has to be done from inside and outside. You up to speed?'

'What's four?'

'Four is we think alike — believe in conventional war. But I'm not sure these shmos understand that. Biological stuff, mind-fucking . . . God knows what they've got. That's why I want you to find out exactly what's happening. It's why I'm putting my full weight behind you, plus any leads I've got. You receiving me, hard-arse?'

'Hell, they'll rub us.'

'Maybe. But think of the stink if they do. No, we might just swing it.' He leaned forward, voice a little hoarse. 'We risked our lives for our country once. You ready to do it again? Just because we're sixty, it doesn't mean we can stop.'

Braden stared at the rug, jerked his battered head about. 'Oh shit. You bastard. Oh shit.' He covered his face with his hands.

'I know I'm just Dougie to you. But I also have to be the President and I'm trying to live up to that. We both know the world's corruption-cake with pretty icing. But whatever degenerate lands in this office, I believe the job's still worthy of respect.'

Braden removed his now moist hands and immediately wished he hadn't. Because, again, he was confronted by the resplendent rug that symbolised all he'd ever felt about his country.

Jessop followed his eyes and used what he saw to press the advantage. 'If you won't do it for me, at least do it for the rug.'

'Jesus fucking Christ!'

The fire spat and the mantel clock ticked as Jessop milked a pause, then asked in an emotion-charged whisper, 'So? You in?'

He nodded.

7

REUNION

When meal, briefing and checks were over, Blake followed Kate to their tent. The wind had died with daylight so voluble lust was no option. They snuggled together for warmth and he explored her gratefully with his hands, feeling the firm lift to her breasts, the tight flanks, the muscled stomach, shoulders, arms. Her gymnast's body had lost none of its condition. They made love mutely but desperately and her taut, urgent response told him what he had to know.

The cold wind blew outside.

A pony whinnied and stamped.

She stroked his stubble, murmured, 'Thank God for you. I thought I'd never see you again.' He knew the comment was measured against her history. Her past loves had all been killed. 'I've lived on the edge so long I don't expect anything any more.'

'They say if you're not on the edge, you're taking up too much room.' He didn't ask about her mission, knew she could only answer general questions. 'So how are we tracking?'

She didn't reply immediately. She was half-Finn, half-Maori, a remarkably taciturn warrior. 'We've neutralised the petrochemical scam. Now that drug money's out of that area, the pressure's off alternative energies.'

'But the oil companies are still stalling.'

'Because there's an oil glut, although it's never mentioned. We'll have cheap oil for another twenty years. So it'll still take decades to force them into alternatives.'

'Now corporations are flogging the social enterprise initiative.'

'It's more enterprise than social. There's a trinity of exploitation — government, business, finance. But you never hear about it because they control the media.'

'At least America's finally got a half-decent president. You reckon Jessop'll change things?'

'American presidents are still prisoners of the system. Some security decisions never reach their desks.'

He prodded her with words, aware it was weakness in him, unsettled by the silence she preferred. 'So if what we're trying's impossible, why are we putting our lives on the line?'

'It's not enough to attempt the possible.'

A pony snorted. He held her hand and listened to the stream. 'And how come we could be up against the Yanks when the last Company agents we struck saved our arses?'

'Friends today. Foes tomorrow. It's never static. We missed one of Hansen's cronies. A man called Tritter. I've been checking up on him and the CIA may not like that.'

'Why?'

'Because they could be using him for something.'

He hadn't considered that.

'You need to understand the CIA. It's full of bright, well-meaning people who get no outside recognition, just blame. They can't reply to criticism because that makes them a target. They can't announce triumphs because that's called giving intelligence to the enemy. And their projects get washed off course by each political tide. National agendas change and we can't assume they're still our friends.'

'So what if . . .'

'Please don't . . . talk now. Just be with me. Please?'

He held her. Again they made love. It was lazy, sensual, wonderful. After it, he felt the most contented man in the world. He spoke about his hopes for them but she put a finger on his lips. 'Don't. All we have is now.'

He knew his inescapable recall would log every moment here — every detail, word, sigh, sensation, sound. She tried to live in the present. He couldn't escape it — or the past.

She said, 'We need to sleep.'

She was right. She was almost always right. It was difficult loving someone who he reluctantly had to admit seemed . . . more evolved?

No moon. He couldn't see her face. 'I never know where you're coming from.'

'I know I'm not easy to be with. But I do care for you. I do.'

He had to be content with that. He listened to the tinkling stream. From a nearby tent came a snore.

Her voice again: 'One more thing about Tritter. Even mentioning his name's dangerous. So, if you like breathing, keep it to yourself.'

* * *

Three hours later and three tents away, the Brazilian, Conchita, climbed out of her sleeping bag to relieve her bladder. She wore just her camo-patterned T-shirt, briefs and socks but knew she wouldn't be exposed long. As she felt for her boots there was a breath of cold air on her back. Then something fell beside her as if lobbed into the tent.

Her hand closed over it.

Cylindrical. Smooth — unlike a frag.

In a second, she'd ripped the flap wide and flung the thing over the tent toward the stream. As it flew, she heard a hiss from the emission holes. GB? Hydrogen cyanide? She'd remembered not to breathe.

Dark, but she still saw movement. A man with his back to her, running away. He bolted behind the next tent and crouched out of sight.

She knew that if she waited to get her carbine, he'd be gone. And if she ran out and established who it was, she'd be unarmed.

She shook Myers, the man who shared her tent. 'Gas grenade. I throw out.' She stumbled out and moved across the frosted ground. As she skirted the other end of the tent to surprise the man from behind, he heard her coming and rose to face her. Bhutanese from size and outline.

A gleam.

Knife. Single edged but cutting-edge up — to sever the web of a hand that tried to grab it. Not a low or high grip but held in the thrusting commando style, left arm advanced to parry.

Tough to disarm a man in this stance and in the dark. Knife defences were hardest.

'Ambush,' she yelled. 'Backup!'

Where was the fucker on watch?

The man moved in low to lunge.

With boots on, she'd have kicked to the shin.

As the stab came, she thrust her right leg high. It connected, forced his arm to the side. She followed with a left forearm block, moved in, twist-punched his groin.

It was automatic then. Knee into descending face. Knife-hand twisted. Leg sweep — an unnecessary trained reaction.

As the man thumped on his back, she viciously stomped his gut. Air exploded from him. Her hand, cupped to toughen the edge, chopped his throat.

The lookout was beside her now, carbine levelled at the man.

Myers doubling up, pistol out.

'A plant,' she panted. 'Fuck.'

Others piling from tents. A beam shone down.

Yes. Bhutanese — one of the pony tenders. And dead.

When the camp had been roused and all found present and correct, Myers said, 'So why pick us?'

'Perhaps they told him to kill the woman,' Simpson scowled. 'But he confused Conchita with Kate. Cocked up.'

'Whatever,' Myers rasped. 'The takeout is the fucks want a piece of us.'

8

CIA

Braden wondered what he'd got himself into.

After the photo session with the President, the feeding frenzy began. The beat-up in the *Washington Post*, the dissection in the *Wall Street Journal*, the CNN and NBC interviews, the speculation in the *New York Times*. He heard there would be a profile in *Fortune*, an article in *Time*. History was being made — at his expense. He was experienced at massaging the media, braved the fuss as a way to stay alive, then retreated to his Cleveland corporation and consulted the heads of his Defense Systems, Government Information Services, Technology and Avionics divisions.

Calls came in from influential men. One was Frederick Pollock, Deputy Secretary of Defense, whom he knew slightly and trusted less.

'Hi, Chuck. Congratulations. Hope you're getting your head around it all. Anyway, I'm meeting with Bill Stone, the DCI, tomorrow and he suggested you join us for a dry run. Which it will be, with Bill. His heart pumps dust. Funny guy. Vegetarian. Not because he doesn't like eating animals. Hates plants.' An ingratiating laugh. 'You in?'

He reached for his diary. 'What time?'

He'd never been to the CIA monolith. It was eight miles from downtown Washington and referred to as 'Langley' in spy fiction, although the location had long been named McLean. Once past the double chain-link fences, guards with their automatic weapons, guard dogs, pop-up barriers, he was driven through the grove of pines that screened the complex to an off-white concrete pile with slit-like recessed windows.

He left his three-car security detail in the VIP parking lot near the entrance and walked past magnolias into a lobby. Its grey and white Georgia marble floor was dominated by the agency's circular insignia.

He presented his visitor form and was escorted to the Director's elevator at the left of six man-trap turnstiles. His security escort operated the elevator access-key.

On the seventh-floor suite, he was frisked for electronic devices then met the DCI's Deputy for Special Projects, a buttoned-up forty-year-old called Jason. The man led him along an art-lined corridor to a windowless briefing room featuring a leather-covered conference table with polished-wood edge. A video/audio bay and credenza were housed in a recessed service-wall. The credenza supported coffee, sandwiches and fruit.

Jason placed security-stamped documents on the table and poured coffee. 'The Director's on his way. The Deputy's in a budget meeting, might be late.' He passed the sugar. 'We suck up to him. He controls ninety per cent of our funding.'

'About half what the NRO gets.' Braden added three sugars to his cup.

'That's right. And it pisses us off. Because satellites can't do it all. You still need HUMINT.'

'Agree.' Jason, Braden thought, seemed pleasant enough. For a spook.

A grey figure entered the room. Grey face, hair, suit, tie. Even the CIA Director's shoes seemed covered with pale dust, as if he dressed in a warehouse devoted to the packaging of talc. William Stone, Braden had been told, had degrees in politics, economics and psychology and was brilliant to the point of eccentricity. 'Stone. Good afternoon. How are you?'

Braden shook the limp hand. 'Irrelevant. So. You wanted to check me out.'

'I prefer to examine the engine of change before it gets a full head of steam.' His voice had the dry quietness of dead leaves blowing along a sidewalk. 'Jason's prepared a briefing for you.'

'I'll bet he has. But it may not be what I want to hear.'

They sat. Stone peered at Braden over rimless half-frames like an entomologist examining a new species.

'For instance, the President mentioned a bunch called DEMI.' Braden sipped liquid sugar. 'He gave me some press reports on them. Looks like you had a bit to do with them and I'd like to have your take.'

'As you wish.' Stone accepted coffee from his assistant. 'Jason, perhaps . . .'

The other grabbed the baton as instructed. 'DEMI stands for Defence against Enslavement through the Manipulation of Information. They're covert operatives with advanced technology who see themselves as do-gooders.'

Stone listened from afar. 'God's meddlesome little helpers.'

'Why?' Braden said. 'Because they're not ours? Because they're multinational? You object to people trying to fix things?'

'I find them,' Stone breathed, 'rather sad.' He sipped coffee — sugarless and black.

'Their HQ's in an Oscar-class submarine,' Jason went on, 'bought from a cash-strapped Russian navy and fitted with a new propulsion system we're still trying to figure out. As are the Russians, we suspect.'

'Got that much from the papers,' Braden said.

Stone waved a listless hand — non-responsiveness honed to an art-form. 'We get much of our information from careful analysis of world media.'

'And what about these heavies they greased?'

Stone examined his nails.

'A league of buccaneers called The Club,' Jason answered for him again. 'They were manipulating information from a power base in petrochemical companies and testing new biological products on captured illegal immigrants. DEMI blew the cover on certain people they'd compromised in this building.'

'You've weeded them out?'

'As far as we know.'

The door opened again as Pollock was ushered in. He had a high-jumper's gangly body no suit would ever fit. He grinned, pumped hands, grabbed a chair. 'Hi, Chuck. Don't mind me. Keep going.'

'We were chewing over DEMI,' Braden said. 'As far as I know, they were trying to promote alternative energy sources — the stuff you guys have sat on for years. I'm damn sure the three of you know what I'm talking about.'

Stone's tired voice. 'It's not easy to cross swords with the fossil-fuel establishment.'

'When they're paying you to hold the line, huh?'

Stone pushed a cuticle back with the blunt end of his pencil. The skin beneath his nails was also grey. 'Like most amateurs in this field, you begin with a profound lack of faith in the system and a compilation of rumours. Changing things takes time.'

'So are you still working with DEMI?'

The Director glanced at his assistant.

Jason grabbed the ball again. 'They've helped us clean up governments and corporations around the world. Their head honcho's a monk called Ko who certainly has excellent sources. He's even supposed to know the future — which amuses our analysts some.'

'But at the moment,' Stone said, 'we're peeved with our friends at DEMI.'

'Why?'

'They're threatening initiatives vital to our national security.'

'I'm listening.'

Stone's mouth creased to a constricted smile. 'You can't just amble in here and get the keys to the kingdom, Mr Braden. It doesn't work that way.'

'It's going to,' he snapped.

9

RENDEZVOUS

After the attack, the DEMI squad grilled the interpreter. He knew little about the dead man, who was not from his village and who had been hired at short notice like the others. They retrieved the grenade. It was Chinese made, which suggested it was probably intended to be untraceable. The Bhutanese were frisked and their stores searched, but nothing was found.

They stayed on alert with MP5s slung under parkas and other weapons ready to be broken out in seconds. The watch was doubled and, at night, the locals confined to their tents.

The climbs became steeper and, on the third afternoon, the ponies were swapped with yaks. The ponies and their handlers headed back, and the squad was glad to see the last of them. They frisked the yak-herders and checked their beasts and stores before letting them load up.

The yaks were ideal for the high slopes — thick-coated, sure-footed. But, despite their bulk and spreading horns, they were timorous, stupid, and followed the lead animal wherever it strayed. When the line meandered off the track, the herders ran around, shouting and throwing stones until the snuffling creatures plodded back.

Blake glanced from the herders to Kate who was walking beside him. 'We probably can't trust these people either.'

'Yes we can. They're fine. If one of them was after us, we'd know.'

'How?'

'This time, *we* have the mole.'

'We have?'

Two boy monks came down the hill. They were a picturesque sight — framed by stone cairns supporting multicoloured prayer flags, and behind that, bare mountains against the sky. The yaks, nervous even of children, veered off the path. The boys laughed as the herders raced around.

'Funny creatures,' he said.

'We're the funny ones. Use eyes.'

One of the herders, old but spritely, picked up a stone.

Ko. It was Ko! Ko with beard and in local garb, including the cheap blue Wellington boots some of the people wore. He shuffled off, yelling in dialect, threw his stone badly enough to miss.

Kate grinned. 'Even you didn't spot him. We only see what we expect. He's having a great time. So much in character. I think he's doing it to make me laugh.'

Blake suspected that no one in the squad would have met the great man. Simpson, trudging ahead, yelled back, 'Ma'am, you said two days. When do we meet this second group?'

She yelled back, 'Tell you later.'

The sergeant looked puzzled but tramped on.

He said quietly, 'Ko, here? Isn't that dangerous?'
'Very. I only spotted him a while ago.'
'Should we tell the squad he's here?'
'Safer if we don't.'

10

CIA

'I asked if you were still working with DEMI.' Braden glared at the DCI. He knew Stone hadn't forgotten the question and even admired the way the man had deflected it.

Stone breathed out through pursed lips. Had he done that in space, Braden thought, it would have propelled his frame slowly backward until he lodged high against the wall behind. 'We're neither in touch nor . . . doting on their absence.'

'I'm a plain man. Is that a no?'

'Must I restate the obvious?'

Jason, looking uncomfortable, got up to transfer food to the table.

Stone took off his spectacles, began to clean them with a tissue. 'There are things presidents prefer not to hear so that they can legitimately say they don't know. The famous plausible deniability. Precedents date back to Eisenhower and Kennedy.'

'But this president *wants* to know.'

'Then I suggest we eat while we listen to the presentation. We'd normally use the executive dining room but time presses. Jason?'

His assistant lifted a file. 'This summary covers security threats to the USA — ICBM deployments, NATO projections, treaties, proliferation and end-game geometry.'

Pollock gripped his full plate, leaned back and put his feet on a spare chair.

'Many nations now have ICBM capacity and other mass destruction weapons such as blister, blood and choking agents plus delivery infrastructure. These include Iran, North Korea, Libya, Syria, Sudan, India, Pakistan and Egypt.'

Braden munched. 'Funny we never mention the 200 nukes in Israel.'

'Key suppliers of such technology,' Jason droned, 'apart from western nations, are China, Russia and North Korea. Our priorities, in order, are preventive defence, deterrence, then military conflict.'

Stone gave a delicate yawn.

'Item: Space-borne surveillance. Current military sat systems include DSCS, Milstar, DSP, SBIRS, DMSP, FLTSATCOM, UFO, and intelligence satellites employing radar, optical sensors and electronic intercept. The Advanced EHF program is on schedule, so is DSCS SLEP. GPS, secured by NAVWARS to stall enemy guidance systems . . .'

'This is crap,' Braden said. 'It's also history. What about FOAS, China's GPS, Europe's Galileo? And in five years, space'll be vulnerable anyway.'

Jason frowned, slid his finger down the page: 'Item: STRATCOM. Currently the US Strategic Command has authority over wartime use of all US strategic nuclear forces. Nonproliferation treaties . . .'

'. . . Are wallpaper,' Braden said. 'Treaties only work when there's self-interest on both sides.'

Stone said, 'We're boring you?'

'It's kindergarten crud. I'm not the goddamn NSC.'

'Chuck's right about treaties.' Pollock preened his well-trained moustache. 'Most are covertly broken. The fear factor. Political history's just temporary alignments and no one admits it but allies don't exist.'

Stone consulted his watch. 'So what *do* you want to hear, Mr Braden?'

'That we're losing it and arms control's stalled.' Braden lurched from his chair and paced his not too lofty frame around. 'Hackers in the Russian Academy of Sciences have cracked your missile systems and naval codes. You've massaged Congress about a missile shield, first strike and other guff. But you know damned well we'll still get whacked. Any nation sophisticated enough to develop guided rockets with multiple nuclear warheads can deploy enough decoys to . . .'

'There's the airborne laser,' Pollock said through a sandwich.

Braden dry-laughed. 'Which is supposed to shoot down missiles in the boost phase. How many? Got hairs on it. You've faked results, skimped tests. Hardware's immature. Hell, even a B–2's only effective half the time. Keep on that line and you'll ratchet up China and Russia.'

Pollock scowled and Jason looked startled.

Which was just what he wanted. He ploughed on. 'And China's scared you shitless. They've launched over fifty satellites and the Russians have helped their missile program for years. If we try for some half-arsed missile shield protecting Taiwan, Japan and South Korea, they'll flatten our bases in East Asia. Apart from tactical stuff, they have the DF–31 — 5000-mile range — the DF–41 — that's 7500 —

plus SLBMs. And eighteen DF–5/5A ICBMs, each with 5-megaton capacity and a range of 8000 miles. They'll reach this room. So will their SLBMs.'

Pollock did a slow hand-clap, glanced at the deeply frowning Stone. 'I think we're dealing with an expert here.'

'In nature's infinite book of secrecy, a little he has read.' Stone slid his fingers down his ballpoint pen which rested on the table. He up-ended the pen, did it again. 'Please sit down, Mr Braden. No point in us all having heartburn.'

Braden sat as reluctantly as an attack-dog instructed to heel.

'You had us going, Chuck,' Pollock thrust out his loose and prominent lower jaw and scraped his bottom teeth down his moustache. It made him look like a deep-sea fish. 'Yup, Star Wars is a wet-dream. We're losing our superpower clout. And China's the threat. You've nailed it.'

'I'm not sure this is wise.' Stone smeared blue-vein cheese on a cracker.

What wasn't wise, Braden wondered? The man was so prudently imprecise, he could have been referring to the cheese.

Pollock retoothed his moustache. 'China's a missile factory. It used to be Scuds aimed at Taiwan. Now they've got solid fuel ICBMs. Hardened sites. Mobiles. And their silos are hard to spot. They've got IBMs on the Qinghai and Tibetan plateaus and in Yunnan province to threaten south and southeast Asia. Got nine MIRVs in each DF–5 and our strategists . . .'

Stone choked on cheese. A tactical ploy?

Jason rushed for a glass of water which his boss accepted and gulped.

But Pollock ignored Stone's diversions. 'In ten years they'll have parity. We're not changing China.

They're changing us. And once they've assembled the technology . . .'

'It's there,' Braden growled.

'Pretty much. And the cadres have slanted the rhetoric to glorify nationalism. Their military's still corrupt, deals arms, smuggles goods. But that's changing. The economy's growing at seven per cent a year. They're updating their subs, getting a carrier. They're going to be political and military mammoths.'

Braden said, 'And you've got a strategy, right?'

'You bet.'

'Fred,' Stone said. 'Enough.'

Pollock groomed his lip again. 'Before Bill blows gaskets, I'd better point out that I don't have the authority to progress this without consulting others. I suggest we meet with the Secretary of Defense, the Secretary of State, if he can make it, and the Chairman of the Joint Chiefs. What say you, Bill?' He glanced at Stone.

The DCI sighed. 'I say Mr Braden should quit while he's ahead.'

'Is that a threat?' Braden snapped.

'Advice,' the cold voice said.

'Well, blow it out your arse, if you've got one. If you haven't, get someone to change your batteries.'

'Now, girls . . .' Pollock said. 'So waddya say, Chuck? We'll do it in the Pentagon, huh? Fill you in. Happy?'

'Set it up.'

Jason ushered him out of the meeting but the other two stayed behind.

'I can imagine what they're saying,' Braden said. 'If those walls had ears — and I guess they have . . .'

'They're probably in shock. You're amazingly well informed, sir.'

'Not yet, son. But I will be. And, by the way, you can tell them I'm a hard man to discredit. My vice is honesty. I love America. I'm divorced, screw my secretary who I'm sweet on. And that's it.'

The other man said nothing.

Braden kept pressing it home. 'So how will it come? A servo-driven needle in the back of a chair? Causing an unexpected but plausible heart attack?'

'I think that's a little dramatic.'

'Oh yeah? Next time, remind me to swap chairs.'

11

BIVOUAC

By day's end, they were on tundra and threading through a maze of lofty hills. They descended from a prayer flag-studded ridge toward a stone yak-herder's hut. The herders lassoed the yaks around the horns then tied them in a line to a long rope. They unpacked them before freeing them to wander. As usual, the men made more noise than the beasts and Ko was as loud as the rest. Blake had last seen the monk sitting, Buddha-like, in a cabin of his submarine. Yes, Ko had been acting all day, and enjoying it hugely.

There was no fire that night. No wood. A gas bottle fed a camp stove. They shivered around the trestle table while Ko chatted with the herders. Ko helped them cook the food, drank *chhang* and yak butter tea. After the meal, which he ate with them, he looked up and nodded at Kate.

She tapped a tin bowl for silence. 'I'd like to announce a guest.'

The troopers looked warily around.

She nodded to the man. 'Mr Ko.'

Ko stood up, crinkled face smiling, raised one hand slightly as if in blessing.

Simpson breathed, 'Bloody hell.'

The troopers gawked at the small man, as if they thought he might levitate. The locals giggled and slapped their knees, relishing the joke.

Ko lapsed into perfect English, incongruous coming from a figure who looked so indigenous. 'It's good to be with you. Unfortunately, I don't have much chance to meet most of the people who help us.'

As the surprise subsided, Simpson stammered, 'Excuse me, sir. Your being here is dead dangerous, sir. For you.'

'You're squad leader?'

'Yes, sir. Simpson, sir.'

'What you say is true, of course. But there are times when one has to take risks.' He beamed at the soldier but said no more.

'Then, can we know our destination, sir?'

'Just a monastery. One more day's journey.'

'Objective, sir?'

'Nothing to do with our mission at all.'

The troopers exchanged glances.

'The abbot's dying and they've asked me to take his place. A matter of ceremonies, initiations, tradition. A serious obligation. I'm sorry to drag you all here. But some of us live in two worlds, inner as well as outer, and need to take care of both. Then . . . But we'll speak about that later.'

Kate left the table and joined Ko. The excited Bhutanese made space for her. Her eyes glittered as she kissed her guru's hand. Then she perched on a woven saddle-bag, facing him. They talked together quietly.

Conchita turned to Blake. 'You meet Mister Ko before?'

He looked at her attractive lined face and nodded.

'I hear so much about him, is hard to believe he's with us.' He noticed that, when she spoke, only her bottom teeth showed.

He watched Ko and Kate talking in the glow from the pressure lamps. The respect evident between them was unusual — both sitting erect, attentive. Teacher, he thought, and trusted pupil. Then they turned to look at him and Ko called, 'Good evening, Mr Blake.'

'Good evening.'

Ko stared at him a moment. The stare made him uneasy.

After his conversation with Kate, Ko left for his tent. Simpson, in low tones, called for the nightly briefing, organised passive and active security which included a double watch.

Kate came gravely back and when they were together again in the joined sleeping bags he asked, 'Everything all right?'

'Wonderful.'

'When Ko looked at me, it was strange — as if he was telling me something.'

'Perhaps he was. He's never unintentional.'

'With Ko here, and so few of us, we're vulnerable as hell — wouldn't stand a chance against paratroopers or an air attack. No wonder Simpson's worried.'

'I know. But Ko planned it this way.'

'And why am I here?'

'Ko wanted you here. So trust that.'

'I'm afraid I don't have your blind faith in his extrasensory take on the world.'

'It's not blind. And it's not faith.'

He ran his hand along her body as a devotee might caress a sacred object. He respected and adored her but, as usual, lacked words to express it. 'Have you any idea what I feel for you?'

'You mustn't care for me so much.' She kissed him. 'It's best to look at everyone as if you're seeing them for the last time.'

'Why do you say that?'

'Because you may be. People are dangerous places to direct the heart.'

'Kate, I'm human. We're humans. Could you talk to me like another person?'

'Look. We're together. Now. And that could be all we have.' A pause. 'Tomorrow we could die.'

'Or tonight.'

'So love me.'

12

PENTAGON

After Braden returned to Cleveland, he contacted his cronies in the military but found those former convivial relationships tainted by awe or fear. As he followed up the President's leads he became the subject of a media circus. BRADEN GOES TO PENTAGON, the headlines screamed.

He'd visited that pedestrian city often — tramped its broad busy concourses and its numbered spoke-like corridors. Today's meeting was on E-ring — not in the senior command offices he was familiar with but in the lair of the Secretary of Defense. It was an expansive, pleasant space equipped with the usual flags draped from standards. It had clusters of occasional chairs for smaller meetings and a cedar conference table at one end.

Andrew Treloar, the smoothly dressed, smooth-haired, smooth-talking Secretary shook his hand. 'Ah, Mr Braden, your reputation has preceded you. Fred tells me you're extremely well-informed.'

Informed about you, he thought. Treloar had fingers in every pie — arms, oil, media, politics; was the powerbroker's pawnbroker, the tongue for the jaws of the rich.

Treloar introduced him to two other men — the crusty General Carthew, Chairman of the Joint Chiefs of Staff, and Sebastian Bennett, a handsome black man with thinning hair who was now Under Secretary of State for Political Affairs. Pollock and Stone were there too.

After they'd settled around the table, Treloar said, 'Mr Braden, you have the floor.'

He took it. 'Okay. You've read the Presidential directive. I'm not here to tell you what to do. Just to find out what you're up to. I'm a simple man, loyal Republican, support the NRA, manufacture weapons, believe in the sanctity of war . . .'

''Scuse me, Chuck,' Pollock cut in. 'Okay if I precis where we got to last session for those who weren't around?'

'Fine.'

The gangling man filled them in. 'We established that China's missile program threatens our bases in Asia and our mainland. We know they're not about regional defence but want superiority over the west and see us as their principal enemy. Just as we see them as our future threat.'

'Don't discount Moscow.' The Under Secretary turned to Braden. 'The Kremlin still sees the old Warsaw Pact nations as a buffer. And disarmament's stalled. We're supposed to shrink our arsenal to a third by 2012. But we can withdraw at three months' notice, redeploy from storage any time. While the rhetoric's nonproliferation, the reality's unstoppable spread.'

'And they're upgrading what they've got,' the general added, 'at Kozel'sk, Aleysk, Uzhur, Tatishchevo, Dombarovskiy, Kartaly. As for the shield . . .'

'It's bullshit,' Braden growled.

The general sucked his teeth. 'Let's just say that best-case kill is a third of incoming.'

'Still,' Treloar argued, 'it's vital to the economy.'

Braden couldn't disagree with that. The missile shield was a device to funnel billions to prime contractors.

'Their missiles take half an hour to get here,' the general went on. 'Less, depending where their subs are. Gives the President three minutes to respond to an attack. If he's on the can, the country's down the toilet, too.'

'Then we have information warfare threats,' Pollock said. 'Same ones John Deutch outlined to the Senate Committee back in '96. To domestic infrastructure — traffic, power plants, banks. To international systems — funds transfer, transportation, comms. They could stuff strategic world capitals.'

'We've had two players for years,' Bennett said. 'But now we've got terrorists, rogue governments, nihilists . . .'

'And you can't meet them,' Carthew griped, 'with a military dinosaur. We target radars, launch control centres, submarine docks and silo fields. But when the small fry get triggerable fission, it'll come by truck or a low-tech delivery system from near offshore. No shield can stop that. So much for SDI and layered defence. Forget airliners into buildings. Be nukes in pizza vans.'

'Which my people are expected to know about.' Stone's jaundiced look. 'Even if they pick up three vans, the fourth'll get through.'

'Despite the billions poured into NSA?' Braden glared at Stone.

'Money that should have gone to HUMINT. Don't tell me you're also an expert on Fort Meade?'

'I know Echelon's stranglehold on trading partners feeds through the Department of Commerce, the Advocacy Center . . .'

'National interest,' Pollock said. 'Today's ally. Tomorrow's adversary. Shifting sands.'

'But terrorists,' Stone said, 'rarely communicate in conventional ways. As for sophisticated threats, we have the challenge of fibre optics, encoding, the volume of signals. Collecting's one thing. Processing's another.'

Treloar glanced at Braden. 'Perhaps you're starting to see what we're up against. Out there,' he gestured beyond the walls, 'we manufacture "truth" — the usual lost-in-the-funhouse media misrepresentation of reality. But inside this building we acknowledge that national security's a myth.'

'We're even stuffed on small conventional wars,' the general grumbled. 'Surgical strikes now have to be vetted by lawyers. Christ! Then we can't sustain casualties because of the CNN factor. But take a country with run-down technology and government-controlled media. Will it pussyfoot around? No way. It'll take the hits and fight the dirty war we can't.'

Stone stared at Braden as if through the wrong end of a telescope. 'You see the headaches that occupy us here?'

'There's one you haven't mentioned,' Braden said. 'Even with first strike capability and a total missile barrier, if China takes out your bunkers, you're nowhere.'

The general's eyes narrowed. 'Trundle that past me again.'

'Everyone knows where the other guy's command and control centres are. Forget dual delivery and the BLU–116/B, forget the B61–11. China now has a version of Initiative 12.'

'Where the hell'd you get that?'

'I have my sources. You've done your first test and it's worked. It's the projection of force from space using orbiting rods of depleted uranium equipped with small boost rockets and guidance electronics. It travels at hypersonic velocity — like artillery and strike support moving at 25,000 miles an hour — and penetrates hundreds of feet. Shreds the deepest command bunker into metal chips. So much for the billions you've spent to update Cheyenne Mountain. Kiss goodbye to the critical command-and-control mode of North America.'

The general slumped as if he'd been hit. 'Who the hell told him that?'

'I'm in the industry, for Chrissake. You think we don't talk shop? You've got it up. So have they. And if the top brass controlling the war and heads of government can't survive . . .'

Stone mock-sobbed. 'I wish he'd go away.'

Braden growled back, 'Haven't started on *you*, yet.'

'You don't need uranium rods.' Pollock toothed his moustache. 'You just attack ground systems that control space systems. Next step up is jamming. How do you see that, Bill?'

'As part of my nightmares,' Stone groaned.

The Secretary tapped the table. 'Okay everyone. Settle down.' He turned to Braden. 'So every way you look at it, it's a recipe for disaster.'

'Which is the polite way,' Pollock added, 'of saying we're in a fucking hornet's nest.'

'Copy that,' Braden said. 'So what are you doing about it?'

13

DESTINATION

As they rounded a projection of rock high on a mountain pass they saw, nestled into a far slope, what looked like a fortress.

They'd seen no other Dzong at this altitude. It had an elaborate multi-level roof of hand-cut shingles, thick white inward-sloping walls, small high windows. They trudged toward it on slippery alpine pasture. Soon they heard ceremonial horns and, later, a reverberating bell.

The monastery, sheltered by mountains, was inaccessible except for the track. The nearest village, Ko told them, was in a valley, far below.

When they were closer to the building, a phalanx of monks emerged — middle-aged or old. To their saffron robes was added the colour of giant prayer wheels flanking the entrance and the brightly painted woodwork.

While the squad prepared to bivouac in the shelter of the monastery, Ko invited Kate and Blake to accompany him inside. They followed their small leader with his shuffling but stable gait. As he walked between the monks they prostrated, then formed a procession behind.

At the foot of the steps in the courtyard, where the elders waited, was a huge mandala, made from rice and coloured sand. Ko was greeted with ceremony in Dzongkha. Kate and Blake received broad smiles and were treated as honoured guests. He admired these uncynical people, their practicality, their humour, and was surprised they'd admitted a woman to the court.

The monastery's interior was exotic. Intricate painted carvings framed gilt-statues of the Buddha. Butter lamps made shadows leap on illuminated embroideries and mysterious murals.

They sat on a bare-planked floor to join the monks for a simple meal — buckwheat, hand-scooped from a proffered bowl, and salted tea.

When Ko retreated to an inner court, the monks took them to a long gallery where they watched sacred texts being printed from hand-carved wooden blocks. Eventually, with many bows and smiles, they were ushered outside.

It was colder now. Clouds swirled around the peaks. The squad had stacked their packs at the camp's quadrants high enough to shelter a prone man. But, in this mountain vastness, the makeshift redoubts looked pathetic.

Simpson called as Kate passed him. 'Know how long we'll be here?'

'Two days.'

He sniffed the dampening air. 'If it's an air attack, we're stuffed.'

14

PENTAGON

'What are we doing about it?' Treloar repeated. 'I'm happy to tell you. But you won't like it.'

'Try me,' Braden said.

'Well, although the standoff with Russia's still with us and mutual assured destruction's just acquired more players, conventional war — hard war — is under threat.'

'Sounds bad for business.'

'It means nuclear winter or eco-death. That's a tough sale even politically.'

'Then there's the waste,' the general said. 'We've thrown billions at Ivan for that. But at Tomsk, Krasnoyarsk, Dmitrovgrad, they still inject glow-juice straight into the ground.'

'So, for many reasons,' Treloar said, 'hard war's becoming soft. We're looking more at non-lethals, chemical and bio-weapons. Civpol or crowd control elevated to population control. Soft war's the future if we want to survive.'

'Depressing,' Braden said.

'I've asked Sebastian to expand on this more.' He nodded at Bennett.

The black man didn't bother with notes. 'Despite the attempts at birth control in China . . . By the way, female infanticide is 53 million in five years — equivalent to the population of France — and you've got brothers sharing wives. Despite this, their population's still increasing by 16 mil a year. And the strain on agriculture and water supplies is breeding environmental refugees.'

Braden scratched his jaw.

'Right now,' the Under Secretary went on, 'they see people smugglers as outlaws or folk heroes. This reflects government corruption in both China and the target countries. In other words, China's haemorrhaging people. I'll spare you the transshipping details, the setup in Prague and so forth. But a brief case history. Not long ago, one smuggler, the famous Lin Tao Bao in Fujian, smuggled an estimated 50,000 out of the country. And the government covertly encourages this. Why? When the emigrant leaves China, the local official gets a bribe. Later, the settled immigrant sends money back to his relatives. In the late 1970s, Carter asked Chinese leaders to lift restrictions on emigration. They asked him how many million immigrants he'd like! You see it right there. Emigration's their safety-valve against political and social instability. Their government admits to 300 million unemployed. God knows what the real figure is. Then emigration boosts their diaspora which they depend on for foreign investments.'

'Don't get that,' Braden said.

'According to State Department estimates, eighty per cent of all foreign investment in China comes from overseas Chinese.'

'Uh-huh.'

'So China has everything to gain from flooding the

world with people. Several hundred million now want to leave the country.' He waved his hand. 'All kinds of issues hang off this. Human rights. Most favoured nation status and the Jackson Amendment . . . But the bottom line is, they're using emigration as a weapon.'

'So?'

'It's an example of soft war,' Treloar explained. 'Calling for a soft counter-attack. You still with us?'

Braden nodded slowly. 'Still listening.'

'The population bomb's their first salvo. And we intend to turn it back on them.'

'How?'

The silence in the room became oppressive.

Treloar rattled his pencil between his teeth. 'I conferred with the others before you joined us and we agreed this is the place to . . . pause. You now have enough information to inform the President on the situation without compromising him or . . . endangering yourself.' He glanced at Stone.

The DCI's dead-fish eyes found Braden's. 'We're simply trying to convey to you how sensitive these matters are. We consider it vital for national security that you pursue this line no further. You're a resourceful, talented man. You must see the implication?'

Five pairs of eyes watched him. He took it as a threat.

'Okay,' he growled, 'point taken. I'll put what you've said, and your recommendation, to the President.'

The tension in the room relaxed. He was slapped on the back, plied with drinks, told what a superior man he was. Even Stone had the grace to shake his hand and say as warmly as he could, 'You won't regret this. Thank you.'

A tipsy Braden left the rubber-tiled maze with two thoughts in mind:

Defence was a vastly complex discipline.

Curiosity was a dangerous thing.

15

CAISSON

That night, after they'd made love, Kate said, 'Here's one for the walking encyclopaedia. What do you know about caissons for off-shore oil platforms?'

He searched his memory . . . articles seen, documentaries. 'They're reinforced concrete towers with hollow flotation chambers. They're hugely expensive to build — cost more than nuclear power stations or oil refineries. They start the construction in a dry-dock, then float the base to a deep-water shelter, then progressively submerge it while they cast the upper sections.'

'Do you know how big they are?'

'Around a million tonnes with the drilling platform mounted because they depend on their mass for stability. The biggest I read about was as high as the Eiffel Tower and a lot broader at the base. It was designed to survive a 30-metre wave.' He slid his hand across her breasts.

'Let's stick with this for a moment.' She stopped his hand. 'I saw one being built in Java. Just a big central column. It had flotation chambers 60 feet wide and walls 4 feet thick.'

'Uh-huh.' He was used to metric.

'It was a Tritter project — built at a high security site but I managed to get in.' Her hair brushed his face. 'Oil rigs aren't particularly newsworthy but this got no press at all.'

'Where's it now?'

'Six tugs towed it to an oil field in the Timor Sea. They could only make about one knot.' She nuzzled into his shoulder, responding despite herself. 'It's called Deep Six. Probably because it's supporting a rig in waters 600 feet deep.'

'Then it's 200 metres high.'

'More than that. Because the lowest deck of the platform's generally 80 feet above the sea.'

'Why are you telling me this?'

'We're going to bring you in on the Tritter project. We'll be meeting on it with Ko.'

'Uh-huh. So what's so special about this caisson?'

'The inside design. It has a series of levels like the floors in an office building.'

'Why?'

'I don't know yet. It's just one piece of a puzzle. Anyway, enough of that. Do you know I care for you?'

'Do you know I can't leave you alone?'

She kissed his hand, then placed it between her legs.

16

CIA

William Stone looked up from the reports on his desk, removed his spectacles and rubbed his eyes. High-resolution satellite pictures confirmed that the DEMI squad in Bhutan was one person down, not two. Apparently Ko's senior operative, the woman who'd infiltrated the Deep Six construction site, was still alive. He said, 'Still no signal from our plant?'

'Nothing,' Jason said. 'So much for selective targeting. Our analysts think they took him out. Operations are suggesting that we use a Predator to target her.'

'No.' Stone appraised his special assistant who stood in front of the desk — neat, discreet, all upward mobility and inward motility. 'We've tailed her for weeks and she still hasn't led us to Ko. So I've thought of a better way to use her. *Volte face.* We bring her in.'

'For interrogation?'

'Far more devious.' The room, thank God, had no sensors to record his thoughts. They were working on it, of course. The p300-type testing would soon provide the perfect polygraph. And the hard-wired zone system, while initially attached to the skull would eventually . . . His burden was knowing too much about too much.

'But how do we extract her? You can hear a light plane or chopper in those mountains so commandos or paratroopers are compromised.'

'A direct attack.'

'A frontal attack on an elite squad?' Jason looked dubious. 'She could be killed in the firefight.'

'Unless we order our team to hold fire until they verify.'

'How could you ask them to do that? The DEMI squad's a professional unit. They'd wipe our people out.'

'Not if they're turbos.'

'Turbos? Are they operational?'

'Still experimental.'

'So why would the Pentagon deploy them?'

'Because it gives them the perfect test. A turbo squad, theoretically, could take hits and still wait until they'd verified each target.'

'But there's still no guarantee they won't kill her. She'll be in hiking gear or battle dress. Hard to identify a woman.'

'I'll wear that risk.' He pressed his hands together, pleased. 'The mission is to bring her back. And take out the rest. Can you set that up?'

Jason low-whistled, 'Do my best,' and, brain in overdrive, drifted from the room.

Stone rose, entered his personal washroom, moistened a clean face cloth and wiped his face and neck. In a world based on fear and greed, such small amenities mattered. Personal freshness was one of the few comforts left.

He stared at his face in the glass, thinking of the DEMI squad. Now decent, courageous people would die. Damage control.

The strip-lit mirror emphasised his sallow skin. He detested the sun. Cod-liver oil was his sun. He took it with the dreadful-smelling brewer's yeast to prevent the powder from sticking to his palate. The yeast, with its nine micronutritional functions, was his doleful attempt to retard age. Damage control again. Everything was damage control.

He returned to his main problem — how and when to apply it to Braden.

17

INCOMING

They left the monastery that morning heading for the lower slopes. A procession of monks accompanied them for the first hour then turned back, but three elderly men remained. Ko, still in his yak-herder's garb, continued tending the animals but the three monks in their distinctive robes, begging bowls held in the front folds, ignored their toiling superior and walked gravely down the track. Decoys, Blake assumed — prepared to draw fire and die for Ko.

The weather worsened. It started to snow. Everyone was cold and wet. The animals blew and grunted. At Ko's request, Simpson called a halt. They squatted in a shivering circle while Ko, ignoring the hardship, looked at them in turn. For a time he stared at the whitening earth, then looked up smiling. 'Everything is energy. Can energy be destroyed? It's not our place to dictate outcomes. Only to contend. And that can be . . . a joyful study.' He beamed at the listening monks. One bowed low. Then Ko glanced at Simpson.

The mercenary, unused to such a briefing, opened his mouth to speak, thought better of it.

Ko smiled at the man's washboard frown. 'Yes, the practical aspect. Of course. I feel we may soon have visitors. Time to check weapons and have them ready. I appreciate all you've done. And thank you for being here.'

Blake stared at the bleak terrain. In this isolated place and this weather, nothing seemed less likely than an attack. But he'd been surprised by Ko's insights before.

Ko stood, glanced at Blake with his strange, empty gaze. 'Yes, wet, wild, miserable, nowhere . . . hardly the place for a battle. Yet . . .' He shuffled back to the yaks.

Simpson barked orders and cranked up alertness. Equipment was unloaded, weapons openly worn.

The snow swirled and stopped as a fierce wind roared up the valley. Moving downhill was hard on the now slippery ground and rain-squalls with drops like thrown pellets made the track more treacherous still. The yaks paused each few steps to sniff the track. Boots slithered on stones. Blake had wet pants from sliding on his rear.

They reached a lower ridge with a spine of rocks to one side. Beyond, a landscape of jagged boulders rose from the earth like leaning tombstones. The yaks, for the tenth time, had strayed from the track and the handlers were coaxing them back. Blake, needing to take a leak, retreated to a cranny in a pile of granite and shale. He stood there, cursing the weather, rain dripping from his nose and chin, while the procession inched past him down the slope.

The thock-thock of the chopper was drowned by headwind and the mountains behind. It came over the ridge, a twin Huey, becoming rapidly more distinct — dirty-grey chipped paint and dents. It settled almost alongside him, skids holding a foot off the slope, and disgorged ten men in flak jackets, visors and full combat gear.

As Blake stuffed himself back in his pants and shrank against wet stone, a man ran toward him carrying what seemed like an ammo box with stub aerial. But he was looking down to keep his footing. Blake, still unspotted, moved back into the cranny. If he hadn't just emptied his bladder, fear would have been running down his leg.

The chopper lifted off and headed down the slope. He glimpsed a man behind a pintle-mounted door gun as the blur flashed overhead.

Above the noise of the aircraft, a fusillade of fire. From the squad?

His residual image positioned the man on the other side of the rock. He tore at his parka, freeing the MP5K. Weapons weren't his skill but he knew this type well enough. He unfolded the stock, shaking with cold, and pushed the selector to burst.

The firefight echoed off the hills. They were outnumbered, outgunned. And he'd be expected to help them fight.

He edged around the rock, saw the man less than 2 metres away, facing away from him, crouched beside his box. It wasn't a field radio because he had no headphones. A line of switches and LED readouts flickered, like heartbeats, on the device.

Another attacker slithered down the hill, half on his back, firing. His slide was checked as his foot found a half-buried rock. Something lobbed near his legs and exploded. Dirt and flesh flew as his body bucked in a shower of its own blood.

The man was on his back, his legs bloodied strips of cloth. A mess of pale worms below him slithered between the stones. But he lived, his face above the shredded battle jacket not contorted with pain but rage. Then his expression went blank. He slumped — as if turned off.

Blake registered it in an instant, time slowing as he edged forward. He seemed to have an age to act, every step eternal. He aimed at the back of the man working the box.

The man half-turned.

Their eyes met.

The man rolled, brought his weapon up.

Blake fired.

The 9-millimetre rounds slammed body armour, travelled up the chest. As the neck pumped red and the eyes dilated in death, his adrenaline-fired satisfaction was eclipsed by his fear for Kate.

The chopper came around again, death's shadow in the sky. He expected to see flame from its nose and door. But it didn't attack.

The squad must have waited till the craft turned, exposing its exhausts. He didn't see the SAM connect. But he saw the craft disintegrate. Rotors flying off. Fuselage shattering to spinning scrap. Tail boom smashing on the cliff-face. What was left bounced down streaming rocks.

And he saw something else, his recall inescapable — three buttons alight on the control-box beside the man he'd killed. One had lit as the grenade exploded at the feet of the man on the slope.

He mentally played it back. The man had pressed the first glowing button down. And the disembowelled warrior on the slope had slumped as if turned off.

As if turned off!

He lunged forward across the corpse and grabbed the box. Three buttons were still alight with one pressed down. He pressed the other two. Did lights signify hits on the men?

The rattle of fire from below.

He peered further down the slope, spotted two dead yaks and four bodies but no survivors.

An explosion and a scream. Bullets chipped rocks near his head.

He ducked behind the outcrop. He'd seen nothing move so where the hell was it from? And how far? His squat anti-terrorist weapon was ineffective at long range.

A far-off figure inched into sight around a rock. Simpson — with a grenade launcher fixed to his gun.

Now Simpson's target appeared. Darker clothes against the rock. The squad leader, who'd outflanked him, fired and the man staggered before the sound arrived. But the dying assailant turned like a bull and charged at Simpson, firing. How? He'd taken a close burst. No body armour was that good. The shocked squad leader, lunging too late to evade, went down.

But the shot man, incredibly, still stood.

Another switch glowed on the panel.

Blake punched it.

And the distant enemy collapsed — as if turned off!

A ricochet beside him. A rock splinter flew past his head. The sniper still had him pinned.

Blake punched all switches down. All lit and their readouts went to zero.

Firing stopped.

He waited, listening. Nothing.

Just the sound of the rain and the wind. And the wrenching of his breath. He knew he'd have to go down there.

God! Was she still alive?

Then he heard a second chopper coming in.

18

OPTION THREE

For the second time, Chuck Braden, adorned with Pentagon security tag, was filtered through the vestibule and panelled outer office into the sanctum of the Secretary of Defense. The security men, aides, staff were less friendly than before. Tough, he thought. Dougie had insisted he find out more.

Treloar and the loose-limbed Pollock were there, both exuding gloom. Treloar said flatly, 'You're back.'

'Did my best for you. No dice.'

A third man, near the conference table, tapped a white stick on the floor. He was thin, had a crumpled shirt, two hearing aids, thick spectacles.

Treloar introduced him. 'I'd like you to meet Professor Turner, from Strategic Population Studies, a division of the Future Planning Unit which, because of converging research, is now linked with DARPA.'

Braden knew of the Defense Advanced Research Projects Agency — knew they were spending millions seeding microelectromechanical systems and test-flying one-seventh-scale aircraft.

Turner peered around for Braden, held his hand out too much to the side. Braden fielded the hand and shook it. They sat around the end of the long table.

'So,' Treloar said. 'We've reached a point of no return. Is that absolutely clear?'

He nodded.

'Shame it's come to this, Chuck,' Pollock said. 'Anyway, we've asked Professor Turner to give an outline.' He raised his voice to double volume. 'Professor? Your cue.'

Turner had both hands to his hearing aids. 'Where is he?' He peered around, bottle-lens glasses distorting his eyes.

Treloar pointed at Braden — seated directly opposite.

'Ah, yes.' The magnified eyes squinted. 'The major world problem is population growth.' Like most deaf people, he spoke too loudly. His hand knocked against a remote control on the table and he fumbled with its buttons. 'Is it there?'

Pollock yelled in his ear. 'It's there.'

A slide, rear-projected on a wall screen, showed a graph dating from AD 1. Population growth was negligible until 1750, then rose steadily, and from 1950 became near-vertical.

'This forecast,' Turner brayed with the reticence of a broken muffler, 'has been in the too-hard basket for years. You note that from the 1900s, the curve is exponential. It took a century to go from one billion to two. Twelve years to go from four to five. Now it's a million every four days. A second China in ten years. World population, now over six billion, will double by 2150.'

'Whatever we do, Chuck, we're doing for America,' Pollock said. 'Tackling the primary issue.

Never been done before. Political dynamite. That's why it's under wraps.'

Braden felt like a man being sucked into quicksand.

'This unchecked growth,' Turner bawled on, 'is more dangerous than a nuclear threat and affects everything from global warming to resources. Pollution, the ecosystem, water and food supplies, biodiversity . . . The planet is finite. We're destroying it and ourselves.' He peered in the general direction of Braden. 'Before things become irredeemable, populations must be pruned.'

'War does that,' Braden said. 'A fucking great war. Probably what it's for.'

'Not effective enough,' Pollock said. 'It hasn't been for centuries. Disease kills better. But now we're victims of medical advances. Live too long. Crazy, huh?'

'I didn't hear that,' Turner bellowed.

'People live too long,' Pollock yelled.

'Far too long. So what are the alternatives? One: reduce births. Two: increase mortality. But reducing births through government coercion isn't efficient. China's tried it and cut growth by millions. But it's still out of control.'

Treloar grimaced at the shouting match. 'To expand on that a little — sterilisation's certainly efficient and it's been covertly tried in several Third World nations. But it's unpopular, difficult, expensive and a political disaster. We could engineer a chromosome deficiency. But it weakens the breeding stock, takes a generation before it has an impact, and you can't hide it because it's statistically obvious.'

'Jeez.' Braden examined the walls as if searching for relief.

'Let's now look at increasing mortality.' Turner cleared his throat at peak volume. 'Euthanasia is still opposed. But end-point planning is imperative. Because, whatever the birthrate, by halving the lives of people you halve the population.'

Pollock toothed his moustache. 'Don't get that.'

'What?' Turner cupped hands to his ears.

'Don't get it!' Pollock yelled.

Turner nodded. 'It seems fallacious, but it's true, I assure you. The mathematics are elegant.'

Trying to follow the labyrinthine thinking had tightened Braden's whole body. 'Goddamnit! What's this got to do with defence?'

'Everything,' the Secretary said.

Turner pressed the remote again. 'Is it there?'

'Yes,' Pollock yelled.

The new slide read:

POPULATION-REDUCTION POLICY BASED ON CURRENT TECHNOLOGY, SOCIOLOGICAL ATTITUDES AND PROJECTIONS
Sterilisation where possible.
Promotion of biological limiters (such as disease).
Nanobot project.
Selective latency.

Turner peered across the table. 'Now let's examine these options.' He pressed the remote again. More information appeared below the first:

Option 1: expensive because application method is mechanical. Medium-term possibility.
Option 2: cost-effective. Employs natural distribution. Promising short-term but not selective.

Braden cursed under his breath. 'You're going to infect China with some doomsday disease?'

Professor Turner searched for his stick, in a sense-deprived world of his own.

'Well?' Braden snapped.

Treloar said, 'We're simply looking at alternatives.'

'I can see small-town America buying it. They'll call out the National Guard, fire brigade, school band — celebrate the glorious victory.'

'Small-town America won't know. However, I can assure you that option two's been shelved. For one thing, it's far too crude. You need the right disease, an effective vaccine . . .'

'And what's fucking option three?'

'Missed that,' Turner yelled.

Braden roared, 'Option three.'

Turner jerked to life. 'Option three? An advanced technique that ensures death at forty, plus attitude control. It's in development and progressing well.'

'*1984*, huh?'

Treloar said, 'Art and artifice cross-fertilise.'

'Knocking people off at forty? Attitude control?' Braden fought his anger and disgust.

'You need to realise,' Pollock said, 'that we have two populations to consider. Putting it bluntly, ours and theirs.'

'Jesus! You're going to do it to *us*?'

'Not the same way. Ethics prevent us sterilising or infecting friendly nations.'

'You talk about ethics? You're turning us into ants!'

'Hold it, Chuck. Back up a bit. If you have to chop populations, you can't expect them to do it to themselves. And option three's a humane method. Costly? Difficult? Sure. You've heard of Fulbright's "impotence of power" thesis? There has to be another way. And there *is*.'

'We're in the fucking Pentagon.' Braden pounded the table. 'What happened to honest war?'

'We've tried all that. Hell. Since 1945 we've bombed China, Korea, Guatemala, Indonesia, Cuba, the Congo,' Pollock was ticking them off on his fingers, 'Peru, Laos, Vietnam, Cambodia, Grenada, Libya, El Salvador, Panama, Iraq, Sudan, Afghanistan, Yugoslavia . . . About oil, of course. Always has been.'

Braden cursed. 'No wonder the world loves us.'

'What did he say?' Turner shouted.

'Nothing,' Pollock yelled in his ear.

'What?'

'He said,' Pollock yelled, 'that the world doesn't love us.'

'What girl?'

'World. The WORLD.'

'You don't have to shout,' Turner bellowed and tweaked his hearing aids again.

Treloar ignored the madness, face grave. 'You need to measure all this against our assessment on China. After their charm-offensive with Taiwan, their subs will block key ports. Then they'll try for political reversal. If it fails, they'll attack with their Dong Fengs and follow up with an invasion force.'

Turner yelled, 'What's he saying?'

Treloar ignored him. 'Then you'll have a pre-emptive strike on the USA. These people have a mind-set that makes Russia's duma look cuddly. They'll absorb enormous losses to achieve the imperial dream.'

'So,' Pollock said, 'a pre-emptive strike hard war's fine against minor countries. But, with China, it means all-out nuclear exchange. Means our one option, apart from nuking them first, is soft pre-emption.'

Treloar nodded grimly. 'We're saying hard war capacity half-works — as shield, defence, deterrent. But all-out nuclear war equals biosystem destruction. Forget full spectrum dominance. The only practical way now to control a hugely populous foe is to do it without firing a weapon.'

Pollock chipped in, 'And before they target us.'

'You're talking to an old soldier,' Braden said. 'This stuff's . . .' He waved his hands helplessly. 'You're saying hard war's now passive defence and soft war's a pre-emptive strike?'

'It sounds strange, I know,' Treloar said. 'But except for skirmishes, it holds. Soft war's pre-emptive but needs lead-time. The question is, do we *have* that time?'

'Assuming we do,' Pollock pointed to the screen, 'effective birth control's essential. And for allied nations, option three's the future.'

Turner, hand to ear, caught the word. 'Future? Without this, none at all.'

Braden said, 'Jesus H. Christ. So what are goddamn options three and four?'

The Secretary fondled one of his gold American Eagle cufflinks. 'Option four's hypothetical — a possible combination of two and three. But option three's a current project. Unfortunately descriptions won't help. It's something you have to see.'

'Spare me. When?'

'We're arranging a demonstration for you now.'

19

CARNAGE

Blake watched the second chopper, another battered Huey, land further down the slope behind rocks. Now he could only hear its racket. Was it bringing in more men? Rapid fire rattled from small arms and he heard a grenade explode.

He waited, drenched and shaking with cold.

The firing stopped. The chopper spooled up and lifted off. It hugged the ground and vanished down the slope.

He listened for sounds of life.

Not a shot, shout, groan. Only wind and rain. Soon, the fear of being killed seemed less miserable than crouching where he was. He moved around a glistening outcrop, dashed to the next.

No one fired.

On the second reposition he fell and slithered down the rocks, exposed. His shoulder bashed against a rock, and the impact numbed his arm. He was no seasoned mercenary, just an ex-photographer who'd stumbled into hell. He examined his scratched hands, panting.

Kate! God! Was she all right?

He lurched from rock to rock until he reached a patch of reddened rubble — blood dispersed by rain. And the man Simpson had shot.

Simpson, nearby on his back, was a horror minus cheek and eye.

He edged around the rocks, found a dead yak, its load of pots and food scattered on the shale. Near it were the monks. The hand of one clenched air. Another was doubled beside his shattered bowl. The third, badly chopped up, was on his front.

Then he spotted the man who'd shot them. He looked unharmed, was propped against a rock, legs splayed, weapon near his hand. Instinctively, Blake fired. The body shook but was too trussed in battle harness to collapse.

Turned off?

'Kate?' Jesus, where was she?

The next body had been minced by the chopper's heavy calibre rounds. It was Conchita, her face a mask of pain — fixed grimace, lips drawn back, upper teeth exposed at last in death.

He moved from corpse to corpse but found no one left alive. Just bodies abandoned like puppets, their staring eyes flooded with rain.

'Kaaaate!' he yelled in despair, a cry snatched by wind. A startled yak, now high on a streaming ridge, stared down.

Something blue — moving. Wellington boots.

He stared up at the bloodied man.

It was Ko.

His right arm hung useless by his side and the sopping red sleeve of his jacket was badly bound with a sock. He swayed from loss of blood. He said, 'They took her.'

20

FIELD TRIP

Their destination was Kansas, an easy 900-mile leg from Wright-Patterson in Dayton, Ohio, where Braden's gunship was based. He liked nothing better than cruising above the clouds — free of toll roads, traffic lights, billboards — with the Lockheed Legend humming like a top.

He flew it when he could, held a private licence and a commercial one — although pilots over sixty couldn't fly for US airlines. Connie wanted him to ground himself — was afraid he'd scatter gas, guts and gaskets over the countryside. But, hell, Bonzo Von Haven was flying mercenary missions at seventy!

They were heading for Wichita, home of general aviation, and McConnell, the B–1 bomber base. The new routine was good for the crew. Some kick-the-tyres-light-the-fires toned them up.

The base tower called them. 'Six-six-zero turn right to a heading of zero-three-zero for spacing. Maintain 5000.'

'Roger right to zero-three-zero, maintaining 5000, six-six-zero.'

He checked the contrails to port. The weather was fine with high ceiling and no wind shear. It was a visual approach but his copilot, Freddy, gave airspeed and altitude calls, checked the glide slope indicator. He trusted his gung-ho boss but cross-checked him all the way, uninterested in letting the guy in the next seat kill him. Just as Braden wasn't interested in flight crews with subsonic brains.

'Full flaps,' Braden called.

'Flaps 100. Gear down.'

As they drifted in on final, they saw battleship-grey B–1Bs parked on the apron. He knew the 184th had been the first Air National Guard unit to operate the bomber.

They roared down the centre line, sweet and low, settled on the tarmac like bunnies on a rug.

Freddy said, 'Should impress 'em.'

Braden was glad he'd shown the weekend warriors he could cut it. He pulled the throttles to reverse as the nose wheel kissed. Deceleration pressed him into the harness.

He trundled them onto the taxiway and they shut down, as instructed, outside a hangar with words proclaiming KANSAS AIR NATIONAL GUARD.

'I don't know how long this shit-fit'll take,' he told his crew. 'But they'll sort you guys out. Buick and Stick'll watch the bird.' He'd brought the two huge security men to guard the aircraft and told them to let no one on board.

A small group of officials were waiting on the apron. Among them was Jason, Stone's assistant from the CIA. The buttoned-up spook walked forward in welcome across terracotta-coloured concrete. 'Afternoon, sir. The DCI's asked me to assist you personally from here.'

'Big of him.'

'This is Colonel John McKay, 184th BG of the ANG.'

'Nice landing,' the colonel said and glanced at the BRADEN BUNCH patch on Braden's flying suit.

'Practice,' Braden beamed. He pointed to a droop-nosed bomber. 'What's it like flying a Bone?'

'Culture shock after fighters. You need 18 miles to make a 180-degree turn.'

He turned reluctantly from the elongated aircraft. 'So what are we doing here?'

'Nothing here.' The airman pointed to a Black Hawk with sagging blades and an unfamiliar fuselage. 'You transfer to that for the next leg.'

'I don't like unstable platforms with fans on top. Don't you have an aircraft?'

The colonel chuckled dryly and talked about his bombers as they walked to the chopper. He explained that the maintenance intensive B–1 had been conceived for nuclear delivery, a role assumed by the stealthy B–2, and was now restricted to conventional stores. Despite McKay's enthusiasm, Braden suspected they were planes without a mission — too expensive a platform to deliver conventional bombs to standard targets, and now too vulnerable for long range penetration or for strikes without fighter escort.

As he reached the chopper, he understood what was different about it. The windows behind the cockpit were panelled over. 'What's this?'

'Special transport. Still serviced and flown by the 135th but it's our Executive Flight Detachment version.'

'Looks like you're trying to stop passengers finding out where they're going.'

'Got it in one. Have a good trip.'

'Show my crew the hardware, will you.'

'My pleasure.'

Braden climbed in, sorry to see the last of the man. The fun bit was over. Now he had to face the doomsday schemes of Turner interpreted through the guarded mind of Jason. The standard spartan troop seats in the cabin had been replaced by padded ones and the cocoon-like space was unconnected with the cockpit. 'Kansas,' he said. 'So . . . Leavenworth? Riley?'

'No, sir,' Jason said. 'We're going to a detention and research facility partly funded by DARPA and the Alternative Control Technology Lab at Wright-Patterson AFB, Dayton.'

'Detention?'

'Part of the base is a military prison. The other is a molecular manufacturing test-bed for nanomolar chemistry and pharmacytes.'

'Sorry. I speak English.'

Jason smiled tightly. 'That's how I felt the first time I heard it.'

The twin turbo shafts spooling up sounded muted. The cabin had been soundproofed. The machine lifted off and tilted into its heading.

'So explain it,' Braden said.

'It means they implant molecular machines in the human brain which can deliver chemicals or block impulses at the cellular level.'

'You're turning people into robots?'

Jason didn't answer.

21

RETREAT

Ko struggled to be heard against the sound of the storm. 'They've gone.' He swayed, fell on his knees.

Blake squatted to look at the man's arm. It needed a proper bandage or he'd die. The medical kit! He knew the animal and pack. Not the black beast on the slope. A brown one with shorter horns. One of two he'd seen nibbling grass. He tightened the tourniquet, staggered off.

The yak shied as he came up, tried to bolt between two rocks but jammed itself. It backed out, red-rimmed eyes bulging, belched.

He became an automaton, cold efficiency replacing despair. He released the lid of a rattan pannier and dug inside. She'd have wanted him to save Ko and it was all he could do for her now. Try to save the man he now considered responsible for her death.

He cut away Ko's sleeve. The slug had gone through muscle but the bone seemed unbroken. He sprinkled on antibiotic powder, put a pressure-bandage on the seeping holes, bound the arm to the man's side and wrapped him in a salvaged parka. Then he propped a carbine between two rocks and suspended an IV fluid pack from it.

He probed the man's forearm for a vein and worked the needle in, exactly as the nurse had done the one time he'd given blood.

There were spare ropes in the load of the dead yak. He found one, then approached the animal that carried extra ammunition. He made the clicking sound the herders had used, repeated their unintelligible words. The village yaks had nose-rings but not these. So he roped the beast around the horns, led it to the dead one and tied the rope to the horns of the carcass. The yak grunted, snuffled, unperturbed.

He unloaded ammunition from its panniers so that he could replace it with essentials. There was no riding saddle. Ko couldn't walk but could be tied between the in-sloping baskets.

He stumbled back.

Ko showed no sign of pain.

Another man padded toward them. Long tunic, rubber boots. An apprehensive native herder — perhaps the last alive.

Ko beckoned the man close. He whispered to him in his native language then turned to Blake.

Blake bent again to hear.

'I've told him to round up some yaks. Now. One thing we must find — a communications device. Black metal box. You know where it's packed?'

He nodded.

Ko shut his eyes.

He stumbled away to salvage what they'd need, and was careful to leave nothing that indicated survivors. He examined the attackers' faces but recognised none. He searched their bodies for papers, scanned them, replaced them in the same pockets. He knew where they were — knew each step of the return journey and twist of track. Knew it would take three hours to reach the nearest farm.

The yaks' steep spines and low-held heads made them unnerving to ride. But they lifted Ko onto the beast, placed one of his legs in each basket and lashed him on.

They set off down the mountain in streaming rain with two snuffling supply beasts following Ko's yak. Ko, wrapped in a waterproof groundsheet, dozed much of the way. The herder knew no English so communication was by signs.

Blake trudged through the downpour, stumbling on flinty earth, almost oblivious to the cold and his sodden clothes. He'd become a beast himself, bludgeoned to emotional numbness.

They had her.

That meant they'd torture her.

Then kill her.

22

BUNKER

When the door of the chopper slid back, Braden expected flat Kansas plains. But they'd landed on an underground pad with sides of concrete and steel. The square sky above the slowing rotor blades was ringed by blowing wheat — and was being shut out by metal covers on rails closing from both sides. Yellow stalks at the edge of these covers showed they doubled as vast planter boxes. The dull clang as they joined echoed in the cavernous space. A compressor on a wall rack started up as hydraulic jacks raised them level with the field.

The chopper was now flanked by four guards in navy-coloured fatigues. They carried automatic weapons, had headsets and wore security tags.

'Some place!' Braden said. 'Let me guess. We're in the salt mine vault under the wheat fields near Hutchinson?'

'No, sir. Nothing so obvious. No, we dug this to order. A poultice of site-risk analysis went in here. I think they picked the dreariest spot around.'

'In Kansas, that must be something.'

He followed Jason to a duty-room built into one of the walls, where they stared into iris scanners, then stood on a plate for further scanning. Braden was requested to check in his clasp knife. They gave him a tag marked VISITOR with a clear plastic back that revealed an electronic circuit.

'We'll visit the detention block first,' Jason said.

The metal pressure door in front of them hissed open, exposing gas-tight seals at its edge. They stepped through into a reinforced-concrete corridor with a domed ceiling and fire sprinklers down one side. They climbed aboard an electric buggy and the armed driver put it into drive.

The buggy whined along the bleak tunnel and stopped outside a security office fitted with rows of mimic screens and winking buttons.

Beyond the checkpoint a series of iron grilles successively opened to let them pass. Once inside, they were escorted by two guards with duress buttons on their belts — black devices designed to set off an alarm if pressed or if they fell. They walked over a metal grating. There were more gratings on levels below. It looked like a factory for battery humans.

'The grunts in here,' Jason said, 'are total psychos — self-obsessed, irresponsible and utterly ruthless.'

'Good soldiers, huh?'

They passed bare cells with seatless steel toilets and metal beds. Surveillance cameras high on the walls had Plexiglas shields scratched by thrown objects. In the cells were men wearing orange T-shirts and shorts. They'd hung towels on the bars for privacy. They didn't look like crazed killers. Most were slumped on their beds.

'So who knows about this place? Are you sharing development with any of our allies or working with their people?'

Jason shook his head. 'When you see what we do here, I think you'll agree it's not the kind of stuff you share.'

23

KO

At dusk, they reached the simple, three-roomed farmhouse where they'd bought potatoes on their way up. The owner and his wife helped them get Ko inside. They propped him near the low stone hearth. The wall behind it was black from cooking and the crude room mercifully warm.

Ko revived enough to speak to the farmer and herder, who listened respectfully. The herder unloaded the supplies and left with the yaks.

Blake protested. 'We need him to get you out of here.'

'No,' Ko whispered. 'They'll torture him if they find him.'

Blake checked Ko's arm. The bleeding had stopped but the wound was inflamed. 'We have to get you to hospital. You're a moral for gas gangrene.'

'If you find a doctor in this country, you're doing well.' A bout of coughing. 'Life is brief. And death an observant thief, as you've seen.'

He probed Ko's wound, wondering what to do. For Kate's sake, he couldn't let the monk die. He squatted in the puddle that had come from his drenched clothes, while the farmer's wife placidly cooked mash.

'Well, if you insist I live,' Ko placed a poker in the coals, 'fight fire with fire.'

'Cauterising the outside won't help. The bullet's infected it right through.'

'So push the poker through. Can you do that?'

'If I could, and you could stand it, it still mightn't work.'

'But worth trying, don't you think?' He thrust the poker deeper into the coals.

The woman offered them battered iron bowls full of what tasted like bitter porridge. After they'd eaten, Ko gravely, intently, handed her back his empty bowl and turned to Blake. 'Now. It's hot enough.'

'When we get you dry and you're rested a bit, we could try it. There's morphine in the kit.'

'No drugs. And you're evading. Do it now.'

Blake checked the poker. 'I'll have to give you something before we . . .'

'No.'

'Not sure I can do it like this.'

Ko stared at the fire impassively. 'You do it now. And do it well.'

Blake bared the damaged arm again. The poker was thin enough to go through but represented rough surgery indeed.

Ko waited.

Blake retrieved the poker and blew off ash. The heat warmed his face. He held the glowing tip over the wound then gripped Ko's elbow firmly, gritted his teeth, and pressed.

The metal seared into the flesh. The smell of cooking meat. The woman shrieked and covered her eyes.

Ko's sizzling, charring arm seemed completely relaxed. He didn't change expression or flinch. Blake forced the red-hot iron right through his arm like a spear. Then, revolted and gagging, withdrew it.

Ko looked suddenly withered and old.

Blake packed the mess with antibiotic powder, got Ko into the second room and undressed him. He towelled the strong peasant's body and helped him into a dry sleeping bag. Ko's murmured 'Thank you' was like a voice from the grave.

24

NANOBOTS

Braden followed Jason through the detention block, wondering what he'd see next. Or wouldn't see. They were still playing along with his demands. But further probing could be terminal.

Still, he was safe enough here. They wouldn't wipe him on an official visit. Or target his home, because his domestic security was phenomenal. And his high profile was jamming them, too. One whiff of an attack and the media would take them apart. No, he decided, they were baffled. They'd had official bloodhounds before — but not one with supreme power to snoop.

A guard punched numbers into a keypad. A door slid open and they entered a room with a stepped floor and plastic seats. Instead of a screen, it faced a one-way window. Through it he saw an empty space with doors each end. The only object there was a riot baton in the middle of the floor. In front of them, closest to the window, two men sat behind a console.

'Control room,' Jason said.

One of the technicians turned to face them. He was intense and cadaverous-looking with a sharp jaw and dark hair. 'Good afternoon, Mr Braden. We are honoured to have you here. I am Velimir Korac, resident genius.' He laughed at his joke. He had a middle European accent. 'Please sit.'

Braden sat.

'First let me tell you what you'll see.' He turned back to his console. 'Send him in.'

Jason murmured details. 'Korac started with the Department of Bioengineering at the University of Utah, then he . . .'

A man entered the test area encased in what looked like a fire-entry suit. It was white and so heavily padded he could barely walk. Huge mitten-like gloves extended almost to his shoulders and the visor of the helmet was shielded by a metal grid.

Korac twisted back to address them. 'This is a warden — an unpleasant man our subject hates. Our subject is a Vietnam vet who committed terrible acts on women and children. Like all psychopaths, he's a moral imbecile — lives in a world of momentary obsessions and is completely unable to relate to others.'

'Could do well in local government,' Braden said.

Korac grinned. 'He was a sergeant with a medal for bravery — now court-martialled for multiple murder of civilians. He's normally — or you could say abnormally — a raging animal and extremely strong.' Korac pointed to his head. 'In his brain we've introduced by diapedesis — that's transendothelial migration — cytonavigating by a combination of triangulation and functional methods, nanobots able to block the receptors of particular groups of cells. In other words, we've introduced neuro-compatible interfaces that can suppress neural firing and much more.'

Braden didn't hide his displeasure. He detested technology he couldn't understand.

'By *ex vivo* communication, or what we call in-messaging, we can communicate with his neurons, neural connections and synapses at the molecular level — that is, far more precisely than by introducing any drug — and control the on-board computers of the bots which are, as you can imagine, little more than a series of transistors. By this means we adjust the functioning of our subject's brain. To begin with, we'll introduce him as he is — without any adaptation.' Korac turned back to his panel, checked parameters with the other man.

'Internal subsystems?'

'Stable.'

'On-board sensors?'

'Positioning positive.'

'Power?'

'Holding at three picowatts.'

'Conjugation?'

'Acceptable limits.'

'Field strength and frequency?'

'Corresponding.'

The genius rechecked screens. 'Dum te dum te . . . Seems in order. Okay. Let him in.'

A door opened. The man who bounded in wore regulation orange clothes. He had sly, close-set eyes, a bullet head, thick hairy limbs and seemed manic. He scooped the baton off the floor and, yelling with fury, rushed at the padded figure, as if homicide were his standard greeting. He brought the baton in low and slammed it up between the man's legs hard enough to emasculate a bull.

As the padded form tried to push him off, the maniac grabbed one of the long mitts and yanked it so violently the anchoring shoulder-strap parted. The gauntlet came off, exposing the man's unprotected arm. The warden turned to the window and yelled.

'Watch now,' Korac touched a control.

The madman dropped the baton as if no longer sure why he was holding it, stood passively, smiling, as if filled with good will.

The warden punched the subject in the face. The man fell back on the floor, clutched his face and began to cry.

The warden retrieved his missing gauntlet and dragged it on, then picked up the baton to attack again.

Korac leant toward a stalk microphone. 'Enough.'

The snarling man reluctantly stepped back.

Korac cut the sound to the room and twisted around to face them, grinning sourly. 'The hardest thing is controlling the non-bots, as we call them. Which illustrates the reason for this project.'

'Fucking hell.' Braden stared at the floor.

Jason said, 'We'll visit the warfare section next. Need some coffee?'

'Coffee? What's going to be in it. Nanobots?'

Korac stood up. 'Curious you should say that. We have, in fact, used coffee to introduce them into the body. They're capable of natation.'

'Great.' Braden stood up slowly. 'Hold the coffee. I need a Scotch. And I want to see the seal on the bottle.'

25

DEBRIEF

Blake sat with Ko half the night, mopping his brow with a rag. The monk refused pills for his fever so there was nothing more he could do. Near dawn, Blake climbed into his own bag and slept.

It was sunny outside when he woke. Ko was shivering and the woman was bending over him.

Blake felt his brow. Clammy, but the fever seemed less. 'How do you feel?'

'Not good. But not good is also good. In our tradition, no one helps you. If you die or live, that's fate.'

'Hardly reverence for life.'

'It is. For cosmic life. Not to attach to form is suchness.' A ghost of a smile. 'We call this our life. But it's only lent to us for experience.' He shut his eyes, weak from loss of blood that they had no way to replace. He whispered, 'Everything leaves us. Until we see the wisdom of not being attached. Then everything rushes back, desperate to be with us again. We chase after our shadow till, one day, we turn to the sun. Then, wherever we go, our shadow submissively follows.'

'Fine words. But they won't bring Kate back.' He unbound the man's arm. The skin looked less angry. 'Why didn't they just kill her?'

'I don't know. There's only so much I see.'

'Well, do you have an opinion?'

'I suspect they'll try to use her to get at us.'

Blake repacked the wound with antibiotic and covered it again. 'Can you imagine what they'll do to her?' He covered his face with his hands.

The next day, Ko was well enough to walk. Blake helped him to a stone-and-shingle barn further up the hill, well away from the farmhouse and track. He made a fire. The smoke filtered from cracks around the ramshackle door but was not enough to asphyxiate them or signal where they were. He trudged back to the farmhouse, ferrying what they'd need. On the last trip he brought the black box. Ko hadn't told him to open it.

It rained again and he rigged a poncho to divert leaks from the roof.

Ko, huddled in a blanket, stared vacantly at the door. The wound had reduced him to a mortal. But as his strength grew, his inner cohesion returned. It had been difficult enough with Kate. Now, jammed in this shed with her super-boss, Blake felt immature and resentful. His mind supplied a D. H. Lawrence quote: 'The only authority is one of consciousness.' He listened to the rain and spitting fire. 'Life's a game to you, I suppose?'

Ko stared at the door.

'I'm trying to understand you people. Don't treat me like a child.'

'Life's a field of endeavour. But painful if you believe in it. You need a foot in both camps.'

'What's the other camp?'

The monk didn't answer immediately. 'The other camp has beautiful surroundings but a high entry fee. You have to pay . . . with everything you own, love, want. Everything you are. Inside, there has to be nothing. Then, the blessing. To be everything, one has to be nothing. Very difficult.'

'Impossible.'

'Doing what's possible isn't enough.'

'Kate said that.'

'She did?' His pensive look.

'Well, you may not be infallible but you see things. So, is she still alive?'

'Yes.' Ko shifted painfully and changed the subject. 'You searched the bodies?'

He nodded. 'I was trying to find out who they were.'

'And what did you discover?'

'You tell me.'

'A few papers. A photograph. American.' It was a statement. And right.

Mind reading? He didn't know. 'They were careful. They had no letters or identification on them. I found lists of radio code clicks and a receipt that might have come from somewhere in Pakistan. There was a photograph of a woman. That was the most significant thing.'

'Why?'

'She was standing near the fork of a two-lane road. There was a sign saying HIGHWAY 50. The sign had bullet holes in it. There was flat farmland all around and a side-road went off behind a field of grain.'

'Go on.'

'I saw a late night doco once called *Journey Into Mystery*. It was about a trip through west Kansas. They were flogging it as an ominous place. They showed the presenter driving along US Route 50, showed Holcomb and the house where the Clutter family was killed, flashed through a place called Lakin — and stopped just before that sign.'

Ko stared at the door but seemed to be visualising the scene. 'Go on.'

'The presenter said everyone was leaving the area, that the old cow towns were boarded up or dying, but up there — and he pointed up this side road — they were building a new settlement. He said he couldn't show it because it was some kind of high-security area. Next, they showed the pickup driving off and, as they panned it through, there was this sign with the bullet holes.'

'The same bullet holes?'

'Exact match.'

'You amaze me.'

'I sometimes amaze myself. Kate said you wanted me on the Tritter project. What I want to know is who's got her? Tritter? Or the Waffen CIA?'

Ko stared into space for some time, then said slowly, 'I think they're working together. It may have been a CIA operation. But I suspect Katherine will end up as a guest of Tritter.'

'Then I want to get the bastard.'

'Be careful what you wish for.'

26

DEATH WATCH

Braden was slightly drunk. After a double Scotch and more booze at lunch he was taken to an anteroom and issued with a white smock, canvas overshoes and a cap.

Korac said, 'We don't like dust. Dandruff's the killer in this environment. And there are positive pressure clean rooms you can't enter.'

'I'm used to labs.'

'Not like this one,' Jason said.

He put on the cap.

They went through a blue-lit airlock plastered with warning signs. The hospital-white underground laboratory had a ceiling supported on thick columns. They walked between red lines on the floor past glassed-off sections and exclusion booths.

He was shown the mass spectrometer, nano-centrifuge, molecular assembler, the PET and mechanosynthesis sections. He was introduced to protein engineers, designers of proximal probes, chemists, physicists, microbiologists. He saw microscopes that looked nothing like anything and had three-letter names — SAM, SEM, SPM, SFM, STM . . .

'Each has its shielded area,' Korac said, 'because it's affected by surges or changes in the magnetic field. We're doing well with our scanning force microscope — got tubes to four nanometres thick. We've gone to three, but they're unstable. We cap them with a hemispheric fullerene and it gives us a chemical probe.'

'Is this something to do with buckyballs?'

'Yes. A perfect container. Made of carbon, so tolerated by the body. The tubes are extruded from graphite rods — vaporised by electric arc in a helium filled chamber. Helium from the south-west of this state. This next section refines nanolasers. You have to be a polyhistor to run this place. They don't call me genius for nothing.'

'How much do you pay them?'

Korac got it instantly and grinned. He took them into the laser section. 'We've shrunken these smaller than the wavelength of emitted light. Get a boost from quantum effects. They're thresholdless. Semiconductor diode lasers aren't even thirty per cent efficient. These are ninety. Almost every photon adds to the fundamental mode or output light.'

After half an hour of this, Braden, his learning-curve vertical, was led to a briefing room. When he sat, the alcohol hit. The concentration needed for the gunship flight had caught up with him as well.

The lights were dimmed and Korac took the floor, using projected diagrams and slides to emphasise points.

'The scale of nanomolar chemistry's difficult to describe. If picomolar represents, say, 10 kilograms of sugar dissolved in a harbour then femtomolar is ten to the minus fifteen molar — equivalent to a handful of sugar in that harbour. Now ferritin . . .'

Braden, at the end of his intellectual rope, peered dutifully at the slides.

'Let's start with the Niels Bohr atom. At this level, you only affect electrons. You're familiar with shells, exchanging and sharing of electrons, charges, unstable, radioactive?'

He tried to stay with it. 'I did basic chemistry. Covalent bonds, ionic bonds — sodium chloride, that stuff.'

'So you know that, when we come to physics, the orbital theory doesn't relate?'

'You mean the status of the nucleus?' He was pickled enough to sleep.

'Exactly. Isotopes and so on. You can have isotopes of hydrogen, for instance. You realise the nuclei are different but the electrons the same?'

He nodded.

'Good.' Korac skipped through slides. 'Do you understand peptides? Fragments of proteins made up of amino acids? Forget neuro-peptides which have five to fifteen amino acids. We're talking peptide hormones active at one part per billion or trillion.'

'You've lost me.'

'So we'll start here.' The slide read PROTEIN ENGINEERING: THE BASICS.

'Just a minute, Velimir.' Jason leaned toward Braden. 'How much of this is helpful to you?'

'How much is there?' The booze was shutting him down.

'An overview takes two hours. The general summary goes for ten intensive one-day sessions.'

'My mind's out to lunch. I'm hammered. Can we cut to the chase?'

Jason said, 'I think Mr Braden has a working understanding of what we do here. Could we just run the warfare tapes?'

'But without a broad idea of the techniques . . .'

'I appreciate what you're saying. But he's completely new to this and there's only so much you can absorb in a day.'

Braden's lids were drooping. 'Look, I don't need to know how it works — just need to see what it does.' On the flight back, he thought, I'll need Freddy in the left-hand seat.

'A shame.' Korac seemed distressed. 'For a layman, you're very bright, and you would have appreciated the scope of what we've done. However . . .' He dimmed the lights, pressed a button on the player. 'These tapes have no commentary for security reasons. I'll explain what's happening as we go through.'

The first scene looked like a junkyard — cars piled high on each other, pieces of rusting machinery. A soldier crouched behind some drums, ready to attack. A time-code flickered in the corner of the screen.

It cut to the reverse angle — across an access lane. A second soldier crouched there. Both had carbines and helmet-mounted headsets.

It cut back to the first soldier as a burst of fire came from across the potholed alley. The soldier grimaced with rage.

Korac paused it. 'You're seeing the remote-control stimulation of the aggression response. This man doesn't know his weapon's adjusted to jam. In a moment, you'll see the other soldier — a control soldier with functioning gun but no receptors implanted — leave cover and attack.' He hit the button.

The hidden soldier came out firing. The crouching man in the foreground tried to shoot him, glared at his jammed carbine enraged, and bounded out, still intent on attack.

The normal soldier shot him.

But the conditioned man staggered on and wrestled the weapon from the other's hands.

Korac paused it again. 'Note what's happening here. Our turbo trooper — that's what we call them — is insensible to pain, doesn't know he's dying. Rage carries him along. As well, he's astonishingly strong. Insane people are. Have you ever seen four strong male nurses trying to restrain a frail old lady in a psych ward? We still don't understand the mechanism there. Now watch.'

He stop-framed the next section. The turbo ripped the carbine from his opponent with such force that the gun-sling almost dragged off the man's helmet. As the conventional soldier fought for his gun, the turbo chopped him in the throat until he fell. The turbo, blood pouring from his chest, stood over him, kicking him.

Braden fought to keep his lunch down. 'Fuck.'

Korac paused it again. 'At this point, our man is kept alive by the chemical momentum of rage. He has perhaps ten seconds to live. However nanobots also facilitate cytocide — the killing of living cells. What's more, it's instant. Here we send the signal. Watch.'

The tape rolled again and the turbo pitched forward — dead, it seemed, before he hit the ground.

Korac ejected the cassette, put in another. 'It may not appear that impressive. But consider the implications. Super soldiers untroubled by fatigue, cowardice or pain who fight on even when mortally wounded and who can be terminated by remote control. A squad of these soldiers has just been used for a limited, covert operation. At this stage, of course, the control mechanisms are cumbersome and technician-intensive. But that'll change. We're developing carbon nanotubes for body armour that increase ballistic protection tenfold and SMRT telemonitoring to . . .'

'What the hell's that?'

'Nanosensors that monitor metabolism by analysing exhaled breath.'

Braden choked down his bile. 'These guys are . . . automatons.'

'Virtually.'

'What the fuck happened to loyalty, courage, pride?'

'Things have moved on,' Jason said.

27

SUB

Blake braced himself against the wheelhouse of the heaving, stinking boat. The smell of rotten fish was almost bearable now. The rusted hull was a sieve and the sweating diesel below, as well as pushing them along, had to power the pumps. For a while, despite a stern wind, they'd barely made five knots and he'd given the peevish Bengalis extra money to raise the sail — a filthy rag on a mizzen, the one stick the boat had left. It was ripped near the gaff but the hot wind added two knots.

It had been arduous getting Ko out of Bhutan unseen. The airport was too risky. So he'd used the maps of the subcontinent imprinted in his mind. They'd ridden the bizarre narrow-gauge train from Darjeeling to Siliguri. It shared the roads with bullock carts and sand was sprinkled on the wet tracks by men perched on the front of its engine. The second train, to Calcutta, offered luxuries to those who could afford them. He chose rail to confuse their attackers. With luck, they'd be written off as dead.

The cruise down the Hooghly from Howrah had been an interminable chug. The variety of craft on the river was as diverse as India itself — from primitive *nouka*s and jute-loaded square-rigged boats to battered old ferries and freighters. They'd survived tidal flows, silt banks, a collision with a dredge, drifted past settlements, ghats, mangroves. Then, beyond the Sagar Island lighthouse, they passed the last of the flotsam — a bloated dog and a broken thong — and headed into the Bay of Bengal.

The boat's rudimentary wheelhouse didn't run to an echo-sounder but after puttering for two days they'd decided the bay was deep enough. That morning, Ko had opened the black box and trailed a device like a fluorescent tube in the sea. Blake's relentless mind belched up an article he'd read about a plasma aerial:

A RADIO WAVE SHOT INTO A DIELECTRIC TUBE OF GAS BY A METAL ELECTRODE, MOVES UP THE TUBE, STRIPPING ELECTRONS FROM THE GAS AND IONISING THEM TO FORM PLASMA. THE ELECTRONS OSCILLATE, FORMING ELECTRO-MAGNETIC RADIO WAVES. WHEN POWER IS OFF, THE ANTENNA IS NEUTRAL, AS INVISIBLE TO RADAR AS AIR.

The attempt at contact was dangerous. It took all their technology to conceal the sub's position. Did the device transmit a VLF microburst on prearranged frequency for machine decoding? Was the burst received by a floating antenna trailed behind the sub?

He walked from the wheelhouse to the stern, bracing himself against the movement of the boat. The swell moved sluggishly, like thick soup. Despite unbroken cloud the monsoon rain had stopped.

Ko sat straight-backed against the transom on a pile of fish-net, like an icon. His arm was healing but he looked frail.

Blake squatted beside him. 'Do we have an ETA?'

'They'll pick us up tonight.'

'If we don't hit a storm and sink.'

Ko glanced at the puzzled Bengalis in the wheelhouse. 'You did well to get them out to sea. They're not brave.'

'Avarice is a wonderful thing.'

'You've been most resourceful and I thank you.'

He stared at a battered winch. The time with Ko had been tough. Even a saint, he suspected, would become peeved if exposed to Christ night and day for a week. 'I hope it was worth it.'

'Everything's worth it. If you're intentional.'

'Morphic resonance?'

'Existence is conditional.'

'Subject to dependent co-origination with nonsubstantiality?'

A look of contempt. 'I detest your famous memory when it's connected to your ego.'

'Sorry,' he lied. 'So you're saying that everything matters?'

'I'm saying that life's an infinitely malleable dream. And the smallest thought, intention, act, affects it.'

'Like the loss of fifteen people?' He still blamed Ko for the attack on the squad. For days, what sleep he'd snatched had been disturbed by the nightmare of what might be happening to Kate.

Ko stared at the sea, expressionless. 'Everything visible changes. Only non-existence endures. Therefore nothing and everything matters. One needs both aspects. Compassion and sunyata.'

He didn't want them at all. He just wanted to sleep. 'I'm sick of Buddhist sophistry. I took it from her. But you don't have her . . . redeeming physical attributes.'

— 105 —

The monk's face became stone. 'And you think I'm a stupid old man for wasting my breath on you. You have the memory of an elephant, the mind of a grub and you're so caught in your reactions you can't see that I'm addressing your potential. But when you've lived more, discarded more, you'll remember.' He twisted a strand of net around his finger. 'My time's valuable, Blake, and like it or not, you have the misfortune to be in it.'

Reams of Buddhist texts scrolled through his mind from a book he'd once scanned. He couldn't resist another gripe. 'In the Kashyapa chapter of the *Sutra of the Great Mass of Jewels,* it states, "Emptiness does not make phenomena empty, because phenomena are themselves emptiness."'

'Do you see what a smart-arse you are?'

'Does it matter? If I don't exist? So. Address my potential. What's it mean?'

Ko's look would have wilted cactus. He tapped the deck with his good hand. 'This boat exists. Suffering exists. If they didn't, emptiness wouldn't exist. And emptiness isn't a blank, but a fullness of potential. The manifest and unmanifest are two sides of a coin. So what is to be abandoned?'

'Search me.'

'Attachment.' The word was snapped out. 'Living is dying. Dying to everything now. To "I" or "mine". For instance, to your concerns about Katherine. Not clinging is an aspect of sunyata. It's also the root of Buddhist virtues and the gateway to reality.'

'Easy to say. But I happen to love her. And someone's probably tearing her apart.'

Ko nodded slowly. 'You see how difficult simple things are?'

* * *

The wind died with the day. The night was breathless, stifling, moonless. They told the Bengalis to throttle back until the prop just kept them bow-on to the swell. He could see nothing on the water but knew the submarine could see them.

The first sign of contact was the sound of muffled outboards. He heard it seconds before the grappling-hook clanged on the rail. The taciturn clearance divers from the sub were barely visible — just the sheen of their black wetsuits in the dim wheelhouse light. Their sophisticated semi-submersible, with its sonar, satnav, mortar launcher and negative buoyancy engines, was fully inflated.

The men helped Ko on board as if he were the Dayspring From On High. Blake handed their bundles over the side, climbed the rail and, when the next wave forced the craft against the hull, jumped down. A diver moved behind the centre console and the craft churned almost silently away.

As the jabbering of the boat's startled crew faded behind them he saw phosphorescence ahead, like a shoal, that marked the edge of the submarine's enormous hull. Its huge beam was due to its unique design — external missile tubes mounted between the pressure hull and the outer casing. In the slight swell, the great shape looked solid as a rock.

They lowered a harness for Ko. Blake climbed the jumping-ladder dangling on the casing, felt the welcome coldness of sea against his skin. There were the usual square gaps on the vast cylinder where anechoic tiles had worked free.

As they reached the base of the fin, hands hauled them up. They helped the monk into the fin, then down the hatch into the pressure hull. Blake descended next into the blast of cool air coming off the scrubbers. Again he stood in the red-lit cream and white world of blowing air and ubiquitous piping, wiring, panels, gauges.

The COB greeted him, his red hair crew-cut and wearing trademark soiled skivvy and work-pants.

Blake said, 'Gordon Kelly.'

'You remembered.' The man shook his hand, frowning and sympathetic. 'But then, you remember everything, don't you? They say you've done a wonderful job. We're devastated, of course, about Kate. The CO wants to see you. But not till you feel ready, he said.'

He heard rumbling water entering through ballast vents. 'I need to crash.'

'Right. We'll get you dry clothes and feed you.' He looked concerned again. 'I'm sorry.'

Blake descended ladders through the machinery maze and headed for the racks. He peeled off his sodden clothes, put them in a laundry bag and tagged it. He fumbled in his kit for something dry, avoiding the locker of spare clothes salvaged from the dead. He found a vacant bunk, yanked the curtain across. Alone at last, he lay thinking of her again, tears seeping from closed eyes.

He slept.

Hours later, clean, dry, rested, he climbed to the top deck, trudged past command control, sonar and entered the control room.

He'd toured the curve-roofed cavern last time. Planesman, helmsman, ballast control, fire control, nav suite. He recognised many of the crew — committed people from nations around the world.

Pale in the glow from the automatic plotting table was the thickset officer of the deck, Lieutenant Yuri Apollonov. The OOD straightened as Blake came in, held out his hand. 'The hero returns to join us. What good work you have done.'

People looked around from their consoles, smiled, clapped. 'What's that for?' he asked.

'Without you, perhaps Mr Ko not now alive.'

'Did my best to get rid of him, but you can't knock the bugger off.'

Apollonov's lopsided grin looked odd on one so morose.

'I'm told the skipper wants to see me.'

'Is true.' He picked up a ship's phone, rang through and told Blake to report to Hale's cabin.

As he walked forward through the creaking hull, the CO emerged to welcome him. 'Blake. Thank God you made it. Wonderful stuff. Come in.' Hale, a distinguished-looking ex-RN officer, had a slight American lilt, a relic of an exchange program early in his career. He wore casual clothes like his crew. But his were notably clean — not rumpled or greasy but pool-side party smart.

Blake entered the compact cabin. Fold-down desk, bunk, communications wall with annunciator, and — the supreme badge of office — a tiny en suite shower/washroom.

'Grab a pew,' Hale said. 'Fancy a G & T?'

'Could use one.'

The CO opened a miniature cold-locker and mixed drinks. 'So, we live to fight another day.'

'Who attacked us?'

'Still working on that one. But it's definitely connected with a certain Adolphous Tritter, whom I believe you've heard of?' He handed a glass across. 'Chin chin.'

Blake raised his glass.

'I'm sorry about Katherine.'

'Can you imagine what they'll do to her?'

'I know.' He shook his head sadly.

Blake gulped his drink.

'We've lost so many over the years. Wonderful people. Now a whole blessed squad. Not our finest hour.' He sighed. 'So, a debrief if you don't mind.' He placed a mini-recorder on the desk. 'Take your time.'

An hour and three drinks later, Blake had recounted the details of the Bhutan expedition. Hale switched off the recorder. 'All grist for our *contemptus mundi* analysts. So are you ready to have a crack at Tritter?'

'I want his guts. Kate must have left notes, leads. Could I see them?'

Hale stared at him keenly, then lifted a wall-phone.

28

SITREP

'Human robots. Fuck!' The President paced his office, swearing.

Braden sat by the fire — unlit today. 'So that's about the size of it. So far.'

'It's out of hand,' Jessop bellowed.

'They call it influence technology. They see it as a form of non-lethal warfare. Of course, the tactical potential's enormous. And those are just the penal and military applications. With plastic bullets and foam, people know they're being controlled. But if they don't know, you've got total control.' He stared up at the curved cornice, stared down at a bust of Lincoln sculptured in unpolished sapphire. 'We're talking about information controlled by the government from inside people's heads.'

'Fuck! The CISS could have a ball with this.'

'And there's something that goes beyond that. Called negative externalities.'

'What the fuck . . . ?'

'It's economic double-speak for social disruption.'

'They've crossed the line,' Jessop spat. 'Soft war! Fuck! Can't sell soft war to the constituency.'

'The way they're going, you won't have to.' He stared at the rug. The wonderful rug.

'Jesus fucking Christ!'

'Can you pull their funding?'

'Not effectively. The appropriations are masked. That's why hammers for the military cost 200 bucks each. How much more of this is there? What's this option four?'

'They say it's hypothetical. Some combination of the others. Not sure I buy that. You can bet they're not telling us everything.'

The President stood trying to control himself, a big man with white knuckles. He dropped his shoulders, as if he'd read somewhere you should do that, turned back. 'Chuck, you're doing great. I'm not sore at you, understand?'

'I know.'

'Okay. No action yet. If we bore into them too soon, we'll only drill out half the decay. Agree?'

He nodded.

'So keep digging presently. And get a handle on everything you can.'

29

TRITTER

The submarine's intelligence section was on the bottom deck between galley and torpedo room. It was the size of a domestic garage and crammed with metal drawers that moved vertically on cogged rails. Blake was admitted by a peculiar woman — elderly, with overcurled blonde hair and wing-frame spectacles. Her floral dress belonged in a circus. So did the slippers with pompoms.

'This way.' She turned side-on to squeeze down one of the two narrow aisles between the stacks. Her ample breasts almost jammed her. To follow, he had to breathe out.

Beyond the stacks, three bolted-down swivel chairs faced a bench crowded with computer terminals. In one chair sat a fiftyish Japanese man.

'This is Kazuya,' the woman said.

The man nodded, looked back at his screen.

'And I'm Flora. Sit there.' She thumped a pile of files and papers on the bench. 'Background on the oil industry, Tritter and the Fiji deal.' Her accent was South African. 'Katherine's latest notes are on this machine. When you're through, we'll talk.'

He scanned the stack, turned to the computer, glanced at each screen a split second, turned back to the woman. 'Is that it?'

She glared. 'Are you taking this seriously or not?'

'I am.'

'Like hell you are.' She grabbed a file at random, read, 'Why do OPEC estimates of cumulative production contain systematic errors?'

'By overstating their reserves, they're allowed to export more oil.'

She flipped pages. 'At the end of '96, how much conventional oil was there in P50 reserves?'

'The *Oil and Gas Journal* reported 1019 giga-barrels of oil, *World Oil* 1160 Gbo. The actual figure was 850 Gbo.'

Baulked, she grabbed another folder. 'Explain sensor feedback in directional drilling.'

'Mud pumped through the pipe rotates the bit, carries out rock fragments and also goes through a rotating valve which converts data radioed to the tool from various sensors into surges in the mud-stream. At the surface, these pulses are converted to a 10-bits-per-second digital signal.'

Kazuya said, 'Wow. We give you job here. Great condition. Are lock in each shift, work eight hour on, eight off, eat tin pea, never see sun.'

Blake said, 'Bit cramped for three.'

'Like summit of Fuji at daybreak. I go now to void body's waste.' With a space-constricted bob, he edged between the racks.

Blake swivelled to face the woman. 'I have questions.'

'Thank God for that.' She found a jar on the cluttered desk and removed the lid.

'Tritter married one of the engineers who designed his rigs. Would she be a lead?'

'Unlikely.' She rubbed cream on veined hands. 'He left Louisa Tritter years ago for a ballet dancer half his age. I don't have much on his personal life. Even the mug shots I have of him are old. These people protect themselves.'

'So we know about the caisson. We know his past business links. We know about a possible mysterious project tied in with the CIA. And that's it?'

'That's background.' She replaced the top on the jar, crossed her stockingless muscular legs. Their pale skin was covered with fine hairs. 'To find out more, we have to crack Infandus.'

'What's that?'

'Latin for the unspeakable. And a licence to print money.'

'I'm no wiser.'

'It's a kind of club. A recreational facility for the megarich. It does two things. It indulges their vices and keeps them hidden. It has branches in Hong Kong, Argentina, England and it's run by a Chinese called Tan.' She linked her hands above her head, straightened them, palms up. Her superstructure became stricture but it was exercise, not display. 'The megarati are hysterical about keeping their fetishes private — fixated on preserving that last surviving anonymity. Which explains Tan's power.'

'You mean he blackmails them?'

'Far more subtle.' She lowered her arms. 'He has the dirt on them, but, you see, he needs them. And they need him. Let's say he sometimes asks them for favours. In the sweetest way.'

'Symbiotic relationship.'

'Exactly. Now he's a personable type — a Cambridge don, which gave him his connections.' She grabbed another jar and scooped out colourless gel.

'So he provides the rich with a safe way to indulge any vice?'

She nodded, rubbed gunk into her cheeks.

'And where does Tritter come in?'

'Tritter uses Tan as a facility — for connections, dirty work.' She gelled her lips. 'I don't use lipstick. You'd be surprised how many pounds of lipstick the average woman eats in a lifetime.' She replaced the top on the jar and moved her dangling foot in a circle. 'This is Tritter.' She punched up a personal profile. He saw a European looking man, blond with a goatee beard. 'It's an old shot. He stays away from the media. And this, by the way,' she changed the frame, 'is your new boss. Elina Luna, who happens to be the head of our branch in Argentina.'

Luna had the eloquent face of a South American — expressive lines around the mouth, lively eyes.

'She'll be running you.' Flora re-crossed her legs and circled the other foot. 'She was working with Katherine on this project. They intended to use you to get at Tritter through Tan. That's all I'm authorised to tell you.' She slid off the chair. 'I'll let you out.'

Blake padded back through the long coffin, considering it all. Hunger led him to the wardroom where Apollonov was wolfing curry.

He filled a plate, sat beside the Russian, nodded.

The big man grinned. 'Your boss Luna now?'

'Some security you've got.'

'I have good friend during many years.' He cupped his hands in front of his chest. 'Bigggg. Good tune on old fiddle.'

'Luna. What's she like?'

'Brrrr.' His jowls shook.

'What?'

'Some people get ducks in line. Hers do trapeze act, then cook dinner.'

Kelly looked through the door, saw him. 'You're wanted for a briefing. Ko's cabin. Half an hour.'

Ko's cupboard-like cabin had no chairs, just three hard cushions in a triangle. Ko sat on one. A loose robe covered his damaged arm. Hale sat on a second, his expensive boat-shoes neatly placed behind him. Blake took the last cushion. He hadn't forgiven the monk.

Ko exuded force. Energy built in the room. Finally, the empty eyes turned to him. 'I know I wasn't easy to be with. And, without your resourcefulness, I wouldn't be here. You have my gratitude.'

'Any news on Kate?'

'No. I'm sorry. Did the Intelligence Section give you the background you need?'

'Some.'

'Tell me, old chap.' Hale's friendly voice. 'Have you heard of a fellow called Charles Braden?'

'The old fart Jessop's using to . . .'

'Yes. It seems you're about to meet him.'

'Oh?'

'Mr Ko has more on that.'

Ko began to speak as if in a trance. 'You'll go to the place in the photograph. You'll meet Braden there. You'll mention the word Tritter. It will interest him. He'll help you.'

'How could you *know* that?' Blake asked.

'Some things can't be explained.'

'Well, since it's my life on the line, I'd like you to try.'

Ko sighed.

The sound of blowing air and a creak from the hull.

Hale said, 'Mr Ko can . . . see things. The more you are, the more you know. Perception depends on the depth of self-abiding.'

'That's not an explanation.'

Ko's eyes became black holes. The air in the room seemed to shimmer as if he were providing a wordless demonstration. 'Diversity,' he eventually said, 'is the other side of unity. So the world's *in* us, not outside. It means that, at a certain level of intensity, we're outside manifestation spatially. As the fundamental ground includes everything, when Being stops time, consciousness expands as space.' He pulled out a handkerchief and loudly blew his nose. To destroy the atmosphere deliberately? Kate said he did nothing unintentionally. 'Explanations are pointless. But I've done as you asked,' he replaced the handkerchief, 'and you'll just have to accept that I'm able to see you and Braden together in that . . . monotonous part of America.'

Blake looked sceptical. 'Well, even if he's in Kansas and I somehow get to talk to him, how do we know he's heard of Tritter?'

Ko looked pointedly at Hale.

'We're financed by prominent people,' Hale said. 'Many in the USA. We've asked one to mention Tritter to the President.'

He nodded. At least that made sense. 'But why team up with this flag-waving redneck?'

'The media image isn't the man.'

'Come on. A megarich wacko who's into gunships . . . ?'

'It's true,' Hale said, 'that wealth's mostly in the hands of the unfit and that Braden's obscenely wealthy and the victim of an American education. But he's still decent. And no fool.'

Blake scowled at Ko. 'So all this is based on prophecy?'

Ko glanced at Hale. 'He's resented me for a week.'

Hale interceded. 'Really, old chap, I know you're hurting and all that, but . . .'

'Just a minute, Julian. It's a reasonable objection. I've explained to you, Blake, that everything we do or say is altering our future — this moment. And if I could trust what I see completely, Katherine would still be here.' It was probably as close to an apology as the guru of DEMI came. 'So, we try again.'

'And there's nothing more you can tell me?'

'Be careful on the road.'

He stared at the monk, bewildered.

'You'll find Elina helpful,' Hale said. 'She's very efficient.'

They said nothing more, just watched him.

It was over.

'Well,' he said lamely, 'I suppose you only live once.'

'If you're lucky,' Hale smiled. 'I know how unclear it all must seem. But it'll work out. You'll see. And Elina can fill in the squares.'

To his surprise, Ko rose and escorted him to the door.

'So if the world's an illusion,' he said, 'and nothing matters, why are we in a bloody great sub?'

Ko opened the door for him. 'What part of you thinks we are?'

30

CLOSE CALL

Cleveland's most exclusive businessman's club had a name as nondescript as its entrance. It was a retreat from public scrutiny and matriarchy, a sanctum for the wealthiest men in Ohio. And its restaurant was superb. Braden felt like dining there tonight.

Bodyguards weren't allowed on upper floors. Only members and trusted staff went upstairs.

After Braden's three-limousine cavalcade was checked into the basement, his security squad saw him to the elevator. As Stick and Buick rode with him to the second floor they re-checked his pocket alarm. It was slaved to their receiver in the security room downstairs. They watched him enter the club proper and rode the elevator back to the lobby as Braden walked to the opulent washroom to tease his thinning hair.

Zack Zimmer stood at the urinal. The man had the death game sewn up — lawn cemeteries, crematoriums, funeral homes — but his takeover tactics had hurt people. 'Good God! It's the famous Chuck Braden who's never off the box. You've sure been making waves, Chuck.'

Braden made noncommittal sounds as the door to one of the cubicles behind them was shut. Anyone could be in there and he didn't want to say too much.

Zimmer shook himself and went to the basins which were hollows in a thick marble slab. 'The way you're going, you might meet me next time in my professional capacity.'

'You disapprove?'

Zimmer took a thick hand towel from the pile and dried his hands. 'Look, we pay the military to handle the dirty stuff. And I say, let them get on with it.'

'You're entitled to your opinion.' He walked to the basins.

As Zimmer left, he half saw in the mirror the cubicle door behind him open. A man in dark clothes came out.

But the toilet hadn't flushed!

The man's arms were by his sides and the angle of his right hand was strange — the thumb pointing down and something extending just beyond it. Too thin for a knife. More like the tip of a spike.

Sounds faded and the lighting seemed to glare as his alertness centred in his eyes. He wheeled around, finger hard down on the button of his alarm.

Just as the outer door banged and the inner swung wide. Two more patrons entered laughing.

The man, by then an arm's length from him, veered away and hurried out the door.

He stayed in the toilet, chatting to the men and combing his hair, hoping they didn't spot his shaking hands. Then Stick and Buick barged in.

He was too shocked to say anything coherent. 'Someone on the can. Dark suit. Looked like he had a spike or something. Gone now.'

They hustled him away. By the time he gave them the full story, he was in the elevator heading for the

— 121 —

basement where the other members of his squad had weapons out covering the carpark. Buick joined him in one of the limousines. His three-car convoy cleared the building and sped off.

'Could've been nothing,' he told them later, cradling a drink in the fortress of his home. 'Hard to see in that mirror. But it didn't *feel* like nothing. And if the others hadn't come in . . . Guys, you don't tell Connie, right? Don't want her worried more than she is.'

His bodyguards nodded.

Buick folded arms the size of hinged watermelons over his flak jacket. 'So, no more fun trips. You here. You at the corporation. Or you doin' stuff with the military. Finish. Otherways, they whack you, man. Figure out an MO for sure.'

Stick said, 'That's a given. You only leave here if it's unavoidable. Sorry. But after this . . .'

'Message received,' Braden said. His two security supremos were button-bright and the least he could do was cooperate. He gulped the drink.

He felt cold right through.

Jeez, he hadn't felt like this since 'Nam.

31

LUNA

Blake was unused to America, had been to Manhattan twice. But this wasn't JFK. It was Mid-Continent Airport, which, according to maps in his head, was 10 kilometres west of Wichita and roughly 240 kilometres southeast of the geographic centre of the 'conterminous' US.

His body's time-clock had been disrupted by the sub's eight-hour watches. Then, after being smuggled ashore near Bombay, by the flight via Rome and New York. He left the UA plane, longing to sleep.

He dragged his bag from the conveyor, asked questions at a rental car desk and found the shuttle to the airport Hilton. The five-floor pile was mostly a conference centre for corporate aircraft conventions. He checked in, showered and slept five hours. When he woke at 2 pm, he ordered a room service snack. It was huge.

He ate in front of the TV, which told him there was 'a sixty-three per cent chance of precipitation'. He switched to a twenty-four hour fundamentalist channel that offered to pray for him if he sent money.

Luna was flying London–Washington. He set the alarm for six and tried to get more sleep.

At 7 pm he was back in the terminal, watching people leaving her flight. Tired businessmen, waddling housewives, demanding, overweight children. Then he saw her ahead of two fleshy men in cowboy hats.

She was a slim-bodied woman with dark, wary eyes. About thirty-five and small. Beside the giant Americans she looked little bigger than a child.

He walked forward and extended his hand. 'Colin Blake.'

'Good to meet you, Colin.' Her soft-accented voice went hoarse. She coughed and touched her neck. 'Strep throat.'

He ambled beside her, shielding her from people hurrying to the baggage claim. 'We can drive to Lakin tomorrow. Take under five hours.'

'I'll need time here to set things up. So I think we should fly most of the way.' She frowned. 'Must go to the rest room.'

He watched her walk off. Strep throat . . . rest room . . . So she was familiar with this country where everything looked the same but wasn't. He was glad she knew the ropes.

At the hotel, she said she wanted to 'freshen up', said she'd meet him in the lounge 'at ten of'.

He said, 'You speak like an American.'

'I lived here for ten years.'

He inquired about flights, found a secluded nest of sofas, ordered a Bloody Mary, waited, jet-lagged and fretting about Kate.

Luna came down in a form-fitting dress. Its halter top showed a tempting curve of breast. She was certainly attractive but, right now, he couldn't care less. He ordered drinks.

She held her glass in both hands, said, 'I'm so sorry about Kate.'

He didn't want her sympathy. 'There's a commuter flight into Garden City but only once or twice a day. I suggest we fly to Dodge late tomorrow and get a hire car from there. Should take us an hour and a half to Lakin.'

'Fine. But I've booked us on USAir Express to Dodge tomorrow evening.'

'You don't muck around.'

'So, let's see — you're John Vincent, an Australian medical rep on a working holiday. Is your cover story straight?'

'I don't forget.'

'I'm supposed to be visiting my sister in Holly, Colorado.'

'Uh-huh. And what if you have to produce her?'

'There's a woman there ready to swear I'm her half-sister. The story is, you and I met in Manhattan four years ago and you've written six times since. I have all your letters in my case. Do you have them?' She held out a hand.

He gave her the envelope.

From her handbag she produced what looked like a powder compact. 'The latest detector. It picks up most bugs and pinhole cameras — even optical fibre types.'

'You think they'll be onto us this fast?'

'No. But best to be alert. Try not to look so sad.'

'Sorry. I just can't stop worrying about her.'

'So!' A bright smile. 'We'll have a pleasant dinner and appear to get on very well. Then you'll visit my suite and leave about 4 am. Then they'll think we're, as Americans say, an item.'

'Right.'

She looked at him with concern. 'I know you're frantic about her, but please try to act as if you like me.'

Over dinner, she was charming. Attentive, responsive, amusing. Her lively South American nature, softened by a warm sense of humour, made her reputation as an organisational whiz seem out of character.

He forced himself to make conversation. 'Blueberry pie à la mode? What's that?'

'With ice cream.'

'So why don't they say that?'

'You're in the land of hype.'

'We call it bullshit in Australia. So tell me about Argentina.'

'Which one? Buenos Aires or the rest?' She said a little about her home city. 'Appearance is everything. Plastic surgery, gyms . . . It's Paris at half price.'

'You're supposed to be a sophisticated lot.'

'We're Italians who eat beef, speak Spanish, live in French houses and think we're British.'

'I read an article that said you had 37,000 shrinks in the country.'

She laughed. 'Yes, we love discussing ourselves.'

'You know Yuri, the Russian in the sub?'

'Yes, a wonderful man. All that technical knowledge. So gruff but marvellously kind. Russians are such genuine feeling people.'

'He told me you're tremendous at getting things done.'

A delicate smile. 'I am.'

In her room, she walked slowly round the walls, using the bug-buster. 'Clear.' She put it carefully back in her purse. Her gentle but deliberate movements implied a certain self-possession. 'I need to go to bed now. I'll set the alarm for four. You sleep, too.' She pointed to the bed.

'With you?'

'There's plenty of room. But no forced entry, please.'

'Last thing on my mind.' He undressed and got into bed.

She came back from the en suite in a shift and got in beside him. 'Goodnight. And try not to be sad. It never helps. I know you're hurting and I'm sorry. But no one can help you with that.'

For once in his life, the proximity of an attractive woman left him cold. He lay beside her in the dark, worrying about Kate.

32

CIA

The DCI finished his shower in the apartment adjoining his office. He sometimes stayed at the Agency overnight. At times of national emergency. Or when he needed peace.

At home there was no peace.

No peace in his wife's dreary conversation. Or in servicing her flaccid body — once tempting but, after three children, as lush as, responsive as, dough.

No peace walking his unloved dogs along the electrified boundary of his property. The two Alsatians and the poodle had been chosen by his security adviser, a South African. Apparently poodles were the alarm system for waking the attack dogs.

He disliked all three animals.

He disliked things that breathed.

He plucked a towel from the hot rack, patted his scrawny frame.

He was sick to death of it all.

Sick of the hostile Executive.

Sick of his punishing job.

Sick of this political-gesture-governed point-and-click world.

He discarded the first towel, wrapped himself in a second, heard the secure-line buzzer and returned to the bedroom. A light on the red phone winked and the duty desk readout showed the caller — the Secretary of Defense. It could have been worse. Treloar, though vain and expedient, saw things sensibly. He picked up.

'Stone.'

'Hi, Bill. Working late?'

'Avoiding domestic bliss.'

'Try divorce. As a remedy for marriage, I've found it most effective. Now, tell me. A friend of mine's a member of Braden's club. I believe there was some kind of incident there. Was that an Agency initiative?'

'If it was, it didn't work. So you'd hardly expect us to admit it.'

'Unless it was meant as a warning.'

'It'll certainly serve as that.'

'We need to be together on this, Bill. Because . . . Can I speak to you frankly? As I see it, our little band of do-gooders completely lack perspective. Because they're trying to get rid of the one solution that's practical. You with me?'

'Totally.'

'Now we've put vast resources into it and we've got to defend it. I'm being absolutely honest with you, Bill. I expect that back. We've got to defend it. You agree?'

'One hundred per cent.'

'Good. Because it basically comes down to the two of us. So — are we in tune?'

'In perfect pitch.'

'Now try to follow my thinking here. Hell's paved with good intentions and grouted with sentimentality. You agree?'

'I do.'

'Which, being interpreted, means that virtue potentiates evil because it's impractical and produces entirely the wrong result. Makes the last state worse than the first. You agree?'

'Agree.'

'So what's needed is hardly sweetness and light but an efficient blend of good intentions and bad methods. You follow me?'

'You're saying the end half-justifies the means?'

'Beautifully put. I love your mind. I wish I could have said it so well.'

'Ethically, logically . . .'

'Bill, do try to be simple for a moment so we lesser mortals can relate to you. I'm basically saying that if something were to happen to Braden, we'd be much better off. Even if the method has to be conventional. Yes, it could cause a media storm. But if it's not done soon, that storm could become a tempest. You agree?'

'Agree.'

'You *do* agree?'

He said nothing, giving the other time to grasp this not really so difficult issue.

'I respect you, Bill. And I expect you to help out here.'

'I heard you. I agree with you.'

'Thanks, Bill. I needed to hear that. Good to talk. Very good to talk. Appreciate all you're doing. The end half-justifies the means! God, that's beautiful. Beautiful. After forty years — eureka — a genuine mission statement. Though I guess I better not hang it on the wall. You're a wonderful man. Enjoy your evening.'

'And you.' He put the handset down thoughtfully and practised his bladder sphincter exercise. Best to do it several times a day. No point in being captive to urgency. Life provided humiliations enough.

No, it hadn't been a warning. A quiet heart attack was intended. With needle withdrawn, forensic evidence suppressed, Braden's high cholesterol, weak heart and stress in his new capacity . . . Plausible.

But the best laid plans . . .

Treloar was right. The next attempt mustn't fail.

Braden had to be despatched.

33

KATE

It was a bare metal cell — very small.

The floor vibrated. It was warm.

She was naked and shackled by both hands to a pipe that ran up the wall. The shackles slid up the pipe. It allowed her to stand, squat or sit. But never rest.

A remote-controlled camera on the ceiling watched everything she did. She had to lie in her own filth until blasted with a fire hose.

The racket was continuous. The rattle of winches. Metal clangs. The sound of turbines, pumps, the yells of men. The glaring light above became a torment. If she nodded off they'd come in and beat her with soft truncheons that pained terribly and left huge bruises but broke no bones.

When none of that worked, they kept her kneeling for hours, a black hood covering her face.

Sometimes they threw her into walls.

It was standard 'stress and duress'.

She told them nothing.

Then it got worse.

There were two eyelets in the ceiling and two large cleats on the wall. They put a broomstick behind her bent knees and bound her ankles to her wrists. Then they hauled the stick into the air by ropes until she hung.

The pain was unendurable. Each time they did it, she passed out.

Then they gave her Sodium Pentothal.

Interrogations went on for hours.

Finally, she'd no idea what she'd told them.

But she noticed they were careful not to cause any permanent injury.

That was what worried her most.

It meant there was more to come.

34

FACADE

They got the keys from the Avis desk at Dodge City regional airport and walked from the hothouse of the terminal into a bone-chilling wind and flakes of snow.

They found the Ford Thunderbird by the numberplate. He said, 'I'm used to right-hand drive. I hope you're driving.'

'Would look better if you did. And you'll probably need to do it later. So this is a good time to get used to it.'

He shrugged. 'Your funeral.' As he backed the car out of the space, he automatically looked over his left shoulder then switched sides. 'Everything feels wrong.'

'Turning's worst.'

'I'd better practise in town first.'

'The rule is — whatever you do, keep your bottom in the centre of the road.'

Dodge City was marshmallow tough. Brick-paved streets, cottonwood trees, the vaunted Front Street a tawdry recreation. The battlefield of Wild Bill Hickok and Bat Masterton was now a cheerless cattle centre with cow horns over doorways, museums, bored-looking tourists. They passed baseball-capped farmers, ranchers in boots and cowboy hats, feed and produce stores. He'd read that the hell-raising town once had nineteen saloons but had buried its lurid past under a parking lot and Buffalo Burger signs.

He drove around the block, practising turns. Left-hand drive felt dangerous but his instant recall made it simpler. And the car was automatic — which stopped him trying to change gears with the door handle.

They headed west on Wyatt Earp Boulevard in a stream of cattle trucks and campers. Highway 50 carried a constant line of vehicles. It appeared to be the truck route across the flat monotonous plains.

He said, 'They've cornered the market on wheat silos.'

'They call them grain elevators.'

Soon, the browns, greens, yellows and tans of endless fertile fields became grey with snow, then sombre with approaching night. He turned the heat up.

As they went through Cimarron, she said, 'Put your headlights on.' She yawned, shut her eyes. 'Call me when we get to California.'

They passed run-down cow towns, some with boarded-up buildings, their names high on rusting water towers, their populations thinned. As the highway became each Main Street, signs on cafes, diners, drug stores importuned the traffic — as if the mom-and-pop businesses were dying, like the towns, for lack of trade. They cruised past cattle pens, road signs reading 'Eat Beef — Keep Slim', through the feed-yard and abattoir centres of Garden City. Now the line of headlights formed a bright ribbon across the plain.

She stirred. 'How are we doing?'

'We passed Holcomb a while ago. What a limbo-land.'

'They call this the loneliest road in America.'

They reached an old railroad town and truck stop — a huddled clutch of buildings, pulled in to a 'gas station' festooned with fluttering pennants. A sign for PROPANE hung by one bolt. Others said TIRES. NO CHECKS TAKEN. The spelling grated.

They stepped out onto slushy concrete. The snow had stopped but it was bitter. They bought some 'soda' and visited the 'rest room'.

The proprietor drawled, 'Be cold again for a few.'

'So this is Lakin?'

'You're standing in it. Home of the Little Britches Rodeo and the Jelly Bean Jamboree. Good place for overnight. Recommend Cynthia's Pizzeria. You're in mountain time, now. Gained an hour. Where you from, bud?'

'Australia.'

'Seen pictures of there.'

When he got back in the car, she said, 'We could stop here.'

'Got to find that sign.'

'Too dark now.'

'Just to the next town, okay?'

He'd become used to overtaking vehicles — edge out on the wrong side, check the wrong side mirror — but mostly stayed close to the shoulder. Then he became sandwiched between cattle trucks — couldn't pass the one ahead and had a blocked view front and back. Ko's comment echoed in his mind. 'Be careful on the road.'

The mercury lights of another rest area loomed ahead. He swung off the road to wait for a space in the stream of traffic behind.

Ahead, on the highway, tail-lights flashed. The first truck braked, its tyres juddering on the wet road. The second, about to overtake, slid into the back of it. With a hiss of air-brakes, tortured tyres and twisting metal the rear truck jack-knifed, swayed, but, remarkably, stayed upright.

But the car behind the rear truck locked brakes and crumped straight in. The truck-bed tore its roof off.

If they'd stayed between the trucks they'd have been minced.

'Oh my God.' She was shivering, face pale in the glow of the lights.

It took time to ease past the wreck. Men were peering at it with horror or self-importantly directing traffic. In front and underneath the first truck were the remains of a Black Angus. The beast, the cause of the pile-up, had strayed onto the road.

She covered her face. 'Please stop at the next place we come to.'

Then two miles ahead, he saw the sign.

Just another shield-like route sign.

But the bullet holes matched exactly.

'Shit. That's it!'

He turned into an unmarked side-road that went off into the plain between feed-lots and drove for a couple of minutes until the tarred surface turned to gravel. He pulled over, got out, and gazed back over the dark prairie at the distant long-haul transports thundering on the treeless expanse. A squad car, siren blaring, red lights flashing, speeded by heading for the smash. 'Whatever we're after's right here.'

'We're too tired now,' she called from the car. 'It's too late. We need food and somewhere to stay. Look. There are lights up ahead.'

'A farm?'

'I think they're street lights.'

A mile along the unlit track, the headlights played across a sign reading MINTMINE.

'A mine?' He checked details in his head, maps, documents. No such name.

As they turned a bend, the headlights floodlit a farmhouse. It had two stone chimneys, green shingles, a boarded-up door and broken windows. Now the lights were brighter. Sparse streetlamps, buildings.

Mintmine was ramshackle. There were last-gasp frame houses with loose siding, sagging porches. There was an implement dealership, a grain elevator, a closed convenience store with the inevitable ice dispenser and a cut-limestone Baptist church in a sea of grass and weed. Next to the block-shell frame of a locked and boarded petrol station was a mobile home surrounded by rusting monsters from Detroit.

The only action seemed to be the Bar and Grill and the six-unit motor lodge. The wind-shaken sign of the last read CHEAP RATES, CLEAN ROOMS, FIRM BEDS, AIRCON. Its pink-gravel compound sheltered two cars and three plastic flamingoes.

Blake drove back to the motel, parked near reception and got out. The air was ice.

The woman behind the screen door had dull eyes and a mouthful of gum. She said, 'Per room and not per person. Breakfast extra. Menu in the room. You pay up front and checkout's eleven. Got ID?'

'So this is Mintmine?'

'Beautiful downtown Mintmine. Where nothin' happens all day long.'

The room was tired. The toilet-seat strip reading SANITIZED FOR YOUR PROTECTION was stained. TV on pedestal. Bible on nightstand. Elina said, 'We need to eat. Could we walk there? I've forgotten what my legs are for.'

They dumped their bags, zipped their jackets and walked toward the grill. As they neared it, a battered convertible stopped outside and its two occupants went in.

The front of the place had a sign: PRIME RIBS WITH SALAD BAR. MALTS. He opened the door and she walked in under his arm. The walls were hung with farm ironmongery. The tables had chequered cloths.

'Jest set yerself right down, folks. Plenty of room,' the twenty-five-going-on-fifty waitress said. She wore jeans, a too-tight blouse and had makeup more cracked than her skin. 'Jest passin' through then?'

He said, 'Trying out Route 50.'

'Used to go all the way to San Francisco. Then they made it Interstate 80. So what brings you to Mintmine?'

'Got to stop somewhere.'

'Ain't that a fact.'

'Got a mine around here?'

'Nope.'

'How'd the town get its name, then?'

'Figure it jest happened. So where you folks headin'?'

'West.'

'She's goin' to turn tonight, looks like. You be good now.'

Near a wooden bar at the back with a jukebox, two men were playing pool. They were young thickset types intent on the game and their beers.

There were two other patrons — a middle-aged overweight man sitting with a faded, round-shouldered woman. They finished staring at the newcomers and continued eating.

The waitress came back with iced water. Blake ordered a prime rib with fries, Elina a mushroom omelette with baked potato. They made good use of the salad bar but avoided the factory-white bread.

Elina said, 'What do you make of this place?'

'Doesn't add up. The floor's a concrete slab — like the motel and the other buildings. But they don't build them around here like that. And did you see the strips across the road when we came into town? Then, Mintmine's an anagram for imminent.'

'How on earth did you work that out?'

'Got that kind of brain.'

'Imminent. Meaning . . . what's coming?'

The men had begun to quarrel. One slammed down his cue, abused the second, shoved him. Soon they were grappling, slugging.

But the couple at the table continued their dull munching with the facial animation of Easter Island statues. And the waitress fronted their table as if nothing were happening. 'Food all right? You be good, now.'

One of the men had a split lip. The other's eye was swollen. But, suddenly, they were buddies again, hugging each other, chuckling. And they left, cracking jokes, arm in arm.

After their meal, Blake and Elina walked to the far end of town. Most houses they passed looked respectable — neat front lawns and fresh paintwork. They heard someone playing the piano, doggedly but well enough.

Elina stopped to listen. 'The Goldberg Variations. Strange thing to hear in the middle of the prairie.'

THE INSOMNIA OF COUNT HERMANN CARL VON KEYSERLINGK — A STORY SINCE DISPROVED.

He said, 'This place gives me the creeps. It's a stage set. Nothing's real here. Let's get back.'

The grill had Tyrolean-style windows on the street side. He peered in as they passed.

The stone-faced couple were rutting doggy-style on the floor. Her bra was around her neck and her breasts hung like water-filled balloons. They'd knocked over the table in their ardour. Blake doubted two cans of Coors were that emancipating. The waitress calmly wiped tables.

He moved aside so Elina could see.

'Normal?' he asked.

'No.'

They walked on.

He said, 'I reckon it's a series of tests. The people are controlled in some way. They can make them do anything they like.'

'I think you're right.'

The same convertible passed and stopped behind them outside the grill. Two men got out again. Different men. He said, 'Same car, different cast.'

When they reached the motel, the other cars had gone. He got his flashlight and they walked further along the road away from the town. Well beyond the last streetlamp, he pointed down.

There were foot-square plugs of earth on either side of the potholed gravel joined by two strip-like bands. He climbed through the wire fence into the field beside the road, shielding the flashlight with his hand, and found filled-in holes with even spacing. 'There's been a double security fence here. And the posts were concreted in.' He got back through the fence. 'I'd say there's a good chance they're onto us. Our room'll be wired for sure.'

As they reached the motel, the two cars that had been parked there passed them on the road and stopped in the compound. One man got out and walked to the office. The other parked near the same unit. He wore a suit with a string tie held at the neck by a silver toggle. The generous drape of his coat disguised his paunch and flab but did nothing for his double chin. 'Stayed here before?' he called.

'No,' Blake said.

'Forget the motel breakfast or you'll have the stomach of a poisoned pup. Eat at the grill. That's my advice.' The man went into his room.

When they'd shut their door she walked around the walls as if searching for something in her handbag. Her eyes met his and she gave the faintest nod. The room was hot.

It was play-acting after that. They exchanged the comments of tired lovers. When he sat on the bed to take off his shoes, she nestled between his legs and kissed him.

He held her close.

She said, 'I'm so tired. Let's get to bed.'

He brushed his teeth and stripped bare before getting into bed. She came back from the bathroom in her shift. Her body was certainly good. She might have the breasts and butt of a teenager but all he could think about was Kate. She climbed into bed and turned off the lights. He pulled her gently to him, knowing they could be watched on low-light or infrared. They kissed again.

She said, 'Darling, I've still got my period. We'll be right tomorrow night.'

Smart comment, he thought. 'Goodnight.'

'Goodnight.' She gave him a last peck.

Next morning, they were about to venture out when there was a knock at the open door — the businessman in the same suit, black shoes shined to perfection. 'I'm off to the grill for sausage, hotcakes and then some. Wanna schlep along?'

The bad weather had passed. An endless sky with wisps of stratus made the earth seem squalid. As they walked the man asked where they came from, then switched to God's covenant with the faithful. 'Only Jehovah can solve man's problems. Read Romans 11:13–36 and Revelation 4:11.'

Blake quoted part of the first text: 'For who hath known the mind of the Lord? For of Him and through Him and to Him are all things, to whom be glory forever. Amen.'

'Hallelujah, brother.' The man looked at him, amazed.

They passed an excavation. It hadn't been there last night. It was fenced off with metal stakes and plastic strips. In the small hole rested a mattock and long-handled shovel.

Their companion stopped short, said like a small boy, 'That hole needs digging.' Then he was over the plastic tape, a blur of enthusiastic blubber. He hung his coat on a stake and grabbed the mattock, his pristine shoes forgotten.

She called, 'What about your hotcakes?'

'You go on.' He dug like a man possessed, face red, shirt buttons straining.

Blake nudged her. They walked on.

The waitress in the grill wore the same clothes. She'd either been up all night or hadn't changed. 'So two eggs up, hash browns, tomato juice, grits, toast, grape jelly.' There was no one else in the place. She flounced off with their order.

The sound came suddenly, as if the helicopter had been hugging the ground. Heavy concussions of tortured air. By the time he got outside, the thing was somewhere close behind the building. Then its turbines became muffled, which he didn't understand. He walked two buildings along and peered through the gaps between them. But all he could see was a barn and an empty field. The machine seemed to have disappeared.

The man in the hole down the road was still digging like a madman, the pile of earth around him growing. His shirt now stuck to him like cling-wrap.

Blake went back to her. 'Couldn't see a thing. But I remember sounds. And that chopper was a big job — a medium-lift twin turbine. This place is a definite worry.'

After breakfast, they walked back. A sparrowhawk high on a pole, flared its tail. It was genuine at least.

The man was still digging — clothes ruined, face purple. He'd uncovered a slab of grey concrete at the bottom of the hole and his shovel screeched as he scraped the top. 'Can't find the edge. Gotta find the edge.'

As they walked on, he told her, 'Whoever's controlling this is probably under that slab and monitoring everything we do. I reckon we've seen enough. I'd say we get out of here fast.'

She said, 'We can try. But will they let us?'

As they neared the petrol station, its rusted shutter opened smoothly. Two men in orange boiler-suits and holding foam guns stepped out. They had helmets with plastic visors, shoulder mounted mikes and heavy leather belts supporting snap-out batons, pepper spray and gas grenades. Inside the petrol station, behind old engine blocks and scarred benches, he saw the shiny metal cage of a lift. He said, 'Pleasant morning.'

One glanced at the sky. 'Yup. She's turned all right.'

'Nice to meet you good folks at last,' the other drawled. 'Now we'd appreciate you comin' easy 'cause gettin' thays foam off is hell on a stick.'

35

TURN-OFF

The big chopper with the covered rear windows circled the ramshackle town. Jason had opened the door so Braden could see it. Then they descended below the prairie into another sub-surface pad.

When they powered down, Jason became the centre of a sober-faced huddle but broke free long enough to introduce the base director.

'This is Major-General William P. Homan, formerly with Air Intelligence.'

Homan had the anxious attitude of a man promoted sideways. 'Welcome to Project Mintmine, sir. How're you feeling today?'

'Lousy.'

'Hope it's nothing to do with us, sir.'

He didn't answer. The guy was petrified and could stay that way. Intimidated men were malleable men.

'Must excuse myself,' Jason said. 'Something they want me to check.'

Braden was glad. Jason as nursemaid was a pain in the tit.

The tour began in a shabby briefing room housing a table-top replica of the town. The walls were plastered with room layouts, strip photographs and charts of utilities from phones to sewerage. They walked from there to the control room — a doughnut-shaped tube like an abandoned metro walkway. Faded paint and grimy fittings showed it had been there years. Teams at workstations monitored each experiment.

'This first subject,' Homan droned, 'is a Caucasian male aged fifty-two, overweight and inclined to idleness.'

'You mean he's lazy?'

'We've tuned his brain to relish hard physical labour.'

'You mean you've turned his brain to relish.'

'Since 0800 hours he's been digging this trench. His pulse and heart readings are now critical. He's working more consistently than his body can stand. If not returned to normal mode, he'll have a coronary infarction.'

'That's a relief. Thought he might have a heart attack.'

But sarcasm, Braden realised, was wasted on the washed-out, washed-up airman, so he turned his attention to the screen and watched the exhausted, gasping man who was working with the fury of an earthquake victim trying to reach his buried family.

The next workstation was monitoring an equally exhausted young woman playing something classical on the piano. Whenever she made a mistake she repeated the difficult section. The circles under her eyes weren't mascara.

'This girl,' Homan explained, 'suffers from attention deficit disorder but she's been practising fifty hours straight without food or sleep. Every three hours we make sure she drinks a little.'

'Proving what?'

'That diligence and exceptional skill can be induced.'

The tinkling left him cold. To him, classical brilliance was Harry James playing 'The Flight of the Bumblebee'. 'Some town you've got. Why not get them to paint it, rather than bashing the piano and digging holes?'

'That's a practical comment, sir . . .'

'I majored in good sense.'

'. . . but we don't want the place to look inviting. And we've all kinds of experiments here. For instance . . .' He pointed to the next screen. It showed an ugly old couple in a bathroom. The man was face up, lying on the tiles with the woman's flaccid body moving up and down on top of him.

Braden said, 'Gross.'

'These two hate each other. The man's almost impotent and the woman's frigid. But it's possible to make even people this age copulate consistently.'

'Prefer screwing, myself.'

More screens followed. People fighting. People being provoked yet remaining passive. 'And here,' Homan said, 'a special demonstration. I believe you've been briefed about the nation of the future requiring people to live shorter lives — that, according to projections, it's best if we die at forty.' The screen showed a bearded man with tattooed arms and pigtail seated in a scruffy mobile home smoking pot and petting a white rat. 'This subject is thirty-eight. We're advancing his termination-time to thirty seconds as of now.'

'You're going to cream him — for my edification?'

Homan nodded to a technician. The man turned back to his panel and red lights flashed a countdown. Braden watched in horror as a long buzzer sounded.

'Don't worry,' Homan said. 'We're doing him a favour. It's as painless as turning off a switch.'

The man on the screen slumped forward, mouth open, eyes oddly locked to one side. The rat ran up his beard and peered into his mouth, as if that cavity had always intrigued it, then scuttled out of frame.

Homan searched Braden's glazed eyes, more desperate for approval than a dog that had jumped through a hoop. 'Now, er . . . I've scheduled a coffee break and discussion.'

Though disgusted and appalled, Braden hid his bile. There was no mileage in telling this human debris how he felt. In a lounge with sagging armchairs, he moistened his sugar with coffee. 'So this is your vision splendid? This cockamamie town?'

'It's just the test bed.' Homan tapped shaking fingers together. 'The state-of-the-art stuff's back at the lab. Which you've seen, I believe.'

'And this is all to turn innocent Americans into short-lived breeders or workers?'

'Non-breeders, more accurately.' The airman stirred his cup. When he put the spoon down, it rattled. 'The sex side's simple enough. We can enhance or inhibit that area. We have young couples in their prime whom we've made asexual.' He glanced at the door, as if hoping Jason would return and take the heat. 'The problem's control without surveillance. We can't monitor cities with teams of technicians in basements. We need life-limiting implants with variable twenty-four hour time coding and semi-bio — powered from body systems. There's considerable progress on that but the delivery system's crude. Until the dweebs and geeks get something better, we're marking time. We're just the coalface here, you understand. Most of our funds have been diverted to the lab.'

Braden fumed but scratched his knee and tried to look relaxed.

Life-span limits ... mind control ... military robots ...

Fucking hell!

What else?

36

INTERROGATION

Blake was stripped, searched, weighed, fingerprinted, photographed, measured for height and cheek-scraped for DNA. They gave him back his clothes but kept his socks and shoes. Two guards took him to a bare room with a metal table and two chairs. They told him to stand against the wall. Opposite was one-way glass.

He stood on the cold floor, face flushed, hands sweating. His mouth was dry. He wanted to pee.

And, in another room, he knew, this would be happening to Elina. They'd interrogate them separately, then compare stories. How it was done.

A man came in. He had deep lines at the sides of his mouth and eyes like slots. He sat and put some articles on the table — Blake's wallet and fake ID. 'State your name.'

'John Vincent.'

'State your name.'

He clenched his hands. 'John Vincent.'

One of the guards unhooked a baton from his belt, a baton with a projecting handle.

Blake clenched his jaw, neck muscles rigid.

'State your name.'

'John Vincent.'

He expected the baton to be swung back or raised. But no movement telegraphed the blow. The end jabbed like a piston into his gut.

He doubled, winded, dry retched, was on the floor, gasping for breath.

'State your name.'

He had a high pain threshold but was terrified of torture because the damage to the body was gratuitous, profane. This was what they'd done to his brother. Probably what they were doing to Kate.

Another man entered.

The man he'd spotted at Paro airport.

'You see,' the inquisitor said, 'we know exactly who you are.'

They'd brought the man in to show they knew about the squad.

'State your name.'

'You know.'

'State your name.'

'Colin Blake.' He got painfully to his knees. 'And you shits are CIA.'

The first man said, 'State the names of your backup.'

'Get fucked.'

It felt as if they'd thrust a spear through the arch of his right foot that pierced his body to his neck. He realised why they'd kept his shoes. So they could slug the soles of his feet.

He moaned, rolled, writhed.

'State the names of your backup.' The voice seemed far away.

Agony in waves.

Ko was right.

Tritter was working with the CIA.

37

ALLIES

In the lounge with sagging armchairs, Braden stared into his cup. He felt angry and sad that his country had come to this.

During his latest visit to the White House, Jessop had said that a retired judge of unimpeachable integrity had mentioned a name to him: Adolphous Tritter. 'My informant,' Dougie had confided, 'says the name's a can-opener, Chuck. That's all I've got. But pick your time and use it on these guys.'

He thought about it now. But the name would be wasted on Homan.

The man was waffling — treading water until Jason returned. 'What sustains me is Chomsky's remark about indoctrination being the essence of government.'

'You sure he was recommending it? Think you're a bit off-message there.' Christ, he thought, where do they find them?

Jason entered, his careful lack of expression advertising trouble.

The relieved Homan sprang up. 'Thought we'd lost you.'

'How's it going?' Jason asked.

'Covered everything.' Homan sat again, shuffled and dry-coughed.

Jason sat, too, as if exhausted, lifted a flask from a cork mat and poured a coffee.

They're waiting for a sign, he thought. A sign that the President's watchdog condoned what they were doing. Well, he could fake sincerity there. He spread his arms along the back of the lounge and announced, 'So, I'm impressed.'

Some tension left Homan's face but Jason didn't trust it.

Braden assessed them, the bright, much-promoted Company fixer and his antithesis. The weak link was Homan, a man of merited low esteem. A disappointed man. A man who said too much.

Homan lifted the cookie plate. It shook in his hand. 'So can you er . . . understand our mission?'

Time to soften them up.

'Well . . .' He used the drawl and knowing smile, '. . . we know war's legalised murder, death life's little triumph — all that jazz. I thought you guys were being bad boys. But control the population, eliminate negative externalities . . . ? Has a point.' He took a cookie from the offered plate. 'I'm overweight but what the hell?' (Put out chaff.) 'Better make hay while my best girl's not here to monitor my diet.'

Homan attempted a smile and crossed his arms to hide his tremble. 'So what do you think of our town? The sophisticated security — no fences or signs. Do you appreciate what we've done here?'

'Clever.' He bestowed a sunny smile.

Its beam, as intended, burnished Homan's dark opinion of himself. 'Down here, despite what we do, it's in the service of our country. And we're proud of that.'

'So you should be.' He beamed again. 'I'm always mighty impressed by the dedication of the forces. People in difficult jobs who never get the adulation or the gongs, but do a vital service. It's admirable. Admirable.'

The uncharacteristic approval had Jason frowning his distrust. But Homan melted in its glare, gratitude priming his mouth with drivel. 'Very kind of you to say so, sir. I take it as a compliment for all my men here. Good men. Despite the routine, they're always on the alert. For instance, today they identified two snoopers. Two DEMI agents sniffing around.'

Annoyance grooved Jason's face but Homan saw it too late, and said to him, 'Sorry. This off-limits for you?'

Jason covered well. 'Mr Braden's up to speed with DEMI.'

Homan realised he'd unbagged a cat. The shaking of his fingers became extreme. He knew the young CIA apparatchik vastly out-scored him in influence and intelligence. 'Don't know how they got wind of us. The good news is we've got them.'

Braden leered and turned to Jason. 'Mind filling in the squares?'

Jason, for once, looked unbuttoned. 'It's an Australian called Blake and an Argentinian woman called Luna. One of our agents here was recently assigned to check on a DEMI operation in Bhutan. He recognised Blake from the screens. Blake was also involved in the Hansen operation. He's not a hard case — not a pro — but has total recall.'

'They seem to go for weird types.'

'DEMI? Yes. No cookie-cutter recruitment strategy there.'

'So,' he said casually. (Low, ground-hugging approach.) 'You grilled 'em?'

'Preliminary so far.'

'What happens next?'

'We get all we can, then turn them off.'

'And what if more of their people know about this place?'

'We need details of their backup.'

'So if you're sprung?'

Jason said nothing.

'And this pair are here now?'

'We brought them down this morning,' Homan blabbed.

'Interesting. I'd like to see them.'

'I don't advise that,' Jason said.

He aired his grade-one lazy smile. 'Indulge me.' (Locked on target.)

'I'm afraid it exceeds my authority, sir. It's a decision for the DCI.'

'Now listen up, fucker.' He bounced up. (And — fire!) 'You've paved enough hell with good intentions — given me a pain in the ring for weeks. I outrank everyone here. I can shut this dugout down and tack you to the wall. I wanna see them.'

'Bad idea, sir.'

'Wheel them in or I barbecue your balls.'

He suspected that brilliant young CIA men, dedicated patriots though they might be, remained unblooded by the consummate boardroom shit-kick. He raved on — bellowing loud enough to pound shock through Jason until the man's spine sagged and the petrified Homan went pale. (Two hits confirmed.) He knew his targets lacked supporting fire in this isolated sewer. They had no DCIs or Chiefs of Staff to shelter them. Sure, they could reach their gods on DSN — interrupt their crucial meetings — if they relished offering themselves for blood-sacrifice.

'Well?'

'Sorry, sir,' Jason said. 'I'm afraid it's off-limits.'

He patted the man's knee in the most patronising way he could devise. 'Understand, son. Understand. Just doing your job. Turning good guys into robots. Which is nothing to what you're doing to the slopes.' He clicked his teeth. 'I mean this memory-man and this woman have just blown your master plan for America. Some comment on your security!' He looked across at Homan, drawled, 'Hope they don't know about Tritter!'

Jason jerked as if stung. (Direct hit! Major damage.) The man's features wouldn't rearrange. He staggered from his chair. 'Have to ring the DCI.'

'Screw you, Jason. Your turn to take the heat.' Braden's voice became abrasive as a saw. 'Front them now or I'll make sure the fleas of a thousand camels infest your armpits and your left ear withers and falls into your right pocket.' He ended in a rasping yell. This was early stuff. He had routines to frighten dogs off chains.

Jason clung to a wall-phone and talked to his local CIA contingent while Braden lounged in his chair, hoping to survive the day.

Jason came back, nervous as a box of butterflies. 'They're bringing them.'

'Fine.' He leaned back, became expansive. 'No cure for life, son. No pat solutions, to society, war, anything. I distrust earnest men who think they can order a disorderly world. And I don't buy dinky arguments for distorting minds and wills. They say laws are devised by the old for the control of the young. And that may be. But you're beyond law here. And beyond the Bill of Rights. And you think you'll get away with it? Believe me, conditions still apply.'

Two orange-clad security staff entered. Two more stood outside the door guarding a strange-looking couple. The prisoners were pushed in. Homan ordered the guards outside. Braden examined the arrivals. The man — tall, athletic, good-looking. Pain behind the eyes. He was carrying his shoes and could barely walk. His face had a grey sheen. He clutched the wall and almost fell.

The woman was around five foot two. Trim but sexy body. Nice face. She looked terrified. She held her left hand under her right wing.

The Aussie slumped on the floor and cradled his foot with shaking hands.

'So you're Blake — the gumnut and memory magician?'

The man nodded. 'And you're Braden, the President's bloodhound.'

'Better believe it. And the little lady is . . .'

'One of their senior operatives,' Jason muttered. 'We know quite a bit about her.'

'So what's Tritter's specialty?' the Aussie asked. 'Robot people? Or worse?'

Braden whistled low. Then lower. He stared at Jason long and hard, rolling lugubrious eyes. 'Oh, *my* . . . !'

Jason, jaw sagging, stammered, 'I — have to make a call — outside.'

'You do that, son,' he shouted. 'And if you're not back and spilling your guts in three minutes, your next bout of 20/20 hindsight'll have you staring out your arse.'

The airman watched Jason leave with the look of an abandoned child. His turn now. 'So what do you know about Tritter?'

'Never heard of him.' A bleat.

'Figures.' He turned back to the couple. 'Want some coffee?' He poured the woman a cup.

She thanked him in a whisper. Her whole body shook.

He poured another for Blake. For a man who'd clearly been worked over, he seemed to take everything in. He didn't like foreigners much. But Aussies were okay. He said, 'This room's wired, so it kinda limits conversation.'

The woman gulped her coffee. She looked ready to throw up. Her hand was still under her arm. 'If we stay here, Mr Braden, you won't see us again.'

'Them's the breaks.'

'So if you're interested in Tritter . . .'

'I'm not dumb, okay?' He slapped his knees, turned to the airman. 'Right. I'm off now. Fire up the chopper. And these folks come along for the ride. When we get back to McConnell, they get a joy-ride in the Herc.'

The big Aussie blipped on that. The bastard had it in one.

Homan lurched to the phone to raise Jason. 'I can't compromise this base, sir. These people have to stay here.'

Braden ignored him. 'Do hope you folks can stand outdated military aircraft.'

'Better than having your feet pulped,' the Aussie said.

'Then we'll get along just fine.'

Jason burst back into the room, eyes darting. The security men were still outside.

Braden got up. 'As I figure you've just heard, I'm heading home. And giving these folks a ride.'

'There's just — so far you can push us, sir.' He sat as if determined to stay put.

'Is there a Commander in Chief in this country?' Braden roared. 'Who the hell do you people think

you are? If this cockroach hole ever saw daylight —
if you were ever dragged through a court — you'd
end up on a gurney with straps on it and tubes.
Think you can shit on this nation?' He cranked the
tone higher, higher till the woman cringed. He'd
studied the Hitler newsreels. Lunatic only had one
ball but he had talent. '. . . Think you're above the
fucking law?'

Jason looked up, momentarily defiant. 'Yes.'

He'll be quite a guy, Braden thought, in twenty
years. Caught in the middle but growing up fast. He
dropped his voice to a bear-like growl. 'You . . .
insouciant . . . bastard.' It carried the contempt of a
crowbar through the heart.

Jason coped with it, hung on. 'We c-can't let you
take them, sir.'

The woman said softly, 'I think I can settle this.'

The room became suspended in time. Everything
hung on her move.

'Let us . . . fly with Mr Braden. You know we
can't get away. We'll be in a slow old plane that you
can track the whole time. You'll know exactly where
it lands and be waiting. And then . . . you'll have us
back. But at least we could talk with him privately.
Which I think is what he wants.'

Homan looked at Jason, stammered. 'What's the
DCI say?'

'Couldn't raise him.'

Didn't want to be raised, Braden guessed.

Jason glared up at him, tight lipped. 'You accept
those conditions?'

'Fine with me.'

He stood up. 'I'll need an hour to get things
watertight.'

'Take your time. We're no threat. An old prune
with two unarmed tourists. A creaky old gunship

with dummy ammo. Hell, if the US Armed Forces can't handle that . . . What's it like in the hot seat, son?'

The CIA man flashed a look of angry resentment, hurried out.

Braden eyeballed Homan. 'That coffee's cat-piss. Seeing we're waiting, got any Scotch? I may hunger after righteousness but I refuse to thirst.'

Homan, too stunned to order it, too demoralised to remain, hands uncontrollably trembling, left the room.

Braden said to the pair, 'Wouldn't want him to take out my appendix.'

The woman turned to Blake, who was peeling off his socks. His feet were swollen, the soles blue. She gasped and touched his hand. 'Oh, Colin.'

'You okay?' The Aussie touched her arm.

'Almost.' She held out her left hand.

Braden winced.

The nail of her little finger — half pulled off.

38

GUNSHIP

Blake was strapped to a seat in the chopper's cabin and handcuffed behind his back. But it was a thousand times more comfortable than standing. The pain in his feet was bearable until he tried to stand or walk.

They hadn't cuffed Elina. He glanced at her, got a quick look back. The organisation woman. Somehow, she'd swung this trip. A few quiet, strategic words and the ducks had done the high-wire act.

Now they were in this vibrating, padded cell with Braden, the blustering tycoon, Jason, the CIA clone, and four guards who looked like their frontal lobes had been removed. But it still wouldn't help them — unless the old guy was prepared to stake his life on them.

The chopper settled on its shopping-cart wheels and the door was slid back, letting in grey light from low cloud. He saw a squat old C–130 across the dirty-orange apron. The business side of its fuselage faced them, bristling with sensors and cannons. Joining it to the chopper were two lines of Air Police, immobile as garden gnomes.

Braden turned around grimly. 'Let's go, folks.' He helped Elina down.

As Blake was unstrapped and stood, pain shot to the base of his skull. On the walk to the plane, every step stung like hot coals. He hobbled between the guard of dishonour, saw parked bombers, felt a drop of rain.

The crew door near the nose of the big aircraft was filled to half its height with armour plate. Above that was some kind of optical sight mounted on a stalk. They were heading for the lowered ramp at the tail, a ramp which also seemed loaded with equipment.

Beside it stood two alarming men. The black one was enormous, like a wrestler. The white one looked 7 feet tall. They both wore green tuxedos and held sub-compacts.

Braden asked them, 'Any flak?'

'No sweat, boss,' the black one said.

'Crew's ready,' the tall one said.

'Right. This guy's got bad feet. Better give him a hand.' Braden helped Elina onto the ramp and turned back to Jason who'd followed them. 'See you other end.'

The gorillas helped Blake up and, half-supporting him, got him inside. The fuselage was jammed with so much gear it looked like a fabrication plant. As the ramp went up, he caught a last glimpse of the stymied Jason. Then there was just the dim lighting in the hull and the whine of the GTC.

He said, 'Got to sit down.'

They sat him on a box. He panted with relief. 'It's like a factory.'

Braden nodded. 'Out of the ark but still works. Got four Vulcan 20-millimetre cannons. But I'm thinking about swapping the rear two for Bofors.'

He pointed out features enthusiastically. 'Flare launcher on the ramp. Press the wrong button, you launch the launcher! That's the light-set. Six-million-candle power. Later versions had low light level TV.'

'What's the shovel for?'

Braden touched it. 'Size ten coal-scoop. Essential. These are ammo cans and the disintegrating belts come out here and here. Expended brass collects in this trough. So you gotta scoop away the brass or it jams the guns.' He pointed out more features. 'Side-looking radar dome. Swings inboard. Two 7.62-millimetre miniguns up there. Smaller versions of the Vulcans. More up front. So we talk when I get us off the deck. Cut those cuffs off him. Hacksaw's in the toolbox.'

The tall man moved back toward the ramp.

'No,' Braden said. 'It's up front now.'

The two bodyguards helped him to his feet. He followed them along an aisle beside a large boxed-in section to the front of the crammed fuselage. Braden pointed to a locker, then climbed the flight-deck stairs.

The men helped him onto a seat on the starboard side of the fuselage. 'You're official right scanner,' the tall one said.

While the black man rummaged for tools, the tall one took over the tour. 'Ox-bottle storage. Ammo racks. Infrared target acquisition . . .'

His companion returned with a hacksaw, a bolt cutter and two large pairs of pliers. 'Turn around.'

Slicing the chain was simple but getting the bracelets off harder.

There was a thing like a large telescope mounted on the converted crew door. The tall man saw him looking at it and drawled, 'Night Observation Device.'

When the last bracelet was severed, Blake rubbed his wrists and nodded thanks.

Now, with arms free, he could support himself. As the engines started, they led him back aft, opened a door at the rear of the container-like box and waved him in. It had stretcher bunks at the rear, three each side. Elina sat on one. Ahead of her were two operators in headsets facing displays. All the crew seemed Braden's vintage. He slumped gratefully on a bottom bunk. The tall man handed them foam earplugs, then went out and shut the door. The racket was less with it shut but when Elina shouted something, he still couldn't hear it. With a ponderous jerk, they started to move.

He was amazed such a roomy airframe could be so jammed with gear. Braden had to be worth billions to keep a thing this old and complex flying.

He was yelled at to lie on the bunk. He braced himself as the engines wound up. The props bit, brakes released. The vibrating scrapyard gained speed. He wanted to cover his ears but needed his hands to hold on.

As they thundered off the strip, he glanced across at Elina. She looked petrified. Ko, he thought, was on the money so far. The accident. The meeting with Braden . . .

The airframe shook and its contents rattled as they hit the layer of cloud. A drop and lurch. He visualised Braden on the flight-deck, doing his gung-ho thing.

After the roar of taking off and gaining altitude became the drone of level flight, Braden entered the compartment and waved the others out. He found them headsets and jacked them into intercom outlets. 'Got a fighter escort now. We're the best-tracked aircraft in the nation.' He turned to Blake. 'So, what do you know about this Tritter guy?'

'He was one of the leaders of the oil cartel. The CIA's running him. And that's why they attacked us.'

'CIA attacked you? That confirmed?'

'It is now. We were on an operation in Bhutan. They wiped us out. While they were grilling me, they wheeled in a man I saw watching us in Bhutan. They . . .'

'The CIA's in bed with Tritter? Fuck.' He glanced at Elina. 'Sorry. So what's he up to?'

'He's got something happening on a rig in the Timor Sea.' He looked at Elina for a lead, unsure how much to say.

She said, 'Tritter's connected with a kind of vice club called Infandus.'

Braden rubbed his jowl. 'I've heard of that.'

'And we're working on that angle. So what can you tell us from your side?'

'I'm interested in the CIA–Tritter connection. That's all I'm prepared to say just now.'

'Do you think Tritter's involved with that . . . town down there?'

'Don't know.' Braden stared at them both in turn, as if assessing his next move. 'What I'm after is hard information on Tritter. If you can get me that, I'll try and help you.'

The plane hit a thermal and shot up. Elina grabbed for a handhold. 'But they won't let us go now we've seen what they're doing. Even if Tritter's not involved, they'll still kill us.'

'How brave are you, little lady?'

'I'm a coward.' She burst into tears. 'Such a terrible . . . terrible . . . coward.'

Braden patted her hand, won over. 'Only difference between a brave man and a coward is the coward thinks faster.' He looked at Blake. 'There's one way out of here for you two. It's all I can suggest and you'll have to learn fast. Now people have spent their careers jumping out of these things and . . .'

'I couldn't,' Elina shrieked.

'You want to live?'

'I've never done a jump,' Blake said. 'And my feet . . .'

'Shame about the feet but that's how it flops.'

'And if we jumped out of this, wouldn't they see us?'

Braden scratched an eyebrow, thinking. 'They'd spot you on static line. But we've got cloud at 7000 feet. So you jump in cloud, deploy at a thousand. By then the fighters are miles ahead. Get away with it. If you don't bounce.'

'Wouldn't they suspect?'

'No way. Either of you been to jump school?'

She said, 'They forced me to do a tandem once. I said I'd never do it again.'

'Good. No training. Forty per cent chance you don't make it. No, I don't think they'd suspect.'

Elina covered her face. 'Oh, God!'

'We tell you what to do, what the count is, how to land. Simple as warming up canned soup. We've got standard military chutes. Paratroopers use them — drop their heavy stuff down just before they do their landing fall.'

She shuddered. 'I couldn't do it by myself.'

Blake said, 'You'll have to.'

She bleated excuses. '. . . and even if we landed safely, they've taken everything we had. Our ID, credit cards. We'd soon . . .'

Braden produced a wad of hundred-dollar bills.

'. . . and if you help us they could kill you.'

'They've tried. And after my shit-fit down there, they'll try again. I'm ready for that. Still. Up to you. You don't have to jump. But stay here and I'll have to hand you back.'

Blake looked at her. 'Take the money.'

She covered her face again.

He took the wad from Braden. 'Deal.'

'I'll get Stick and Buick to give you contact details. They're the two big guys who showed you around. Both totally reliable. If you get out of this, raise them when you can, and arrange a two-way connection.'

'Right.'

Braden stood up. 'I'll get someone to brief you and sort out the kit. Got to get back to the office.' He extended a hand.

Blake shook it.

'Have a good one,' Braden said. But his level, speculative stare didn't indicate encouraging odds.

They stayed in the booth while a bull-necked elderly crewman instructed them. 'Skipper says to tell you everything I know — so listen up. First thing. Parachutes are over-designed for safety. And when the canopy opens, whoompa! You stop so fast, things go through the bottoms of your pockets.'

Elina's face was tense with fear.

'So you get a tangle and the chute don't open, you try pulling lines in and releasing them — might clear it. Pull in all the material and try and undo the knots. Got the rest of your life to clear a malfunction.' A sardonic grin. 'Got to get the skirt of the chute into the mainstream. With me?'

'Oh God,' she groaned again.

'You see a figure-eight above you, that's a partial inversion.' He held up an orange-handled hooked knife with a lanyard ring on the end. 'Standard USAF shroud-cutter. Cut no more than four lines.

Better still, forget it. You tug on a line looped over the canopy, could cut the chute in half. Other way, just costs you a broken leg.'

Elina groaned again.

'Now if your risers twist, you'll know 'cause you can't lift your head. Try pulling 'em apart above you or move your legs like you're on a bike. Got to counter-rotate, see? Watch out for trees, wires, water or buildings. These chutes steer like barges but if you tug a bit . . . Aw, forget it. But you're going backwards, you look under your shoulder to check you're clear of trees. So much for late-life maintenance. Now we get down to the jump . . .'

When he was fully kitted up, he felt like Quasimodo. She stood beside him, goggles and helmet on, petrified. The instructor tightened their leg-straps more. 'If it don't hurt, it's too loose.'

They shuffled to the jump door. The aircraft was pitching and yawing now as Braden dropped them into cloud, fuselage creaking, tail swinging. The crewmen spoke into their headsets.

'Set,' one yelled. 'And waiting on the skipper.'

Someone held up three fingers.

Blake clung to something to steady himself, pain shooting up his legs. The crewmen watching weren't smiling. Their faces said 'Better you than me, pal'.

'Opening door.'

The panel moved up, letting in the dull glare of cloud, the thunder of the engines. A blast of cold wind.

'Stand in the door.'

He inched forward as they pitched and yawed in the turbulence, braced himself against the frame. He could see nothing but grey, hear nothing but the tumult of the turbines. Elina clung to the fuselage behind him. She knew she'd have to do it next.

The green light came on.

He felt the tap, pivoted left, grabbing the door edges, leaped with all his strength.

The engines' roar and the freezing blast of air plunged him into sensory overload.

His brain fused.

He was meant to assume the best 'exit position' he could — head down, hands across his chest, elbows in, legs locked together, toes pointing down.

He couldn't do it, fell out of control, ears popping, moist air bellying his cheeks.

The count.

He had to do the count.

He couldn't breathe but, for some reason, didn't need to.

'One thousand. Two thousand. Three thousand . . .'

They plummeted through cloud.

The plane seemed long gone. Not even the sound of engines in the distance.

A sudden clear view of half the world.

Through battering wind he drifted toward spinning fields below.

'Seven thousand. Eight thousand . . .'

He was surprised to find no sensation of falling. He forced himself to get with it, tried to tuck a little, preparing for the shock, pulled the cord.

No shock. Hell!

Then a sweet pop and a jerk that seemed to cut through his thighs and tear his guts loose.

He craned up at an unfouled spreading canopy — the most beautiful sight in the world.

No snags.

Clear.

He took grateful breaths.

He was drifting placidly down. The sound of wind through suspension lines. No more spinning. He looked up and around. He couldn't see her. Had she jumped?

Where were the front risers? Were these the lines they'd meant? Had Ko also foreseen this event? If so, he'd had reason to keep it to himself.

It was like a ploughed field below — brown.

And looked more like it fast.

He drifted to the side and pulled tentatively on a lift web but there was no way to steer the thing, nowhere to steer it to anyway. He concentrated on landing.

As his feet took the shock he almost passed out. But managed to roll as they'd told him to. His legs swung over his head on wet soil. Graceless. But nothing snapped.

He gasped for air, breath knocked out of him.

He lay for long moments, enduring the pain in his soles. He looked at sky, rain on his face. He was alive.

There wasn't much wind so the chute didn't drag — 'turf-surf' the man had called it.

He popped the harness release, got out of the webbing, rubbed his sore limbs.

Where was she?

Fields. A farm roof with a windmill and far off barn.

And, some way across the furrows, the billow of another chute.

She was down.

Thank God for that. But in one piece?

A small form stood up and struggled with her harness.

She'd made it!

Still on his knees, he tried pulling in the chute. Should he bury it? He threw dirt over it to stop it bellying, then walked painfully toward her on the soft earth. She'd taken her helmet off and was kneeling on the ground.

As he neared her he called, 'You all right?'

She looked like someone who'd faced a firing squad only to discover they were using blanks. 'I think so.'

'We're still here. Wherever here is.' He looked at the sodden fields. 'So now we're playing it by ear. Guess it beats being tortured, then killed.' He grimaced at the pain in his feet. 'I'm not sure I can walk far.'

The remark seemed to change her. She regained poise, self-possession. She was no longer the terrified woman. The transformation was extraordinary.

She touched his arm gently. 'Don't worry. I'll take care of things now. I'm good at that. Remember?'

He knew she'd get them out of this.

39

PENTAGON

It had rained for days. Soaking, depressing rain. In the inner courtyard of the world's biggest office building, sodden trees dripped gloom. The gloom persisted in the sanctum of the Secretary of Defense, where two men sat motionless, listening to the third.

Stone endured Jason's debrief, feeling greyer than the sky. He glanced at Treloar — groomed and grave behind his monumental desk.

Stress had raised the Secretary's voice half an octave. 'And you don't even know how he did it?'

Jason shook his head. 'I'd say they bailed out. Only possibility left.'

'And you've picked up nothing since?'

'The clamps are on. Coast Guard. Commercial flights. But you can't monitor every yacht that leaves a marina. If they're alive, they've skipped.'

Treloar, who could recognise a debacle when he saw one, looked ready to take Jason apart. 'Why the hell did you let Braden take them in the first place?'

'My fault,' Stone sighed. 'I gave him enough latitude to expose his intellectual and occupational ceiling.'

Jason glanced at him as if stung. He took it as a betrayal, and it was intended to be.

'Braden's past his use-by date.' Treloar picked up a pencil and snapped it. 'Bill?'

Stone detested histrionics. 'True. But decisions should adjust to time and chance.' He probed a molar with his tongue where he'd detected a jammed scrap of food. He flossed after every meal and had several small devices for that purpose — two-pronged plastic things with reels of tape in their handles. The nearest was, unfortunately, in the side pocket of his car.

Treloar stared like a bull. 'Time and chance?'

'For the race is not to the swift nor the battle to the strong.'

'Fuck. I'm looking at hard facts here. Braden and DEMI know about Tritter. So Jessop does, too!'

Jason, still smarting, put the best spin on it. 'I suspect they've heard of the name. But that's all.'

'Then it's got to stop now. No way we can let this drift. Don't snow me about time and chance. I want to hear from you, Bill.'

Stone probed his tooth. 'DEMI's now seen option three and could be on the trail of option four.'

'Means Braden has to go. We pull his plug.' Treloar turned back to Jason. 'You damned fool. What made you think that . . .' He cut it off. Jason wasn't his employee. Lucky for him, Stone thought. He watched his squirming subordinate with interest. Would he dare speak again?

Jason risked it. 'Wouldn't retiring Braden be obvious now? His profile . . .'

'The alternative's worse. And we don't need your advice. You've done enough damage already. I want to hear from you, Bill. Not this klutz.'

Why, he wondered, had he accepted the job of DCI? Masochism? The lust to prove himself a fool? And what could he say to the man? 'Hypothetically . . . is it enough to silence Braden?'

Treloar wasn't sure what he was hearing. 'You mean take out . . . the President?'

'No-oo. Purely as hypothesis — a coma? We have this thing that — well — destroys short-term memory.'

Jason watched him, amazed.

Treloar screwed up his lip. 'What the hell are we saying here?'

'Just freeing the mind with hypothesis.' Stone tongued the worrisome tooth. 'So! Do we reject that course as insane?'

Treloar cradled his head. 'Jesus, Bill, be serious.'

'Funny, isn't it,' he said, 'how everything boils down to ethics. I know brand image has replaced the image of God, but if you just rely on tolerance you eventually have to tolerate everything.'

Treloar looked stumped. 'What the hell?'

'The greatest good for the greatest number. Is that enough? Mere happiness and satisfaction? Good intentions are destructive because they're agenda-based. But virtue has no motive.'

Careful evasion? Elliptical ploy? They were trying to understand him.

Treloar said, 'I'm lost.'

'All of us are,' he smiled, 'because, in our present situation, virtue's its own retribution.'

'All I know is that doing the right thing never got me far.'

'And I'm pointing out that, in this predicament, doing the wrong thing won't either.'

'So what's our move?'

'I'm not sure yet. It's check. But is it checkmate?'

'Sorry,' Treloar growled, 'but that doesn't wash. Right now, I want Braden off the board. Your department, Bill. But if you don't do it, we will.'

He sighed. Treloar had missed his point. But then, almost everyone did. Now it would blunder on predictably. Strike and counter-strike. Stupidity squared.

The contract was out on Braden.

But it was too late to kill him.

That'd only make it worse.

40

LEARNING CURVE

Elina was living up to her reputation. She seemed able to handle everything and everybody while making it seem effortless. She'd got them out of Kansas. Out of America as well. Now they were jammed in an aircraft container for the flight across the Atlantic.

They had a small fan to recycle air, two rudimentary floor-cushions with backrests and restraining belts, emergency oxygen bottles, a can toilet and barely room to scratch. The battery-powered light died on takeoff and left them talking in the dark. They were exhausted but the thing was too cramped to let them doze. She'd told him they were heading for Heathrow, then said more about the terrors to come.

'We'll be met and driven to a house in Putney. The place is a blind. We're watching a man across the road, an art and antique dealer called Peter Mair, who Tan wants to refurbish part of Infandus. And before Tan's people interview Mair, we want to swap him with you.'

'I'm supposed to become this bloke?'

'Yes, I'm sorry, and it's happened so fast you've got hardly any time to prepare.'

'And this is to get me into Infandus . . . ?'

'That's the plan.'

'Back up a bit. How does it connect?'

'I'm sorry. I'm forgetting how much you don't know. There's a woman called Gwen. She's our plant in Infandus. She works in the office of a Marcia Traill. Traill runs a kind of palace of pain for ladies.'

'S & M?'

'I suppose that's what it is. But with a kind of schoolmistress slant. She's wealthy, weird, bright, well-connected and into Art Deco. Mair's a world authority on that period and she wants him. She's asked Tan to organise it.'

He shifted uncomfortably on his rudimentary seat, longing for room to stretch, feet still aching. 'Why ask Tan?'

'Everyone does. Whatever you want, if you have money, Tan makes it happen. And, as he owns Infandus, he's also Marcia's landlord. Now Mair divides his time between London and Sydney. They apparently contacted him in Australia just before he left.'

'So he's Australian?'

'Right. Which saves you having to learn some Midlands accent. And he has lots of interests. You'll have to know about each one — as well as become an expert on Art Deco.'

'And Tan's people have never actually seen him?'

'Not here. He's just flown in and they're meeting him in three days. By then, we have to swap him with you. You're the only person who could possibly learn everything he knows before the interview.'

'And how do you do the swap?' He massaged his feet. He didn't need the crutches now.

'We'll make you look as much like him as we can — dye your hair blond and so on. Superficial but enough, we hope. They could have snapshots.'

'I realise your thing is organisation, but this sounds pretty hairy.'

'It is. And, to be honest, a lot could go wrong. But we're continuing Katherine's project. Doesn't that matter to you?'

'What matters to me is getting to Tritter.'

'Which is what this is about.'

The house was no High Street mansion but a free-standing brick home with a small back garden featuring pond and potting shed. Inside the front fence, a car stood on brick-paved strips. In the basement was a listening post manned by two DEMI agents.

She showed him a desk piled with books and photocopies. 'Information on Art Deco, investigation techniques ... Mair used to be a private investigator ... life history, business contacts. You'll need to absorb it all.' She rubbed eyes red with jet lag.

He glanced at the dossier. 'So he's an antique dealer. That means I can't just know one art period. I need books on old furniture, pottery, glassware — general stuff.'

'We'll get it.'

A buzzer.

'His front door,' she said. 'We've wired it. Quick. This could be the only chance you'll get to see him.'

They crossed to the window in time to see a man leave a house across the street. He had a slight stoop, a shuffling walk and wore a sportscoat with leather-knot buttons and leather elbow and pocket-top patches. He looked too pommy for a lad from Oz.

'Well, he's around my age and weight but our faces aren't that alike.'

'A rough match should do it. We'll morph his photo ID so it's halfway between the features of both of you, then get rid of him.' She moved to the door. 'Come on. We'll trail him.'

'Painful. How far do I have to walk?'

'Not far.'

Mair went to the shops and, to Blake's relief, entered a pub. They followed him inside and sat down. The place had heavy beams, wooden benches and pictures of Putney rugby teams on the walls. Mair ordered a pork pie with chips and a Foster's, then settled beneath a shade-umbrella on a bench outside the door. They ordered a counter lunch then perched near a window to watch him over mugs of Guinness.

While he noted the man's mannerisms, Elina blinked with tiredness. When Mair eventually strolled off past trendy shops, she said, 'Let him go.' She put down her half-empty glass, 'I shouldn't have drunk that,' and yawned. 'I have to get back to the house. I'm fading fast.'

'Me too.'

Once inside the door, she swayed. 'Got to sleep for a while.'

'We should sleep for a couple of hours.'

'You don't have time. Mair lives in Putney six months of the year so you need to know this area. Car keys in the hall-stand drawer. Go out and get to know it. Go!'

He drove around the suburb, occasionally leaving the car to walk the mizzle-melancholy streets under a brolly he'd found in the hall.

He noted street names, pubs, churches, sighted the Thames walk, strolled on the common. Putney's natural joys cost nothing, the rest too much. When steady rain began, he returned to the house and scanned the dossier.

Mair had gone to Melbourne and Ballarat Grammar Schools, then Melbourne Uni, where he'd gained a BA. He'd spent the next five years working with his uncle, as an apprentice private investigator. He was famous for an inquiry into thefts from a fine-arts auction house in Sydney and that detective work had been widely reported. The auction house job had fired his interest in art and artefacts. He abandoned sleuthing, opened an antique shop in Oxford Street and built it into a four-shop business. He was divorced, had two sons, liked jazz, was an expert in veneers. There were examples of his handwriting, lists of friends with potted bios, folders full of contacts . . .

He flipped through an Art Deco book. His only knowledge of the style concerned a Clarice Cliff plate which his father, lacking foresight, had bored a hole through to hang it on the wall.

He scanned the sleuthing material:

> . . . but with skid marks, the striations run parallel, starting faint then darkening as the vehicle advances into the skid. With equal braking, the marks should be equally dark and equal lengths . . .

He yawned, jet lag shutting him down, then heard her behind him.

She said, 'Are you sure you can do this?'

'Remembering isn't the problem. The problem's not getting sprung.'

On the second day, Mair was 'disappeared' and he moved across the street to the man's house. Mair's clothes didn't fit him but they'd procured duplicates that did. He tried to work into the role, practised the art dealer's drifting shuffle.

On the fourth day, bilious with dread, he caught the tube from Putney Bridge to Saint James's Park. Impressions of London engulfed him — dark skins, dirt, a beggar near an automatic teller machine . . . He walked to the Athenaeum on the corner of Pall Mall and Waterloo Place. Its portico was surmounted by the gilded statue of Athene. He shuffled inside and announced himself to a porter who opened the glass window of his vestibule to talk to him. He asked to see Cooper.

'Very good, sir. I'll inform him.'

He stood near a stand holding the *Telegraph* and waited.

ATHENE (OR MINERVA) WAS TOO VIRTUOUS FOR VULCAN, WHO SPATTERED HER WITH SEMEN, WHICH SHE WIPED AWAY WITH WOOL, ONLY TO BEGET THE DEFORMED ERICHTHONIUS.

Did celibacy generate distortion? Was that the point of the myth? He fought free of intruding recollections as a man came down the palatial red-carpeted stairway to meet him — a rakish old boy in beige suit with mustard pearl-buttoned waistcoat. 'Mr Mair, I presume? I'm Milton Cooper. Do come this way.'

The walls of the comfortable public rooms groaned with academic paintings. He glimpsed a splendid library. He was ushered into a private sitting room with velvet curtains and chandelier where several men rose from chesterfields to greet him. Cooper introduced just one — a knowing type with curly hair and beard. 'Ashley Andrews, barrister at law. The other two gentlemen shall be nameless but they're experts in various fields.'

Blake slumped in his chair as Mair had at the pub. It was genuine. He needed to sit down.

'Now,' Cooper said, 'Paul will have covered much of this but, today, there's the chance to go into it in detail.'

Paul? Who the hell was Paul? There was nothing about him in the briefing.

Cooper glanced at his notes. 'I see you went to Ballarat Grammar. Curious that.' He turned to one of the others, an elderly man with large teased eyebrows.

'My father ran a plantation in Borneo,' the man with the eyebrows said. 'My brother and I were sent to Ballarat Grammar as boarders. So, in a sense, I'm an old schoolmate of yours. I suppose you were too late to encounter that supreme headmaster, Mr Dart?'

'Renney was there in my time.'

'You remember old Harbourd? And Jimmy and Lofty?'

Was it a trap? He felt the cold sweat of funk. The dossier hadn't equipped him to cope with detail like this. Don't go there. Stick to what you know. 'What I remember most was peeling spuds and cutting hedges.'

'Fatigues. Lord, so do I.' A chuckle. 'I see you were involved with the National Theatre.'

Firmer ground here. 'Yes, I was in several plays Jenny Strickland produced.'

'Strickland. I remember her vaguely.'

'An exceptional woman.'

'Were you a reasonable amateur actor?'

Where the hell was this heading? 'Not bad.'

'Excellent. That could be useful.'

Cooper nodded and turned to the second unnamed inquisitor, a ruddy, multi-chinned man.

He took the cue. 'So you spend half the year in London.'

'I've come here in summer for years now. I give occasional lectures, do consulting work, evaluations. But basically I'm sourcing new items and shipping them back.'

'And this assignment will still allow you to procure items for your business. I see you live in Putney. Some excellent pubs around there.'

'I'm quite a fixture at the Jolly Gardener.'

'And there's the common. You know the meadow north of Queens Ride?'

'Yes. The yarrow. Most pleasant.'

'Now you used to be a private investigator. Specialising in?'

'All areas — asset recovery, public liability . . .'

'I have some knowledge of that field myself. By the way, what kind of video camera did you use for investigative work?'

That was easy, part of his turf. 'A Canon XL1. It has 2 lux with a one-sixth second shutter speed. And the interchangeable lens was a help.'

'Congratulations on your success with that auction house business. By the way, how did you work out it was arson?'

'The usual signs. Absence of stock items and account books. Uninsured items moved to a safe area . . .'

'Of course. Of course. Yes, er . . .' He turned to Cooper. 'I don't think we'll have much difficulty there.'

Meaning what? What did all this have to do with redecorating some upper-class dive?

The man with the eyebrows continued. 'Now your expertise is Art Deco — the pruning of lyricism and what-have-you. Remarkable period. Such a sense of the future.'

'One feels that.'

'What's your opinion of Franz Marc?'

'Well, he's so much the exponent of stylised tension. The precursor. I mean, when you consider he was killed at Verdun in 1916 . . .' He chatted on about sun rays, rainbow motifs.

'Quite.' The man displayed his nostrils, as if puzzled that a colonial could appreciate such things.

He fielded questions for another five minutes, not understanding the motive for them. It was like being dissected in public without benefit of anaesthetic.

Cooper surveyed his experts. Heads nodded in turn. 'Thank you gentlemen.' He rose, a signal for the jury to file out. The barrister remained, twirling a finger in his beard.

Cooper sat again. 'So! Andrews and I, as you know, are specialised employment agents who find people for exacting purposes. And I must say that when we were commissioned to contract you — at Ms Traill's request — we were most taken with your attributes; to whit, a good-looking man with expertise in the art of the thirties and an investigative background.'

'Why that combination?'

'I thought Paul explained that.'

Shit. It was going pear-shaped. What to say? 'He was reasonably vague.'

'But the proposed remuneration. As a man of the world, you surely . . .'

The back of his shirt was damp. What could he say without blowing it? State the obvious. 'I'm here.'

Cooper smiled. 'You have every right to be cautious. I'd also want to know precisely what was involved. Ostensibly, you're assisting an extremely wealthy woman to refurbish her establishment.'

'Original pieces?'

'Reproductions acceptable.'

'But as Paul told you,' the barrister leaned forward, 'we work for a Mr Tan, not her. So it's Tan who's directly employing you.'

'That's clear.'

Cooper glanced up from his notes. 'You're divorced with two children, I see. So I assume you find women attractive?'

He nodded.

'Splendid. Because we hope you'll not only become Ms Traill's interior decorator but also her intimate friend.'

'For a particular reason?'

'I assume, from what Paul told us, that you have the general idea of that. And that's all you really need. Fear not. The lady's quite fetching.' A sidelong smile at Andrews. He turned back. 'You'll report on her activities to an employee in her establishment, a transsexual called Rita. Yours not to reason why.'

'Merely to do or die?'

'I couldn't put it better. Now you're entering a rarefied stratum where the stick looms as large as the carrot. And while you fit our requirements admirably, the question is, do you accept that?'

'Well, you're buying lots of loyalty.' He hoped that would fly.

'Quite. But significant money implies significant risk.' Cooper glanced at the lawyer.

Andrews gave Blake a cold stare. 'This is a sensitive initiative, Mair, involving utterly uncompromising people. You're familiar with the seedy side of life, you take my meaning? So if you commit . . .'

He nodded, appeared to decide, said, 'I'm in.'

'Capital. Capital.' Cooper beamed. 'I'm sure we'll get on swimmingly. From now on, exchanges of information go through Rita. The establishment's Mandel Court in Kent. Drive there, will you?'

He nodded.

'It's off main roads so I've drawn you a simple map. And you'll need this.' He handed over a piece of paper and a smart card with an embedded chip. 'Your entrée to the establishment. In more ways than one.'

'Interesting.'

'Believe me, it will be. But, as Andrews explained, this requires absolute loyalty or . . .' He spread his hands, 'frankly, your life may be — not to put too fine a point on it — curtailed.'

41

ROBOTS

Braden lounged on the plush seat of the limo, cradling a Scotch. He would have been home by now if Stick hadn't vetoed him commuting by chopper. A standard helo was a sitting duck for Stingers. And Stick, an ex-SAS commander, insisted that the convoy was safer because they could swap the position of the three identical limos to make his location a pea-and-thimble guess. They'd even suggested a decoy convoy, which struck him as overkill. He'd told them he wasn't a head of state but a private citizen, for Chrissake.

The wind hadn't died at nightfall. Gusts buffeted the heavily armoured car. They varied times and routes and this one avoided major roads. They were somewhere south of the Ohio Turnpike, heading for Medina, escorted by two four-wheel drives carrying Mk19 heavy machine-guns. They also had a communications van and ambulance.

Buick, beside him, pressed his earpiece. 'Fuck.'

'What is it?'

'Detour.'

He found a spare headset and plugged in.

'All units — four.' That was the comms van. 'Unscheduled according to the recce. Verify and report.'

'All units — five.' The leading four-wheel drive, which travelled five minutes ahead, was acknowledging. 'Road blocked by barrier with flashing lights. No sign of incident or vehicles. Isolated area. Visibility low. Potential hostiles. Checking detour now.'

Buick said, 'Four — one. Copy. Can we divert?'

'One — four. Negative. Last turn-off's a mile back.'

'All units — two.' Stick's voice from the limo behind. 'Losing mobility's the worst possible move.'

'Two — four. Roger that. Five — acknowledge.'

A crackle.

'Come in, five.'

Empty air.

Braden finished his Scotch and returned the glass to the circular hole of the cocktail cabinet's rack. 'If it's a rumble,' he told the frowning giant beside him, 'at least the weather's on our side. Attacks never go the way you think. And bad weather makes it worse.'

'All units — four.' The comms van calling now. 'Regard detour as ambush.'

'Four — two. Copy.' Stick again. 'Three, assume position Bravo and prepare to ram. Six, assume position Delta.'

'Two — three. Wilco.' The driver of three, like all of them, was familiar with split-second anti-ambush drills and the stretched saloons had hydraulic-dampener-backed steel bumpers to shunt blockades aside.

As six acknowledged, the third limo overtook, its fog lights glaring, risking a head-on. God help any vehicle that hit it, Braden thought. But no traffic had passed the other way for minutes.

'All units — four.' The comms van. 'Five still out. Full alert.'

Braden peered through the bullet-proof rear window as the four-wheel drive moved in directly behind them. The decoy limo was now ahead of them and the gun-buggy behind, followed by the limo with Stick, the comms van and the ambulance.

'Three — two.' Stick again. 'Report situation.'

'Two — three,' the lead limo called back. 'Can see barrier but no visual on five. No sign of bad guys. Do I ram?'

'Three — two. Affirmative.'

'Two — three. Wilco.'

'One — two. Assume command.'

'Two — one,' Buick acknowledged. 'Wilco.' He glared ahead through the downpour. Their car, closer to the action, had the call.

Debris flew over the hood of the dimly seen car in front. A piece bashed against their windscreen. Yellow, striped, jagged. The barrier.

Then a flash beneath the lead vehicle and a crump. Its kerb-side wheels seemed to lift as it skidded off the road and almost flipped.

They swerved to avoid the crater but it was under them too fast. A rear tyre caught the lip and the suspension drummed with the shock.

'Floor it,' Buick yelled.

The driver dropped a gear and the supercharged engine roared.

'One — all units. Three hit by road mine. Bugging out. Three — four. Report.'

'Four — three. Taken out.' The car but not the driver, Braden noted with relief. The limos, as heavily armoured as any executive movers made, had self-sealing petrol tanks, anti-mine blast plates, run-flat tyres . . .

Looming in the headlights, a large black-painted van parked across the road. They were going too fast to avoid it.

'All units — one. Blocker. Blocker.'

They broadsided into the van. Braden was hurled against the side of the car and felt as if his head had come loose.

The four-wheel drive stopped in time and laid down a carpet of fire — high-explosive antipersonnel rounds with a casualty radius of five yards.

Their driver spun the wheel and tried to bulldoze his way around the van. A flash in the dark. As the big car jerked ahead, there was an explosion where they'd been and the back of the van erupted. Debris slammed into the car and the rear window became opaque.

'Fuck.' Buick roared. 'Antitank.'

The battered limo slid into a ditch, climbed the other side, tyres spinning, engine roaring.

Braden, pop-eyed, stared out the side window. What the hell were they using? From the firing flash, it could have been an M72A2. The throw-away tube had a suicidal signature and, from the racket, the machine gunners were on it.

The limo demolished a fence. His head hit the roof as the car banged and bounced across a field.

Another flash and a shock that knocked him back against the seat. The windscreen view was now obscured by a twisted and vertical bonnet. They slid to a stop, the engine scrap. The driver went for the smoke grenades. Their launchers were hidden under flip-over panels in the guards. They worked, thank God, but the rain limited the effect.

Through the murk he saw approaching shapes — masked figures in black combat gear.

Buick yelling for backup.

Jeez! It was like 'Nam.

An explosion behind.

The 4WD?

'Frags,' Buick yelled.

Those took longer to deploy because their launchers were concealed behind the retractable headlights and panels side and rear.

Black figures all around them.

Where were the fucking grenades?

The 40-millimetre antipersonnel went off in a close preset pattern, pocking the windows and tearing through the panels into the blast plates. The bulletproof glass showed the impacts but the blast-resistant net curtains hung untouched.

The attackers staggered. Most fell. But the closest man still stood, his ripped uniform exposing the glistening red mess of his chest. Incredibly, the downed men started to get up.

'Sonofabitch!' Buick went for the Jackhammer in the weapons bay beneath the cocktail cabinet. The ugly combat shotgun had a rotating magazine. He cleared it as the man with the mashed chest staggered three steps forward and clamped a square device against the door.

'Breaching patch,' Buick yelled. He thrust Braden to the safe side of the car, then jammed the riot gun's wedge-like snout into the concealed side firing port.

The cabin rang with earsplitting noise as three rounds slammed into the man. The black figure staggered back and fell. But the device still clung to the door.

With the car inop, they had to debus. And fast. But the pinned down gun-buggy couldn't cover them.

'One — two. Coming up on your left. Can you reverse?'

Buick called, 'Negative. Need covering fire and transfer.'

The dim shape of Stick's limo stopped on their left. As Braden dragged off the headset, ready to get out, he saw their driver was now cradling an MP5.

Phantom shapes of more attackers trudging over the bodies of the first. The machine-guns hammering. A distant flash and explosive charge. The gun stopped, as if taken out.

Their car took shrapnel again as the other limo used its frags. The smoke came second to hide the transfer. But it wouldn't hold long in this wind.

As Buick bundled him out of the wrecked vehicle, shielding him with his body, the driver hosed the mist, emptying his mag on auto.

Then the frame-charge on the car door exploded and the wave of heat almost burnt off Braden's ears. As he was shoved into the second vehicle, he saw, with horror, blood and brains spurt from the back of the driver's head.

The door slammed shut.

Stick yelled, 'Bug out.'

He crouched on the floor as they churned and banged across the field. The suspension bottomed as they hit an obstacle. The car recovered, tyres spinning.

They slithered up a slope to firm road, the rubber gripped and they left the killing field behind.

While Buick handled the comms, Stick checked him for damage.

He hadn't taken any hits but shook like a guy with the DTs.

Five minutes later, reasonably sure they were clear, they started to talk themselves down and to wonder how many men they'd lost.

'. . . but if we'd fallen for the detour,' Stick growled, 'we'd've taken three tubes of antitank.'

Buick still gripped the shotgun, ready to smoke anything that moved. 'Those motherfuckers weren't human. Just kept coming. Fucking droids!'

'Same as the zombies I saw in Kansas,' Braden said. 'That lot were supplied by the Pentagon.'

42

INFANDUS

The over-green Kent countryside was picturesque but depressingly wet. Blake drove through its ancient sodden villages, jittery about this double game. How long would he fool them? And how dangerous would it get?

He'd read that Kent had once been a forest sheltering stone-age man and, later, the first site of Roman occupation. Here were castles and fortified houses of all periods and states of preservation. And the Infandus mansion was apparently one — its debaucheries hidden somewhere among these orchards, hop gardens, farms.

The further he drove, the smaller the roads became. The last was no wider than a lane. It had an overgrown hedge on one side and venerable trees on the other. Near an ancient chapel with a brood of leaning tombstones, he pulled over to let a tractor pass. Its potato-filled trailer was surmounted by a yapping dog.

He lowered the window. 'I'm looking for Mandel Court. Know it?'

The rustic thrust his cloth cap back, scratched his skull. 'Might. But around here, we keep the eyes shut, the mouth closed. And a good day to you.'

He drove on. Through misty rain, he saw what looked like a square forest — close-planted poplars stretching along the road and over the fields with other trees behind. As he drew level he saw, through gaps in the branches, a wall topped by electrified wires.

Halfway up the next rise the trees parted to expose metal gates with moulded escutcheons. He turned in, left the car, found a wall panel, inserted the card. The gates ponderously opened.

He drove through but was stopped by a raised-spike barrier big enough to disable a close-combat vehicle. Two uniformed security guards circled the car, checked it with portable detectors, peered inside. He was asked to open the boot and produce identification. His dummied-up documents were examined and the details entered on a clipboard before the barrier hissed into the ground.

He drove on past oaks and elms. Beyond the wood was the mansion's forecourt — lawns, manicured hedges and statuary. The pile itself had mouldy brickwork and an intricate slate roof with spire-like chimneys.

Signs instructed him to follow the drive around the side. Behind the original structure spread increasingly modern buildings linked by porticos. The additions increased in size until the last was as large as a hangar.

At the rear of the structure was a second formal garden. Grottoes and pavilions partly screened more buildings behind. A drooping windsock on one indicated a helicopter pad.

A guard directed him to a parking bay, then waited to conduct him in.

He breathed deeply. This was it.

The entrance to this section had a suspended-glass wall that framed a view of the grounds. Behind the marble reception desk elegant women posed. 'Good afternoon, Mr Mair. Please take the lift to the second floor.'

The lift wafted him to what could have been a movie house lobby in the thirties. Bronze and ivory girls on onyx bases struck extravagant attitudes for mythical reasons unexplained. A white baby grand lurked in a far corner and overstuffed sofas propped walls papered in variegated stipple. In recessed arches, light filtered through geometric smoked-glass panels.

A nymph dressed like a maid pattered toward him. She was grossly afflicted with eye-shadow and had long plaited hair. She whispered, 'This way, sir, if you please.'

She ushered him into a library of elderly books. Many were gripping yarns for girls. *Janice of the Lower Fourth. What Katy Did.* Chairs and bureaux in varnished rosewood continued the Art Deco theme.

'Please wait here. Mistress won't be long.'

A hinged section of bookcase swung wide, releasing a hint of Chanel No. 5 from the red plush interior beyond. He walked into a combination sitting room/office. Its green baize walls supported large paintings in gilt frames top-lit by brass strip-lamps — early academician versions of half-naked women. A pyramid-design clock ticked on a stained wooden mantelpiece and a gramophone in a corner had an Aztec-temple lid.

A woman leaned against the desk, arms akimbo. Generous mouth, perfect teeth, clear challenging eyes.

'Welcome, Mr Mair.' A plummy drawl. 'I'm Marcia Traill.'

She was at least thirty-five years beyond the age of consent but her rangy body hardly showed it. Beneath the clinging black gown her legs and hips looked trim enough to model jeans. She had the firm arms of a swimmer and her blonde hair was going attractively grey in streaks. She extended a hand older than her body, that dated her at fifty-plus.

'Please sit.' She subsided behind her desk, exuding provocative ease, her air of sex and wealth unmistakable.

'You certainly like the thirties.'

'A way of life whose passing I personally mourn. But re-creations are comforting. You must be wondering what we do here.'

'I'm told it's a facility for certain . . . indulgences.'

'A facility? How circumspect.' An ironic smile. 'True eroticism is art. But I can't expect you to share that perspective. So, yes, it's a facility, as far as you're concerned. For personal tastes. And mine, as it happens, is discipline.'

'Typically British.'

'Indeed. We nurture our fine madness into intimate depravities. So tell me, Mr Mair. Does bondage appeal to you at all?'

'I wear a watch-band. That's as far as it goes.'

'Disappointing in such a good-looking man. So. To business.' She touched her diamond-studded halter. 'Despite all efforts to develop the unerring eye, I remain curiously unafflicted with good taste. But I understand you possess a flair I cannot begin to approach.'

'I know a good thing when I see it.'

'How fortuitous. Now, this establishment has over sixty rooms, most with specific uses. However they lack cohesion. Artistic overview, that is. I want to extend the feel of the thirties throughout. But the nature of our activities makes that a challenge.'

'Could I could see the rooms?'

'Are you prudish?'

'No.'

'I'll show you one or two areas. A caution. No speaking. It interferes with concentration. One more thing. Some of our guests are . . . eccentric! Hush my mouth.'

He smiled at that.

'Avanti.' She rose, opened the far door to reveal a woman kneeling in the corridor beyond it. She wore nothing but black leather boots and studded belts. Her wrists were secured behind her to her boots and her leather collar was held down by straps secured between her legs. A plastic ball in her mouth silenced complaint.

Traill fondled her hair as she passed. 'Such a good, good girl.'

The first room featured a curved leather pommel horse. A prone half-clad woman was tied to it. A masked, dark-skinned dominatrix caressed the welts on the woman's buttocks with a cane. Another victim, a crone in frilly underwear, waited in a cage.

Traill pointed to the bold-patterned wallpaper. 'Notice that decor is cursory or absent.' She held out her hand for the cane, bent it to test the spring, then brought it down.

The victim flinched with pain, dragging at her bonds. 'Thank you, mistress.'

'At a certain point, a certain intensity, one melts.' She gave another stinging blow.

The woman's cry was orgasmic.

Traill caressed the quivering flesh, murmured, 'Did you melt, dear? I believe you did.'

As he followed her to the next room, she pointed to a side door. 'Enema suites. Best not before lunch.'

The room was full of wooden frames — manacles, ropes, pulleys. Two middle-aged naked men were suspended, feet almost off the ground. A third was spreadeagled like a hide hung out to dry. Three inadequately clad young women were tying the complex knots.

'Gentlemen's suspension room,' she murmured, once they gained the outer corridor. 'The knots are an art. I've sent two of my girls to Tokyo to study the technique. We believe in matriarchy here. But also in femininity. You may think that hard to reconcile but a moment's thought shows how one can. Culture has lost much since the thirties. Well, that's enough to give an impression.'

They glanced into a third room on their way back — a recreation of an early schoolroom. Women in school uniforms were jammed behind small wooden desks. The female 'teacher' had one forty-year-old 'girl' bent over her table, the woman's short skirt lifted to expose a plump bare rump. The teacher wielded a leather strap. Two other women waited in line. On the blackboard was a maxim:

Pleasure and pain flow like two springs. He who draws the right amount from the right spring at the right time lives happily.

— Plato, *The Laws*.

They returned to Traill's den, settled again into overstuffed chairs.

'So, Mr Mair. Are you shocked?'

'At the wallpaper?'

She half-smiled. 'At what we do here.'

'I'm trying to decide whether it's laughable or pitiful.'

'Neither. At best, it's purifying. Cleansing. Unfortunately, few who come here are wholehearted. Most are isolated souls seeking romance in fantasy, delusion. But I don't need you to understand — just to become familiar with the area, then provide your proposal.'

'Budget?'

'Money's no object. But I demand absolute discretion and loyalty. You will discuss this place with no one.' She smoothed a hair from her brow then spread her arms wide as if needing to stretch. Elbow wrinkles showed her age. 'I won't influence you initially. I prefer to see fresh concepts. We're open around the clock so you can choose when you work. We'll make each room progressively available. We have a small administration area and they've cleared an office for you. I've asked one of my best girls, Rita, to act as your guide.'

She took him to the office. It looked normal enough. Neatly dressed women in workstation cubicles. No rubber suit or mask in sight. Elina had shown him a photograph of Gwen, their mole in Tan's organisation, and he spotted her immediately. She didn't look up.

Traill waved to a small, bare office. 'You'll work in there.'

'Fine.'

The black-leather-clad dominatrix entered, removed her cat-woman mask to expose a young, attractive West Indian face with full lips ringed with a tattooed line. She called to one of the clerks, 'Can you book Lady P in again next Thursday? Ta.' Her voice had husky undertones.

Traill said, 'Rita. This is Peter Mair. He's doing the redecorations. Take care of him will you?'

'Yes, mistress.' She flashed him a smile. 'I'm knocking off now so if you can wait a mo . . .'

'Sure.'

'Smashin'. Just have to change. Meet you by the lift then?'

She re-emerged in tight top, jeans and leather jacket. He followed her warily into the lift. Fooling Traill was relatively easy. But this creature was a Tan employee and a slip-up with her could be fatal.

When the lift door closed, he said, 'So you're my contact with . . .'

'I'm your future.'

'So Traill doesn't know you work for . . . them?'

'She suspects the whole staff. The toffs who use us are paranoid. 'Cause we've got the dirt on them, see?'

They left the lift on the second floor and walked along a wide corridor.

He said, 'Big place.'

'Three sub-floors and main carpark below.'

They reached tall scene-dock-type sliding doors with wooden rostrums stacked nearby.

'You make films here?'

'Nah. It's the fantasy department.' She opened a small access door in the large one. 'Have a butcher's.'

It looked like a sound-stage. Sand and rock began at the doors and sloped up toward the back of the set. A diorama effect behind the centre hill suggested a bare land of olive groves and mud-brick buildings. A track wound up toward the hill-top and in the foreground was a village. Then he saw the wooden crosses stacked near the door. 'Calvary?'

'You've tumbled. Right bit of old misery, this lot.'

'What's it for?'

'Well, if you were a rich geezer who thought you were Christ Almighty and happened to be dying of terminal cancer and had a bee in your bonnet about heroic death and could afford extras, lightning effects, Judas, Herod, the lot . . .' She led him to a side door behind the permanent cyclorama. 'Nah, they've locked it. But Herod's palace is through there. And the set for the Last Supper, too.'

'This is all for some crazy who wants to die like Christ?'

'Some lark, huh? Daft bit is, he's C of E.' She guffawed. 'Only religion that worships social standing.'

'What happens at the end?'

'We tack him up, do the spear-and-vinegar bit and he's a goner.'

'You — crucify him?'

'What he wants. He'll cark it anyway. No sweat. Place is soundproof. Come on.'

She took him past what looked like an exclusive Paris restaurant, then stopped outside a bistro with cubicles. 'Could you come at a coffee?'

He nodded and squeezed in opposite her.

They ordered and he examined her closely. She wasn't recognisably male. Small-boned, twenty-something.

Her quizzical smile. 'Do I pass?'

'You're remarkable.'

'I'm pre-op in case you're wondering.'

'Saving up . . . ?'

'For the kindest cut? Nah. Happy like this.' She pushed her breasts high. She was bra-less and it showed. 'Part hormones, part implants. Had me cheekbones done, too.' She inclined her head to show him. 'Like 'em?'

He nodded. 'So what's a tranny doing in a sanctum of female domination?'

'They like novelty in our caper. I'm not much into discipline, mind. Don't even whip cream.' She grinned over her cup.

He sipped hot chocolate. 'So, how do I get friendly with Traill?'

'Easy. I saw how she looked at you. Her bacon strips are simmering now.' She shrugged out of her jacket. Soft brown arms and nipples clear beneath the thin material of her scooped top. 'She's had boyfriends. None now. She's lonely.'

'But she likes beating women . . .'

'Most mistresses get off on masochism, too.' She stroked his fingers. 'What's your thing?'

'I'm straight.'

'So? I mostly get bonked by straights. And you're dishy. Who knows? We might both fit you in.'

'What does Traill do when she's not spanking people?'

'Runs Traill Cargo.'

'No wonder she's loaded.' He hadn't associated Marcia Traill with the international air cargo company.

'Her da taught her the business — left it to her when he croaked.'

'So she doesn't want to end up in the tabloids?'

'Or be shopped for manslaughter.'

'Meaning what?'

'Well, what we do is supposed to be safe, sane, consensual, see. But it goes a bit beyond consent. You gotta push it. There are inner depths to this racket. Something you find out from experience. Anyway, every so often we top one of her trussed chooks. Make it look like an accident to keep her on a string. We video everything that happens here.

Slaves love replays and so do the toffs who run the projects. Two-edged sword.' She grinned.

'Why tell me this?'

'You cooked your goose when you took this job.'

'You mean you've . . .'

'Topped one?' She nodded. 'Do my next soon. You'll have to prove yourself too, ducks.'

He gaped at the dark-skinned, sexy face. 'Murdering people wasn't part of the job description.'

'You don't get megabikkies for nothing.'

'Why didn't they . . . ?'

'. . . Tell you? Those guys you met are supply side. Not part of the scene. You work for me. I own you.'

'You mean, I've been press-ganged?'

'Give it a rest. You knew it wasn't kosher.' She took his hand and looked at his palm. 'I see money, sex and death. Sounds like the average life.' She pouted. 'Look, mercenaries get paid to kill people and who complains? At least you're here and not in some cruddy African war. And those punters upstairs are pathetic.' She stroked his hand. 'Don't blame me. I'm just part of the sodding chain of command.' She placed his palm between her warm firm breasts. 'And I want us to be friends.' A sensual look. 'Bet you've gone around the world with chicks. So . . . ?'

'No offence. But I like women.'

'They're fun. But not like the real thing.'

He looked at the seductive fake — this cynical cockney who required him to murder on command.

To safeguard the operation, and his life, he knew he might be forced to do it.

43

ARCS OF FIRE

The sun shone benignly on Braden's 100-acre kingdom and the private army patrolling its grounds. After the attack on the convoy, they remained on full alert.

Stick sat in the solarium, his M–4 across his knees, the spare mags in his combat vest warm from hours against his chest.

He glanced at Braden, who sat in his favourite cane chair, reading the *New York Times*. They kept the chair against the corner of the colonnade to limit angles of attack. The boss was tough but he wasn't young. He could imagine what the guy was going through.

Two shadows advanced across the flagging beside the indoor pool. Buick was escorting Connie, Braden's significant other, back from the garden. It was like a battleship escorting a schooner. The old girl was in a one-piece bathing costume. Buick wore military fatigues and his Argentine Special Forces vest: knife pouch under one arm, pistol holster under the other, map pockets, ammo loops, pocket for cigars. The poser's vest was a joke but not the wearer. He was the toughest hard-arse in the game.

Connie called to Braden, 'Chuck, this place is turning into Sing Sing. Yesterday I had to practise my putting in the trophy room. Now Buick won't let me use the outside pool. We're hiding away like mice.'

They hadn't told her about the second attack.

Braden glanced over his paper. 'Man's just doing his job.' Buick glared at her and rumbled, 'You got two pools. But you only got one life.' He turned and padded around the colonnade, eyes never still.

She perched on the arm of Braden's chair. 'We're living like cornered animals.'

'It won't be for ever.'

'Wish you'd never started this.'

He patted her hand. 'Someone had to.'

She said tearfully, 'I don't want to lose you. Wouldn't you be better hiding somewhere?'

'No way.'

Stick watched as he showed her the article they'd vetted in the control room that morning. Incoming mail was checked for incendiary or explosive apparatus. He remembered the headline: BRADEN DUBS SECRET PROJECT UNCONSTITU-TIONAL. PRESIDENTIAL INQUIRY TIPPED.

She scanned the text then gasped, 'Oh-my-Godddd. You went for it, didn't you?'

'I need the exposure. Could be the one thing that keeps me alive.'

He tried to ignore their talk. Get distracted, people died. Braden had paid heavily for letting Blake and Luna dive out of the bird. Still, popping the boss was no cakewalk. He went over it again in his mind.

Their perimeter security included foot patrols, infrared cameras, seismic detectors, radar, dogs and anti-intrusion. They had four concealed snipers and had increased ground sweeps to four a day, with stress on bombs and unauthorised entry. The team was back to forty strong. Experienced, dedicated men. Short of mortar rounds or biological attack — uncommon in rural Ohio — Braden was secure enough at home.

The mansion, called Sans Souci (that always cracked him up), had a series of safe rooms and elaborate detection devices. Exterior doors worked on an airlock system and the control room had twenty monitors feeding off two hundred cameras. They worked on the inner and outer cordon principle, with emphasis on power supply, dead ground, suitable firing points and observation posts.

Not even the CIA knew all they had up their sleeves. But no attack went to plan. You had to expect the unexpected.

They'd try to get at Braden somehow.

The question was, how?

And when?

44

TRAILL

Blake's first task at the palace of pain was to assess it. He measured rooms, drew plans, designed concepts, sketched. The sourcing of antiques and materials and the commissioning of reproductions would come later.

He used DEMI's mole, Gwen, as his secretary. She taught him what went on. She was an odd person, like many of their field staff — buck-toothed with a built-up shoe, a hint of chin hair, a figure coarsened by British stodge and a mind grooved by indiscriminate metaphors.

She told him that the office staff called the clientele GPs or Gluttons for Punishment and that, except for the filming of people's obsessions, internal security was poor. He mentioned Rita's intention to kill a GP and she said, 'He's done it before. He reports to Tan directly. Don't cross him.' She classed the transsexual as a man.

'You must find this place one hell of an assignment.'

'It's disgusting. That enema room! My God!' A grimace made her plain face ugly. Yet what she condemned seemed to intrigue her.

'What's Tan like?'

'An octopus with a finger in every pie.'

'And the connection between Traill and Tan?'

'He exploits her and she fears him — sees her employees as snakes in the grass, Tan's watchdogs.'

'Are they?'

'Some will be.' She tapped her protruding teeth with a pencil. 'Marcia knows Tan's been riding roughshod over her, but she's onto him now. She was thick as thieves with Louisa Tritter. All reasons why Elina, and Tan, want you to be . . .' she blinked, searching for a bearable expression, '. . . intimate with her.'

'And now Rita wants me to murder someone.'

'To incriminate you.'

'Great.'

'Don't blame me. My job was to infiltrate this place and get someone installed. I can check the computers, see things going through, but that's it. The rest's up to you.'

He stood in the empty schoolroom, wondering how to reconcile wooden desks and a blackboard with Art Deco. Even the water-torture chamber offered more scope. He gave it up and walked back down the corridor.

Through the slightly open door of the female suspension room, he noticed Rita adjusting an obese woman's bonds. The client hung from a frame, face down, 5 feet off the floor, the folds of her stomach and thighs projecting below the slings. She was gagged and her limbs secured by leather straps. Weights hanging from thongs were cinched around her breasts. Rita tightened the spiked collar, hauling back her head to bring extreme pressure onto the thick and flaccid neck. The woman's face became blue and her eyes bulged like a frightened steer's. Her body jerked as he watched, hands and feet trembling in the cuffs.

Rita left the room impassively, as if she'd tied up a parcel. 'Hello, ducks. Notice my subtle interaction with the slave?'

'Subtle? She's strangling!'

She glanced back at the bulging eyes, now blank. 'Dying happy. No loss. Ugly self-indulgent bitch.' She closed the door on her crime. 'I'm actually doing her a favour. Giving her the chance to be reborn as a human.'

He wanted to loosen the collar and let the woman breathe. But Rita was watching his reaction. He returned to his office in turmoil and tried to work on his concepts.

A scream, running feet, hoarse discussions in the corridor. One of the two large Dutch women who were Traill's lieutenants stomped into the office and summoned the staff to Traill's den.

He stared through the glass of his cubicle at the vacated workstations. He had an appointment with Traill tomorrow to present his ideas.

He wondered how receptive she would be.

When he entered Traill's room next day, layout pad under his arm, she looked her age and her jaunty air was gone. 'Do come in, Mr Mair. Though I doubt I can do you justice. I'm so dispirited I can barely groom myself.'

'I've made rough sketches — enough to show the intention.' He opened the pad on her desk, showed her three revised views of the foyer. His photographer's eye and good draughtsmanship had made the drawings professional enough.

She nodded, rubbed her brow. 'I can't do this now. I'm sorry.'

'Up to you. I'll leave the written submission. The drawings are numbered in the text. When you want more input, yell.' He put it all on her desk and left.

He'd slept for a week in the one village pub that offered accommodation. His room had a creaking bed, chintz curtains, water pipes that rattled, and a view across the street to Sainsbury's. He'd just got back when the phone rang.

'Hello?'

The elegant tones of Marcia Traill. 'I'm sorry about today. Just couldn't cope. For reasons you no doubt know.'

'That's okay.'

'Are you comfortable in that fleapit?'

'It's medieval. But it's close to the manor.'

'Where I still am. There's a restaurant downstairs. I'll eat there tonight. And I thought, if you have no other commitment, you might care to join me.'

'Love to.'

'Excellent. Shall we say eight?'

He was pleased she'd made the first move.

Infandus seemed mysterious at night. Hundreds of hooded garden lights made its jagged line of buildings resemble a cliff rising from a phosphorescent sea. Furtive Nigels and Cynthias exuded from expensive cars like nocturnal sea creatures emerging from their shells.

Although the swanky in-house restaurant was moderately full, alcoves with cut-glass snob-screen inserts gave it an intimate air. He asked for Traill's table and was deferentially conveyed to a private booth.

Traill's backless black sheath emphasised her figure. Her drawn look was half-repaired by make-up, her longish hair caught back. The venerable perfume hung about her. As she leaned forward for the menu, her gown's discreet but deep cross-over neck suggested more than it concealed.

The waiters were well spoken, unobtrusively eager. The expansive menu featured French, Greek and Italian fare. He ordered souvlaki. It was superb.

He noticed she hadn't brought his sketch-pad. 'Did you have a chance to check my submission?'

'No. And I don't want to discuss it. This is simply a get-to-know-you.' She asked about his interests and past as if schooled by a royal equerry.

He refilled her glass. 'How long has your . . . establishment been here?'

'Too long. And I never discuss my inclinations. People see them as perversions instead of a cleansing release. Do you consider me perverted, Mr Mair?'

'I see you as curious.'

She laughed.

'At least you believe in yourself.'

'I've never believed in anything. But art's a substitute for religion. Just as well because, according to Yeats, women lose their sanity in the presence of the abstract.'

'You consider yourself an artist?'

'In my fashion. I've been born, fortunately or otherwise, to fate's fleeting tribute — success. Which was my father's achievement, of course, although I've embellished it. But did I eat the bread of idleness? No. I've worked very hard. I'm also an artist of desire. And all artists are anarchists.' She'd drained two thirds of the first bottle while barely appearing to touch her glass, ordered a second. 'I need a sedative. You heard what happened today?'

'Someone died.'

'A prominent someone.'

'Who became . . . too enthusiastic?'

'So they say. Though I don't believe it.'

'You think it was murder?'

No answer.

The fresh bottle came.

When the fawning waiter had backed off, he said, 'You're an attractive woman.'

'Beauty and wealth are afflictions. One becomes a target. And when one has something to hide, one can be misused. I'm exploited, for instance, by this place. And determined to do something about it. Speak of the devil . . .'

An Asian man approached their table, wearing crisp casual clothes and with laughter lines around his eyes. He looked a handsome forty but was probably older. 'Marcia. They told me you were here. We are flattered.'

She smiled back.

'And who might your companion be?'

'Peter Mair — antique dealer extraordinaire.'

'Oh, yes. The expert we found for you. Welcome to Infandus, Mr Mair.'

'Peter, this is Mr Tan.'

Blake rose and shook the man's smooth hand.

'So you're finding your way with each other?' Tan smiled.

'Doing our best,' Blake said.

'Well, I mustn't disturb you. Dear, dear Marcia.' He bent and kissed her cheek. 'Do take care of her, Mr Mair. She's one of our treasures.'

'I will.'

'Wonderful. *A bientôt*.'

'Smooth bastard,' she slurred when he'd gone. 'The *ipsissimus* of Infandus.'

Latin was beyond him. '*Ipse*? Himself? So . . .'

'Masculine singular due to the "us" suffix. Superlative by virtue of the "issim".' She smiled at his perplexity. 'Yes, a cruelly inflected language. When ironically applied, it means "the bigshot".'

'And you detest him?'

'Adore him. He's utterly likeable, brilliant, charming. And infuriatingly dangerous.'

By the end of the meal, eyes as empty and glazed as her glass, she became conspiratorial. '. . . and I can't trust a soul. I'm even suspicious of my personal staff. People can be planted.'

'By Tan?'

She nodded, ran a finger along the tablecloth. 'Can I trust you, Mr Mair?'

'I hope so.'

'So do I. You're here on a specific job. May I assume you're not part of Tan's web?'

'Obviously.'

'Nothing here is obvious.'

'I'm an antique dealer.'

'And I'm an antique.'

'I've seen few pieces from your period in such excellent condition.' Drink had blurred his edges but not his ethics. If romancing this woman brought him closer to Tritter and Kate — he'd have to do it.

'Ah yes. Snow on the mountains,' she touched her hair, 'but warmth in the valleys. I have everything going for me. Except someone I can trust.'

When the bill came, she signed the chit, despite his vague protests. 'No, I asked you. Mind if we go back to the club? Some things still to do.'

Her enclave looked the same at night. Except for foyer and office, the rooms were windowless. He stood woozily in her den as she checked her desk-pad. She turned back to him, hips thrust out, slid her arms clumsily around his waist and tilted her face to be kissed.

He did it.

She laughed. 'Can't you do better than that?'

'Do you usually ridicule men?'

'A woman's right. And good looking men should be made to feel ridiculous.'

'I thought you got off on dominating women.'

'I enjoy a little give and take. If I'm taken with the giver.'

'As blessed to receive as to give?'

'Both have delights. Sex is such a problem.' She spoke slowly, trying not to slur, her pickled brain still formidably sharp. 'Promotes marriage, children, divorce, obsession, perversion, murder, war, transmission of painful and fatal diseases . . .' She took his hand and placed it inside her dress. Her nipples were hard. 'I thought I should claim you before Rita does. She's alluring. Intriguing. And many of our sturdy British yeomen prefer the tradesman's entrance. You haven't . . . done it with her, have you?'

'I don't see the male anus as an object of adoration.'

She chortled and swayed to the divan, kicking off her shoes. 'There are condoms in that drawer.'

Once he would have relished this.

As he helped her undress with the enthusiasm of someone peeling a banana she glanced at him archly. 'Don't I conform to your dream of . . . petal-scented love?'

He realised he was watching the scene at one remove, emasculated by his love and fear for Kate. Yet the one practical way to help her was to shag this woman as if he meant it. He began to act the part, hoping his body would respond. He fondled her still firm breasts and flanks with simulated boozy delight, swayed with her onto the divan. She was now out of it enough, thank God, not to sense how he felt. She insisted on helping him strip and he realised with relief that the intrigue of his younger body distracted her. She made him lie on his back, straddled him and caressed him. 'Am I the perfect English Rose?'

'No. But you're perfectly positioned. And I've risen.'

She speared herself on him and he took it from there — did a reasonably workmanlike job and she seemed satisfied enough. At least she came.

After it, he held her while she snored.

Gaining Traill's confidence was one thing.

Riding her tiger would be another.

45

SHIPMENT

Within days Blake was installed in her home, one of the few Park Lane mansions not converted to an office or hotel.

They were wafted there in her Rolls-Royce Silver Seraph — a computer-stabilised leather and walnut cocoon with a chauffeur as regal as the car. He recalled Cooper's words about Infandus being his entree to the Establishment. When they reached the building's inner court, uniformed lackeys insinuated his bags within. Behind its iron railing and ornamental balconies the place was a time capsule of *objets d'art*, patchily chosen, ineptly placed.

She conducted him through gloomy ground-floor reception rooms. 'Your assessment?'

'Looks like a props department storeroom.' He examined a wall mask. 'Beswick?'

'One of his finest.'

He upended a geometric vase. 'Fielding Crown Devon. Not worth much.'

'So how would you improve this?'

'Send the less valuable pieces to the manor. Then

you'd have half what you need over there. And room here to display the best of your collection.'

'What a marvellous solution. I agree. Now, we must get you ensconced. Sophie, take him up, dear.'

'Yes, Madam.' Her personal assistant, a woman in a rayon-crepe dress, led him to a creaking lift with a folding metal grille.

The top floor guest suite had a carpet with Berber motifs and furniture featuring lacquered wood, metal and burr veneer. The PA showed him around. Bedroom, study, period bathroom and dressing room. His cases were already in the last. 'Madam says you'll be our guest for some time.' She paused beside a door guarded by an odalisque on a plinth. 'This connects with her suite.' A sly look. 'She has the key.'

After she left, the butler knocked. 'Excuse me, sir. Dinner is served in fifteen minutes and madam requests the pleasure of your company.'

The dining room had murals reminiscent of Renaudot. Its table featured Baccarat candlesticks and Russian porcelain plates by State manufacture, Leningrad. Traill had changed into a bead-embroidered flapper dress with sleeveless side-slits open to the waist. The material clung to the part of her breasts still not exposed — proving that the twenties flat look had been the biggest tease of all.

When the butler and maids left the room, she suggested he propose a toast.

He raised his glass. 'To William Morris. Truth to the machine.'

'Most appropriate. You've no idea how delightful it is to have someone who relates to all this.'

They chatted about the Glasgow Four, Hoffmann, Nevinson, the evolution of the cinema wall sconce and the effect of the 1907 invention of Bakelite. She told him that as well as the Rolls she had a 1928 supercharged Bentley, and a blue 1937 Bugatti in the basement. He mentioned that Bugatti had studied art, which pleased her greatly, and that Rolls and Royce had modelled their radiator on the Parthenon. By the time dessert wine was downed, she was semi-drunk. 'A pleasant meal. But nothing ever tastes the way you wish.'

A knock. Sophie came in and spoke to her in a whisper.

Traill frowned. 'Excuse me a moment.'

She followed her into the adjoining reception room through large double doors. One door remained ajar and he could see her standing there. He heard the butler usher someone in, whom she moved out of sight to greet. A conversation with a man. He couldn't make out the words. She rang for the butler again. The visitor was shown out. The sound of an envelope being opened. The flash of her crossing the door gap.

She returned frowning. 'Sorry about that.'

'Bad news?'

'Yes. But disappointment should be taken as a stimulant.' Sophie came back and whispered to her again.

'Switch it through to the study.' This time, she left by the side door.

Blake replayed the glimpse of her he'd seen as if in stop-frame. She'd carried an envelope and read a single-page letter. Her fingers at the back of the letter had held something that shone — a key. She hadn't brought the key back with her. And why the pause? Was she hiding it?

He went into the adjoining room, registering everything from the grained woods to the naked bronze women petting greyhounds. He superimposed it over the earlier matrix in his mind. Nothing had moved. Except the curtains were now drawn. Against the wall ticked a modernistic grandfather clock. Its pendulum door had a glass inset and a brass ring knob that was now a fraction more to the right.

He opened the door, stopped the pendulum and felt around. She'd placed the letter upright and out of sight against the side of the case. In the envelope was a security key with intricately cut bit and, at the end of its round shaft, a circular handle bearing the word 'Chubb'. He scanned the letter.

Marcie,

You know damned well what Adolphous is capable of. My solicitor will explain the rest. The bank is the Barrack St branch of Westpac in Sydney and the box number is 1666. I intend to get him for that tizzy, brainless, corps de ballet bint. Here's my full signature which you'll have to practice to get in. Get the contents to MI5. If you get this letter, it was nice knowing you. Keep the signature but burn the letter. Old times. You were the best.

Lou Tritter.

He re-examined the key then put things back as he'd found them, restarted the clock, moved the handle to exactly the same angle.

When he returned to the dining room, he gulped wine from his glass to make it seem as if he'd been there all the time. Continuity mattered. Not that he expected her to notice. People didn't notice much.

She came back looking drained.

'Something wrong?'

'Everything.'

'Anything I can do?'

'I don't wish to discuss it here. Dark matters require dark rooms.'

He returned to his suite, undressed, got into bed. He heard her key turn in the connecting door. In the mysterious gloom of streetlamps through curtains, her pale body approached. She reached the bed, swaying slightly. 'Not a good day. I need to forget this lousy world.' She fluttered hands along her breasts and thighs. 'Am I your after-dinner fantasy? Or do you find me too decayed?'

'I like mature, full-bodied wines.'

'Splendid. Age is what you make it. To let one's era . . . dictate one's Eros . . . is . . . error.' She slid into bed. 'Am I again to be sacrificed on the altar of your lust?'

He cradled her breasts, feeling their weight. 'Sex is very important to you, isn't it?'

'Naturally. Or rather, unnaturally.'

He knew he wasn't indulging all her appetites but he'd told her straight sex or nothing. It was bad enough betraying Kate. He could do without her manacles and whips.

She drew his head to her breasts. 'Take heed of this large privilege.' She'd quoted from one of Shakespeare's sonnets, his memory advised. She tossed off scholarship as one might discard a coat. Her hand went around his penis. 'This appears to indicate unconditional positive regard.'

'I thought you were a feminist.'

'No one less feminine than a feminist. Most men treat women like dirt. So why should a woman allow herself to be psychologically colonised?' A grin. 'Don't understand me, do you?'

'I spend my life not understanding women.'

'You're sweet. But I'll cure that.'

'So you're not in favour of the Women's Movement?'

'I hate it when they just lie there.'

After they'd done it, he said as casually as he could, 'So what's the bad news?'

'I have an old friend. Her solicitor delivered a message. Which might just suggest she's dead. Then that ultimate anarchist, Tan, rang to borrow one of my aircraft. Again. Asked so politely. Even offered guarantees. Why are anarchists so bloody responsible?'

'What's he want it for?'

'He never explains. I never complain.'

'Why not?'

'One submits to blackmail because one has much to lose. But some of us have vowed to fight back.' A thoughtful pause. 'He's loading his cargo at Zurich. And I intend to discover what it is and where it's going.'

'How?'

'Simple. It's my airline. My pilots never know when the corporation's owner will appear and install herself in the observer's seat. It builds loyalty, commitment and one discovers what's going on. Now, I could use some support on this junket and, as I don't trust anyone who works for me, I wonder if you'd care to come?'

'Sounds an adventure.'

'But safe enough. Tan won't attack me. I'm too valuable to him. And I know too many influential people. You see, Tan depends on us, too. But, unfortunately, we lack firm information about our benefactor's dirty washing. Of which, be assured, there's plenty.' She fondled his penis again. 'Good heavens. Do tell me your brand of multivitamins.'

When she finally left, he went downstairs again in the dark. The aftersight of his memory steered him through doors and past projections as if he saw them.

Now the mouldy smell of the pitch-black reception room had merged with the aroma of burnt paper. That told him the letter's fate but he checked the clock anyway. He unerringly found the brass ring. It had moved position again.

There was nothing inside the clock. He wondered what she'd done with the key.

Next morning, she announced they'd be flying her executive jet from Heathrow to Zurich and told him to pack enough for several days.

He rang Gwen on his cell phone and, in veiled terms, explained the situation, then called Rita, who said she'd check with Tan and get back.

Her orders, when they came, were specific: 'Go along with whatever she does. Someone will contact you at Zurich.'

A section of Traill's Gulfstream V had a workstation featuring SATCOM link, computer and fax. From an oversized swivel armchair he watched her governing her empire. She'd become the businesswoman. Chic suit. Single strand of pearls.

She looked up from her screen. 'I've contacted a top man at Cargologic. He's called the Zurich hub and told them to investigate the consignment on the quiet — commercial and customs invoices, export declaration, certificate of origin and so on.' She removed her large-framed glasses, the first time he'd seen her wear them. 'I'm one of their key accounts. We generally operate out of Basel where most of the freighters land. But I suspect he'll move *Himmel und Erde*. Our contact's a woman called Sulser.' She frowned at the pile carpet, thinking. 'Suppose I could raise the aircrew from here.' She rechecked the screen, 'Martin Armstrong. John Stevens. Doubt I've met them personally. They'll recognise me, though.'

'What if someone picks up the transmission?' It didn't matter but sounded good.

'Mm.' She removed the glasses, sucked the end of an earpiece. 'A point.'

'First time I've seen you as the business baroness.'

'Don't be too impressed. Airfreight profit's down the toilet. Fees, fuel and personnel costs are killing us.'

He looked at the plush cream-leather interior of her personal aircraft and smiled.

They stepped into freezing rain under monogrammed umbrellas and dashed for the business-jet terminal. When they cleared customs and Swiss immigration, she said, 'Cargo's a three minute walk down the service road. Chop chop.'

The cargo hub was inside the runway triangle, a huge warehouse with a high centre-section. A sign on its corner read *Fracht Ost*.

They reached the land-side delivery ramp awning, and closed their umbrellas. She dodged a forklift as if she'd done it all her life. 'We rarely fly in here. They don't handle many freighters, mostly do belly and bulk cargo. Where's our contact? Ah.'

A smartly dressed young woman walked from between lines of metal-roller conveyors. She carried a two-way, seemed furtive. 'Ms Traill? I'm Valda Sulser. I'm most most honoured to meet you.'

'Please, don't be, dear. I defecate just like you. We're all flawed in this idiot world.'

The woman survived the eccentric language and gave them plastic visitor tags. 'Please clip these on

now. We think is best to call this an inspection tour.'
She pointed to a glassed-in office on a higher level.
'So best, please, you leave your bags up there.' A
passing security guard provoked a language change
in mid sentence. 'We will not talk here *an der
Aufgabenrampe, aber später. Dieser Weg, bitte.*'

They walked beside conveyors, climbed metal
stairs. Their guide handed their overnight bags and
umbrellas to a clerk in the office then led them up
more stairs beside huge goods lifts monitored by
cameras.

She swiped a card beside a door labelled
ZUGANG VERBOTEN! and took them higher into
a maze of narrow aisles and soaring steel racks.
Here, computer-guided vehicles on rails moved and
lofted cargo to the distant roof.

'A cathedral for robots,' Traill drawled.

At least they weren't human, he thought.

The woman communed with her two-way, '*Jetzt
sind wir bei dem Sendungssystem. Ja, gut. Der
Zwischenboden, nicht? Verstanden. So, fünf
Minuten? Ja.*' She looked around to make sure they
were alone, raised her voice above the whine of the
machines. 'So now we talk. The cargo you seek is
being prepared in the outer station. The consignment
is from two sources — Credit Suisse and two
pharmaceutical companies. The paperwork is, how
to say, not regular? The customs clearance is
countersigned by officials of Swiss and American
governments and, in fact, represents an exemption,
no?'

Traill raised an eyebrow. 'What's the cargo?'

'Is classified as metal ingots. However, many
shippers use generic terms such as garments,
instruments, opticals, aluminium foils . . . But at
Cargologic we insist that a description contain the

phrase "not restricted" or we class it as hazardous material. This consignment is unrestricted and not classed as valuable cargo, although it must be.'

'Why?' Traill asked.

'It came in armoured cars from a bank and has security officers guarding it as we pack and load.'

'So it's bullion?'

'Strange if so. Because bullion is handled by our special security area. But, for some reason, not in this case. Is also a large consignment. And, we think, not insured.'

'In a country that spends more on insurance per capita than anywhere in the world?'

The woman shrugged. 'They are in the area now where we load cargo by destination. We believe a US Government official is with them there also. I can take you through if you wish, but please to be careful.'

CIA, he wondered? The Company helped American interests strategically and commercially. So what was the interest here?

They walked down more stairs and entered a cavernous space. Forklifts were lifting pallets and containers onto roller conveyers.

At the far end of the hall at least thirty armed guards stood around a loading station watching warehouse staff handling a pile of low-stacked pallets. On each pallet were two light green metal boxes sealed with what appeared to be embossed aluminium bands. The boxes were being wrapped in clear plastic and banded again with steel strapping.

'What happens to this now?' he asked.

'It will bypass our stacker and go to the airfield ramp. There we tow it to the aircraft an hour before takeoff.' She got back on the two-way, asked a

question of her informant, '*Eine halbe Stunde. Gut.*'
She checked her watch, glanced at them. 'So, given
flight time, they dispatch in an hour.'

Traill touched her finger to her chin, turned to the
woman. 'When it gets to the aircraft, does a
Swissport team load it?'

'Yes.'

'Mm. You've been most helpful and I appreciate
you bending the rules. Now, may we go back and
lurk in your loading dock office?'

'Of course.' The young woman looked relieved.

'And could you get me out to my aircraft just
before the cargo goes?'

'My pleasure, Ms Traill. I'll watch loading
through the security monitors and deliver you to
your freighter on a tractor before we tow the dollies
out.'

'*Wunderbar,*' Traill said.

They returned to the hub office, drank coffee and
cooled their heels.

Traill lazily stretched. 'Do hope you're not bored
silly.'

'No. Interesting to see you in action — and see
this amazing place. Quite a setup.'

'You've no idea. Electronic tags, container X-ray
systems, nitrogen sniffers . . . Air cargo's another
world. Did you know that, without cargo revenue,
no international passenger flight would make
money? In fact, we simple, nocturnal cargo movers
are the stalwarts of commercial aviation.' She
examined her expensive shoes. One had been scuffed
on the metal stairs. 'Do you like me?'

'Yes, I do. You're an extraordinary woman.'

'Who wants to take you to bed. I made love on
main-deck cargo once. Was bruised for a week.'

'Perhaps there's a car on board with soft seats.'

'A printing press, more likely.'

Sulser came back. 'And so. It's time.'

The tractor that took them out was towing a line of loaded trailers. The driver diverted to her aircraft, let them off, then headed further down the apron.

The rain had stopped but it was bitterly cold. They walked through puddles to the windowless twin-engined 767. It had the distinctive T on the tail and TRAILL CARGO in huge letters on the side. Its cargo door was shut. A mobile ladder stood against the closed crew door. She said, 'Tight as a clam and they won't see us if we wave.' She hurried to a tanker that had just filled the plane with fuel. The driver was by a panel near the front wheel, headset plugged in.

She tapped him on the back. '*Ich bin Marcia Traill. Traill Cargo ist mein Flugzeug. Verstehen Sie?*'

The surprised man spouted a stream of words ending with one Blake understood. *Verboten.*

She showed him her passport, business card, something with a letterhead. The man squinted at them, then looked up at Blake, unconvinced, as if expecting a male to make more sense.

Blake tried schoolboy German. '*Ist recht. Es ist Ihr Flugzeug.*'

She let her coat fall open to distract him with her cleavage. '*Ich muss Kapitän Martin Armstrong sprechen.*' Next, a searchlight smile, all part of her progressive attack on the crumple zones in the man's psychology. '*Geben Sie mir das, bitte,*' and she'd plucked the thing off his head. 'Captain Armstrong, please. Traill here. Marcia Traill? I'm downstairs. For God's sake, let me in.'

The blur of a face behind the gold-blue sheen of the cambered window high above. It disappeared and, as they reached the top of the stairs, the crew door was swinging open. A surprised pilot stood there — short, fifty-plus, grey-haired.

'Ms Traill. What a surprise. I saw you ten years ago at . . .' He was English.

'We've met?'

'. . . a company function in Paris.'

'Sorry. Don't remember.'

'Stupid of me. You must meet so many people.' His deliberate way of talking echoed his slow movements. 'So you still fly the backside of the clock with the bats? Amazing. Never thought you'd get around to us.'

'Into each life some rain must fall. This is my assistant, Peter Mair. May we come in?'

He stood back, embarrassed. 'It's your airline.'

'Sometimes I wonder.'

They passed a galley on the right, a toilet straight ahead, turned left into a spacious crew compartment. The flight deck had just two crew seats and several display screens.

Blake said, 'Two-man job? So this is the famous glass cockpit?'

The captain nodded. 'No more steam gauges. Supposed to make things so simple you barely need living help.'

There was a jump seat behind the first two and three seats in a row along the rear bulkhead. On one was a copy of *Aviation Week*.

The thirty-something second officer climbed from under computer-generated flight plans and en-route weather charts. Traill greeted him crisply. 'You'll be Stevens.' She picked a map off the seat. 'NY. LAX. Then?'

'Hawaii. Port Moresby,' the copilot eagerly explained, probably amazed that the illustrious owner had bothered to look up his name. '. . . but we leave this flight when we dock at LAX.'

Moresby, Blake thought. Close to the Timor Sea.

'Manifest, please.' She held out her hand like a schoolteacher demanding an assignment.

The second officer passed it. 'Seems all right. No explosives, corrosives or radioactive materials.' His eyes strayed to her breasts and legs, as she read it.

'No chemical oxygen generators,' the captain said, 'and no livestock. I flew a rhino once. When it butted its stall, you felt the shudder.'

Traill read, 'Bullion ingots. Forty tonnes.'

The captain nodded in his slow way. 'The rest looks unremarkable. Pharmaceuticals. Wristwatches. Cameras. Cheeses.'

'So.' She handed back the file. 'May we join your lonely odyssey as you rake the midnight sky?'

'Delighted to have some company. But rather depends how far you're going. Have you talked to the security people?'

'No.'

'We're technically on charter from JFK. All the cargo's offloaded there except the bullion and pharmaceuticals. And they've already been very particular. For example, this ship's just out of major maintenance and they had four engineers double-check it.'

'Did you watch them?' Blake asked.

'Was done in London. But I doubt they did much damage.'

He saw movement outside the window, a mobile lift ramp approaching. 'Here comes the cavalry.'

'This should be interesting,' she said.

46

FLIGHT

Blake watched the intent, deliberate pilots entering route coordinates into their flight computers, checking and rechecking each entry — waypoints, projected wind speed ... Their intricate plotting charts, a delicate tracery of curving dotted lines and details, reminded him of needlework on hand-embroidered cloth. He admired these careful lonely men whose lives depended on attentiveness. They made his own craft of photography seem almost irresponsible.

Traill lifted her overnight bag and headed for the toilet. 'Tracksuit and sneakers time. Wearing anything else on these flights is stupid.'

He glanced through the manifest, registering items and codes in an instant. The pilots were checking weight, balance figures and fuel load. From the fuselage came the rattle of containers on rollers.

He walked through the door in the bulkhead that protected the cockpit from shifting cargo. The lift ramp was level with the main deck and, through the gaping cargo door, small box-loaded pallets were still coming on. The loaders were dogging them down to a red-latch-studded floor of steel castor bearings and roller track.

Below and beyond the lift truck stood the security escort — a dark crescent of bulky men with automatic weapons held across their bodies. Most faced the aircraft but every third man faced back toward the terminal. Their nonreflective uniforms glistened with the latest shower of rain.

One of the loaders approached him, waterproof jacket streaming. 'Peter Mair? Message from Rita.' He was a bony-headed type with stubble and stained teeth. 'You and Traill are to leave this aircraft, either in New York or LA.'

'Not so easy. If I push her, I could lose her confidence.'

'Could lose more than that.'

The man moved back to his work just as Traill came through the bulkhead. She looked stylish even in the tracksuit. 'How much more?'

'Almost through.'

'There's a delegation on the crew-door steps now. Care to join me?'

He followed her forward.

The captain was talking to two sodden men who, except for their German accents, could have doubled for FBI. They stood at the top of the mobile steps in now-pelting rain. They were either careful not to enter or Armstrong hadn't asked them on board. The older man glanced at them, rain dripping off his chin. 'We know you had passengers on board. For security reasons, we require them to leave this aircraft now.'

Traill arched her manicured brows. 'Then your consignment stays on the ground. This plane doesn't fly if I'm not on board. Right, Captain?'

'If you say so, Ms Traill.'

The German's expression would have turned sugar to salt. He produced a cell phone, spoke into it fast, glared at his colleague, swore. Both retreated down the steps.

Traill looked at Blake serenely. 'I think we warped their vestigial psychologies, wouldn't you say?'

'They appear to be in full denial.'

'So. Let's get on with getting off.'

They were cleared onto the main runway.

'Flaps five,' Armstrong called.

The first officer confirmed it, acknowledged clearance from the tower.

Armstrong advanced the throttles. The cockpit remained quiet as they began to gather speed. But, somewhere far behind them, the two big General Electric fans were screaming.

'Eighty knots. Vee one.'

'Rotate.' The captain pulled on the yoke and the freighter lifted off the deck.

'Positive rate of climb. Gear up.'

Blake heard and felt it retracting.

'Flaps one.'

The tower called the departure.

Soon they were high above the weather. A vista of sunlit cumulus. The computer was now flying them, maintaining programmed course and altitude. Traill unstrapped from her seat, said, 'Peter and I might go for a stroll, then try for some rest.'

Armstrong called back. 'Sorry. No relief crew bunks on this ship.'

They unbuckled and went aft. The hold was now lit by dim safety lights. He was surprised to find it airconditioned, then remembered that freighters often carried livestock. They strolled the narrow outboard aisles at the edge of the cargo until they came to the squat boxes of bullion, like a valley in the load.

'We need to open one of those,' she said.

'What with?'

They scoured the eerie, windowless hull for something to use. Strange shapes shrink-wrapped in heavy plastic, netted and tagged with coded routing labels. They went down to the lower deck. It was jammed with shaped aluminium containers and pallets.

She shrugged. 'Nothing remotely useful.'

They reached the bulk cargo hold at the rear of the lower deck. He lifted a long cardboard box bound with packing tape. 'Samples of gardening tools.'

'How do you know?'

'Was on the manifest.'

'And you remembered that? Then remembered the right label? Then spotted it in all this?'

'Sure.' He opened his small pocket knife and slit the heavy cardboard.

The tools were up-market implements, precision made, with yellow handles. A tree-saw with extension, a long handled pruner, shears, fork, trowel, and a three-pronged scraper. He took the pruner and saw extension. 'Let's do it.'

The pruner was sharp and the extension strong. But it still took half an hour to jimmy the box. When the mangled top of the metal case yielded, they saw tightly packed brown cloth bags, each with a yellow drawstring. He lifted one out, released the drawstring, glanced at her, then slid the heavy ingot from the bag.

There were three numbers stamped into the face and a centre hammer and sickle emblem above the words MADE IN THE USSR. The number at the lower left read '99.97%'.

She frowned at the metal which looked like brushed stainless steel. 'What is it?'

He pointed to the letters 'Pt'. 'Platinum. Forty tonnes of platinum.'

She took the bar from him, curious. 'I wonder what this consignment's worth.'

'We're sitting on half a year's output of the world's most precious metal. It's generally twice the price of gold. I'd say on current prices, you're looking at roughly 800 dollars an ounce. So 40 tonnes brings that to almost a billion dollars.'

'How come you know all that? And work the figures out so quickly?'

'Used to be a quiz champion.' It was the best lie he could think of.

She weighed the ingot in her hand. 'Tan, Prince of Darkness and Duplicity. I wonder who he's paying off.'

'He won't let you find out. And he knows you're on board, so this is as far as you'll get. This plane's on exclusive charter to him from JFK. So we'll get off in New York if we're smart.'

'No.' She handed back the ingot. 'That would be giving up. Even if I start to stink and my skin cracks for lack of moisture, I'm staying with this consignment until it's taken off.'

'Not a good move.'

'I'm doing it anyway.' She strolled back along the main deck cargo. 'All this excitement's made me feel deeply receptive.' She climbed the irregular front of a plastic and net-wrapped load. The plastic — opaque to guard against theft — was cushioned by half-soft cardboard boxes.

She threw her shoes down at him. 'Come on.'

Afterward, she said, 'It's years since I was crazy enough to let someone screw my arse off on cargo.'

She wanted him again on the trip across the Atlantic. She talked a lot, slept little and even acted as stewardess — setting out food trays and clearing away. Despite his concerns about the journey's outcome, he found the loaded freighter far more commodious than Braden's artillery-stuffed museum.

He watched from the jump-seat as they neared JFK. Traill lay asleep across the three seats at the rear. The air-traffic became dense and contrails streaked the sky. Controllers harangued inbound aircraft constantly, sequencing them into an orderly line that would end on runway zero-four.

'Traill freighter zero zero seven, increase speed to three two zero please.'

The instructions continued until Armstrong set the vertical speed control to descent at 2600 feet per minute. At 10,000 feet, the pilots did the pre-landing checklist.

As they followed the glideslope in, he woke Traill and told her to buckle up.

At 1100 feet he could see through a broken cloud base to a grey-white expanse of ocean. They broke free from the last fleecy puffs and headed for a long black strip of tarmac.

Stevens called out the altitude. 'Five hundred.'

'Minimums.'

'One hundred.'

'Fifty, forty, thirty, ten . . .'

The wheels touched — the enormous weight pressing on the struts as lightly as a car coming off a speed ramp. He looked at Armstrong with admiration, glanced back at Traill who nodded approval.

'Speed brakes. Yellow. Green. Eighty knots.'

The controller's voice cut in with taxiing instructions. The soaring silver miracle had become a truck once more.

They were again surrounded with security officers. Three of them came on board to watch the cargo unloaded. They immediately spotted the breached box and checked the contents. Two stayed while the third went. Blake watched uneasily. Traill remained up front, thumbing through an issue of *Vogue*.

One of the men approached him. 'Mair?'

He nodded.

'Rita asked me to talk to you.' He pointed to the damaged box. 'Your handiwork?'

'Traill made me open it. And she won't get off while that lot's on board.'

The man moved off and talked to his companion. Soon the third man rejoined them. They talked together, glancing at him. The man who'd spoken approached him again. 'New instructions. You both stay on the aircraft. That includes the stops at LAX and Hawaii.'

'Well, seeing there's no transit lounge for cargo flights, we could use a shower.'

'You'll get that soon enough.'

'Where?'

The man just stared at him.

'So where do we get off?'

'You don't.'

47

CLEANUP

The conference dragged on — a management meeting in the Braden Aerospace Corporation boardroom. Stick tried to concentrate. He and Buick were short on sleep.

The long room had a full-length suspended glass wall overlooking acres of factory roofs. He was watching the meeting from the security booth behind the wall near the window. The bolthole, concealed by a one-way glass wall-mirror that opened as a door, was used by the close-protection team and their latest innovation — Braden's double.

The double resembled the boss and dressed like him. But beneath his expensive suit was a Kevlar vest with front and back ceramic inserts, holsters for an Uzi SMG and a Browning 9-millimetre HP pistol. Although he wasn't as thickset as Braden the body armour added stoutness.

Buick spotted trouble first. He jerked a salami-sized finger at a monitor. 'Get this. Waddya say?'

The view from an external wall camera showed two window cleaners in a cradle. It was being lowered from a remote-controlled dolly that moved on rooftop tracks. It was now inching along the wall toward the boardroom windows.

'I say we stop it.'

Buick buzzed admin and told them to cancel window cleaning on that wall. Admin replied that the cleaners hadn't checked in.

That was it.

He yelled, 'Live one. Changeover,' and punched a button that sent an alerting tone to the earphones of all other team members in the building.

In a moment, burp guns at the ready, they'd both charged into the room. Buick assumed a combat crouch between Braden and the window. Stick ordered the executives to freeze, then hustled Braden into the booth where they could watch developments unseen.

As the double reached Braden's chair, the stairwell and lift detail rushed in. Buick waved the four men to the shadowed far-side wall. He briefed them, then covered the booth, his specific job. Their contact-front-or-rear drills were well rehearsed.

Stick stood beside Braden, watching the cradle approach on the monitor. He knew glass glare would confuse the attackers for a single precious moment. And knew Buick couldn't watch the window. That left him to give the order.

'What the hell's going on?' Braden growled.

'Window cleaners. But they haven't checked in.'

'You're going to grease my cleaners?'

'If they're on government business, I am.' He turned back to watch the room. 'Here they come.'

The cradle, moving quite fast now, was half across the boardroom window. A man on it dropped to his knees and stuck a black circular object on the glass. It wasn't heavy enough for a limpet bomb, which would have meant a suicide mission. There was no rope attached to it, so it wasn't some steadying device. It was connected by electrical cables to an object half-hidden by the cradle base-board.

His pulse increased from its usual fifty to perhaps fifty-five. He yelled, 'Engage,' into his throat mike. By their code, the word 'fire' meant selective fire. But 'engage' meant 'smack everything in sight'.

The glass wall shattered in a cascade of falling shards as three M4A1s and an M1014 opened up from the inner wall.

The double twisted in his chair, Uzi out, firing.

The moving cradle jammed.

The object fell with the glass and dangled beneath it, useless.

The two men on the cradle died in a mess of broken glass and blood. One slumped over the rail, head and body pulped. The other dangled by one foot like a butchered pig.

Their team, hot to trot, still covered the shattered wall. If a bird had flown past, they would have changed it to atomised soup.

Buick came back into the booth. 'Sweet as pie, man.' Behind him, the corporation supremos were under the table or in shock. The mammoth strolled back to them, talked them down. 'Thanks folks. You did great. Just a drill. Show's over. No big deal.'

Considering the dangling carnage outside, he didn't win a gong for subtlety but by then the department heads were dazed enough to believe in the tooth fairy.

Stick turned to his favourite tycoon. 'You okay?'

Braden sagged against the control panel. He looked grey. 'And w-what was *that*?'

'You're the expert. You tell me. A high-powered acoustic beam weapon that puts out energy waves? A microwave that fries your guts? A sound generator that purees your lungs? Some Los Alamos nifty — something they could easily deny. Except they left the evidence. And I bet your nerds in Research can work out exactly what it is. You wanted physical proof? Well, this time . . .'

Braden pumped his hand. 'My God . . .' He raised a victorious fist. 'We got 'em by the balls!'

48

TRITTER

Adolphous Tritter sat in the bare bright room stroking his long blond beard. The walls, painted in slapdash candy shades, looked quaint.

He didn't like quaint.

He rose and walked to the window. The outlook was dismal — a narrow view of Darwin Harbour. He ignored it and thought about the consignment. The plane with the second load of bullion carried urgently needed drugs. Some things had to be flown in. Ships were easy to pilfer and slow.

The surgery door was still closed. Cassie had been in there an hour. He'd vetoed her third trip to Melbourne and flown her surgeon up. He'd also ordered Tan to leave his cesspool in Kent and appear in this tacky room at three. No point in spending time on the surface unless several objectives were achieved.

But Tan was late — and would pay. Time was not only money. It was life.

The door opened. Marcus Yul, President of the Australian Orthopaedic Foot and Ankle Society and the Performing Arts Medicine Society, beckoned him into the borrowed surgery.

Tritter glanced at the specialist's sobbing patient who cradled her distorted, callused toes. He took the spare chair. 'Well?'

'I'm afraid damage has been done,' the nervous doctor said. 'Apart from the lost nails, corns and so on, she has severe hallux rigidus, an arthritic condition around the base of the big toe that restricts dorsiflexion on *demi-pointe*. She also has chondromalacia on one of the sesamoids and the nuclear bone scan shows . . .'

'Spare me the jargon. What's the verdict?'

'No operation will solve her problem. Stress fractures of both second metatarsals and one tibia. Loose bodies at the front of the ankle joint . . . She started *pointe* work far too early and she's wrecked her feet. They now need complete rest with time on crutches. Her career's over. She should never dance again.'

She turned her tear-streaked face to him. 'Dolfie?'

He gave her his neutral look. He believed in the neutral look. In indifference to all that occurred. To this intimidated doctor he'd dragged from his expensive rooms in Melbourne. To the woman-commodity sitting on her only real talent. Although thirty and a mediocre dancer, she still yearned to shine in the period pieces she witlessly considered the essence of ballet.

Tears wet her leotards. 'Dolfie? What will I dooooo . . . ?'

'You'll do what you're told.'

'Taglione has a lot to answer for,' the surgeon sighed.

'Who?'

'She was the first classical dancer to stand on her toes. Couldn't you persuade your partner to find another interest?'

'Eagles don't catch flies.'

When they left the room a smiling, sweating Tan was waiting.

'You're late.'

'Desperately sorry,' Tan said. 'The flight was delayed. And I'm afraid I'm not myself today.'

'Must be a relief.'

'Please, please forgive . . .'

'Restrict your requests to the possible.' He ordered one of the bodyguards outside the door to escort his crippled bedmate to the car. He hustled the jittery doctor out, waved Tan into the surgery, joined him, slammed the door. 'Schumann's nagging me about Fong.'

'Senam will make sure he cooperates. Now she knows we have her children, she'll do anything we say.'

He glared at the frantically smiling man. 'The shipment . . . ?'

'Arrives in three hours.'

'The body's on board?'

'As requested.'

'No one saw it?'

'No one who'll survive.'

'Meaning what? And this better be good.'

Tan squirmed. 'A development that got out of hand. Marcia Traill's on board. But she's being monitored by one of our people. Of course, it makes no difference. They'll all die.'

49

MAYDAY

Blake was in the aircraft's toilet, trying to freshen up. Although a contortionist could have done better, he was now too exhausted to care. He braced against the unsteady wall and rubbed his gritty eyes. They'd been prevented from leaving the freighter at LA, Honolulu and Moresby. After so much time in the windowless tube of dried air he felt like a corpse with a pulse.

He left the booth and glanced past the flight crew — their fourth — at the view ahead. The setting sun they were following shed splendour on the upper clouds. Through gaps in a lower bleaker layer he saw the darkening washboard sea. From this height it looked ominous, inert — proving that distance lent tranquillity, not enchantment.

Traill had been asleep across the spare seats. Now just her handbag was there. She'd been confident most of the flight and animated about her business — had talked about the big twin jet's extended-range capability with lowered payload and how long hauls required a fuel/cargo weight trade-off. She'd expounded on cost-plus-profit, APEC and WTO.

But, as she became more jet-lagged, her commentary had dwindled with her confidence.

The Moresby stop had been a shock. Nothing had been offloaded. As they'd refuelled, they'd discovered that the new pilots were flying them on to Singapore.

She'd accepted the news darkly. 'It makes no sense. We've already come halfway around the world.'

Blake, touching the load to steady himself, walked aft to find her. The main deck looked cavernous with most of the freight gone. Only the bullion boxes and a few stacks of netted goods remained.

She was crouched near the rear of the dimly lit cylinder where they'd found the pharmaceuticals. From the palleted load she'd removed more of the small cartons — each holding peculiar vials made of toughened finger-thick glass, numerically labelled and packed in shaped styrofoam. Now she'd hacked at a long cardboard box at the base of the stack, still determined to unearth Tan's scheme. She called to him, 'Something wrong here. Look.'

He smelt it before he reached her.

She gagged. 'Oh God. You'd better do the rest.'

He forced down the outside to expose ripped plastic wrap. Inside the plastic was a chicken-wire cage.

'What can you see?'

'I need a torch.'

'I've got a penlight in my bag. I'll get it.'

He followed her further up the drumming deck to get away from the stench.

When she returned with the torch, he held his breath and shone the beam into the gap.

An eye stared back, embellished with false eyelash and mascara. It was dissolving from the iris and surrounded by mottled flesh. The body had been frozen and had thawed. He grimaced. 'A woman. Anyone you know?'

She took the torch and knelt to peek, averted her head in disgust. 'God, it's Lou.' She retreated from the smell. 'Louisa Tritter. God.'

'So, you know her. Does that mean Tan killed her?'

'It means more than that. It means Tan's working for Tritter.' She slumped on a bullion box.

He faked ignorance. 'Tritter? Who's Tritter?'

'An oil tycoon I met through my father years ago. You've heard of the seven sisters? The seven major oil companies? He's supposed to control three of them. Big oil runs just about everything and he's a man with enormous power. Louisa was a design engineer on one of his projects. Even after she married him, she never learned much about him.'

'Too much by the smell of her.'

'I'm sorry to involve you in this.' She was trembling. 'Tritter. My God! No wonder I'm feeling labile.'

He'd never heard the word but felt sure he felt the same. 'So, what now?'

'Think, Marcia! Think!' She stood up and leaned against the fuselage wall. 'We know Tritter, or Tan, will have more people waiting for us at Singapore. So I'll tell the captain what we've found and ask him to divert to another destination. Should spike their guns. What say you?'

'Worth a shot.'

He followed her back to the cockpit and its view of the outer world. A vista of fan-thin clouds. A lower sun. They should be somewhere north of Timor, he thought and scanned the flight displays, registering their readouts at a glance. They seemed to be too far south.

The pilots were concerned, were resetting dials, dragging out checklists. Traill was too upset to notice. She shoved the torch back in her handbag, gripped the back of the jump seat and announced, 'Gentlemen, we have a problem. There's a body back there that's not on the manifest.'

'Be more here,' the captain said, 'if we don't fix this.'

'Fix what?'

'Autopilot's gone bonkers. We've disengaged it but it's still flying us.'

Blake smelt it first — an acrid polymer stink.

Then saw it.

Suds — exuding from the edge of the cockpit floor.

In seconds, they'd filled the flight deck to the height of the pilots' chests. Before the dumbfounded crew could release their belts, their heads vanished under foam.

He and Traill were standing — all that saved them. He hauled her back through the bulkhead, shoving her through the door so hard that she went sprawling.

The cockpit had filled with a wave of foam as high as the overhead instrument panel. As it rolled toward them, he slammed the bulkhead door.

She sat up, half-covered in the stuff, tried to brush it off. 'What is it?'

He looked at the foam boots on his legs. 'An aqueous barrier-foam. Some kind of soft-kill special.'

'The pilots?'

'Suffocated by now. It could be poisonous to inhale. I've read up on nonlethals. This looks like one but it isn't.' He grabbed for webbing as the aircraft suddenly banked. 'Feel that? You're getting your diversion.'

The bank flattened, the nose dipped and the engine tone changed. They'd throttled back, were slowly descending, heading into turbulence.

She looked amazed. 'How could . . . If they're dead . . .'

'I reckon Tan's engineers did more than check for fatigue cracks. They've knocked off the pilots for a reason. We're now an RPV.'

'A what?'

'A remotely piloted vehicle. They've rigged things so they can control the plane. Standard technology. That's why the pilots couldn't . . .'

'Controlling us? From where?'

'Anywhere. Could be a ship.' Or Tritter's oil rig, he thought.

'Can they land us?'

He remembered the comment of the man at JFK. 'They won't bother. They'll ditch us.'

'With this bullion on board? That's insane. Besides, if they did, we'll die. They wouldn't *dare* do that to me.'

'They did it to your smelly mate.'

She went pale. 'God! What can we do?'

There was no point pretending. 'Nothing. Follow me.'

It took a while to get to the tail because the aircraft was lurching badly. He checked the load of cartons at the end of the cargo hold. 'We'll be safest back here, facing back. We need to brace ourselves against the boxes and hang on to the webbing.' He showed her how to do it. 'You stay here.'

'Where are you going?'

'To try and get into the cockpit.'

'Why?'

'That ooze could be dissolving by now. I'll try and get some life jackets.'

'Well, for God's sake don't be long. And get my handbag. It's on the seat.'

Women were aliens, he thought. She'd die, but wanted her handbag. He heard the whine of servos. The flaps were extending so they had to be low.

He worked forward again to the bulkhead door and opened it slightly. Foam oozed around his legs but the stuff had stopped expanding.

He held his breath, shut his eyes and pressed into the stinging, crackling mess, mentally seeing the cockpit, aware of the number of steps, the exact spacings. He extended his hand and unerringly touched the edge of the first spare seat. From somewhere in the grey mass he heard the strident recorded voice of the ground proximity warning system. 'CAUTION. TERRAIN. CAUTION. TERRAIN.'

He felt below the seats. Surprisingly the jackets were there. Her bag was to the left of seat two. Where she'd left it.

As he cleared the flight deck, the warning changed: 'TERRAIN! TERRAIN! PULL UP!'

He stumbled back to the rear of the load, still blinded but able to breathe, viewing the hold from previous images.

He felt her hands reach out to him.

He found his handkerchief, cleared the last of the stuff from his eyes and gave her one of the jackets. 'Get this on. We're going in.' But she put the strap of her handbag over her shoulder first.

He secured his life jacket, expertly replaying the demonstrations he tried to ignore on commercial flights, and efficiently helped her with her tapes.

The deck changed its incline to nose-up. The engine pitch didn't change on the flare. The big fans were barely ticking over.

He said, 'This is it. Hang on.'

'Oh God,' she sobbed. 'Oh God.'

When they hit the first crest it sounded like landing on gravel. Fittings crashed from the overhead and the airframe shuddered as if coming apart.

As they smashed into successive waves, he heard thunder and knew what it was. Bullion boxes breaking free and hitting the forward bulkhead like an avalanche. The lighter rear load had less inertia and stayed secure. But their bodies were so jammed into it by deceleration they could barely breathe.

Blackness.

Metal screeching like a truck hit by a train.

The taste of death in his mouth.

Light and salty wetness flooding in.

Water up to his thighs.

The great cylinder wallowed.

He craned around the edge of the stack and saw what looked like a grotto — a crescent of light above slopping sea. The freighter had broken its back.

He grabbed for her. 'Come on.'

They tried to haul themselves along by the side webbing. Against the influx of water it was hopeless.

The arch grew smaller.

They were sinking — going down.

He yelled, 'Hold your breath.'

He didn't know what happened then. The invading sea's backwash must have flushed them toward the rent.

He coughed saltwater, blinking into glare.

He saw the aircraft briefly, a broken tube settling by the nose. The proud tail, high against the cloud, had already begun to tilt.

He pulled the cord on the jacket. It didn't inflate. Whenever his head surfaced he blew into the mouthpiece until the bladder filled.

Now the wreckage was hidden by the swell.

Traill gone.

Aircraft gone.

Just mountains of moving sea.

But he was buoyant enough to rise on the steep approaching waves.

As he felt down to take off his shoes, he saw half-submerged cardboard crates, loose inside their webbing, slide into the next trough. Traill clung to the net, long hair like seaweed across her face, life jacket slack.

He yelled, blew the whistle on his jacket, but the flotsam vanished over the crest. He struck out after her but the size of the swell made it useless.

The chopper must have observed the crash. He didn't hear it until it was almost overhead — a smooth-bellied red and white Sikorsky S–76 with rescue hoist. Before blinding spindrift blew off the crest he saw two bodies dangling from a sling — a crewman in a yellow survival suit and Traill.

The rotor-slap and turbine whine faded. The machine was hidden by the swell.

Had they seen him?

Did they want him?

He heard it approaching again.

Thank Christ.

It hovered above him, flattening the sea to spume.

He stared blearily into the gale at the harness coming down. No crewman this time. Just a man above, working the winch.

It took them several attempts before the sling was close enough to grab. It took him more time to get inside the thick canvas belt and cross his arms in the recommended fashion. Trailing wire jerked from the sea, jolted him as it took up.

He was plucked from the flattened circle of water, blade-wash turning his wet clothes to an ice pack. On the wasteland of waves, he saw the tail of the aircraft again as it slid forward into the sea, airfoils angled into a V.

He stubbed his toes on the sill of the chopper as he was hauled inside. Traill was between the parallel rows of seats, face down, coughing up brine.

He clung to a seat as they slid the door forward. Three crewmen in the back. Impassive, young.

They gave him a blanket.

'Who are you?' he croaked.

No reply. Were they working for Tan?

They'd been told to get off the freighter, he remembered. And when that tanked Tan was happy to kill them. But as they'd survived, they'd been fished out. Why?

He didn't care. He was alive.

He huddled shivering inside the blanket, more from shock than cold. The low sun, partly masked by storm clouds, painted a silver path across the swell. They flew barely above safe-operating height for just minutes before the rig appeared.

It was a factory city — perched high above the sea on four huge legs. A multi-platformed oblong of gantries, air ducts, extraneous metal, cocooned in a web of handrails, walkways, dangling hoses and ropes. Near its derrick a slanting tower belched yellow flame. Huge prefabricated steel units were painted red and yellow. Lifeboats hung from davits. Drill sections were stacked in a great well. They were heading for the chopper pad on top of the accommodation block. Lights on the pad, the derrick . . . Lights ringed the thing on every level. And burning gas from the flare boom turned the dark waves red.

He felt the gear doors open as the city above the sea grew bigger. Large words painted on the pad read PACDRILL–1. They touched down.

Two men helped Traill out. He went to follow her but they prevented him. She stumbled on the rope mesh covering the pad. She turned back once, called something to him, eyes despairing. He couldn't catch it. Then they shoved her down a metal stairway.

He kept his eyes moving, trying to take in as much as he could, knowing he could replay everything exactly later. A discarded ballpoint pen rolled out from under his seat, then back again. On the pad outside was something pink mashed into the grating.

A stunted, pitching workboat wallowed close to the rig. The boom of a crane from the rig hung over the vessel, spotlights on its end glaring down. Its load, a large metal sphere, hung above the boat's plunging deck. As the freighter rose on the swell, cable drums spun on the crane. The load settled on curved chocks built into the afterdeck. Men scrambled to uncouple it. And when the boat sank into the next trough, the freed hook hung high in the air. He realised he'd just seen an extraordinary demonstration of skill.

Then the chopper lifted off and headed back over the sea. He looked back at the metal city as it became a cluster of far-off lights.

He yelled, 'Where are you taking me?'

No answer. Just cold stares.

50

SECRETS

They flew Blake to Darwin and drove him to the Holiday Inn. At the desk was a note to say he'd be contacted by phone that afternoon. He spent some time buying clothes in Smith Street Mall and sweltering on the Esplanade, then retreated to the coolness of his room.

He gazed out at the palms and occasional yacht, thinking about Marcia, then Kate. Was Kate on the rig? He fretted to think how near to her he might have been. Useless, of course. There was nothing he could have done at the time. But they were closing in on Tritter. It wasn't over yet.

The phone shrilled.

'Mr Mair?' It was Tan.

'Speaking.'

'Did you have an interesting trip?'

'You were happy to kill me, you bastard. And Traill, too.'

'Yes, I suppose I was. I'm so sorry, but events can be so unexpected. And one can never be quite sure how things will play out. Purely circumstantial, I assure you. Not intentional.'

'Jesus.'

'There can be no sentiment in business, as I'm sure you understand. You see now why we pay well. There are definite risks. Please don't take it personally. So what did you find out about dear Marcia?'

He reported on the trip, the dead woman, and also mentioned the letter and the key. He didn't say he'd examined both and didn't mention the code. Tan listened, then said brightly, 'Very good. We were aware of some of that through separate channels.'

'So. What now? Do I go back to Kent?'

'Er, no. That's rather on hold. I'm afraid Marcia's . . . indisposed. But there could be another way you could help us. What do you know about holiday resorts in this region?'

'Which region . . . ?' He was fishing.

The slightest pause. 'Australia. I have in mind a holiday for a couple very much in love. Probably on an island.'

'Most islands cater for that.'

'But this needs to be a kind of . . . unspoiled place. Secluded.'

He'd only read about most of them but had been to Lord Howe Island some years ago, so mentioned it.

'Lord Howe? I'm not familiar with it. Tell me more.'

'It's about 700 kilometres noreast of Sydney. Small. Beautiful. Mostly national park. Hardly any cars. A limit on tourists. Expensive to get to, so reasonably up-market. Coral reef, rainforests, mountains . . .'

'Perfect,' Tan sounded delighted. 'Just the ticket. Now, as you know this place well, I wonder if you could nursemaid our couple there? Find them accommodation, show them around, take care of them for, say, two weeks?'

'What couple?'

'The man's Chinese. The woman's Korean — and our accomplice, like you. They met at Infandus. We engineered that, of course. Her assignment's to keep the man her slave. Yours will be to make sure the course of, er . . . true love . . . runs on greased wheels.'

'What's the catch?'

'No catch. Well, there may be Chinese nationals keeping an eye on the man. But I doubt it's a particular concern.'

'So who's this man?'

'A scientist called Fong. He's attending a biotechnology conference at the University of New South Wales. They'll have their holiday after that. I'm going down to have a meal with them on Wednesday and I'd like you to join us. You'll have a few days to prepare. Fong's important to us. We need him content, compliant. A delicate operation, you might say, requiring a certain finesse.'

'So I don't have to survive another plane crash?'

A polite laugh. 'Noooo. Just have a pleasant holiday. I'll have a plane ticket and full details sent to your hotel this afternoon. I'm sure you'll be happy to be home. And Mr Mair . . . ?'

'Yes.'

'We're all very pleased with your work. You've handled yourself extremely well. A good job well done. So let me convey my very best wishes and do enjoy the rest of your day.' He hung up.

Blake stared at the bay which looked inviting but sheltered crocs and deadly box jellyfish. It served, he thought, as a fitting analogy for Tan.

The details of DEMI contacts in Australia were filed in his brain, together with the current sixty-page book of area codes. He decided on a single alerting call from a public box. He encoded the message in his head. It consisted of a long series of numbers that would be recorded at the other end. Old technology was often safest. Purely electronic methods were prone to sophisticated detection.

He went out, sent his report, then strolled back to the hotel.

Two weeks on Lord Howe?

If something sounded too good to be true, it was.

51

RIG

Marcia Traill stumbled on the metal walkway, exhausted and near collapse. A roaring flare and a soaring derrick dominated everything. Stinking fuel oil. The racket of generators. The crash of waves far below. She was marched past metal walls and machinery and into an accommodation module.

The racket changed to the hollow sound of people inside a steel can. She was led into a clinic where a medic checked her over, then taken down a rubber-carpeted corridor to a cabin. There were clothes on the bottom bunk — boiler suit, sweater, thick socks, gumboots . . .

She stripped, aware a man with a gun was waiting outside the door. She showered, towelled herself, then took the vault key from her bag. Should she hide it in her vagina? Too predictable. So she put it in her mouth between her cheek and her teeth, knowing she could still talk without them spotting it. She dragged on the clothes, but was too exhausted to fix her hair. The guard stuck his head around the door. 'Get a move on.'

It was dark outside. They took her down more dank stairs past flat-stacked rust-streaked piping. The racket was oppressive. They marched her along a suspended gangway flanked by huge pipes and lit by far-spaced globes to another iron shed. They pushed her in.

The module was soundproofed and resembled a modern apartment. It had elegant furniture, subdued lighting and southeast Asian carvings on the walls. The floor still vibrated but the racket was now just a hum.

Two men lounged in the chairs. Tan, in an unmarked boiler suit that looked designer-made.

And Tritter.

She said, 'Hello Adolphous. Still too mean to eat your own lunch? Your beard's longer. It confirms your exclusive relationship with yourself.'

The cold-fish eyes didn't blink.

'Love the Ugh Boots. A sense of style isn't one of your virtues. In fact, you have no virtues I know of.'

'That tongue of yours was always too sharp.'

She sat down, exhausted. 'So what now? You kill me? Shouldn't be hard after murdering your wife.'

'Curiosity's killed you.'

'You rank bastard.'

He opened the hinged top of a small antique silver cylinder, selected a tiny silver spoon, inserted it in his ear, twirled it, dragged out wax. He wiped the spoon on a handkerchief pulled from his crumpled pants.

She said, 'That's disgusting.'

'You have more to worry about than my manners. You seem to think you're untouchable.'

'Lou gave me the key to her bank box.' She pushed back a strand of hair. 'If anything happens to me, my lawyers will open it and expose everything she had on you.'

'Not true. We pay your lawyers a retainer. They've got nothing. We pay your butler, too. He recorded the conversation with the solicitor. And we know where the box is from Louisa's bank statements. She sent you the key and the box number. Hand them over and you'll die fast. Mess me around and you won't.'

She felt as if the wind had been knocked out of her.

Tan moved forward as if to put a hand on her shoulder, thought better of it. 'Marcia, dear. I wouldn't have wished this for the world.' He turned to Tritter imploringly. 'Marcia's a beautiful person and my friend. Couldn't we come to some arrangement?'

'You were happy enough to kill her an hour ago.'

'Expediency. Circumstances change. And as I look at the dear lady now, I feel mortified. Couldn't we . . . perhaps I could offer you . . .'

Tritter probed beneath his nails with another ivory-handled implement. 'I'm not the Mafia.'

'No,' she spat. 'You lack their ethics.'

He returned the probe to the silver étui. 'Useful or not, she dies. How slowly's up to her.'

Tan almost curtsied. 'I agree. But she's important to Infandus. And as she's survived, I rather think . . .'

'If you can't keep your customers out of my business, that's your problem. She dies.'

'But she's an extremely influential woman. And I'm sure, with sufficient inducement, I can ensure that . . .'

'She dies.'

She got wearily up. 'The key and the number are in my cabin.'

'Go with her,' Tritter ordered.

Tan opened the door and let her out. The men

outside stood back. She leaned over the rail and spat the key into the sea.

Tan yelled for the men to grab her. They dragged her back into the module.

Tan said, 'We should have searched her. I'm afraid the key's in the sea.'

She stood defiant. '*Now* what will you do?'

Tritter laughed. 'All you've done is help me. Now no one can open the box as long as the rental's paid.' He rose, took a machine pistol from a cabinet and held it out to Tan. 'She's useless now. Shoot her.'

Fear swamped her. Time seemed to slow.

'I'm not certain I can do that.' Tan's face worked with dismay. 'I'm fond of her. And I certainly didn't want to harm her. Or for any of this to happen. Isn't there some way we could . . .'

'Do it.'

Tan took the gun gingerly. She realised he was a coward. He could order third-hand executions but was too squeamish to participate himself. But, surely, they wouldn't really kill her? She gasped and backed against the wall.

Tan levelled the barrel at her. She could see the frightening hole in the end.

He grimaced and squeezed the trigger.

Nothing happened. It was like a terrible dream.

No. They were simply trying to scare her. She dashed for the door but it was locked.

Tritter glared at Tan. 'It's not cocked and it's on safe. Are you that dumb?'

Tan plucked at the bolt.

'Give it here.' Tritter took the gun, hauled the bolt back, released it, thumbed a lever on the side. She watched in horror as he handed it back to Tan. 'Get on with it.' He sauntered out of range.

'Dear love, I wouldn't wish this for the world.' Tan aimed at her again. 'I'm so terribly, terribly sorry.' He screwed up his face as if afraid to hear the bang.

She lunged for Tritter. It was all she could think of. Then, if Tan fired, he'd hit them both.

Hideous pain ripped through her belly.

She slid to the floor and writhed.

Tritter held a triangular-pointed blade. It gleamed red.

With her blood!

Her head exploded before she heard the shot.

52

EXPOSURE

Braden had expected to die for weeks. But, after the botched assault on the boardroom and the evidence of the acoustic beam weapon — now dissected for its technology and kept in his corporation's vault — he doubted any government agency would dare attack him again.

DEMI's latest information had been damning — implied Stone was behind the whole business. So he called a meeting at the CIA and instructed all panjandrums to attend.

Again the rigmarole of the double chain-link fences, guards, dogs, pop-up barriers. Through the forest, past the magnolias, over the grey-and-white Georgia marble . . .

He entered the small seventh-floor conference room half an hour late, to tone them up.

Their urgent voices died. He eyeballed each in turn. The nervous Jason — carpeted by Stone, he supposed. The smooth-haired Treloar, meticulous and grim. And Bennett, the Under Secretary, who looked like he'd sniffed shit.

He grabbed a chair. 'So which one of you tried to kill me this time?'

Stone peered over his half-frames, remarked with studied politeness. 'May I ask the purpose of this meeting?'

'It's your final chance to come clean. I'll spell it out one last time. You've fed me soft war, population reduction, the nanobot obscenity, but nothing about option four — your scheme for wrecking the East. Spill your guts or you're gone.'

Stone said. 'You're operating in an empirical vacuum.'

'Plain language.'

'You don't know what you're talking about.'

'You hope.'

A glass jug steamed with coffee but no one offered him some.

Stone looked at Treloar. 'Your question, I think.'

Treloar disengaged a cufflink from the sleeve of his suit. 'We, uh . . .' he cleared his throat, 'have initiatives in place to — selectively target the subcontinent.'

'Details.'

Stone removed his glasses, set them gently on the table. He stared at the ceiling as if epiphany shone there. 'Strange how we suffer from the notion that evil is entirely bad. Sometimes treachery can be compassionate — and selective indignation's kinder than outright condemnation . . .'

'Careful, Stone. I've had it up to here with your malarky.'

Bennett spread his hands, revealing pink palms and gold rings, 'Mr Braden, can't you cut us some slack? Persisting in this way isn't fair to the people present. Everyone in this room is a patriot.'

'I'm questioning methods, not motives.'

Treloar fiddled with his second cufflink. 'This great nation has its faults. Violence. Intolerance. Simple-minded worship of success. But it's still . . . it's *still* . . .'

'. . . the best democracy money can buy. I know that,' Braden said. 'I'm rich. I'm smart. And I don't tolerate crud. The roof's gonna fall on you arseholes.'

Stone replaced his glasses. 'Unless we get top cover from the White House . . .'

'Not your call. You get thirty seconds to come clean.'

Treloar looked at Stone who looked at the ceiling. Treloar examined his fingers and frowned. 'We've contracted a third party to . . . uh . . . develop a new soft weapon. It's still highly experimental.'

'Tritter. You deal with him through Tan.'

Treloar's eyes rolled up. 'You have no hard information.'

'You've just given him 40 tonnes of platinum bars.'

'Tritter has nothing to do with us,' Stone said.

'Bull.'

'If you think you can start a media stampede,' Treloar said, 'forget it. They won't touch it.'

'Jury's out on that one. Meanwhile you have a Presidential directive to give me the full signal here.'

'We have no intention,' Stone said, 'of divulging anything more. There's a point beyond which the most determined inquiry from the administration must never be allowed to go. You're beyond that point.'

He thrust out his jaw. 'And a persistent cuss. I'll crack this — with or without you.'

'Without us.' Stone's languid voice.

'You fucks,' he thundered. 'You're dead. The moment I kick Tritter's arse, you can kiss yours goodbye.' He bounced up, pounded from the room.

As the door closed behind him, he heard a heartening sound.

Someone had smashed a chair against a wall.

53

BRAINWASH

She'd been moved from the fetid cell. This new place was like a hospital room.

The tortures had stopped. The live wires on fingertips, between her legs . . .

She remembered screaming to the man who fed her, a man who smelt of diesel oil and soap. 'Please help me kill myself.'

Each time, the man had laughed.

Now she was strapped on a kind of table. The walls were hospital white. She couldn't focus. The hum of the aircon. Murmurs.

Something attached to her arm. A drip?

Her body was healing. She knew they wanted her alive because they were doing something to her mind. Because it was getting harder to think.

Shock treatment?

Some new drug?

Every so often, she'd become dizzy and feel an excruciating pain in her head.

Then she'd wake up stiff and thirsty.

After each session, she seemed to lose a little of herself.

Then she'd howl her name.
Over and over again.
Kate Retki.
She was Kate Retki.
She had to remember who she was.

54

VAULT

During the flight to Sydney, Blake decided to open Lou Tritter's bank box. First, he recalled the signature on the letter he'd found in Marcia's clock and practised it until he could exactly reproduce it. He knew the staff wouldn't connect the name for such a rarely used box with a woman. He also knew the number of the box. Now he needed the key. He drew precise scale drawings of it that matched the matrix in his mind.

It was years since he'd been in Sydney. He was struck again by its rat-race mentality. The beautiful city was cold, despite its ever-welcoming sun. He avoided Mair's expensive home, although he had the man's credentials. He couldn't pass as Mair in his home suburb. He booked into a North Sydney motel, then took a train to Bondi Junction to ask a favour from an old schoolmate.

John Hankin — Hanky to his friends — was a locksmith. Blake found him at the back of his shop in a display room full of safes. He produced his sketches and persuaded Hankin to try and duplicate the key. As the man worked on the blank he requested adjustment after adjustment, removing it from the jig and turning it in his hand until sure that, from every angle, it exactly matched the original.

Then he caught a train back to Wynyard, in the city's centre, and walked to the bank. The entrance to its basement vault was a blast from the past — imposing stairs with thick brass railings that curved down to a marble anteroom. A clerk pushed a slip of paper toward him under a heavy brass grille. He wrote the number and signature. The man compared the slip with his files. No computer matching. The place seemed frozen in time. Satisfied, the man pressed a button, opening the outer grille.

He walked over thick carpet to the gaping vault door, then over the floor-level inset that bridged its opening well.

The guard inside took the slip, led him to the box, turned his master key in it, then left.

He inserted the dummied-up key and tried to turn it. It stuck. Heart sinking, he jiggled and forced it until it reluctantly scraped around.

He swung the small steel door wide, slid out a long flat metal box and took it to a table with a modesty strip in the centre. Inside the box was a sheaf of intricately detailed plans. He glanced at each, refolded them and slipped them inside his coat.

In the train back to the motel, he composed another coded message in his head. He sent it from an internet cafe at North Sydney and waited for a response. Thirty-six numbers came back which he instantly decoded using the stored pages in his mind.

The reply showed that he'd got their attention. Elina would meet him in Sydney. She was also flying in from Darwin — which made him wonder if she'd been investigating Tritter's rig.

Tan had directed him to present himself that evening at a harbour-front mansion at Darling Point.

The home was an ugly building from the thirties but the site was superb. He spoke into the intercom. The tall spiked gate slid open.

He walked down the paved drive, looking at the lights from across the harbour. Tan stood at the front door, beaming. 'Mr Mair.' He shook hands warmly. 'How delightful to see you again. Do come and meet our loving couple.'

He found the pair of them rather sad.

The beautiful Senam was the most exquisite woman he'd seen. Compared with her ethereal face and slender body, Fong was unprepossessing. He had a small paunch, bags under his eyes, hair thinning at the crown. He was clearly besotted with her and she played up to him but nothing disguised the coldness of her look.

As they talked before what appeared to be a catered dinner, he discovered that Senam was from North Korea and she'd had a difficult time escaping. But Tan adroitly switched the conversation to health topics and world affairs.

They moved to the dining room which made the most of the spectacular view.

While superlative service and food spun a cocoon of delight around the table, Tan presided with wit and perfect manners, the consummate host. 'Mr Fong,' he told Blake, 'is renowned for his work on the human genome.'

'Really?'

Fong rolled his eyes. 'I not that special.' He was holding the woman's hand under the table.

Her attentiveness to Fong was anxious, as if Tan were prodding her with spikes to perform. But her lover was too infatuated to notice he was being gulled.

The conversation shifted to the holiday and Tan asked Blake to describe the island.

'There is coral reef, is it?' Senam asked.

'On both sides.'

'You see fish swim?'

'Beautiful multicoloured fish.'

'I love to see.'

'Sound wonderful,' Fong said. Whatever pleased the woman he agreed with. Then Tan started to talk to him in Chinese and the conversation became strident. One word was repeated several times. It sounded like 'Schumann'.

Senam listened for a few moments, then lost interest and turned to Blake, 'You unstand Cantonese?'

'Not a word.'

'You handsome man.'

'And you're very beautiful.'

The calculating eyes moistened slightly, which surprised him. 'It make worse.'

'Well, at least you escaped from the North.' He wanted to keep her talking so that he appeared oblivious to the foreign conversation, knowing his brain would still faultlessly recall each sound the two men spoke.

She nodded. 'Many see children starve. People make sausage with human flesh, then sell. People sell children as slave.'

'That's terrible.'

'People too poor to feed children. Some pay bribe to go over border — put children to bed, kiss goodnight, then leave. Know never see them again.'

Fong and Tan were arguing.

'And you?' he asked her.

'I get over border with my girls. Live in dugout in mountain. Put girls in illegal nursery where they never allow outside. I work illegal on tobacco farm, sell body for rice, flour, corn. No way am see children. If they find me, find them too and we all killed.'

He knew a lot about the Chinese Government — re-education through labour, summary executions . . . 'Terrible.'

'Even in mainland China, people pay to ship children to Netherland as hope they have better life there. When only can help children by sending away . . . You imagine . . . ?'

He couldn't. 'And where are your children now?'

Tan must have heard the question. He abruptly stopped the unintelligible conversation and smiled suavely at Blake. 'So it's settled. Lord Howe it is.'

'Right. I'll set it up.'

'Excellent. I suggest you go over a day or two ahead so everything's arranged.'

'Fine.'

He decided to parrot the Cantonese conversation into a recorder as best he could, reproducing every word and inflexion, then give Elina the tape. Although he didn't understand a word of it, someone would.

'Mr Mair,' Tan told Fong, 'is one of our most useful employees.' His smile dripped with so much affection he appeared the sweetest man in the world.

Elina flew in next morning. She'd warned him not to meet her flight. She came to his room at the motel.

She looked concerned as he let her in. Concerned yet relieved. She let the handle of her wheeled suitcase go and impulsively hugged him. 'I thought I'd lost you there for a while.'

'Can never tell with plane crashes.'

She shuddered and shut her eyes.

He brought in her luggage and closed the door. 'You look bushed.'

'Bushed?'

'Whacked. Worn out.'

'There's been a lot to set up.' She took the bug-buster from her purse and walked slowly around the walls.

He said, 'I don't think they see me as a worry, but if you want to go somewhere else . . .'

'Clear.' She collapsed into a chair.

'Reckon you could use a drink.'

'And a year's holiday. Thanks.'

He got two plane-style half bottles from the fridge and twisted off the screw-tops. 'Any news of Kate? And don't give me the need-to-know line. I need to know.'

'We've heard nothing. That's the truth.'

'Shit.' He poured the wine and handed her a glass, not hiding his disappointment.

'I'm sorry.' She raised her glass. 'Confusion to our enemies.'

'And freedom for Kate.' He gulped wine. 'So, tell me, are we getting anywhere?'

'I can tell you this much. Two days ago Braden met the Special Group and stuck them with some of your information.'

'Braden's still helping us?'

'He's been tremendous.'

'And what else can you tell me?'

'That's it for now. Because if things go wrong again and they catch you . . .' She didn't need to complete it. 'So fill me in. I want every detail.'

As the wine dulled the edge of his hurt he described the evening with the lovers then produced the mini-recorder. 'It's all here.' It was a meticulous elaboration of the reports he'd sent. He played her the start, ejected the tape and played part of the second tape he'd recorded — his reproduction of the Cantonese conversation. She said she'd take the tapes and analyse them later, then asked him about the plans.

He spread them on the bed.

The first showed a single huge cylindrical tower surrounded at the base by what looked like a circle of small domed mosques. 'This is the caisson. It's 600 feet high. Check the scale.'

She examined the diagram, intently. 'This is wonderful, Colin.'

'Here's the overview of the inner construction.' He unfolded the second sheet. 'Floors and compartments. Kate was right. It's a series of accommodation levels. Nothing to do with oil production.'

'But it's under Tritter's oil rig.'

'Wrong. The rig *looks* like it's on a concrete base but it moves. Not much but a little.'

'How do you know?'

'When we landed on it, something on the floor of the chopper rolled around.'

'That could have been the chopper. And surely oil platforms move — even if they're supported on concrete columns?'

'Might shudder a bit if they're hit with a killer wave. But not in an average sea. And this is a single column design. But the rig's on four supports that look like a metal template platform. So Deep Six is somewhere else.'

She nodded slowly, thinking. 'We checked the GPS coordinates you gave us for the plane crash. We estimate you ditched about four nautical miles southwest of it.'

'That makes sense. It has to be somewhere near it because it's powered by a sea-bed cable from the rig.'

'You know that?'

'No, but it's obvious. Rigs are full of pumps and they get their power from old jet engines. And it'd take a lot of power to run the caisson.'

'Unless it's got a nuclear reactor.'

'It doesn't have. Because that's a major component that would have gone in when it was built. And there's nothing on the plans like that at all.' He sipped wine, thinking it through. 'I've been trying to nut out how ditching Marcia's plane fits in. All that bullion and the pharmaceuticals at the bottom of the sea . . .'

'It's shallow there. Eight hundred feet.'

'You call that shallow? It means the top of the tower's still two hundred feet down. So how do they get out of it? Or get the stuff from the aircraft into it?'

She shook her head.

'You see this?' He pointed to the circle inside the top compartment of the caisson. 'It looks like the metal sphere I saw them putting on the workboat. I think it's the way they transfer people from the rig to the caisson.'

'How would it work?'

He found the detailed sheet he wanted. 'Look. The compartment below the sphere's a winch room. I'd say they attach its cable to a buoy. They float the cable up to the surface, secure it to the sphere, then winch the sphere down into this top compartment which looks like some kind of sealock . . .'

'You mean it's like a sub-sea lift?'

'Right. But in calm seas they wouldn't detach it. They'd just send it to the surface then ferry people between it and the rig with the chopper. These plans are yours, by the way.'

'You've made a copy?'

'No need. They're all in my head.'

She folded them up carefully, slid them into her bag and lifted out two electronic devices. 'I've brought you some goodies. Bugs for listening in on Senam and Fong. And a voice ciphering unit you can use with a phone. It adds key bits, uses TDM encryption, reverse readout, high security. You'll hear a synchronisation tone first. Keep messages short.'

He took it. 'I've used this model. I remember.'

'So they're using Senam to sweeten up Fong?'

'Or compromise him in some way. I've checked with the university. Fong's legit. A famous microbiologist.' He noticed he was scowling. It was becoming a habit. 'Senam seems scared stiff of Tan. I'd say he's got something over her.' He shrugged. 'So many loose ends. And how does Deep Six fit in?'

'Braden's helped us with that side.' She paused as if considering how much to tell him. 'We think it's where they're developing a thing called project four — which is some kind of soft weapon — probably biological — that they plan to use against Asia.'

'They might need Fong to help them develop it.'

She nodded slowly. 'Could be.'

'Must be a real nasty if they keep it at the bottom of the sea. So what do I do now?'

'Do exactly as they say. You're right inside their operation and they trust you. You could hear something that makes all the difference. So get over to the island, keep your ears open, find out what you can. We know a lot now but there are still huge gaps. And the nearer we get to Deep Six, the more dangerous that gets.'

55

ISLAND

The Dash 8 turboprop came in low and circled the island to give the tourists on board their first view of land since Sydney.

From the air, Lord Howe was magnificent with two sheer rocky mountains at the south end, both around 800 metres. The crescent of land, mostly rainforest and wooded slopes, cradled a coral reef.

They turned in for the approach to the short strip belting the narrowest part of the island. As they crossed the breakwater, the pilot got it down fast, hit reverse-thrust almost as they touched.

Blake left the plane, breathed sea-fresh air and gazed at the microclimate mantle of cloud above the soaring peaks.

He longed to be here with Kate, not a coerced woman and her deluded lover. He collected his luggage and found the courtesy bus for his lodge.

The building was on a hill in a grove of ferns and had a garden enlivened by bush orchids. But self-catering units were too basic for the love-struck Fong.

He took a complimentary bike and rode off. The visitors' centre was closed so he bought food at the northern shop and asked about renting a house. The girl gave him phone numbers and addresses of two houses above the palm nursery on the hill.

The first was a mess. The second looked well-kept and had a cabin with loft window. A spider's web low across the path told him he was first to examine it that day. An elderly man wearing a Marks & Spencer-type tweed cap stepped over a low rock wall from next door. 'Can I help you?'

'This for rent?'

'It's booked till the end of the week. Then there's a three-week gap. Cancellation. Then it's booked the rest of the year.'

'That'd be fine, as it happens.'

'Right. Well I'm the owner. Thompson's the name.'

'Mair. Can you show me through?'

'I suppose so. I saw them go out a while ago so I don't think they'd mind if we sneak in.'

The rooms were tastefully furnished. And the French windows of the living room at the rear opened onto a garden sheltered by a thicket of shrubs and stunted trees. The man led him along a track to a clifftop lookout. 'Neds Beach on your left. You can see the sunrise from here.'

He paid the deposit and rode back to the lodge, relieved to have found what he wanted so soon. The tide was ebbing and a line of breakers bathed the reef in foam. The sun had set. The twin mountains were misted silhouettes.

He rang Fong. Senam answered. He told her they could come at the end of the week.

He then sent a coded message to DEMI and got one back. The Cantonese altercation at the dinner was about a scientist called Schumann. Tan wanted Fong to work with the man, but Fong wasn't keen.

He thought about it for a while, then glanced at a copy of the *Bulletin* that he hadn't read on the plane. It contained a picture of Braden and his crew posed in front of his gunship. The headline was FLIGHT OF THE WARRIOR. He read the article, intrigued.

The President's eccentric envoy was flying his superannuated warbird to Canberra. The satirical tone implied that it was a pointless goodwill junket. One Australia could well do without. He ignored the spin.

The article confirmed what he suspected. Braden was involved in the hunt for Deep Six.

56

FREIGHTER

Braden had arrived in Canberra with due fanfare, but now was determinedly incognito. He'd flown to Broome on a commercial jet, then transferred to a Pilatus Islander. As it landed, he noticed the sign on the small terminal building: WELCOME TO DERBY.

So Elina wanted him to fly the Lockheed Legend up here? Well, this strip wasn't long. But long enough. C–130s were STOL and he'd landed on postage stamps. Hit full flaps, smoke the main gear just over the end line, yank the throttles to full reverse, stamp on the brakes so hard you relied on the antiskid to protect the tyres. Tough on old planes and old pilots. After landing on one regional skidmark, his flying suit had needed cleaning.

He swatted flies and sweltered, surprised it was so hot. The taxi waiting at the terminal had air, thank God. It drove him through curious Australian bush, through a town that seemed half-Aboriginal and had streets lined by trees that looked like bottles. Then out along an elevated road with vast mud flats on each side. The long causeway ended at a crescent-shaped steel and concrete jetty. The height of the structure told him the tides here were huge.

There were crates on the wharf being loaded by a crane into a truck. He knew the crates — had selected them to be nondescript. As he left the car, flies covered him again.

The ship was a flat-bottomed coastal trader of about 300 tonnes. It had a stern deckhouse and a single battened-down hatch with a tarpaulin covered by ply sheets. The ply sheets told him she'd brought the stuff in as deck cargo.

Where was she? Then he saw her slim figure near the deckhouse. She didn't recognise him, which delighted him. He had a skinhead haircut and black clothes — rude T-shirt, ripped pants. The effect was completed by granny sunglasses, five-day stubble, fake tattoos and cotton wads in the cheeks. He loved his new persona of dangerous old fart.

He grinned and waved.

'My God, is that you?' She looked incredulous then laughed. 'You made it.'

'Some trip.' He touched a crate. 'No trouble with these?'

'Lots. But we've swung it.'

The way she'd handled things amazed him. 'You wouldn't call this a pretty place.'

'Not here. But it's beautiful out in the sound. Come down.'

Slinging his bag strap over his shoulder, he negotiated the slimy steps, clambered over the bulwark, skirted a ventilator and shook her hand.

She giggled. 'You look amazing.'

'I am amazing! And why waste energy acting your age? So I've done the diplomatic dance in Canberra but we're sticking our necks out here. You know that.'

'Yes. And we've got a lot to catch up on.' She led him through a door below the bridge. Somewhere a generator thumped. They entered a curved-walled cabin at the stern that had two portholes, a bunk, a fold-down desk, a chair and a wash basin. It didn't even have a fan. The tub was an oven. Sweat was running down the back of his neck and his feet were baking in his boots.

'This is the captain's cabin,' she told him. 'He said we could use it for now.' She had a set of the plans she'd sent him ready on the table — Louisa Tritter's working drawings of Deep Six.

He pulled the wads out of his cheeks and stowed them in his pocket. 'Are you sure you can find this thing?'

'We've got a fair chance.'

After they'd swapped their latest information he said, 'So what are we using? Some kind of hydrographic sonar?'

'Better than that. I'll show you.'

He followed her down two flights of ladder-like stairs and through an open bulkhead door into the stifling hold. A single light further forward showed what was under the hatch.

The submersible rested on chocks. It had vertical and side thrusters but was shaped like a mini-sub. The top section was painted orange. It had handrails, a hatch but no connection for an umbilical. Auxiliary equipment filled the space around it.

Fitted into the steel sphere that formed its lower front were three circular windows — thick Plexiglas wedges. A canopy around the sphere sheltered halogen lights, mechanical arms, cameras, sample bins and other devices.

He whistled. 'You organised this?'

'My job is getting things done.'

'Where do you score a submersible in a hurry?'

'Russia. They've built over fifty for the Ministry of Fisheries, the Navy and so on. This one's free-floating and safe down to 3000 feet. But it only makes four knots so you have to know where to launch it.'

'Why not use your sub?'

'It's in Murmansk for repairs. Bits are wearing out. Evaporators, seals, ballast valves . . .'

'So your head office is in dry dock on the other side of the world?'

'Yes. But there are ways around everything. If we can find the caisson with this, we'll save time.' She led him back to the cabin. 'And your gunship's still in Canberra?'

'Yup. My double's seeing the sights under heavy security protection.'

'The flight got lots of media attention.'

'Thank God for the media. They're keeping me alive. But I had to risk this Hell's Angels caper. With bodyguards around, you look obvious.'

'I really appreciate all you've done.'

'Mutual. Besides, I'm having a ball.' He chuckled. 'Haven't felt this free in months.'

'So you're happy with the details on the strip?'

'I could use the one I came in on.'

'It's too obvious.'

'So the other one's 35 kilometres inland?'

'Yes. It's an unmanned RAAF base with a security fence around it. It's been used for domestic flights but they don't do that now. I'll run you out to check it before we sail. I'm sure you can pull strings in Canberra to get clearance.'

'That's under control. Amazing what you can swing when you've got the backing of the White House.' He mopped his brow. 'This bucket could really use a fan.' He went to open a porthole. It was open. 'So we head for where Traill's aircraft went down?'

'That's right. We leave with the tide. It only does 12 knots but we'll be there in twenty hours.'

57

TRYST

The lovers came on the commercial flight. Blake watched the Dash 8 land, heard the racket of its turboprops die, saw the hostess lower the door and the first passengers straggle out.

Even at a distance, Senam was unmistakable — flawless skin, perfect face. Fong, nondescript beside her, looked what he was — another out-of-shape Asian on the downward slope of life's curve, unused to relaxation, uncomfortably festive in bright shirt.

The sun was on the mountains and the far sea misted into sky. But Fong saw only the beauty beside him. And she, compelled to pretend she cared, responded with tight smiles.

If Ko and Hale were right, he thought, about human love being the greatest disaster, then the second greatest was the vanity of assuming it was returned.

He installed them in the house, showed them the cabin where he'd stay. They pecked at a salad he'd made them while Senam studied a tourist map showing the walks.

That afternoon, he led them around the northern cliffs. As he climbed the grassy slope from Neds Beach she kept up easily, barely panting, while Fong struggled behind, hindered by his small paunch and short legs.

How much did the woman know? And how much did he dare ask? 'So where are your kids now?' he said casually.

She glared at him. 'You friend of Tan. You tell me.'

'You don't know?'

No answer.

'You mean Tan's got them?'

She looked away.

When they reached the high cliffs, she looked back at the island's expanse — the wooded valley where the village nestled, the line of breakers outlining the reef and, far off, the twin mountains, shaded now by passing cloud.

He said, 'Beautiful, isn't it?'

She nodded sadly, perhaps wishing her children could see it.

While they waited for Fong to catch up she said, 'I think you know where are my kids?'

'No.'

'I think you know.' She checked that Fong was out of sight, then leaned forward and dragged down the neck of her knitted top. She wore no bra. Her breasts were small but perfect. 'You tell and I nice to you.'

The cold directness of it startled him. 'I honestly don't know where they are.'

'I not believe.'

Fong came around the bend.

She smiled and took his hand.

The climb up Mount Eliza, easy for the slim woman, had her out-of-condition lover gasping.

Fong had trouble with the trip back and reached the house all-in. He flopped in a chair and told Blake not to appear before eleven next morning.

When he did, they were having breakfast at the small garden table. The map was open beneath the coffee cups. Senam told him they wanted to climb Mount Gower.

He doubted Fong would make it. But he seemed ready to do anything to please his love. Except work with Schumann, Blake wondered? Was that the agenda here? He explained it was a seven-hour trip that could only be done with a guide. 'Gower's 875 metres. Partly vertical climbing. Difficulty level ten. You haul yourself up by ropes fixed in the rock.'

Fong just looked resigned and the woman wasn't discouraged at all. She said, 'We not want other tourist. You can guide?'

'Not supposed to. But I can.' He'd done the climb years ago but remembered every step of the way.

They packed a reasonable lunch, got a lift to Salmon Beach and walked to the rock face. By the time they reached the goat-track that wound around the cliff, Fong was showing strain. He clung to the safety lines, his feet sliding on hard volcanic rock.

When they got to the palm valley between the two peaks, Blake called a halt. They opened their day packs and ate their sandwiches by the creek.

She asked him, 'Why we see no one else?'

'Unless the guide has enough masochists he doesn't go.'

Fong already had blisters. Love's dream was becoming painful. Blake gave him Band-Aids and the man plastered his feet while Senam gazed at the stream. She wore shorts and a simple top, every line of her perfect.

Once, she glanced at him boldly. It told him why she'd suggested this trek — to ditch Fong.

The slope rose sharply from the valley and Fong tired fast. They reached the saddle between the steep peaks, the vegetation changed to tight-knit hardy bushes and ferns, then to a misty wonderland of entangled, mossy trees. The rest of the way was almost vertical.

Fong was well behind and limping. They waited. When his head finally appeared above the last rock ledge, she said, 'You too slow.'

'Too much for me,' he panted. 'I stay here.'

Blake remembered the sound the guide had made to coax wheeling petrels from the sky. He repeated the call exactly, wondering if they'd come for him, too. The inquisitive birds landed and flapped around their legs, webbed feet sliding on the muddy slope.

'Why they do?' the beautiful woman asked, amazed. 'Why come when call?'

'They're mad.'

As the creatures, clumsy on land, spread their wings to balance, she touched the feathery sea around her feet.

'It's not far to the summit,' he told Fong. 'Don't you want to see the view?'

'No. I stop here. You two go.'

'Okay, but we could be an hour.'

The gene-jockey shrugged and pulled a plastic jacket and sweater from his pack. Senam said something to him in Chinese and started up the path.

She was ahead on the last stage. Blake watched her dangle off the ropes above. She straddled rocks, making sure he could see up her shorts to the curve of her rump.

As they paused at the foot of a rock face, he said, 'So Tan's using your kids as leverage?'

'You know that, bastard.'

Confirmation.

'Is Fong meeting Schumann here?' It was a guess.

She didn't answer.

They reached the summit wetland of scrub, moss-covered trees and ferns.

She said, 'Is like fairy place.'

'Lookout's ahead.'

'When Tan come?' she asked.

'You mean here?'

She nodded.

Tan was coming here, too?

'He didn't say.'

'I not believe you.' A wary look. She trudged ahead.

They reached the small clearing. The mist had lifted from the peak. The island stretched below, banded by sunlight and shadow. Beyond the jagged silver thread at the edge of the reef stretched endless sea. Petrels floated on the updraught in darting, cawing clouds.

She said, 'Oh, wow.'

'Worth the climb?'

'Worth to get away from *him*!' She stood close to him and put her hands in his pockets, a frigid smile on her upturned face. 'You tell me where my kids are and you get to screw me right now.'

He pulled her hands out. 'It's a long way back and getting cold.'

She pouted. 'You not want me?'

'Let's keep it to business, shall we?'

They sipped some water. When he tried to ask her more questions she ignored him. As they trudged down, he said, 'I really don't know where your kids are.'

She tensed her face as if trying not to cry.

58

SCHUMANN

Tritter waited with the three CIA-funded scientists in module six — an elaborate facility for an oil rig sickbay, but PACDRILL–1 had more functions than pumping crude. He waited for the dysfunctional Schumann to cease his love-affair with the door.

Schumann had returned five times to check the door was shut. He was a remarkably ugly man — shapeless as if padded for a pantomime. His mouth would have looked better on a groper and long hair straggled from the sides of his bald dome.

'You have here,' Tritter told the visitors, 'a psychological cripple. Interesting how brilliance blends with the dysfunctional.'

Schumann shuffled up for the sixth time, thankfully not hopping. He hadn't hopped since the lino had been replaced. They'd got rid of the chequerboard pattern because he was treading on alternate squares. Afraid of bears? Tritter didn't know or care. All he cared about was option four — and persuading Schumann's damaged mind to perfect it.

The microbiologist stopped just short of them, tapped his fingers on his lab coat as if playing the piano accordion. 'So! We begin.'

He led them to the first bed where a comatose-looking Asian man lay strapped down. As he removed the clipboard from the foot of the bed, the drowsy man slurred words in Chinese. Schumann ignored him and told his audience, 'This man's brain contains a neural-compatible interface called GE-MOD6. MOD6 is a peptide-based psychotoxin first synthesised in Russia and re-engineered using molecular design. The recombinant is nanobot controlled and triggered without external commands.'

A dubious expert said, 'You mean a kind of *in vivo* computer?'

'A biological computer,' Schumann said. 'For example, protein A can inhibit the transcription of protein B. So simple digital circuits can actually be compiled into a string of DNA. Through RNA transcription you can build logical gates inside a living cell.'

'So would you call that physical transduction or a biological recognition mechanism?'

'Ah!' He waved a dismissive hand. 'The gears-or-goo argument. Neither. Think of it as computing goo running on blood sugar. Or as engineered biotechnology. Biotech's the future of nanobotics. Is it not true? Is it not utterly, utterly true?'

'So you're working with Korac's project?'

'No. No. *No.*' The human blob pounded his fist on a cabinet. 'Korac's lab is providing nanobot input to *my* project.'

'So you're saying you can program cells within living organisms?'

'Yes,' Schumann blustered. 'By modification of genes.'

'And you've achieved this?'

'Experimentally. Of course failure rate in the field is unacceptable and computational speed very slow. So, as a demonstration, I've preset this patient *ex vivo* to activate in the next few minutes. We pass on.' He touched the wall behind the bedhead and his nervous fingering stopped. Touching flat areas, Tritter knew, relieved the man's compulsions. As he bustled to the man on the next bed, someone asked, 'And transmission?'

'I wondered how long it would take you to come to that.' He surveyed them like a teacher confronted with simpletons. 'Transmission is complicated, obviously, by the need to limit the effect to specific regions. A virus is best. For instance, years ago, we looked at the female anopheles mosquito because it's widespread in south China.'

'And transmits malaria — a parasite, not a virus,' one of the men smiled.

'Which I am well aware of,' Schumann huffed. 'We had hopes for regional limitation but couldn't make it work. So we chose flu.'

Which, Tritter thought, was not before time. The stench from racks of mosquitoes in fetid muslin cages had made the caisson reek.

'Amazing creature, our spiked friend.' Schumann's fingers tapped again. 'Always changes its hemagglutinin to frustrate antibodies. Antigenic drift and shift. Mutability. A microscopic marvel. Is it not true? Is it not utterly, utterly true?'

The visitors now had a subject they could comment on with authority. '. . . supervirulence and the core polymerase gene . . . soon recreate the 1918 virus . . . reverse genetics . . . Hong Kong strain's NS1's point mutation at position 92 . . . unstable . . . antiviral era . . . bacteriophages in Georgia . . .'

Finally someone asked the key question. 'But how can you restrict this to Asia?'

'Ah.' Schumann scuttled to a wall-chart documenting gene types of native populations. 'As you see here, genes for different races show considerable differences in allele — that is, alternative forms of a gene that occur on the same site on a chromosome. Hence, one can target specific areas. Is it not true?'

'But that could infect allied populations,' a visitor said. 'American Asians for instance. I presume you have a vaccine?'

'No. No. *No*. You're not listening. The virus is simply the carrier. The agent, GE-MOD6, is nanocomputer-controlled.'

'But that means it's dangerous to Asians everywhere.'

'So? There are always casualties in social engineering.'

The visitors murmured with concern but Schumann ploughed on. 'And we're developing strains for other races — currently only in injectable form.'

Tritter agreed, for once, with the infuriating man. Great initiatives were always criticised by people with immaterial concerns. But these overeducated dolts didn't see that disaster was prescriptive. That, in fifty years, when the lines of population growth and food production crossed, what they were developing here would be nothing less than . . .

The first bed began to shake.

'Come. Come.' Schumann beckoned them back.

The first patient had gone berserk. He fought his restraints and yelled like a maniac, eyes bulging with homicidal rage.

Schumann waved a hand at the bed. 'The primary trigger's acted. If he got free, he'd kill you. We've set the second trigger to act immediately. Watch.'

The raving man slumped as if switched off.

'Cytocide,' Schumann said. 'Causing death in seconds. A triumph. Is it not true?'

'So what we're looking at,' a scientist said, 'isn't a virus but a controlled release psychotoxin?'

'With stand-alone programming. Of course, vectors are needed and several strains of flu. One has to distribute the active agent evenly through the population.'

'You said the computational speed is very slow.'

'A-ha! But it doesn't have to be fast. The on-board computer is simply a rudimentary timer that calculates not minutes but months. It only has two simple tasks and months to years to perform them. Ideally, it will be triggered when there's a vast movement of populations within the region. So the perfect time would be around Chinese New Year.'

Tritter knew the basics. Flu was the best airborne delivery system for a biological weapon and Schumann had adapted it as a carrier. But incorporating the semi-chemical nanobots that controlled the mutation demanded a brilliant molecular geneticist — privy to the human genome.

Fong.

Schumann, still tapping and talking, glanced nervously at the wall. The conversation rose in pitch again as the others pressed their views.

Why, Tritter wondered, did such men let their disciplines consume them? Instead of seeing the full perspective they became lost in the immediate problem or distracted by their tawdry lives. Ridiculous.

Because, after all the years of effort, all the billions, the project hinged on two such men.

The half-mad Schumann.

And the lovesick Fong.

'So how does this vary,' one of the scientists asked, 'from Korac's robot soldiers? Surely it's just another way of turning people into robots?'

'No. No. *No*,' Schumann barked. 'Different entirely. The Pentagon's project turns people into weapons. But this is a pandemic. It turns weapons — into people.'

'Is there a distinction?'

'Of course.' Schumann played the guitar on his sleeve. 'The military produce a few soldiers who fight and die like supermen. But this makes them obsolete.'

'Why?'

'You're not listening. You're not making the connections. You fail to see the scope.'

'I mean, why not just use a nerve agent or . . .'

'Crude, difficult to disseminate evenly, easy to spot and take measures against.'

The scientists looked puzzled. One said, 'So what's different here?'

Schumann snorted. 'Use your brains! This spreads through the country for years until everyone carries the agent. It's undetectable and harmless. Programmed latency. Then, at a predetermined date — a date we choose — it activates. Then their enemy armies fight each other. Their civilians — men, women and children — kill everyone around them. Everyone in the region dies. You can take measures against infections and poisons. But if someone secretly reprograms your cells . . . ?'

One of the visitors murmured, 'My God!'

'You see it *now*?'

'The ultimate soft war weapon,' Tritter said.

Schumann chortled. 'Is it not true? Is it not utterly, utterly true?'

59

DESCENT

As the freighter cruised toward the archipelago, Elina took Braden up to the bridge. It had cabinetwork like a fifties kitchen. And the tattered clothes of the skipper, Jim Morgan, matched the chipped Formica. He was a pot-bellied, laconic Australian who clearly knew the whole plot. He pointed out the simple navigation tools. 'Autopilot. Does most of the work, though we have to correct for drift. Two radars. One up to 16 kilometres, the other to 60. We use echo sounder, sat-nav. She's a strong old girl.'

The view had become spectacular. The muddy water had changed to brilliant blue and they were passing another rugged island. Braden fingered the brass-bound polished wheel, the one elegant thing on board. 'So how do we locate this nine million tonne shitheap?'

'The Ivans handle that. They've got sector-scanning and side-scan sonar. And they triangulate with transponders.'

Elina perched on the captain's chair. 'We're not sure about using those. We don't want SOSUS picking us up.'

'No matter what whizz-bang stuff they've got,' Morgan said, 'it's still a bugger to locate even big things on the bottom.'

Braden frowned, not liking it. 'But if they're guarding the area, won't they see us?'

'We launch at night,' she said.

'And if the caisson has sonar?'

'If we have trouble finding them they'll have trouble locating us. Even if they're looking. The submersible's smaller than a whale.'

He scratched the back of his neck, unconvinced. 'Whales don't have strobe lights. They could have a visual underwater system — low-light video or . . .'

'Water conducts sound,' Morgan explained, 'but absorbs radio waves and light. You can't see things at a distance.'

'And how do we talk to the ship?'

'New gizmo.' The skipper wiped dust from the compass glass with a rag. 'The Ivans have a high-powered Finnish acoustic intercom. The transmitter increases the voice frequency and the receiver lowers it again. Better than two-stage helium unscramblers and all that crud.'

'Still sounds pretty hypothetical.' He frowned back at Elina.

She shrugged. 'Nothing's certain. We can only try.'

'So who goes down in this thing?'

'You and I. Plus Lonya, the pilot. And you'll need warm clothes because it gets cold down there.'

Morgan added, 'And pump the bilge before you get in.'

It was maritime-speak for 'take a leak'.

As they neared the location Blake had seen on the aircraft GPS, they removed the chocks, tarps, battens, then the steel crosspieces over the hold. They spent the last light of that day steaming in a pattern to drop the transponders. Two of the Russians held each buoy poised on the rail. When Morgan signalled from the bridge, they threw it over the side. As it bobbed on the sea they paid out the long tether and finally heaved over the heavy iron weight.

'We've decided we need them,' Elina told him. 'As far as we know, there's no SOSUS here.'

'What do they do?'

'Hang above the seabed as beacons for the submersible. Later you send them a signal and they jettison the weight, pop to the surface and flash a strobe light so you can recover them.'

He watched a deckhand hood the floodlights above the nigger-heads on the mast. As launching the submersible was dangerous at night, blacking the ship out was impossible. Beacons . . . lights . . .

He didn't like it.

The derrick, fitted with a special lifting cradle, was positioned over the craft. A Zodiac with a two-man crew bobbed in the pool of light near the ship.

It was time to board the tiny sub — no more than a pressure sphere embedded in the front of a frame that lent it buoyancy and motion. Lonya, a gaunt blond Russian, entered the small hatch first. Elina climbed the curved ladder next. He followed, knees creaking.

The thick steel ball was jammed with wiring and shelves of equipment. Lonya sat in the central seat facing the largest viewport, checking overhead panels and the miniature oscilloscope for the forward short-range sonar. His cushioned armrests were fitted at the front with small joysticks. There were padded floorspaces behind subsidiary viewports on each side.

Braden crouched on one pad, knees uncomfortably near his chin, trying not to bump switches and buttons. Elina took the other.

Braden didn't like subs. If something went wrong, you died slowly. At least in an aircraft things happened fast.

The hatch above was closed. The pilot rose and turned the inner wheel to engage stainless-steel locking lugs, reducing noise to the sound of the fan moving air inside the sphere. He spoke in Russian through the intercom then said in accented English, 'Oxygen on, blower on. Hold on plis.'

A lurch. The craft swung as it was lifted out of the hold. He stared through the thick port ringed by hexagonal nuts. As light played across it, he glimpsed the ship's scuppers below. They were lowered into inky blue water.

The sphere rolled uncomfortably as the gaunt Russian plodded through his checklist on the sound-powered phone. Now, millions of microscopic glass spheres, called syntactic foam, in the body of the craft held them level with the chop. They waited for the rubber-suited deckhand in the Zodiac to release the cradle above them, then for the inflatable to tow them clear.

Already the spherical coffin felt damp. Their breath condensing on the hull had begun to bead the hatch. The light in the water outside vanished as they were towed from the ship. A bubbling sound.

Lonya said, 'Venting ballast.' He pointed to a gauge. 'Shallow dive a beeech. No time check all system.'

'How fast do we get there?' he asked.

'One hundred feet per minute.'

So they'd be on the bottom in eight minutes. The depth gauge showed the sink rate but he felt no sensation. The pilot corrected the slight nose-down trim and turned on the data logger as the audiophone crackled with exchanges.

He looked at Elina. She had her arms crossed, was biting her lip. Despite her amazing efficiency, he thought, she wasn't very brave.

The sea bottom was grey silt. The probing arc lights made it look like the surface of another world. A pale fish with long whiskers approached the glare as if it offered recognition.

Lonya peered at his scope. 'Is something big ahead. Could be ocean ridge or seamount.'

Braden glanced at the now shivering Elina. 'Unlikely we'd get lucky that fast.'

'All the same,' she said, 'let's look.'

60

NIGHTMARE

Blake wished he had more to send DEMI but the bugged house was a disappointment. What little the lovebirds said was mostly in Chinese and he expected to hear nothing useful until Tan arrived. He'd started to hate his role as entertainment officer. Each day mucking around here was a day lost looking for Kate.

He bought stale bread and took the pair of them to Neds Beach. In the wash of the shore break, the big fish hungrily threshed for the bread while sea-going ducks bobbed above, stealing what they could. As the troubled woman in her skimpy costume fed them, tourists gawked — the husbands with lust, the wives with envy.

They took the free snorkelling gear from the hut and swam out over the reef. He went to sleep that night, still no wiser about events.

A battering on his cabin door dragged him from a dream. 'Mair. Mair.'

The illuminated bedside alarm clock read 3.21.

He left the light off, slung a towel around his waist and peered through the window by the door.

Fong. Alone, his face ugly with emotion.

He opened the door. 'What's wrong?'

'Senam's gone. They take her.'

'They?'

'We go to bed. I hear something, wake up. She dressed. Say she go to see her children, then run out of house. She get in van.'

'Who was in the van? Did you see?'

'Too dark.'

'Be with you in five.'

Lights blazed in the big rear sunroom and the French doors were open wide. He heard Fong's voice protesting about something and a second voice with a different accent. Germanic with French overtones? Belgian?

Fong was huddled on a settee with two men standing in front of him. Tan — and a rubber-lipped man with bolster-shaped body and wispy hair.

Fong said, 'And if I not?'

'You lose her,' Tan said.

Fong delivered a tirade in Chinese.

Blake walked in from the garden just as two men entered from the hall.

A hard-faced goon with tattooed knuckles.

And Jason!

Blown.

Jason's jaw dropped faster than his hand to his jacket. But the other man's gun was out first.

Blake stared at the automatic pointing at his chest. A pistol was as accurate as its owner and this one was extended by braced arms that held its matt-black barrel rock-steady.

Tan blinked at the artillery. 'It's Mair. He works with us.'

'His name's Blake,' Jason said, 'and he works for DEMI.'

Tan looked dumbstruck. 'That means . . .'

'Watch him,' Jason told the bodyguard. 'Need to check this out.' He trotted down the hall.

Blake stared at the wrong end of the gun, energy draining through his shoes.

Tan glared at him, trying to understand it. 'DEMI?'

Fong snapped at the shapeless man. 'Schumann. Your science disgusting.'

'Science takes no sides,' the strange man said. 'It's above ethics and must be bold. War profits from science. Science profits from war. Is it not true?'

'Anyway, I not do it.'

'Then you'll force us to make you,' Tan said, with an air of regret. 'First you'll watch as she sees us kill her children, then you'll watch as we torture her.'

'NO!'

'Then cooperate. There's a good chap. So much simpler. I know it's difficult but everything in life is a compromise.'

Fong looked despairingly at Blake. 'You part of this?'

'Obviously not.'

Schumann's fingers fluttered on his jacket and he stared at the wall, although there seemed nothing of interest there.

'This is nightmare,' Fong said. 'Nightmare.'

Tan looked sympathetic. 'But unfortunately you're awake.'

Schumann lumbered to the wall and touched it, as if making certain the paint was dry.

Jason came back with plasticuffs. He moved behind Blake, secured his wrists. 'I'm instructed to take you along. This time, it's going to hurt.'

*   *   *

The two bodyguards marched them from the cottage-like terminal to an elderly Cessna Citation and thrust him and Fong aboard. Senam was already inside, wrapped in a scarf and knee-length coat.

Fong glared at her as if betrayed and she cried out her answer to the look. 'For my *children*.'

Jason, Tan, Schumann and the bodyguards bundled in. Jason closed the door. The cabin lights were switched off and the man guarding him became a silhouette. The twin turbofans wound up and they lifted into the night.

As they headed over darkness, he glimpsed the sea breaking at the edge of the lagoon. He thought of the oblivious Elina, of Kate. He thought of what he now faced.

Were they flying to the rig or Deep Six?

Wherever it was, they'd want information.

He'd be tortured.

Then killed.

61

SUBMERSIBLE

Braden could sense the pressure of the sea trying to breach the metal sphere. The air was damp now and getting cold. It was better than the heat and humidity of the freighter, but he was starting to dislike the clammy steel ball.

Outside, the dust-like particles had diminished. The terrain was rising, grey silt becoming grit. The motors in their housings whined and whimpered as if arguing with each other as they drifted with dreamlike slowness over the ocean floor.

The first man-made shape to loom into the lights was a section of broken mast. It was covered in tubular marine-worm encrustations and small barrel-like anemones. Cables trailed from its shackles into the sand.

Further on was a small vessel, partly buried and on its side. As they glided around the coral and mollusc-specked hulk he saw that its hatch was off and the hold empty apart from sand.

He swore softly. 'It's a graveyard.'

Further on they found the shattered tailplane of a fair-sized jet.

Elina said, 'There's no T on the tail — so it's not Traill's.'

'Not a 767. Older type.' He stared at the cargo doors. They hung open like wings. 'If those doors opened as it sunk, they would have been torn off. I'd say they were opened down here.' He pointed to indentations that fanned from the plane across the rippled ocean floor. 'That looks like the tracks of a vehicle.'

She nodded. 'Follow the tracks.'

The pilot turned them slowly until they drifted above the most defined.

A glow ahead.

Braden pointed. 'Jeez! We've got company.'

They killed the lights and stopped active pinging. The view outside became ink except for the milky glow. They closed on it, the pilot watching the depth gauge and sounder.

The contraption was a bottom crawler. It had small, down-pointing rear lights and powerful forward floodlights. Their diffusion showed it well enough — crab-claw-like grabs, wide flat tracks on each side and a concave dish at the front with a thick glass port at its centre.

Lonya swore in Russian.

'Doesn't look like an RCV,' Braden said. 'Looks like it's manned. Will he know we're here?'

The pilot shook his head. 'See curved thing above hull? Forward-facing sonar like ours. Lucky we come from side.'

The vehicle's main lights floodlit an aircraft fuselage. The words TRAILL CARGO extended into gloom. The 767.

Braden said, 'Jeez! That's it.'

Lights were moving in the fuselage itself. The thing attached to them emerged — a remote-controlled tracked robot. It had TV cameras and manipulator arms fitted with purpose-made flat-grab claws.

The claws lowered a metal case to the sill of the cargo bay, released it. Then the RCV backed, stopped and its lights died as if the machine had been switched off.

The tractor approached and lifted the case down to a railed dolly. It was close beneath the door, a trailer with towing yoke at one end and sledge runners. There were five cases on its tray.

Elina said, 'They must be the cases with the platinum bars.'

The tractor loaded the sixth, churned sand and repositioned ahead of the yoke.

She said, 'It's like an airport under the sea.'

He watched, fascinated. 'Looks like the guy in the tractor's controlling the RCV. Slow job.'

The tractor backed carefully, using cameras and lights low-mounted on its rear. A moveable grab extended from between its tracks and mated with the dolly's yoke. The tracks churned, taking up slack. Rising silt obscured the view.

Thrusters idling, they followed the retreating lights. The sledge was heavily loaded and the drag of its runners substantial. The sand-grinding tractor made their own slow craft seem fast.

She glanced up from her port. 'He's got to be taking it to the caisson.'

He nodded. 'Must be the only way they can get bulk goods into the thing.'

The loitering pursuit continued in darkness and cold. Nothing to do but follow. And wait.

She produced a vacuum flask, poured steaming hot chocolate into mugs. He sipped, cradling his mug, winked at her. 'You okay?'

She shivered. 'Fine.'

More light outside. They checked the ports. The tractor's forward floodlights now played on the concrete wall of a massive encrusted blockhouse with huge circular perforations in it.

Above the low sound of the blower he heard her murmur, 'My God.'

'He lead us right to it.' Lonya fiddled with something above him. 'Inertial navigation module. I fix exact spot. Later, we check.'

The tractor turned. Its forward lights, now tangential, showed that the wall was very slightly curved. So slight that the base had to be audaciously huge.

'Jeez,' he breathed. 'It's colossal.'

'According to the plans,' she said, 'it's 600 feet in diameter.'

The tractor crawled along the wall, following well-worn sand tracks, veered out again and straightened, heading directly for the concrete rampart.

In its floodlights was a ramp that rose from the sand toward a metal-edged square entrance. The tractor and its load ground up the incline, vanished inside. The ramp lifted out of the sand, cleaning itself with high-pressure jets from its edges, and closed upward to form the outer door of what had to be a sea-lock. The light was cut off as the bottom-hinged hatch met its seating and moved back to lock flush.

Lonya turned to Elina. 'End of loiter time. Batteries to one-third. And carbon dioxide level rising.' He banked them away, angling up, thrusters moaning.

'Could we take it up the caisson?' Braden asked. 'We need to see the top of this thing and test out Blake's theory about the tethered bathysphere gizmo.'

The pilot looked at Elina. She hesitated, then nodded.

They rose beside the fouled blank face, slowly drifting around it. It looked like the ramparts of hell.

She produced a copy of the plans, peered at the diagram. 'He might be wrong. It could be a pressure cylinder for oxygen or something.'

'Nah.' He shook his head. 'If there's a lid on top it's the front door.'

They reached the lip and glided above it, lights angled down. It was so large that only sections of the surface could be seen. Some distance in was a semi-spherical dome with an edge that met a metal groove.

'See that?' He pointed to the groove. 'The gap's free of barnacles. It's definitely a hatch or sea-lock.'

They turned away from the great column and continued, blacked out, through utter darkness.

'Now we've sussed it,' he told her, 'we could use your sub.' His head was aching from foul air.

'It's still in dry dock.'

'So — plan A's still on?'

She nodded.

He blew on his fingers. 'What happens if they take Fong to this?'

'Blake will try to go with him.'

'On his own?'

'It's a deep-cover operation. There's no way we can back him up.'

'And if he's blown?'

A flicker of pain crossed her face. 'He's been on borrowed time for weeks. For an amateur at this, he's amazing, but . . .'

He looked at her keenly. 'I think you're sweet on him.'

'Don't be stupid.' She looked away.

'I felt you were, first time I saw you together.' He grinned. 'Admit it and shame the devil.'

She coloured. 'He doesn't even see me. All he thinks about is Kate — the woman they caught. They were lovers.'

He grinned, delighted with his deduction. 'Well, seeing as how you're the great organiser and it's a sure bet they've killed his squeeze, can't you do something about that?'

'Not much point when he's going to die.'

62

DEEP SIX

Blake was handcuffed during the long flight and confined to the rear seat of the aircraft, well away from the others. A goon watched him from a seat across the aisle.

He reverted to an animal wariness, knowing the one weapon he had left was his recall.

They landed during the night but the window shades were kept down. A refuelling stop. He heard the nozzle being attached. The trip was around four hours. At a speed of 250 knots and a northwest heading toward the Timor Sea, that would put them, according to maps in his head, somewhere near Alice Springs.

On the second leg, Jason took a notebook computer from his bag and gave a demonstration of four-finger typing. Blake watched the fingers, knowing he could remember every move they made. Then a pilot came aft and asked Jason to go to the cockpit. He shut the notebook and went forward. Something was going on. A glitch?

As they flew through the night he dozed once or

twice. Before they landed, three hours later, they tied a black cloth bag over his head.

He heard the others getting out, then was shoved along the aisle and down the stairs.

The air was hot. It was early morning. He heard cicadas, flying beetles, and the shriek of a cockatoo. He'd been in the Kimberley before and his senses told him that was where they were. They led him to another aircraft, placed his feet so he could climb in, then pushed him onto a barely padded seat. He felt others around him, heard a turbine starting up. It sounded like the chopper from the rig.

Jason's voice. 'Have a good trip.' It meant he was staying behind.

The rotors slapped air. They tilted forward and took off. They didn't remove his blindfold until they were over featureless sea.

It was the same long-range red and white Sikorsky S–76 that had flown them from the ditched plane to the rig. He could identify it easily from scratches in the paintwork near the door. This model, he knew from specs he'd studied, was equipped with IFR with weather radar and GPS. He saw the cabin was fitted with auxiliary tanks. He looked at the people on board.

Schumann was drumming his fingers on a medical manual in his lap. Fong, shrunken into his seat, was pointedly ignoring Senam. Tan glanced at him as if betrayed, his urbane veneer replaced by malevolence. The stone faces of the heavies completed the gloom.

The chopper's whine changed pitch. The sea below became more defined. They were descending.

Soon they were flogging over the sluggish chop at perhaps 500 feet. He couldn't see ahead. Were they aiming for the rig?

The pilot hovered the craft and turned it on its rotor axis. Horizon check? He stared through the side window at the revolving sea. One of the armed men plugged his headset into a jack near the door.

When the rotation stopped, the man opened the door, prepared the hoist and fitted a yellow flotation harness to the cable.

The pilot was holding them just above the swell.

He knew what it meant. The seas were calm enough for a direct transfer and they'd be lowered to the sphere directly from the chopper.

It wasn't the rig this time, but Deep Six.

Fong and Senam were the first out. Each looked surprised and anxious as they reached the door. Tan and Schumann, winched down next, appeared familiar with the operation.

They had to uncuff him to position him in the collar. It relieved his cramp and chafed wrists but didn't increase the chance of escape. He clamped his arms over the plastic-covered loop and they pushed him into space.

He dangled in the buffeting downdraught, staring at the thing in the sea.

It was half submerged, a wallowing orange sphere with rungs welded to one side. Too simple for a submersible. Too ungainly for a sub. The same article he'd seen lowered onto the workboat. At its top was an open pressure hatch rimmed by a footplate and railing. A man in oilskins waited on the footplate, staring up.

He looked around for the rig but saw nothing but waves. The movement of the chopper flattened the swell. The man secured to the railing grabbed his descending legs and pulled him in until his feet met the footplate. When he was unhitched, he thought at first of diving over the side, but realised that wouldn't get him far. He descended the dripping internal ladder.

The interior was basic — a circular seat and a panel with simple controls. One of the bodyguards came down the ladder in a shower of water. The man in oilskins came last, shut the hatch and dogged it down. The light was reduced to a dim bulb above them. He spoke into a wall-phone. 'Secure. Two fathoms.'

The thing ceased its uneasy rolling as the muffled wave-slap rose up its side. Then sea-noise stopped. He realised they were moving less because the cable was hauling them down.

The man checked his gauges. 'Seal holding. Retract.'

He visualised the plans again. The upper compartment that had to be the sea-lock for this sphere. Below it, the plant room for the winching gear. Then the main part of the tower — the levels and access stairs that continued to the base of the domed cylinders that circled its bottom. He mentally re-scanned the specifications — plans for compartments, wiring, plumbing, air-conditioning, plant rooms . . .

Yes, he was well informed. Far better than Jason imagined.

Senam turned to the introspective Tan. 'My children . . . under sea?'

Tan ignored her.

Fong spat something at Tan in Chinese.

No response but a seething look from the beautiful Korean. She stared at the rubberised deck, then said to Fong in English, 'I victim here, not you.'

Fong's face remained blank but he emanated hurt and rage.

Blake swallowed to pop his eardrums. The pressure had slightly increased.

A clang of metal on metal and a shudder.

The whine of machinery and the sound of draining water.

The operator checked his panel, climbed the ladder and undogged the hatch. The slight overpressure in the sphere, escaping around the soft rubber seal, lifted the concave metal oval like a kettle lid. Someone outside pulled it wide and bitter-smelling air spilled down.

One by one, they climbed out.

When his turn came, it was exactly as he'd expected.

High above the giant ball was the huge domed hatch — reinforced on the underside with heavy girders like radiating spines. Sea, under great pressure, spraying from one quadrant of it, hit the opposite side of the curving interior wall and ran down the concrete. The slimy floor of the well was crisscrossed with gutters that channelled the water into grid-covered drainholes. The failing seal above showed how much pressure waited to crush them.

He descended the rungs, stepped onto the sodden metal surface and bent to look under the sphere. It rested on curved-rubber buffers and he could see that the cable attached to its base vanished into a stuffing-box. The seal, he thought, wouldn't be watertight but was probably good enough to limit the amount of pumping needed to drain the winch-room below.

'You! Stand behind the line.' The man in oilskins pointed to a yellow circle on the deck.

A hatch flush with the centre of the floor hissed up. The dim bulbs in the sea-lock made the light from the level below seem a glare.

They were herded down a rust-streaked ladder, passed a door labelled PUMP ROOM, then mustered outside the entrance to a lift. A lift that, according to the plans, descended the length of the main tower. Closed-circuit cameras covered every angle. The doors opened and they crammed inside.

The lift lowered them several levels, stopped with a bouncing jerk and opened. Another rubberised floor supported four uniformed guards with sub-compacts. With the reception committee were three men, two in white dustcoats and a third wearing a grey-leather jerkin and thongs who looked like a time-traveller from ancient Gaul. He had a beard but his face roughly matched a shot Blake had been shown in the sub.

Tritter.

As they were herded out, Tritter scrutinised Fong, who gave no indication of knowing him, then he pointed to Senam. 'This one to level thirty.'

'My children,' she bawled. 'My children. They say I see my children!'

Tritter ignored her, pointed to Blake. 'This one's another meddler from DEMI. Give him primary conditioning, then I want him on the rig with Retki so we have the two ready to go.'

She was alive! And not imprisoned in this tomb but on the rig, as he suspected!

The stab of hope and elation soon died.

They'd do *what* to him?

And what had they done to her?

Two guards moved forward. They looked drugged, the inevitability of their movements inhuman. He'd been watching for any slip these people made, any edge of advantage. So far, nothing.

They were shoved back in the lift. Senam cringed against the metal wall, choking on her sobs.

One guard punched a button.

Going down, he thought.

For the count?

63

CIA

The DCI swivelled his chair and the room revolved, replacing his view of his desk with the display on the wall behind — Old Glory and the agency's escutcheon.

Patriotism, the last refuge of a scoundrel? Bennett had called him a patriot. From the Greek word *patris*. Fatherland? Some father! Violent, juvenile, narcissistic, vandalising . . .

Americans couldn't fathom why other nations detested them. Hubris convinced them it was envy, an insularity confirmed on The Hill. Because only one in five Congressmen currently held passports. Despite 9/11, the Land of the Fooled remained self-centric, naive, parochial, quick to assert moral imperatives yet flout them when convenient.

He completed the circle back to his desk. Had the world turned or had he? The evidence for both sides was equal. The inference depended not on physics but oneself — which explained why families, institutions, nations disagreed even while asserting the same proposition.

One of the phones now winked. He checked the

readout for details of the call — Jason, on the sat-link from Wyndham.

He picked up. 'Stone.'

The nervous DSP confirmed details of Braden's flying circus. '. . . will be refuelling at the Richmond RAAF base at 0800 hours.'

'What a coincidence.' He knew Braden's goodwill visit to Australia was anything but that.

'Then he flies on to Darwin.'

'It sounds plausible.'

'It's firm information.'

'Of course it is. They want it to be convincing.'

'I'm taking the next flight to the sphere to get what I can out of Blake.'

'You won't, unless you have a death wish. The scenery's shifted. The DEMI sub's finished its refit. It left Murmansk a week ago. And Braden's in the area. Reflect on that.'

'So what should I do?'

'We've lost information dominance. That means damage to assets valued. I trace it to a subordinate who let Braden take two DEMI agents for a joy-flight. We've also intercepted a phone call from Milton Green — one of the scientists who visited the rig. He's had an attack of conscience and could have told Braden about option four. I want you back here.' He hung up.

The house of cards was falling.

When the President had assumed office and fired his National Security Adviser, the bendable Amy Stead, they'd lost the grease between the gears. Then they'd underestimated Braden, read him as a bombastic fool and been blindsided. Jessop's high-profile ferret was now halfway up their pants. And he, the profoundly gifted William Ulysses Stone, politician, economist, psychologist, had goofed.

Damage control was imperative.

But increasingly less possible.

He sighed and ransacked his mind. Few options dangled there.

One per cent of the world owned more than the other ninety-nine. And Tritter was in the one per cent — untouchable. But if he wasn't shut down, there'd be blowback — a CIA word for a fate worse than forensic accountants. A fate one laboured to avoid. Not that he could. The others in the Group would blame him anyway.

He, William Stone, was pledged to keep information from the public, to divert attention from sensitive issues, to control the now mythical basic freedoms while the Empire of the Buck pillaged on. And to misdirect the Executive as required.

But Washington could stand just so much.

He subsided onto the bed. The whole thing now swung on his decision. He vented a dolorous sigh.

Well . . . if the navy had ships in the area.

A possibility there.

He lifted the phone again and punched a button. 'DCI. Get me the Admiral of the Fleet on the horn. Then get me Tritter.'

'Tritter, sir?'

'You heard me. Secure line. Set it up.'

The duty ComOps officer stammered, 'Give it our best shot, sir. Be a patch job. Got a landline, I guess, sir, from the rig's umbilical?'

'Don't ask. Find out. That's why you're employed.'

'On to it, sir. Right away, sir.'

He replaced the handset and buzzed for lunch. The steward was outside in two minutes with the covered traymobile. At least the Domestic Facilities

Unit was efficient. The man set the small side table perfectly, served the food and left.

He preferred to eat alone. He preferred to live alone. What a paradise the world would be if people never met. 'The day of one's death is better than the day of one's birth.' So it said in Ecclesiastes. Yes, time and chance had now happened to them all. Even to the odious but useful Tritter. Because if this went belly-up, even Tritter couldn't expect . . .

It was unstable.

Could go critical.

The moment a gap appeared in the mass ignorance that protected vested interests and positions . . . Deep Six would have to be deep-sixed.

64

LAB

Fong walked along the corridor past rows of vaultlike doors. His head felt like it was caught in a vice.

Senam had been bait. The shock of it had drained him of life. People were nothing but users, affection a ruse. All she cared about were her children. Her gestures of warmth had been an act.

Schumann, shuffling ahead of him, touched the slight curve of the outer wall. 'On this level were incubators for parasites.'

A parasite! She was a parasite!

'But arboviruses? Useless. And so! We go to the lab.'

'What if I not help you?'

'You lose nails, then toes, then skin. Very slow, painful, scientific.' Schumann led the way downstairs to an airlock and opened the first of several doors. It shut behind them and, as the slight vacuum re-established, he opened the next. 'We are proud of the facility here. Though, to a famous molecular geneticist, it perhaps seems basic, no?'

He followed the madman through the next airlock to the ultra-sterile lab itself. It had a profusion of ultracentrifuges, sophisticated computers, people working with cultures, sequenators . . .

Schumann indicated the mass spectrometer. 'MALDI technique, working on the microgram level. We have a staff of thirty, PhDs in molecular genetics plus trained technicians because it's mostly hackwork, isn't it true? Isn't it utterly, utterly true? Through here is our mini-brewery for growing viruses. And so!'

Fong half-listened, trying to drag himself from the rubble of the once-grand pavilion of his love. People were only agreeable when they wanted something from you. How could he have forgotten? People were rats.

Now he had to think like a rat — become indispensable. First that.

Later — revenge.

65

TRITTER

'Dolfie?'

Tritter ignored her, the phone to his ear.

She hobbled to him, naked, suppliant, and crouched by the bed. A beautiful plaything with crippled feet. In an earlier age he'd have had her footbound.

The line still crackled. How many stages were needed for this link-up? From the CIA, a dedicated optical landline to a transmitter bouncing off a satellite to . . .

'Ooo!' She found the chocolates. Her eyes widened with delight. She sucked one and fingered her nipples in a way she knew excited him.

He'd had women who were intelligent. And women who were ravishing. And women who had everything — passion, intelligence, beauty, depth. But paragons weren't pliable. Perfect women were oppressive. So he'd settled for this toy with its rudimentary mind. Her few brains were in her body, the best place for them.

Indifference to others and oneself.

But not in bed.

Stone's languid voice finally came through. 'Bill here, Adolphous. You're a hard man to raise. Not good news, I fear.'

He listened, stomach souring.

'. . . and had those intelligence estimates cross-referenced. So, on your behalf, I've importuned the Puzzle Palace. A sub and two destroyers will deploy in your immediate area. But they won't be on-station for some hours.'

'And they'll chase the DEMI sub off or sink it?'

'I doubt it.' Stone's trademark sigh. 'It's a Russian Oscar Class — old but rejigged. The Oscar's still the most powerful cruise missile sub in the world — unpleasant enough to send the flag officer of a carrier battle group to the can. And naval intelligence informs us their boat has virtually no signature. Apparently they paid the Russians to practically rebuild the blunt end. They've removed the reactors and put in a plug with some kind of cryogenic hydrogen or reformed methanol fuel system. It could be fuelled with distilled seawater. It's the quietest platform known.'

'It's armed?'

'They may not have SSMs.'

'Have what?'

'Surface-to-surface missiles. But I have confirmation on torpedoes. And that has implications for Deep Six and the rig.'

'What are you implying?'

'The ships we've sent won't worry them much. But if we authorise them to engage, it could worry both of us. A lot.'

'Why?'

'Because a sea-battle can't be hidden. Too much human and recorded evidence. So, if they engage, things become overt and our little secrets scream.

You'll be exposed and I'll be screwed by the Executive. That's how PI — political influence — works.'

'You're saying there's nothing you can do?'

'I'm trying to survive an extremely delicate situation. I'm forecasting blowback. I'm advising damage control. I'm explaining that Deep Six could soon be only good for a mooring. You need to remove all information, sensitive or technical, and all key personnel — as of now.'

'Abandon a two and a half billion dollar investment?'

'The lab can be rebuilt. You need to run Plan F.'

'I've put part of my life into this installation.'

'One torpedo and it'll implode.'

Tritter felt hot rage. 'If I go down, you'll come with me.' He tried to control himself. Indifference to all.

Stone had assumed silent mode.

'Fuck you, Stone. This isn't how it's meant to be.'

'I don't like it either. Plan F's the best I can suggest.'

Acid reamed his stomach. He took deep breaths.

Stone said nothing, which he knew was one of the man's ploys.

'Very well. I'll take Schumann, Fong, Tan . . .'

'Tan?'

'His contacts are useful.'

'And the Korean woman?'

'Expendable. Fong's lost face and wants nothing to do with her.'

'Give me a total. If we need to get you off . . .'

'Probably three senior research staff. I can replace the rest.'

'So seven . . .'

He glanced at the woman. 'Under ten.' He vented a bracket of Dutch swearwords. 'I can't believe that, after all these years of effort and expense . . .'

But Stone merely listened. The lunatic considered himself so exceptional that he treated others like babies — creatures who responded well to routine.

'What if DEMI don't attack?' He tugged his beard. 'Then this is a complete and utter . . .'

'They'll sniff around. Which means personnel left alive pose a security threat. Plan F.'

Plan F was the fall-back. It exterminated meatheads — lab staff, technicians, tradesmen, guards — without damaging the installation. He was comfortable with that because, if no attack came, the tower could be neutralised, scrubbed out, disinfected, recommissioned.

They agreed on details. He hung up angrily, his code of indifference forgotten. He didn't care about the hundreds who would die. But throwing away such colossal resources and so many years of organisation made him furious.

'Dolfie?' She looked alarmed. 'Are you all right?'

He restored his expression to neutral. 'Business.'

'You work too hard.'

He visualised the 14,000-tonne submarine gliding ever closer, saw men in its torpedo room sliding big fish from the racks, heard one churning, released from its tube, wire-guided to its target, felt the shudder as the caisson crumbled under the enormous water pressure. That cataclysmic impregnation was one screw he planned to avoid.

'Dolfie?'

He glared at her eye-candy body. 'Get dressed and pack your things. We're leaving.'

66

LAB

Fong examined the cultures, feigning interest now, suspecting that nothing done here was as complex as his seminal research on higher eukaryotes, his breakthrough in recombinant technology, his contribution to sequencing chromosome twenty. He glanced at the blimp-like man. 'Flu? For drift and shift?'

'No. For airborne transmission of a recombinant psychotoxin.' Schumann's fingers drummed his chest. He stuffed the wayward hand in his pocket and strode past technicians in face masks and rubber gloves who were checking gel strips containing fragments separated by electric charge for sequencing. 'So to business. As you know, the anticodon triplet is in a single stranded environment — needed to base-pair with the codon sequence of the mRNA where the aminoacyl tRNA reaches the ribosome. One problem is . . .'

'You refer to transcription? The structure of transfer RNA and aminoacyl tRNA synthetases?'

'Indeed. Is just one area of concern. But you will solve our dilemma, I'm sure.'

He frowned. 'If I solve, what happen to world?'

Schumann chortled. 'Grand things happen. East

Asia becomes a fertilised jungle. Carbon levels drop. Global warming slows.'

'And China is destroy?'

The shapeless man shrugged. 'Next we confer with my senior staff in detail on our problem.' He blundered to the wall, touched it, came back. 'Follow, please.'

Fong followed. What did he care?

He wanted her dead for dishonouring his love. He wanted everyone dead.

The world could go to hell.

They descended a further level to a conference room with wall-mounted whiteboards covered in familiar scrawls. He saw peptide chains. Genetic codes showing frameshift mutations. Schematic illustrations of ribosomes moving down messenger RNA. An elaboration of the A and B genes of the ABO system.

The scientists in the room were scruffy. Western barbarians, he thought, who didn't care how they looked — who showed their emotions like children and ignored all principles of respect.

A phone rang and Schumann picked it up. His face became progressively grave and the fingers of his free hand cavorted even faster on his lapel. He finally lowered the phone and addressed the room. 'Gentlemen, this must wait. Mr Fong and I are needed elsewhere. And so . . .' He made fists of his fingers to disguise his agitation, blurted, 'You stay here while I collect things. Then you come with me.' He hurried to a door, upsetting a waste bin as he diverted to touch the wall.

Fong stared at the scrawls on the boards — the intricate complexities of life.

He thought of his former honour.

And present shame.

He tasted bile.

67

DEATHTRAP

The light stayed on. No one fed them. They drank from the tap. Blake wrapped bedclothes around her, held her, listened to her shuddering sobs. Moans came from a cell to the right. He'd only heard Asian voices here.

'You not Peter Mair?' she said when a little calmer.

'No.'

'Who you are then?'

'No one special.'

'I frighten. You talk, please.'

'I'm sorry about your kids. Want to tell me about them?' She reluctantly said a little. Her girls, aged five and seven, sounded as brutalised as their mother. She was frantic about them. He said, 'I don't think they're here.'

'Why you say?'

'There's an oil rig near this. I think they're on that.'

'You say you not know before. Bastard.' She pounded his chest with her fists.

'I don't.' He held her off. 'It's just something I saw.'

He told her about the pink thing he'd seen trampled into the oil rig chopper pad. At one end, a tiny foot shape. The mashed plastic leg of a doll.

They must have nodded off, were roused by cries from the next cell. The wail of a distant siren. Then shouts and running feet.

Then, close outside, words he could understand.

'Power outage . . .'

'Or damage to the cable.'

The ventilation died and the strip-light above them flickered. She yelled out her fear.

He tried the door again. It was metal sheet with no handle or inspection hatch. He put his ear to the crack, trying to work out what was going on.

The light went out. She gasped. Panic from inmates around them.

A series of metal clicks. One from the door. It moved in slightly, touched his cheek.

He felt her beside him, said, 'Door's open. Must have a safety mechanism. They've tripped the locks. That means general evacuation. Come on. And don't let go of me.'

They had a chance now, he thought. Slim. But a chance.

She gripped the back of his shirt. 'We go in dark?'

'Don't worry.' He knew exactly where they were. 'Got the plan of this coffin in my head.'

They'd been marched around the core past fifteen doors and three spoke-like passageways. They were level with the domes that circled the central column's base.

He opened the door. People were groping, stumbling past. He edged out and attempted to navigate by touching the wall but the crowd, with the same idea, pushed them along.

She clung to his shirt.

As they went with the tide, he heard her asking questions.

The siren, louder in the corridor, stopped as if cut off. Now just people feeling their way in the dark and an acrid smell. Human panic or . . . ?

'What did they tell you?' he asked.

'Say only Chinese kept here. No children. Once a day they taken upstairs. They do tests and things. Lot of people come back sick and some die.'

At last, thin beams of light. Two guards with torches were climbing stairs to a pressure door. No one seemed to have told them it was a general evacuation. As they shone their beams across the sea of heads, perhaps fifty people surged toward them, those in front going down in the crush.

The men went through the door and began to shut it but the mob reached them and hauled it back open. The guards drew mini-automatics and sprayed the crowd.

The onslaught stopped. The wounded and dying moaned. The guards pulled the heavy door half closed then unaccountably abandoned it. They turned like automatons and began trudging up the next set of stairs. As the beams of their lights retreated, the frantic people followed, scrambling over the shot and the trampled, chasing the retreating light.

She tried to follow but he held her. 'Let them go.'

Pitch black again.

He dredged the fact-file of his mind for details on escape suits. Hooded images flooded his thoughts, the latest resembling the garb of an intergalactic monk. Pressure suits were safe to 180 metres. He did a rough calculation. They could be used for upper levels but not down here. He also doubted Tritter had suits for the hundreds of people in his tomb. If there were a few, people would fight for them — probably tear them apart as they did.

He moved back toward the wall, seeing the layout precisely in his mind, paced it out to the stairwell the men with torches had come up.

His hand found the metal railing. 'Stairs here. Be careful. Hang on tight.'

'Where we go?' Her voice sharp with fright.

He placed her hand on the railing. 'Down.'

Dancing light again, this time from below. Two more guards with torches were trudging up the stairs. Anyone normal would be running.

He pulled her back behind a column.

The two passed silently, faces blank.

Automatons, he thought. Controlled in some way, or drugged.

But the lights had shown him an open pressure door below.

In darkness again, they inched down to it. He pulled her through. 'Careful. More steps.'

Her voice in the dead air, ragged with terror. 'Why we go down?'

At last, a dull red glow above, no brighter than a child's bedside light — emergency lights trying to re-establish.

A crackle. Then an echoing announcement: 'Attention. Attention. Inbound power has failed and sphere recall is non-functional. All personnel to Level Five. Everyone to Five. Immediately.'

Urgent cries from far above. Air in the dying hulk was cooling.

He said, 'We could be the last people down here.'

She shivered and pulled against his hand. 'You crazy man. Should go up, not down.'

'And get killed in the rush? No way. My guess is this thing's been attacked or sabotaged and . . .'

'But when we go down is deeper in sea.'

'Down's the one way out.'

'If true, you think they not know?'

'They haven't sussed it yet.'

Their eyes were now accustomed to the dull glow. They'd reached a dead-end's concrete wedge. But set into the rough-cast floor was a circular hole. And, projecting from it, the inverted U of a metal ladder.

'Down there,' he said.

Her look of terror. 'I not.'

'Best chance to get out of here. Trust me.'

The despairing face. 'You full of shit.'

The crackle again. 'Attention. Attention. Detectors register noxious gas on Levels Twenty-five to Twenty-nine. Levels Twenty-three to Thirty-one will be sealed off. You have one minute to vacate.' The echo died.

He said, 'Okay. Thirty-one was the door we just came through. Your call. Get gassed or stick with me.'

'What if my children up top? You crazy.' She stumbled up the stairs.

A hiss. They hadn't waited the full minute. She reached the door too late, got her hand around its edge but the hydraulic ram closing it was strong enough to sever an arm. She yelped, drew her hand back as it shut. The distant babble of terrified people was cut off.

She cried out with fear.

He listened to her, coldly thinking, the layout clear in his mind. Yes, it still made sense. He called, 'Coming?'

He started down the ladder, knowing she'd follow. The silence was oppressive. Just their feet on the metal rungs, when she wasn't stepping on his hands.

Then the emergency light completely died. Without light, they'd die as well.

His foot found the floor of the next level. 'Floor coming up.' He stood aside until he felt her beside him.

She clutched for him, terrified of losing him.

'There are storerooms down here. And pipes to the concrete tanks around the base. We've got to find the outer wall. Walk with me. Slowly.'

Now not even the ladder's slight comfort. An unknown space. She sobbed as they walked into the void.

Then his hand met a vertical surface. A wall? He inched along it to the right, drawing her with him.

Now something at right angles to the wall. Smooth and cold — a metal panel that moved in slightly with pressure. 'Hold it.'

'What is?'

He felt around. A punched-metal ventilator. Further down, a handle. 'Wall lockers.'

He opened one and felt inside. Some kind of protective clothing on a hanger. There should be a shelf above. Yes. A metal box. He pulled it out. Clinks. Heavy.

He opened it on the floor.

'What you do?'

'I've got a toolbox. This could be a maintenance bay.'

He opened the next few lockers. Hard hats, plastic boxes, riggers gloves. Then in the fourth, at the back, the thick shape of a Dolphin lamp. Heart thudding, he pulled it out and switched it on.

A glare on grey metal. The battery wasn't good. But they could see.

They were in an unpainted concrete corridor around five metres wide and slightly curved. On the inner side were equipment racks and, near them, a spoke-like passage labelled LEVEL 33. PUMP

ROOMS 6–10. SECURITY AREAS 20–30. AUTHORISED PERSONNEL ONLY.

'Come on.' He beckoned her to follow. 'We have to go down five more levels. There's an access shaft with companionways near the core.'

'You mad.'

They walked down flights of metal stairs flanked by huge and complex pipe stacks.

On the very bottom level, abandoned at the base of the steps, its yellow warning lights still winking, was an electric buggy.

'Transport.' He climbed behind the wheel and she perched on the carrying tray. It had no headlights but the warning lights helped. He shone the weakening lamp beam around.

The floor of the corridor was covered in brine. Stagnant seawater pooled around gutters near the walls.

He shoved the cart into drive. It moved off, humming and beeping.

At the end, he turned left into the long gallery around the inner base. They passed large-diameter pipes that sprouted from the outer wall and disappeared into the gloom above.

She clung to him. 'Where we go now?'

'To a sea-lock. It has a sub-sea vehicle in it, like a tractor. If we can get inside and flood the lock, we could get away in it.'

'You full of shit. We still at bottom of sea.'

'But it's got to have an escape device.'

'You mad.'

'Got a better plan?'

He shone the torch on a numbered door: 76 — HYDROACOUSTICS AND FRACTURE MECHANICS, SUB-STATION 6.

Then he found one to the outer cells — a circular

pressure door. The label read: ACCESS TO BASE CELL 14.

He knew that twenty-four compartments surrounded the core — caverns 30 metres in diameter with walls over a metre thick. This honeycomb, connected to the main column by piping, had two functions — buoyancy, when the construction was floated into position, then storage of crude. Except that Deep Six stored platinum bars. And God knows what else.

Noises ahead and a curse, then the sound of rushing water. A torrent of salt water washed around them.

They clung to the buggy as the water rushed past their legs and around the curve. She shrieked and dropped the vital lamp. It bobbed away behind them. The shorted buggy motor sparked.

But faintly ahead was another light — enough to show the influx subsiding. As the level in the huge outer ring corridor lowered to a film of slop he took her hand and pulled her forward.

A small fiftyish man in overalls stood beside an open access door with water still spilling from its knee-height sill. There were warning signs on the door and a control panel beside it.

The man had a torch in his mouth and turned as he heard them coming, blinding them with the glare. 'Good. I need some help here. It's got manual override, thank God. But it's a lake in there. When the pumps died, the water started to build up in the lock. Come on.'

Blake stepped through the hatch into the shallow lake within.

'We drown,' she sobbed. But she followed.

The erratic light from the man's torch only partly showed where they were. It was a tunnel-like space that faced a massive outer lock. The tractor was as large as a World War Two Tiger tank and took up most of the space in the cell. It was connected by charging cables to sockets on the wall. Its spherical pressure-hull had an access hatch open at the top.

'Help me with the door,' the man said.

Blake braced his foot against the bulkhead and hauled the inner hatch closed against the spilling water. The man spun the locking wheel then waded to a panel on the wall. He threw levers, then shone the torch on the power cables. 'See these? Got to get them off.'

Blake helped him unclip them. 'We've got no power, so how do we open the outer lock?'

'With the grabs. But we've got to equalise the pressure first.' The man shone the torch at four numbered, red-painted valves on the wall. 'These are manual sea-cocks. You stay here and when I tell you, turn them full on. That's anti-clockwise. Miss, you follow me.'

Blake watched the man climb the ladder on the outside of the tractor's pressure hull. The terrified Senam climbed after him into the cabin.

For a moment the torch flickered behind the thick ports at the front of the machine, then the cabin lights came on, throwing a beam through the open top hatch. Then powerful forward beams lit up the space, reflecting off the water and almost blinding him.

The man's head appeared above the hatch. 'All set. Open the cocks then get up here.'

As Blake wrenched the first of the wheels around, he heard water pour in from floor vents. Soon it boiled around him, almost washing him off his feet. Before he could turn the third wheel, water was up to his waist.

'That'll do,' the man yelled. 'Hurry.'

He had to half-swim for the ladder. As he hauled himself up, the water level followed.

Once he was in, the man secured the hatch.

Blake gazed at the complexity around him. 'You can drive this thing?'

'That's my job. Stay out of the way.'

He squatted down and the man went to work — turned on oxygen, checked settings for temperature, humidity. The glowing panel lights and chirping instruments were comforting. In the lifeless hulk of Deep Six, they'd found the one thing that still worked.

Rising water turned the headlight beam milky. Senam crouched behind the driver's seat, shivering and drenched.

'So how do we release the outer lock?' he asked the man.

'According to the manual, with the tractor. Never done it, of course. Never had this situation.'

'And if we get out, what then?'

'We crawl along the sea-floor to the rig and jettison the tractor and motors. The cabin's just above neutral buoyancy. So — you two. Did you work in the lab?'

Blake nodded. 'Yup.'

'How come you were down in the bilge?'

'They sealed off the upper floors. Why didn't others think of this? I thought there'd be a queue.'

'I'm the only guy who knows what it can do, apart from the manufacturer. The shits even cut the escape section out of the manual. But I've worked it out.' He pushed levers slightly forward. The tractor moved ahead.

'Here goes.' He stopped them in front of the giant outer door and operated the grab controls. There seemed to be two for each segment of each arm, another two for working the claws. He raised one arm level with the emergency trip-bar inset into the door, got the claws on opposite sides of it and pressed the wrist control. The claw swivelled and angled the lever that drew in the locking bars. But the door stayed closed as if the pressure hadn't equalised. 'Come on, you bastard.' He pushed against it with both arms. The front of the tracks lifted but the door held fast. Then it inched out from the top and slowly fell to form the ramp. 'We're in luck.' He checked gauges. 'Still one atmosphere. Seals holding. CO_2 normal.' He retracted the arms against the hull and conned the tractor down the ramp. 'And we're in business.'

Blake stared through a small forward port. There were none at the side. Small screens showed blurred mono pictures feeding from remote-controlled low-light videocameras each side of the hull. They showed a cloud of silt from the tracks. As they moved further ahead it cleared.

The man tapped a screen. 'See that? The sub-sea cable to the rig. That's where it all comes and goes. All we have to do is follow it.'

As the drifting silt cloud thinned, he realised what he was looking at — an encrusted pipe-like cable emerging from the seabed. It was thick enough to enclose power lines, communication links, pipes for pumping liquids . . .

He glanced at the shivering Senam. Her wet clothes clung to her body. She was frozen, scared, hugged herself for warmth.

The tractor crawled beside the cable with a pitching motion. Despite its powerful front floodlights, the field of view was still limited.

The air was warming. The driver settled behind

the controls. The track levers looked full forward but their speed was barely walking pace.

'Is this as fast as it goes?'

'Top speed. You can't go fast because pressure increases linearly with depth. So hydrodynamic forces increase with the square, and power with the cube, of speed. To increase underwater speed you need enormous power to compensate for drag.'

'So how long will it take us at this pace?'

'Well, it's about 8 kilometres to the rig. So I'd say it'd take us two or three hours. That's if the power holds out.'

'You mean it could conk?'

'That's the worry. It's designed for shuttling cargo, not a traverse.'

They churned on, sometimes passing swathes of refuse that seemed formed by the tide. The interminable cable still vanished ahead into gloom. After an hour, the depth gauge showed they'd risen 300 feet.

The sediment became sand. He could see the sloping floor better now.

At 500, they levelled off and crawled over a featureless plateau. He watched the lethargic world of sometimes curious deep-sea fish.

Senam hadn't said a word since getting in. She sat hunched against the back of the cabin, no longer shivering, condensation running down the modules beside her.

The man checked his panels. 'We've used most of our power. Battery voltage is down, too. We've got an aluminium oxygen fuel cell with nicad backup.'

Blake pointed to a small oscilloscope that had begun to illuminate and blip. 'What's that?'

'That's the positive sonar. We're getting near.'

They stared through turbid water. But it was another five minutes before something appeared at the limit of the floodlights. It was a huge square column of steel, slightly inclined, with massive structural members radiating from its lowest point. The cable ran to the foot of it then up the outside of the leg. The driver turned the side cameras forward for a wider view.

So the rig, he thought, had a conventional platform base. 'Flotation jacket,' the driver said. 'There are two on one side. The other two legs are thinner.' He turned the tractor to follow the enormous bottom brace. But it was almost 100 metres before the next leg appeared.

'What are you doing now?'

'I'm getting ahead of it. We've got a 1-knot current. We need it to wash us back on it, not away.'

'And then we release the pressure sphere?'

'Yup. It just detaches. We leave the heavy stuff — tracks, motors, grabs, down here. They're all one bit, see? And we float to the surface. No bends. We're still at one atmosphere. Simple.' He put the levers to neutral. The whining engines stopped. 'I'd say this is about the right spot. Because if we take, say, ten minutes to surface, that means ten minutes of drift. Hang on. I'll need to think about this and be sure.' He reached down beside him for a pen and pencil, put the stub in his mouth. 'Let's see.' He looked at his instruments. 'We're now . . .'

He stopped in mid-sentence. His jaw dropped and his eyes turned up into his head. He slumped and keeled to the side.

Blake had seen it before. In Bhutan. Somehow, the man had been turned off.

Senam yelped, 'What wrong with him?'

'He's dead.'

'Dead? How?'

'He's dead. That's all.'

She put her hand to her mouth. 'What we do?'

'I don't know.'

He searched the space for the manual, finally found it under the seat. She watched him resentfully, snivelling with fear.

It took him five minutes to absorb the 200 closely printed pages. They included the emergency instructions for manual release of the outer door but there was nothing about releasing the pressure hull of the tractor. The last page, or pages, had definitely been removed. A sliver of paper was still caught in the back of the wire binder and the base of the index had been whited out.

No way back. No way up. Low on oxygen and power. He ransacked the cramped hull for clues, even pulling up the floor mats. Nothing.

She watched him with disgust. 'So what now, smart-arse?'

68

SPECTRE

The gunship, in ferry mode — weapons stowed inboard — circled the Curtin strip three times. The specs showed 3050 metres and also mentioned kangaroo and bird hazards. They'd kept contact to a minimum, were relying on visuals, not wanting to telegraph their position.

'Plenty of error margin,' Freddy muttered, eyeballing the unfamiliar runway. 'Unmanned tower and a terminal.'

'Terminal's the domestic side,' Braden said. 'Not used now. The RAAF bit's on the tower side. Four caretakers and a fuel dump.'

'Thirty-knot headwind.'

'Don't see any roos.'

According to the press releases they were flying back via Darwin. And, after this detour, he thought, they might — just to make it look good. They could top up fuel here, but the live rounds were something else. It would have been a political nightmare to import their long-mothballed cache. It was also heavy and, on a long flight, it was best to stay light. Without Elina's organising brilliance, they'd still be a paper tiger.

Freddy rechecked the field elevs. Even with an approach in good light, runway illusions were possible. If it sloped up slightly, you could be low. If it was narrow, you could land short.

Flaps. Gear down. Braden brought them in, ears tuned to airspeed and altitude calls, planted it on speed and on the numbers. The surface wasn't rubbery and, as the nosewheel kissed, it became a Sunday drive. He held the yoke easily, enjoying it.

Freddy smiled. 'Sweet as pie.'

They came to a standstill halfway down the tarmac. He feathered and killed the outboards to keep them out of the grass, then took a taxiway toward the biggest feature on the military side — a huge open aircraft shelter. It was empty except for a large truck loaded with crates, a four-wheel drive and a forklift. Elina stood beside them, the wind blowing her skirt. She was the first military tactician he'd known who insisted on looking feminine.

He aimed for the next bay and parked half under the big structure. No ground idle in the old bird. Just two speeds — full or shut-down.

As they joined the crew outside the lowered ramp, the beauty was being surrounded by the beasts — old guys with gorgonzola arseholes who thought tact was something you hit with a hammer.

'Behave yourselves,' he told his crew. 'This little lady's our lifeline.' He waved at the crates on the truck. 'She smuggled in our ammo, for one.' He turned back to her. 'So where's your sub?'

'It's coming. But it can't get there as fast as you.' She looked as if something had gone belly-up. 'The caretakers'll let us use a briefing room. And I've brought in some food from Derby. But we need to talk about a few things fast.'

'Gimme five and I'm yours.'

He organised the crew to remount the weapons, then joined her in the waggon.

She drove him along the strip. It wasn't a striking location. Low trees, wattle, savanna. Transportable huts. A cluster of houses.

'Jessop's given me the go-ahead,' he told her, 'to do what it takes. And the Aussie Government'll put clamps on the media if it comes to the crunch.'

'Good.'

'So where are we going?'

'To the briefing room.'

'Don't see it.'

'Most of the buildings are underground.'

He mopped the back of his neck with a handkerchief. 'Did you get any more from Blake?'

'No. Something went wrong. We don't know what happened but we think Jason flew in with Tan.'

'So he's blown?'

'I'm afraid so. Everyone there flew out, so we've got to assume we've lost him. We traced the flight to Wyndham. That's north of here. And they must have got to the rig somehow from there. Or to Deep Six. We're not sure which.'

'Jeez. Means they know the frigging lot. Know we're working together. Might even know we're here.'

'DEMI's a need-to-know operation and I didn't tell Blake about this mission. But they'll know we're up to something. I doubt they'll know about the live ammunition.'

'Hope you're right.'

Her frown persisted. 'There's another complication. We've detected a naval task force heading for the area. The sub's monitored their transmissions. They're coded, of course, but they give us speed and direction.'

'What kind of force?'

'An attack sub and two destroyers. We think it's been assigned to protect the rig and Deep Six.'

'Against your sub?'

'Probably. Though they won't find that easy. The main worry is, they could go after you. Because even if they think you're unarmed, they won't want you snooping. And you'd be easy to spot and bring down. An old slow aircraft with . . .'

'. . . no modern countermeasures. Yeah, our chaff won't cope with an SAM.'

She stopped the vehicle and they got out. He walked beside her, swatting flies, to a bunker-like structure with steps leading into the ground. As he followed her down to the steel door, he thought about the political side. 'Well, I'm too high profile now for them to stage an obvious attack. But Treloar might decide he can stage-manage a minor off-shore engagement. The bird's a relic, which fits the spin. You can see the headline. VETERAN WARBIRD MISSING IN PACIFIC.'

She nodded. 'One thing we know for sure. If they're going to attack, it'll be now.'

They entered a long and mercifully airconditioned room. It had tables and chairs, a whiteboard and a lounge area at one end next to a rudimentary kitchen.

He followed her to the buffet counter, where she'd stacked the cardboard boxes full of food. 'A task force, eh? Bit of a worry. Dougie might smell a rat but he'd have nothing firm to smash their skulls with. So Treloar and Stone might figure they can swing it. Where are these ships now?'

'Five hours steaming northeast of the area.' She started unpacking the boxes. 'It means we don't have much time.'

He helped her with the food, thinking it through. 'What if we pull their plug?'

'I don't understand?'

'What if I get on the horn and crank Dougie up? Get him to veto all naval engagements in the South Pacific . . .'

'Would your president do that?'

'With his ears back. And, if they cross him, their guts are garters.' Then he told her what he'd heard from Green. About the airborne virus that carried a specific psychotoxin — a project near completion that could wipe out most of Asia.

She listened gravely. 'We knew it was something like that. Where's Green now?'

'I've got him under what you might call witness protection. Except there's no way he'll be allowed to testify to anything. You realise that whatever happens, this stuff can never come out. It's too hot.'

'I see.' She nodded slowly. 'So we still go ahead with the attack?'

'That's *why* we go ahead. Because the only way to stop this thing is to take out their lab, their facilities, their key people. The old girl may not be the current 46-million-dollar Spectre but she was a devastating weapon in her time. And we've looked after her like a baby. Hell, we're bored with practice rounds at air-shows. We go for it.'

'Good.' She gazed at the counter, not moving. 'So we're working on assumptions. Projections. Without Blake, they're all we have.'

'Like what?'

'We think Tritter and his team will leave the caisson.'

'You mean before your sub torpedoes it?'

'Yes. And they'll do it fast. Tonight.'

'Using the sphere thing?'

'Yes. The seas are pretty rough, so they'll probably use the workboat to transport it.'

'And what makes you so sure it'll happen tonight?'

'One of our people is . . . perceptive about things at a distance.' She started filling buns with ham and salad. 'They'll get Tritter and his key people to the rig, then take them off by chopper. The rig's manned by Tritter's men and probably CIA nonofficial cover types or even listed agents.'

'So we try to knock out Tritter and his team.'

'Or stall them on the rig till the sub arrives. We have SEAL-trained divers in our crew. They can board the rig and sort things out.'

'After we soften it up.' He sucked his teeth.

'You can operate at night?'

'Our turf, ma'am. It's what we do.' He visualised the gunship, primed with fuel and ammo, flaming off the strip. Jeez! The Braden Bunch in harness again, chopping up an oil rig! Better than tanks. Bigger than a convoy . . .

She set out paper plates on the tables. 'And I need to come with you.'

Like hell you do, he thought. Do you think you're mission control? 'It's organised chaos up there. You'd just be in the way.'

'But we don't know what we'll find.'

He stacked mugs on a tray. 'Very few hills are captured by committees, little lady.'

'But surely flying your plane and finding the target's hard enough? Then deciding what you're looking at and what to do with it . . . Because, if we don't find the sphere, it'll be pretty hard to justify attacking what appears to be an innocent oil rig.'

He dumped mugs on a table. 'You realise I command the aircraft. Period.'

'Of course you do. I just want to be there as a second opinion so we can assess things together before you act. Remember, I got your supplies here, together and on time. I'm sure you know that wasn't easy. I've done absolutely everything to make this a success. We're in this together, aren't we?'

She was a package. Cute as pie and twice as liable to repeat on you. He looked at her slyly. 'So you're angling for another trip in the bird?'

'That's the last thing I want. You know that.'

So he'd heard. He grinned.

Because the day she'd bailed out, she'd frozen when they'd tapped her. So the tap had become a nudge and the slipstream had done the rest. It was what jumpmasters amusingly termed 'Correcting the stand-in-the-door position'.

'Okay. You come. But you do what you're told.'

A little action would tone her up.

69

NIGHT OP

The RAAF caretakers, capable types, wore uniforms that suited the climate — shorts, T-shirt, boots and hat. They linked the bird up to a power cart. And, when the guns were remounted, magazines loaded and ammo stowage double-checked, they told Braden to reposition on the service apron and brought the tanker out. Casey, the flight engineer, muttered about the risk of turning when heavily loaded. 'I know what you guys'll pull on a hop like this.' After they were topped up, he checked struts and wing level then crawled out on the wings to dip and redip the main tanks.

The FLIR and SLR guys seemed happy. But the principal sensor was the Night Observation Device. No NOD, no go. Braden chatted to the operator, then went upstairs where Freddy and the navigator had a headstart on the flight plan. They recommended a vector around storm clouds to the west but he told them not to get fancy. 'We head straight there.'

Things were coming together but their stomachs thought their necks were cut. So he called a break and they made for the briefing room and food.

When he got outside a couple of buns, he pinned a map on the wall, surveyed his grizzled team, yelled for attention. 'So this is a live one. Search and destroy.'

They whooped and jerked fists at the roof.

'Yup! Back in combat after all these years. Do I assume from your dopey smiles that you're content to get shot to bits? Anyone pass?'

No response.

'Hm! Thought the war might have knocked some sense into you but I see you haven't changed. So here's the heads-up.' He stabbed the map. 'Target's here in the Timor Sea — an oil rig and the workboat for that rig. And a gizmo like a floating metal sphere which they use to transport people. We could spot this thing by itself or it could be on the workboat or the rig. The rig, as far as we know, is lightly armed. The objective is to disable everything we can — take out every living thing with total lack of discrimination.'

Goofy grins.

'Sounds a snap,' he went on, 'but may not be. One: we've never hit a target at sea. Two: US destroyers will be in the area and could be unfriendly to our mission. We think we've defused them through political channels but we can't be sure. And we're flying a relic — big, slow, obsolete, so old it doesn't even have flashguards. Which means one hit, we're shit. So, if we're attacked, it won't end up as an entry in the log.'

'You say this force'll be trying to acquire us?' Casey asked.

'And will for sure. But no point making it simple. So we stay off the di-dah machine.'

They had no radio operator on the crew. Freddy, who handled the UHF/VHF, nodded.

'As for the target, we function with traditional night-op strategy. Blacked out. Surprise of the essence.'

'We seem pretty loaded,' someone said.

Braden nodded. 'Target's only 250 miles off the coast. But we're at EWGTW — emergency war gross takeoff weight. Why? We need all the safety margin we can get. First, we could underestimate loiter and length of the engagement. There could be a lot of looking and we don't know what we'll strike. Then we're in the middle of the Timor Sea and choice of pasture's severely limited.'

'Won't we be coming back here?'

'We might have to fly on to Singapore.'

'I've correlated load and temp,' Casey said, 'and we're fine. A four-prop would have severely limited low-altitude performance. But not an unmodified A with three.'

Braden smiled at that. The idealised gunship layout was seldom seen in operations and 'unmodified' was drawing a long bow.

'Endurance with this load,' Freddy added, 'is five hours at 10,000 feet. We're not pressurised and can't close our ports, so we've got the drag of our dicks hanging out and the gas we got now is it.'

'Why Singapore?' someone asked.

'Need to keep our options open,' Braden said. 'If we have to head north after the engagement, we'll be on LOX and at 28,000 feet. Doubles our endurance. I don't like ditching profiles. Three-metre swell with 4-metre waves. Equivalent to burial at sea. And we don't want to land sucking fumes.'

'Masks,' a gunner griped.

'Sorry, but as I recall, useful consciousness sitting quietly is a minute and a half before brain death.'

'He's been braindead for years,' someone jeered.

Elina was trying to understand it. 'You're saying you mightn't come back here?'

'We're Spectre crew, ma'am,' Freddy said. 'Like to put our arses on the line. Otherwise we would have jogged along at MAC driving C–141 Starlifters.'

'Now listen up,' Braden said. 'We'll acquire in the usual way with IR and Black Crow. Rules of engagement. First up, HEI so NOD can help me adjust for windage. Then, if we don't draw flak, we go to flares or switch from IR to white light.'

'Six million candle power should confuse 'em,' the IO yipped, and the others sent him up.

'What if you get so excited your pacemaker switches 'em on before we get there?'

'He can't hear you. Shout it into his good ear.'

'No time. He's due for another leak.'

And so it went on.

After all these years, a combat mission again!

Finally he told them Elina would be in the jump seat. He feared they'd see her as a jinx, but they were so up by then they dubbed her the mission mascot and gave her heavy-handed hugs.

When they could hear him once more, he said, 'Now, we're pushed for time. ETD one hour. So before we slip the surly bonds of earth and stagger off on silvered wings to ruin someone's day, remember, we need full operational efficiency. It's your last shot at this, guys. So stay on track.'

Preflights. Walk-arounds. Everything rechecked, shipshape, stowed. He strapped in, glanced at the overhead fuel panel. Loadings within limits — and a bit.

They spooled up. Thunder shook the ground. Engines at 100 per cent. Brakes off.

This was it.

The four-fan antiquity staggered into the air and, rivets straining, headed for the sea.

They entered cruise profile at a fuel-conserving speed below max and went to autopilot. With checklists and mayhem over, he glanced around the flight deck.

Elina, strapped in the jumpseat looked petrified. Near her, Casey was reviewing switch positions on his fuel and electrical panels and monitoring consumption.

'Cooling air and a 15-knot headwind,' the navigator said. His fingers strayed from his compass selector switch to the search radar, switched it back to warning position to recheck weather build-up.

Braden flicked his eyes forward to his duplicate display. 'Looks like it's clearing.'

The nav unglued his face from a viewing cowl. 'Affirmative. Dispersing.' He grinned. 'You believe this? In business again. Remember that truck convoy trapped in the defile?'

Braden remembered it well. The photo-recon showed fifty-three destroyed and seven damaged. They'd stayed on station to illuminate while F–4 escorts finished off the rest. Those poor stiffs on the Ho Chi Minh Trail had been chained to the steering columns to stop them deserting. When the trucks went up, they fried.

They'd done that job with their four 20-millimetre Vulcan cannons. He kicked himself for not installing 40-millimetre Bofors and thought of the later models with their 105-millimetre tank guns. As for the awesome contemporary gunships, they were still being refined. The new fire control system had dual target capability. They'd developed cool engine exhausts to deter heat-seeking infrared, had a high-intensity beam to blind missiles. DIRCM, LAIRCM . . .

'Colonel Braden?' Elina's tentative voice in the cans. Colonel! My God. It was the first time she'd tried that on him. 'Yes, ma'am.'

'With this kind of sea, do you think they'd risk taking the people off the sphere by helicopter?'

'No way.' As his eyes flicked back to his instruments, he wondered if the sphere would even show.

It didn't stack up. They were depending on the say-so of some psychic, tooling off to shoot up something that could still be under the sea.

The rig was the second problem. They didn't know anything about it. It could be packing RBS70s. Her threat profile was sketchy, too.

The sun had set and the horizon was a glow.

Well, they'd done what they could to be ready.

But ready for what?

70

TOMB

The tractor cabin was rapidly cooling and the humidity rising. He'd switched off exterior lights to save power. Senam sat by the dead body, watching him like a cornered rat. 'We die here. We die.'

'We will if you don't shut up.' He knew hypothermia could finish them before the last of the oxygen became toxic or before the fans and systems sucked the remaining power dry.

'If my children up there,' she sobbed, 'I not see them now. Not ever.'

In this extremity the real woman was appearing — not the calculating stunner but the grieving mother who'd become a frightened child herself. Chinese mothers, he'd read, taught their children *siao-sin* — 'make your heart small'. Asians were careful to preserve face. Did they suppress their inward feelings as well? Was that what she'd done all her terrible life?

He could think of nothing to comfort her. The craft was designed for one occupant, not three, and the lithium hydroxide indicator was already in the red.

He went mentally through the manual, meticulously and unerringly checking off every device in the cabin. Yes, everything he could see had been referred to or described. Except for one trifling thing — a dot of red beneath the black frame of the seat. Red meant caution. So . . .

He felt beneath the seat again and found a bar held by clips — a red crank handle with a large square socket at one end.

He knew immediately what it fitted, had seen the flanged bolt in a recess under the mat. He lifted the mat and connected the crank to the rusted male fitting which was covered by water condensed from the walls.

'What is it?' she said. 'What you do?'

'Don't know. Something drastic.'

The handle wasn't mentioned in the manual so had to be in the missing instructions. It seemed a crude item among all this technology. Designed for a last resort?

'What it do?' she asked again, teeth chattering.

'With luck, it releases the pressure hull and lets us float up to the surface.'

He turned the handle. The bolt was stiff. He kept turning. Nothing.

Nothing happened.

He cranked for at least five minutes. For four of those, the thing moved more easily. Finally he gave it up, looked at her and shrugged. 'I think we're rooted.'

A jerk.

Her eyes widened in terror.

He switched on the floodlights and peered out the port. They were still in one piece, sitting on the bottom.

So why the jerk? Nothing could have hit them.

A tearing sound. The cabin tilted to one side. The floodlights, interior lights and all panel illumination died. Blackness.

She screamed.

He knew precisely where the man had put his torch. He grabbed it and switched on. Their shadows danced as the floor tilted back the other way. He shone the light on the mechanical depth gauge. They were rising.

A rush of triumph. 'Going up. Hope you can swim.'

71

CONTACT

The gunship was cleared for action and holding at 10,000 feet. The weather had dispersed and there was hardly any moon.

The once young but now arthritic IO lay uncomfortably on the open ramp, secured by a length of cable designed to stop him flying out the back if they had to take evasive action to avoid unfriendly fire. In the old days, he'd spent a lot of time in mid-air. Which explained why his joints weren't good these days.

He'd extended the light-set along its shock-mounted guide-rails and rotated the head in the horizontal plane for training on the target. He operated the bulky device from its control panel directly on the ramp although there was a remote box on the flight deck. The two 20-kilowatt xenon lamps could be white or IR screened and he could zoom them to vary the beam spread. When both were on, the heat was like a cutting torch. When they reached the first location he went to IR and they searched in long circular sweeps. No one on sensors reported anything. He was cleared for white light.

He flicked the mode switch right to VISUAL and the lamps turned the night sea to daylight. He waited for the shockwave of an exploding SAM. And remembered with a shudder the AAA shell that, some generations of technology ago, had slammed into their rudder over Ubon. How Braden had got them down safely without rudder control he didn't know.

No SAMs appeared. No Triple A. No target.

Just empty angry sea.

They headed for the second location.

He switched the light-set off.

The NOD operator had a plastic heart-valve and an artificial hip-joint but tonight felt twenty again. He was glued to his huge starlight scope, which magnified ambient light up to 38,000 times and was mounted above a half-height armour-plated panel where the crew entrance door normally was. He twisted in his power-operated seat to look at the dials and needles on the SLADS display. His observation device was aligned with the other on-board sensors and the pilot's electronic gunsight.

'Coming up at ten o'clock.' A voice in the cans. FLR had acquired it but he couldn't see it yet. They had descended to 6000 feet, the useful altitude for 20 millimetres.

They went into a shallow bank.

Then he had it. A multitude of small lights roughly in a cube shape. Lights hooded from above, so not enough to blind him.

Braden's voice on the interphone: 'Tally-ho. NOD, pilot. Description when you can.'

'Pilot, NOD. Medium-sized oil rig with a ship like a big tug standing off. Ship has large flat rear deck-space with sloping chocks and derrick. The main crane of the oil rig's just lifted something off it.

A large round ball.' No other reports in the cans. The whole crew was listening. 'Ball-thing has hatch on top, lifting hooks, rails, ladder. Looks like they're swinging it inboard to the pipe well. Chopper on pad on top level. Rotor stopped and nav lights off. Pad reads: PACDRILL–1. Description ends. You copy?'

'Received.'

Jeez, Braden thought, she was right. The bloody sphere was there. It was a go. From the flight deck, he could see little more than the glow of the rig's lights. They weren't that visible from the air. Some kind of shielding? His brow furrowed and his stomach muscles tensed. It was like the old days. Braced for incoming. He looked back at Elina. 'So we do it?'

She stared back with an almost vacant expression as if examining some place inside herself, then slowly nodded. 'Hit everything.'

'Okay, guys. We whack the lot. Workboat, rig and chopper. Starting with the boat.'

In the hull of the big aircraft the gun crew were poised like rusty springs. They wore flak helmets and gloves and worked in red combat lighting. One man had a penlight between his teeth. False teeth, now. But so what?

On the flight deck, Freddy looked across at his commander with eyes that said, 'Jesus. You believe this?'

Braden gravely winked at him, not believing it himself. The buzz had him now. Their last amazing chance at action. Then he heard through the cans, 'NOD's on. Press the tit.' It was combat-speak for: target acquired and, when your gunsight is aligned with my sensor, you are clear to shoot.

The hairs rose on his neck. The entire operation

now depended on his side-looking gunsight which made him, in fact, the gunner. He centred the two pips in his sight and pushed the trigger button.

In the belly of the airframe the four 20-millimetre Vulcans, each with six counter-clockwise rotating barrels, opened up. Spent gold cartridges flew from their side-stripping disintegrating belts into shell bins. The uproar of the continuous broadside of 20 mike-mike was extreme.

Braden adjusted for the side-push of spewing metal. Flashes flickered on the left-hand window frames as he flew the bank angle, airspeed and altitude needed to match the guns.

The NOD operator had the grandstand view of the stream of fire focused on the ship. The heavy explosive rounds chopped up the deckhouse, then the aft deck. With luck, they could hole the thing or at least knock out the engines. Men were running, dying like ants. He'd seen this all before. He called it. 'Boat's going nowhere.'

The bedlam stopped. The Vulcan's bitter fumes filled the hold. Beneath his flak helmet, through sweaty earphones digging into his flesh, he heard Braden call for a heads-up.

He reported, 'Round ball's on the deck with people climbing out the top. And they're firing up the chopper.'

'Chopper's next.'

They went for it again. The helo shuddered, then exploded, part of the pad disintegrating with it. The tail of the burning airframe toppled into the sea.

'Chopper out.'

'We go for the sphere.'

He screened the crackle of voices. No SAM/AAA break calls. No alarm bell. No incoming or damage reports. Concentrating fire on the thick steel sphere wasn't that successful. Until a shell explosion inside it sent a glow of yellow through the hatch.

'Ball thing holed. Looked good.'

'Going for random fire at rig.'

Just about anything targeted seemed to explode. The tanks seemed full of fuel, not crude. On the higher decks near what looked like accommodation modules, people ran and fell on the walkways while, beneath them, sections of the structure blew out and fell burning to the sea.

Braden called it off but the Vulcans went berserk. The sheet of flame before the belts ran out lit the sky like the fourth of July. The interphone erupted.

'FCO, pilot. What the fuck . . . ?'

'Pilot, FCO. Circuit-breakers on the twenties shorted to closed position.'

Recoil had forced them up and to the right.

'Fuck!' He fought the controls.

The NOD operator had looked away from his scope so as not to be blinded for life. The last thing he'd seen was the huge main crane topple. The gantry had broken loose from its mounting to hang hook-end into the sea.

Incredible. Unbelievable. They'd whacked an oil rig. Christ!

Circuit breakers, Braden thought. Well, something on the old girl had to give. They resumed circling at 3000 feet and sprayed the carnage with the miniguns.

'NOD, pilot. BDA?'

'Total wreck. Blasted to hell.'

Still no threat calls. Damage report was nil.

'Observation run. Stand by for low level recce with white light.'

He took them down to eyeball the devastation. They didn't need the lights. Fires from the huge structure lit the sea, illuminating the wreckage around it. A fuel tank exploded, blasting a gap in several levels, and spewed out flaming metal that fell to flaming waves. The workboat was dead in the water, listing, drifting away.

Bodies in the water, possibly burned to death. No visible survivors. Not that you expected them to show themselves and wave.

Armageddon.

He broke off and banked right, exhausted by the intense concentration. 'Safe the guns. We're outta here.'

The engineer was checking fuel levels.

He heard an elated gunner in the cans. 'Got your shovel.' It was traditional for an officer to help shovel up the spent brass on the gundeck into the waiting canvas bags.

His gut was a knot. He looked at his hands, shaking now. He'd had it. They'd all had it. It was enough for one night.

He handed over to Freddy. 'Fuck Singapore. Take us back.'

He breathed out hard several times, pursing his lips, puffing his cheeks. Connie was right. He was too old for this. They were all too old. Relics — like the bird.

But fuck, they'd done it! Fuck!

He turned to Elina. 'Satisfied?'

She gave a tight nod.

And threw up.

72

RIG

Blake shivered in the tractor's pitch-black pressure hull. Cold had drained blood from his skin to feed his muscles and brain. He breathed fast. The air-supply had stopped and the rising carbon dioxide level had made him headachy, disoriented. For minutes they'd felt nothing. The capsule seemed suspended in oil. Then it clanged against something and reverberated like a gong.

A metallic scraping. Light filtered through the ports. Impossible. It was night.

The light intensified then was gone, leaving an orange glow. Enough to see.

Wave action again. They were almost to the surface. 'Hang on.'

A roll and stomach-loosening drop. The thing became a fairground ride. They were tossed sideways, tilted at 45 degrees. The tilt reversed and light slanted through the ports.

He felt a charge of elation. 'We're there.' He pulled down the simple metal ladder, mounted the first rung and spun the hatch wheel above. 'Big sea. And, when I open this, we could flood and go down like a stone. So you've got to get out soon as it's open. Understand?'

Her startled sob. 'You help me?'

Unequal air pressure stuck the hatch. He shoved it hard and his ears popped.

As he pushed it wide the rim became defined by the glow outside and the trickle on his face became a shower. The blissful shock of fresh salt air. And a shrieking noise he couldn't understand.

They rolled as sea poured in. He fell into knee-deep water. It was warmer than the capsule's frigid air. 'Out. Out. Go.'

She scrambled up the ladder and squeezed through the lurid circle just before another wave engulfed them. He fought up against a torrent, was half out when the capsule foundered. It was sucking him with it when a wave swept him free. He surfaced, lungs bursting, choking, squinted up at the light.

Far above him, perched on its massive four-column base, was the huge upper structure of the rig. Its levels blazed with fires. It appeared to have been bombed. The shrieks came from multiple sirens. As he rose on a wave he saw the flotsam-strewn ocean was aflame.

'Senam!' he bellowed.

Wind blew needles of spray in his face.

He had to get out of the water before the floating fire reached him.

A wave swamped him. Again he surfaced, coughing. Something bumped him. The torso of a man. Yellow helmet. No legs.

He stared up again at the massive supports. Walkways crossed the ponderous lower girders — at least 15 metres up.

Then he saw the crane's fallen gantry. It trailed in the sea like a ladder to the rig. It even had a walkway with rails on one side. They'd surfaced near it, had probably hit it.

He swam toward it but his legs felt waterlogged. It took him minutes of flailing to reach the metal spar. As he grabbed a bracing section, he was slapped by a whitecap. When the sea fell beneath him he saw a head and a raised hand.

Senam.

The next wave submerged them. When the water fell away, she was clinging to the section below him. He scrambled down to her. 'Hang on.'

Again they went under but, despite the shock of the waves, the huge boom barely moved.

They used the next trough to clamber higher. He realised he still had shoes — and why he couldn't swim. But now the squelching sneakers helped him climb. 'Got to get above the waves.'

Exhausted, battered, hauling on the hand-rails, they scrambled high enough to rest. Sea slammed and sucked below. A larger wave would reach them. He urged the terrified woman higher. 'Keep going up.'

He doubted she heard him above the sirens and roaring fire. She yelled something back. He urged her on, staying below her in case she faltered or slipped. The bottom level of the rig still looked impossibly far above.

Finally, they struggled over a rail onto the rig itself — a flaming junkyard of shattered pipes and metal. She swayed against him, shaking with fear and fatigue. 'My kids here? Alive in this?'

And Kate, he thought. Alive?

In this wreck?

An explosion. Fragments filled the sky but the sirens mercifully died. He hauled her under pipes that ran along a module wall. 'You right?'

She was shocked, unresponsive. She stared through the expanded steel-mesh walkway at the ocean heaving below. Her hands and feet bled and there was a ragged gash on her arm.

The metal wall behind them was an oven, its paint blistering with heat. He looked up at the succession of walkways to the higher levels. Walkways built of mild steel. Half, as far as he could see, were twisted scrap.

He said, 'Stay here. I'll come back for you.'

Her terrified look. 'Not leave me.'

'Keep behind me, then.' He moved further along. All he could think of was Kate.

They reached a body jammed half-through the railing. Beyond it was a set of intact stairs. They stepped over the corpse and went up. She called out something. It was drowned in the din. He looked back and waved her to follow.

Now he could see a horizontal rack holding drill-pipes. On top of them, surrounded by rubble, rested the remains of the sphere from Deep Six.

They passed the riser area that held pipes ready for the well-hole. Toppled lengths lay strewn like dropped straws. Flame roared from the smashed top of a gas cock. A module glowed dull-red with inner heat. In steaming mud slurry from a ruptured tank, bodies lay like fossil-art. He glanced at each apprehensively, hoping it wouldn't be her.

They climbed through a tangle of girders, ducked a shower of foul-smelling liquid. Breached fuel tanks flamed. A splintered lifeboat dangled from one davit over the sea. Near its lowering mechanism were the bodies of two armed men.

He examined one man's weapon. Crude all-metal design. Ancient. No flashguard. A venerable M3 grease gun. He'd seen an article on it in *Combat and*

Survival so knew its construction schematically. He opened the ejection-cover flange, reached for the peculiar cocking slot and fingered the heavy bolt back. He relieved the man of a combat pouch containing four long straight magazines.

He retrieved the other gun — a pump-action riot shotgun with cartridges clipped along its butt. He checked it had one in the breech, that the safety was off, and handed it to Senam. 'Come on. Got to keep going up.'

They passed the generator house. A section was blown out. Stripped electric cables sparked off a wall. Above them a blue light blinked. Among the rubble an engine still roared. Something dangled above an inferno — the hook of the drilling derrick. The metal tower reared toward the sky, stark in firelight, like the spire of a bombed church. They reached a control cabin. Its door was blown out and the roof above the consoles had caved in. They glimpsed crushed bodies, severed limbs. Jagged holes showed the force of the blast. From an attack? Explosion?

At the base of a flight of stairs, oil-grimed roughnecks lay like war dead. As they clambered over the bodies, flesh moved beneath their feet.

They reached the living areas. More bodies on the walkways. It was clear to him now that the modules had been riddled with large-calibre HE. A hail of cannon fire. From where? A gunboat? He couldn't work it out. An Apache's chaingun or an A10's GAU–8/A? It would have taken a flight of such aircraft to make this mess. And neither were maritime as far as he knew.

They rested for a moment on the deck outside the accommodation block. Its smouldering industrial nonslip was cratered. On these upper levels, the destruction was extreme. The main module was half flattened under the helipad and a ventilation trunk belched smoke and flames. A door hung by one hinge. Where were the rest of the crew? Dead? Crushed?

Movement. A shapeless figure in torn clothing, face blackened, one arm shredded.

Schumann.

The scientist touched a wall with his good arm, turned, staggered two steps from it, came back, touched it again. He appeared to be in meltdown, his compulsive habit continuous.

Senam raised her gun.

He said, 'Forget him. He's ratshit.'

Schumann here? Then Fong and Tritter were, too. 'Stay here while I recce.'

He climbed a last set of stairs toward the level below the helipad. Through blackened iron and twisted metal he saw the tailless burnt-out cabin of the chopper. Charred shapes hung through the window frames — barely recognisable as the pilots. He inched higher, soles sticking to hot metal, glanced below to check on Senam.

She was sheltering beside a cargo container, gun at the ready. And a wild-haired figure in shredded clothes was creeping toward her along the intersecting side.

Tan. He seemed unarmed.

Before he could wave to warn her, the man emerged from the corner.

She swung the gun onto him, her face contorted with hatred. Tan stopped, aghast, staring into the barrel of death. He instinctively crossed his arms as if to protect his chest.

Whatever she screamed at him was lost in the groan of rending metal, the snapping of tortured rivets, the roar of flames from burst pipes as a length of superstructure behind her fell outward to the sea.

Then the sounds of the stricken rig were punctuated by her gun.

Tan fell to his knees.

She pumped the action, fired again.

Tan collapsed like a rag-doll. Not satisfied, she kicked and kicked him.

Schumann. Tan. Who else? And where the hell did they keep the prisoners? Under the tangled metal covering the walkway he spotted a boat-shoe with an angled graze in the toe. A shoe Fong had worn on the island. Close to it was a combat boot attached to a black-clad leg. Fong and a bodyguard, both crushed.

He understood. The contingent from Deep Six were climbing up to the helipad when . . .

He stooped to peer beneath the wreckage. The bodyguard had been killed by small-arms fire. Fong had a bloody hole for one eye and a rail in the back of his skull.

He climbed the hot junk to what was left of the pad. It had been holed like a cheese grater and its net was white powder now. He examined broken bodies. Tritter wasn't there. There were two men killed by small-calibre bullets. And a third, still alive, had a blade in his ribs.

A tanto blade.

Mutiny on PACDRILL–1?

Blake shook the knifed man. 'What happened?'

The hallucinating agent thought he was one of his team. 'Got to take him out. Company signal. Change of plans. Take him out. Clean site.'

'Take out who? Tritter?'

The man nodded and gasped, 'Water.' Froth flecked his lips.

Water wouldn't help him.

'Where's the woman?'

'Woman?'

'Retki, the DEMI agent. And the kids?'

'Detainees in Module Ten.'

Jesus. His heart thumped. He backtracked to the lower deck, found Senam slumped against the container, staring at Tan. The *ipsissimus* of Infandus was unsuave at last in death. And Schumann, hearing and seeing nothing, still stumbled to and from his wall.

He pulled the woman up, retrieved the riot gun from the smoking deck and gave it to her. She went to the edge of the collapsed landing and tossed it into the sea, almost falling after it. He stared at her shivering back. She'd lost it.

He held his hand out gently to coax her back. She took it like a child. He led her from the jagged rent, searching his memory for somewhere safe to hide her. He'd seen a fire and blast wall between accommodation and production. Yes, the section near the drilling gear seemed less damaged.

Movement ahead.

Two more live ones! Shit!

Two men with carbines crouched near a half-open door. Painted beside the door were large numerals. A ten.

Was Kate in there?

He pulled Senam down behind a pipe stack.

Then, incredibly, a woman with a girl's lithe body came out of the module door.

For an instant, he thought it was her. But she was blonde and hobbled like a terrified hag. She screamed, 'Dolfie, where are you? Dolfie?' She didn't see the men. One fired a burst into her back. She pitched forward, lay in spasm.

Dolfie? Adolphous?

The second man stuck his gun around the lintel, sprayed a burst through the door then leaned back while the other ducked through. A yell that could have been the 'clear' call. Then both were inside. CIA plants, he thought.

He saw it now. Tritter had run out of allies. Including the CIA. And who was the still-jerking woman? Tritter's squeeze?

Automatic fire inside the module. Three quick bursts. Then nothing.

Tritter? They'd shot him?

Then why weren't they back?

He glanced at Senam. She cringed, fingers in her mouth. They waited behind the flaking pipes. It seemed forever and was probably two minutes.

Movement at the door base. A man dragging himself by the arms. The front of his overalls was bloodsoaked and his legs no longer worked. He had two carbines slung around his neck, his partner's and his own.

He bellowed for backup.

Some hope, Blake thought.

The man reached the shuddering woman, sat propped against her, facing the door. He'd have felt nothing when first hit. But now he held his side in agony. The intolerable pain had begun.

Had Tritter shot him? Then why hadn't he finished him off? And why had a dying man bothered to bring out his partner's gun?

The man's hands shook as he dragged out a battered cigarette pack. He lit up, then examined his wound. He bellowed, 'Fuck!'

He took hard draws on the fag, tried to move and couldn't. His head lolled, hand dropped. The cigarette fell from his fingers to the plating.

Blake signed to Senam to stay put. He broke cover

and dashed for the door — ducked in, M3 at the ready, and flattened himself against the wall.

He was in a wide rubber-carpeted corridor barely lit by flickering light. Doors on one side. Listening for movement was useless in the still humming, thumping space and with the bedlam outside. He kicked the first door wide.

A cabin with double bunk. Empty.

He moved on, totally alert.

In the third cabin along, the CIA man lay on the floor. Once again Blake thanked his recall. Hard to identify a man without a face.

Heart pounding, functioning on nerves, he rechecked the corridor.

Still empty.

He stepped cautiously out.

Something hard was shoved against his right kidney.

But there was nowhere a man could have come from. Then Tritter's hoarse, accented voice. 'Throw the gun in front of you.'

His blood drained to his feet. He closed the ejection cover, threw it ahead of him.

'Don't move.'

Tritter walked warily around him into view. He wore a bright orange survival suit, a backpack, held an Uzi. 'Just relax. Too much tension in the world.' He bent slowly, picked up the grease gun. 'Good. And all those magazines.' He pointed the crude pipe muzzle at Blake's chest. A flicker of surprise. 'You're the . . . How did you get here?'

Too shocked and breathless to answer, Blake stood panting, watching the man's eyes. The bearded face looked impassive but Tritter's body was tight with stress.

'Turn around. Slowly,' Tritter said.

He turned to face the far door. A hydrant cabinet stood at an angle from the wall.

'Monk's hole,' Tritter explained. 'Nothing like a custom-built oil rig. Well it's been quite a day — rich, one might say, with unsettling moments. But it's getting better. And, unfortunately for you, I now have a loaded weapon.' He lobbed the Uzi along the floor. 'I emptied that on colleagues who found me uncompromising. Your turn.'

Blake spun, punched, felt the man's nose-bone break. He kneed him in the groin, twisted the ugly weapon from him, flicked up the ejection cover and applied a burst to the belly. 'Gotcha.'

Tritter, face bloodied, fell back on folded knees, but his pack held him partly off the floor. He looked like a champion limbo dancer. Except for the lolling head.

He walked around so the bastard could see him. 'You're not too good with old guns. This flap doesn't fly up with back-pressure. It acts as a safety — locks the bolt in both the open and closed position.'

Tritter didn't comment. Fat .45s had rendered his interest in obsolete weapons academic.

Faint but unmistakable, the wail of a child.

The sound came from a padlocked end door. A metal door with an observation slot. He forced his weary frame forward, riddled the lock and threw the bolt.

Inside, at the far end of a bunk, two small petrified Asian children clutched each other.

He shuffled back to the outside door and waved at Senam to come then dragged back, almost out of puff.

Senam ran past him to the small face peeping from the cabin. The child saw its mother and shrieked.

He only had one thought now. The cries of Senam with her children became white noise.

He reached the second door and shot away the lock.

She was sitting impassively on the bunk staring at the wall. She wore dungarees and her hair had been shaved to her scalp. She didn't turn as he burst in.

'Kate?' He shook her, crouched beside her. 'Kate?'

She looked at him but said nothing. He couldn't see a mark on her. Had they tortured her out of her wits?

Shapes ducking through the door.

God, not more of them!

Armed troopers inside the cell. Rubber suits, Heckler and Koch, laser aimers . . .

One was a diver who'd ferried him from the boat in the Bay of Bengal. He raised his hands, yelled. 'Lynch. It's Blake.' The man looked at him keenly, 'Fuck me dead. Elina reported you MIA. But Ko didn't think so. Hale said to watch for you anyway.' He jerked his barrel at the glazed eyes of Kate. 'Is that . . .'

'Kate.'

'Jesus Christ!' He gave the second armed SEAL the thumbs up. 'Who's the fuck outside?'

'Tritter.'

'Nice one. So move it. We're pushing shit here.'

As he tried to help Kate she stood up. She walked to the door, looking at no one.

A yell from along the corridor. 'Clear.'

A diver was in the cell with Senam. She'd covered the cringing children with her body.

Blake called to her. 'It's okay.' He turned back to the divers. 'Good guys.'

Relief had brought exhaustion. His legs trembled. He could barely stand. Kate let him hold her and guide her but walked as if he wasn't there.

Tritter's legs shook in death-agony. A diver rolled the gagging man and pulled the backpack free.

Blake, blood draining from his head, steadied himself on a doorframe. 'For Chrissake, get us off this thing.'

73

SUB

In the cavern of the red-lit control room the only brightness came from system indicators and glowing VDUs.

Hale listened to the reports — thermal fix, keel depth, sonar. He read the transcript again — the boarding party's return-to-base signal. It reported Tritter dead. And, remarkably, Blake and Katherine alive. He said, 'We surface in ten minutes,' and ordered the sub's deployable tactical mast reeled down by its service cable. Not that an attack still concerned him. The US destroyers and the SSN had diverted far to the north and a coded VHF burst from Braden had confirmed their recall. There was no SOSUS here, no evidence of AWACS. But surfacing again was still a complex business.

'Keep 60 metres.'

'Forward and aft planes up five.'

The vast hull reached the ordered depth. Sonar searched for surface and subsurface contacts.

'Stand by stern arc clearance to port.'

'Port 60 degrees.'

Apollonov vetted the reports, delivered the all-clear.

'Stand by to return to PD. Ten up. Keep 18 metres.' As depths were called, Hale moved to the high-res display on the remote control console. The new optronic mast had multiple functions including ESM. 'Up mast.' He waited.

'And breaking.'

He checked the sweep. 'Burning rig and listing workboat. No other close contacts. Stand by warner clearance ESM.'

The check for dangerous 'rackets'. The wait for warner clearance.

'Captain, ESM. Two sweeps low power. Racket 58 WCSN type 1006, associated with merchantman, bearing 230 60db. End of report.'

Hale switched the attack scope to thermal. 'Returning boats approaching. Two hundred metres. OOW, man the tower.'

The officer of the watch scrambled.

'And . . . stand by to surface.'

All positions readied themselves.

'Surface blow main ballast.'

Over the familiar calls, he barked, 'Yuri has the conn. Captain to bridge.'

When they were on the roof and rolling, he climbed to the bridge, breathed in the salt-sticky night and looked along the casing to the bulbous foam-ringed nose. He listened to the repeater relaying orders from below. 'Right 5 degree rudder, stop main engines. Boat transfer party stand by forward casing. Update inertials.'

The fin towered 14 metres above the sea and half that height was the giant hull's freeboard. So, despite the swell, he was high enough to spot the squad approaching. The sophisticated boats would now be fully inflated. He steadied his night-scope on the weather-shield. Yes, two powering on a crest. And behind them, in the distance, the rig flaming like a torch.

He turned to the OOW. 'All present and correct.'

'Interesting evening, sir.'

'Very. And when we pick them up, it'll get more interesting still.'

The divers passed the sodden children down the access hatch. Then Senam, Kate and Schumann. Then the soaked and filthy Blake.

Blake swayed against a bank of gauges as the sub rolled with the swell, feeling an enormous sense of deflation.

She'd said nothing to him. Nothing.

As if she didn't recognise him.

Gordon Kelly, the COB, grinned at them. 'Still alive, you buggers?' Then frowned as he saw Kate's blank stare.

Blake shoved Tritter's backpack at the Scotsman's chest. 'That's for Hale.'

'What's up with Kate?'

'She's out of it. I don't know what they've done to her.'

'We'll handle it. Get her to the MO.'

Next, he peered at the saucer-eyed children clinging to their mother's legs. 'And here we have . . . ?'

'A family,' Blake said.

'Pre-school's over for the day.'

'Very amusing. They've been through hell. So find them something better than hot-bunking.'

Schumann, the fourth guest puddling the nonslip, had said nothing since they'd found him. He'd compulsively touched the boat's control pedestal on the way from the rig but the sub confused him. Its systems, exposed for access, offered no flat surface.

So he'd fixated on the Russian-labelled cover of a switchbox.

Kelly said, 'Who's crazy-man?'

'He's hard evidence. Lock him up.'

Kelly nodded to the divers. 'MO for him, too. Then the brig.'

As Kate and Schumann were taken along the humming passage, Senam looked up at Blake, eyes wet, and hugged him. 'I not know how thank you. You not know . . .'

He said, 'I'm thrilled for you.'

Kelly led the family off through the nightless labyrinth. The children still clung to their mother and one glanced back at him, thumb in mouth. It was appreciation enough. He turned and walked the other way.

By then the boat was deep and steady. Aching in every muscle, eyes gritty with fatigue, he trudged through its entrails and climbed down two levels to the racks. He showered at regulation-defying length, dried and patched his still-bleeding cuts as best he could, selected dry clothes from the dead men's locker . . .

'They want you now. Ko's cabin.' The ubiquitous Kelly again.

He dragged on the ill-fitting clothes. Shoes were impossible so he settled for bare feet.

There was a red light above Ko's door. He looked into the security camera, pressed the button on the indicator panel and Hale's voice crackled from the speaker. 'Won't be a moment, Colin.'

But it was twenty minutes before the light went green. The Captain opened the door. 'Sorry about that.'

As he sat on a vacant cushion, he noticed blood spotting through his sleeve.

Ko's strange energy filled the room. Finally, he

nodded to Hale who turned to Blake and briefly told him about Elina, Braden and the gunship. 'We've also examined Tritter's pack.'

'Any use?'

'It's damning. Formulas, methods. Correspondence with Stone, batch results, strategies, contacts, money trail . . .'

'Good.'

'Tremendous, actually. We can now expose all the people behind the project — which would have wiped out Asia. You've done a great job.'

He shrugged, worrying about Kate.

'We're standing off Deep Six now. And we need to know the situation inside it.'

He told them about the caisson. His eyes kept closing.

'We've detected two small explosions coming from it. It's hard for sonar to hear through all that concrete but any sounds we were picking up have stopped. There was a reference in Tritter's papers to a fall-back plan — using nerve gas to rub out eye-witnesses without destroying the facility.'

'I reckon they started that while I was there.'

'So do we assume everyone's dead?'

'Tough call, but I'd say yes.'

Hale turned respectfully to the monk. 'We need to get off the shelf, sir. Do I have your permission to torpedo the caisson?'

Ko nodded and Hale went.

Blake half-rose to follow but Ko's finger pointed him back to the cushion. He swayed, the tiredness irresistible.

Ko was looking at him — a look that seemed to emanate from the edge of the universe.

His head fell forward, waking him with a jerk. 'So. Did any of this make sense?'

'To save a continent from a deadly virus?' Ko said quietly. 'That makes sense.'

'All I care about is Kate. I don't know what they've done to her. She doesn't say a word.' The stupid tears came.

'It may be too late for her now.'

'Too late?'

'There are some things you can't mend. Get those cuts looked at. Then get some sleep.'

In the control room, commands, responses.

'Left standard rudder. Steer two-six-zero.'

'Steady on two-six-zero, sir.'

'WSC, Control. Flood three and four tubes.'

'Control, WSC. Flood three and four tubes aye.'

'Commence sequence.'

Behind the glowing screens surrounded by illuminated switches, the fire control team concentrated on their work. Their system now integrated all sensors on the boat, computed optimum target engagement and weapon pre-settings.

But Hale, despite his experience, was unused to actual attacks. His boat was more command centre and refuge than a weapon. Since the sub had been converted it had been used offensively once. Most of the missile tubes were filled with stores and food. But the old Mongo still had torpedoes. And firing drills were regular and thorough.

'Control, WSC. Three and four tubes flooded and ready.'

They rechecked target parameters, depth, speed, sonar type, frequency, background noise . . . With a fixed target, not much applied and TMA — target motion analysis — was superfluous.

'Stand by, three and four tubes.'

'Range 2600. Target speed zero.'

'Quite.' The situation display underlit Hale's wry expression. 'As it's over a million tonnes I doubt it's making much headway.'

Since they'd entered these waters, their arrays had detected no active sonar. No government now seemed interested in anything they did to Deep Six. But the absence of an exterior threat meant an exceedingly cold kill.

'Fire control, do we have a solution?'

'Solution acquired. Master contact zero-one bearing 250, range 2500, speed zero. Bearing rates match.' Range and settings were repeated. 'Computer set.'

A rating flicked a switch from safe to fire and held his finger over a button.

'Fire three and four tubes.'

The finger pushed.

The hull barely trembled as the active/passive homing torpedoes were expelled from their now open tubes.

'Torpedoes running.'

The sonar operator listened to the whine as they raced toward their mark.

'Discharge heard. Sonars blanked.'

'Helm left full rudder.'

The torpedoes — now actively homing, conventional warheads armed — churned unerringly through utter darkness to the monolith. When they hit, shaped conventional charges in their nose-cones shattered the concrete with red-hot slugs.

The holes were smaller than those blown in the side of a ship or submarine but destruction of integrity and water pressure did the rest. A section of the crippled structure began to collapse like a dynamited chimney. Back in the sonar man's earphones, it became a series of dull bangs and crackles.

The citadel crumbled on its base, slowly slightly inclined. A million plus tonnes of concrete imploded and fell in slow motion to the seabed.

Hits were recorded. The attack assessed.

Continuing echoes were mirrored in the sonar operator's face.

A shockwave rocked the 13,500-tonne boat.

No point in surfacing. Nothing to see.

Apollonov confirmed the new course and glanced at his skipper.

Hale, anxious to get off the conshelf, ordered, 'Full ahead.'

74

KATE

Kelly told Blake that Kate seemed physically unharmed. 'She seems to be in shock and they've sedated her. The best you can do is get some rest yourself.'

He went down to the racks, slept for twelve hours, got something to eat. Then he climbed up two levels to the control room and asked Hale if he could see her.

'Not yet, old chap. I'm sorry. I'll let you know when you can.'

To distract himself from worrying about her, he made an attempt to work out what Jason had typed into his notebook computer in the plane. He borrowed a similar machine and asked a crew member to help. They went to the torpedo room, the only space big enough to position the man at the angle and distance Jason had been from him in the aircraft. He painstakingly told the crew member which fingers to move and where, then got him to call out the keys he touched so he could write them down. He knew the sequence wouldn't be accurate but that he could piece it together later by looking at the surrounding keys and making an educated guess.

The emerging text proved useless. Jason was updating his CV. He called the experiment off and went back to fretting about Kate.

It was thirty-two hours before they let him see her.

When he entered the pocket surgery, the MO said, 'She seems better. But we haven't got anything out of her. Don't expect much.'

She was in the cramped two-bunk annexe, propped in the lower bunk, staring at nothing.

'Kate?'

She turned but her face remained expressionless as if the intelligence had gone out of it.

'Do you know me?'

'You're Colin.' Toneless.

'What did they do to you?' He took her hand.

'I don't know.'

'You can't remember?'

'I don't know. Why do you all keep asking me questions?'

'Do you know where you are?'

'In the sub.'

'I've been through hell since they took you. Thought you were dead or they were tearing you apart . . .'

Her other hand plucked at the cotton blanket as if it interested her.

He grabbed both her hands impulsively. 'Kate?'

She didn't respond.

He kissed her, tried to engage her, but she was emotionless. There was no inner contact at all.

Before he left, he said, 'Is there anything I can get you?'

She looked at him for some seconds. 'I think . . . I'd like . . .' she seemed to be trying to remember a word, '. . . a pear.'

As he went back through the surgery, the MO said, 'It may take some time.'

'Have you any idea what they've done to her?'

'I deal with burns, cuts and bullet wounds here. They don't supply CAT scanners on subs. But she's okay physically. And when we get her back, we'll see.'

Kelly was coming along the passage. 'The CO wants to see you. He's in his cabin.'

He went up one deck to Hale's cabin, the one adjacent to Ko's.

Hale let him in. 'You saw her?'

He nodded. 'What have they done to her? God! It's like she's not there.'

'I don't think she is. I've gone over your report on the Kansas project. I'm wondering if it's something to do with that.' The annunciator winked on the wall and a buzzer sounded. He picked up a handset. 'Hale.' He listened for a moment, frowned. 'Arm the squad and search the whole boat.' He pressed a button. 'CO. General alarm. A diver's been stabbed and a sub-machine-gun and a silencer stolen from the armoury. Security will monitor all bulkhead doors. Section alert.' Another light winked. 'Hale . . . So we're looking for Retki . . . Because they must have programmed her somehow.' He turned back to Blake. 'She's broken the MO's neck and gone.'

'Kate?'

'She's also knifed a diver and taken his clothes. We've got a human bomb on board. God knows what they've programmed her to do.' He unlocked a drawer and lifted out an automatic pistol. 'You stay here.' He opened the cabin door.

As he stepped into the passageway, Blake heard the crack of the automatic, then the stutter of a silenced gun.

Through the gap, he glimpsed Hale's flannels. And blood spotting the rubber matting.

As the captain collapsed outside the door, a dark shape brushed past.

A second muffled burst.

Then a bang. As if a door was being kicked in.

He picked up the intercom handset. 'It's Blake, in the CO's cabin. Kate's shot him. Security to Ko. Immediate.'

He got to the door, hesitated, listening.

Just the blowers and hum of the systems. He had no doubt she'd shoot him, too.

He got behind the door.

Just as she kicked it wide.

But he grabbed the squat end of the silencer, before she could spray him, and twisted it up.

Her eyes in the slit of the black balaclava were dead-looking, murderous.

She kicked him in the balls. He grunted as the pain shot through him but knew if he let go, he died. He clung to the warm cylinder, legs buckling, staggered against the bunk.

Ko's voice in the corridor. 'Julian?'

Her head jerked around and she fought with enormous strength for the gun. A burst chopped into the overhead and sparks flew from severed wiring.

She kneed him in the gut. Wind exploded out of him.

Before he fell, she was out the door.

A rattle of fire. Unsilenced.

A return burst from the silenced gun.

As he writhed on his knees, he saw her framed in the doorway, shuddering as rounds chopped into her. But she didn't fall. Just turned a little unsteadily and fired back along the passage.

Then nothing.

Two black shapes passing.

Another rattle of unsilenced fire.

Aching and almost retching, he crawled to the door.

Her gun lay on the matting. She was propped against an electrical cabinet. Blood had drenched the front of her SEAL suit. Her eyes still showed no expression.

A clearance diver bled on the floor of the passage near Hale. The second had her covered and a third was hurrying up. The men, who doubled as security, couldn't understand why she still stood.

'Kate!' The word burst from him, agonised.

She stared at him blankly, then crumpled.

As if switched off.

As a diver scooped up her gun, Ko stepped from a door further down and joined the divers by the bodies of the men.

Blake crawled to her and held her. Her blood soaked into his borrowed clothes — clothes from the dead men's locker.

He felt too numb to cry.

75

END GAME

The crew of the sub passed the news from watch to watch. Apollonov took command and announced they'd surface to rendezvous with a ship.

Blake was summoned again to Ko's cabin. This time there was no good-natured Hale to moderate. But the third cushion remained, perhaps as a mark of respect.

Ko said, 'I've read your report. Thank you. Very helpful.' He touched a battered shape beside him — Tritter's backpack. 'I want you to take this to Elina. She's sailing out to meet us tonight. Then she'll be flying back to Washington with Braden for a closed session with the President.'

He nodded.

'I'm sorry you were put through this.'

He found it hard to look at the monk. 'I'm past the point of cutting my throat. I'm even glad, in a way, that she died.'

'I think she died some time ago.'

'So do I. Which doesn't make it easier.'

'No.' Ko nodded slowly. 'Impossible to be objective in matters of the heart. That's why lovers should be forgiven for the tragedies they create.'

He saw her again in perfect detail, fighting him, dying in the passage. 'I joined DEMI because of her. But after this . . .' He swallowed.

'Of course.'

He fought the tears. 'It . . . hurts so much.'

Ko stared for some time at the wall. Its Formica lining had bellied slightly, which happened in places when the hull was under pressure. Finally, he said, 'You're grieving. And nothing I can say will help.'

'So say it anyway.'

'It won't help.'

'I need to talk to someone.'

'Of course. But I'm the wrong person.'

'You were her teacher.'

He sighed. 'But, you see, I view human love as a myth that causes suffering. People idolise their suffering which is mostly based on ego. And ego is resistance to what is. We crave continuity, fulfilment. And that stops us knowing our lives now.'

'She said something like that once. I remember everything she did and said. I was talking about the life we'd have together. She said, "Don't want. Don't hope. Don't fear. Just be."'

'It's true. We try to fix things from the outside. But the real warfare's inner.'

'Hard to see it that way when they're shooting at you.'

Ko smiled. 'Or pushing a poker through your arm.'

The incident in Bhutan played through his mind in vivid colour. He smelt Ko's searing flesh, knew the monk embodied what he taught. 'Perhaps one day . . .'

Ko raised an eyebrow.

'. . . I can live the way she wanted me to.'

'But you need to do that for yourself. Not for her.'

'Do what? I don't even know what to do.'

'Live now.' A sad smile. 'Living now's the hardest thing.'

'I don't understand what that means.'

'To move from knowing a thing to being the knowing itself. It takes years to understand.'

'So help me.'

'You can't help people. That's one of the most difficult things to bear.' Ko lifted the backpack and placed it between them, paused as if unsatisfied with what he'd said. 'Psychological death is the present. Dying to yourself each moment until there's no person left and no time. Just the energy of naked observation. At that level, attention is virtue.'

'You mean empty my mind?'

'Can you do it?'

'No.'

'Because the way to do — is to be.'

'I know you think I'm stroppy. But it's because I never understand what you're saying.'

'But suddenly you're ready to listen, and that's already a big change. So you've come some distance. It sounds cold-hearted, but her death's helped you.'

He covered his face with his hands. 'Why do you bother with me?'

'If people are sincere, you have to respond. And you may not understand what I say yet — but you'll remember.' He passed across the backpack, radiating affection. 'So can you put up with us a little longer?'

Ko had finally met him as a friend and he felt grateful. 'If you can put up with me.'

Ko gripped his shoulder. 'Good. Very, very good. Now you need to see Kelly and get ready for the transfer. We surface in half an hour.'

A pitch-black night. The ship was an old freighter. It had just enough way on it to hold its nose into the chop. As the inflatable bumped against the side, he lunged for the rope ladder. He struggled up the rungs, grazing his knuckles on the rusted plates, heard the muffled motors of the commando boat putter as it headed back to the sub. A wave drenched him and tugged at the backpack. Pale faces stared down. Rough hands pulled him over the bulwark. His shoes squelched on the metal deck.

Elina said, 'I never thought I'd see you again.'

'Which means you were happy to send me on a one-way trip.' He shrugged off the backpack and handed it over.

'I had a job to do, Colin.' Her eyes showed instant hurt, as if he'd betrayed her.

When he got dry and joined her in her cabin, the backpack's contents were spread across the bed. She said, 'This stuff's incredible.'

'Should help Jessop shaft a few people.'

'With this he can purge the administration — even outflank the Congress if he wants to.'

'Sorry I yelled at you up there. It wasn't fair. I'd have gone through hell for Kate.'

'It's all right,' she mumbled, looking uncomfortable. 'It's not easy sending people into danger. And it's harder when you're a woman. It's been tough for me too, just so you know.'

It was best to change the subject. 'They filled me in on Braden and his gunship. You certainly made a mess of that rig!'

'Yes, we couldn't have pulled it off without him.'

'Why didn't you tell me you'd . . .'

'Need to know. If they'd tortured you . . .'

She was right, of course. He noticed her fingernail was growing again. She looked very feminine tonight, had done something to her hair which, at such a time, struck him as odd.

'Braden's quite a character.'

She smiled. 'He seems so gruff but he's a dear. We're all amazed you got out of Deep Six. You even found Senam's kids.'

'What happens to her?'

'We'll set her up in Osaka. Lots of Koreans there.' She came to him and took his hands. 'I'm so terribly sorry about Katherine. It's appalling. You must feel . . .' Impulsively, she hugged him.

He held her tentatively, enjoying her warmth. 'Why's everyone nice to me suddenly? Even Ko's being half decent.'

She held him off at arm's length. 'Has it occurred to you that I might . . . like you?'

It hadn't. 'No.'

'Men,' she moved back against him, 'are so dumb.'

76

STONE

William Stone left the boxes in the car. He had the rest of his life to unload them. To unload the trophies, the books, the contents of his desk drawers. He'd destroyed the incriminating files they hadn't found.

The security men, who were packing their equipment to leave the house, told him his wife was at *a cappella* class. Her absence never worried him. It was her presence he deplored. And if music removed that burden, then it had a function after all.

He undressed in his overneat separate bedroom, a man severed from his career. A man void of responsibilities. A man who had been fired. As had Treloar, Pollock and thirty-six others. He'd found the news of Tritter's death amusing. But, on balance, it had been a degrading day.

He chose the master bathroom, less constricted than the rest, longing for small comforts. The touch of hot water and the sweet slime of soap.

He was about to have a shower when he noticed the peculiar bottles his wife kept on the room-length vanity — an example of female suggestibility he'd ignored a thousand times.

He picked one up.

Madame De Pompadour Foaming Bath Salts.

Since childhood, he'd never had a bath.

He removed the top, sniffed the blue gel. It stank of opportunity.

He ran the bath too long, thinking how wise they'd all been. But their foresight was now tagged genocide which he considered a synonym for war. For a soft, effective, cleansing war. But Jessop didn't understand — saw them as patriotism's scoundrels. 'Be not righteous overmuch,' said the preacher. Such wisdom. Such insight.

He tested the water — perfect — turned off the taps, read the label on the bottle. No recommended quantity mentioned. Just mellifluous nonsense. *Enriched with terebinth and thyme.* Wasn't terebinth another name for turps? He emptied the bottle into the bath, added himself. His displacement almost filled it.

Joy enclosed him. He wriggled his thin frame. No moderate comfort, this. The thick scented bubble-layer foamed from the overdosed bath and carpeted the floor-tiles. He found that droll.

He made a circle with finger and thumb and gently blew.

A bubble grew — expanded into a shimmering foot-wide orb. Then it rose in hot air and hung above him, reducing the world to a gossamer sphere.

Thrilled, he watched it rise.

He felt enormously, irrationally content.

77

DELIVERY

In the security room of Braden's mansion, they monitored the transfer.

The van at the main gate looked ordinary enough. But with its outriders and Special Group escort, it was commotion city out there. And the one person oblivious to the whole production number was Braden.

Stick watched the solarium's VDU. The boss was still in his favourite cane chair, planning the surprise party for his gunship crew.

And that was where they wanted him.

Because this was the day.

Stick eyeballed the other displays. They'd let the van through the perimeter gate and were checking it with detectors and dogs. He'd put fifty men on this project, had been planning it for a week. So far everything looked kosher. But you could never drop your guard.

He swivelled his eyes to the indoor pool monitor. Yes, Connie was still in position. And, if Braden left his chair, her task was to steer him back.

The threat to Braden was no longer extreme but they still had primary and secondary defences. So in the unlikely event that the van had been accompanied by assassins, and not legitimate government employees . . . He drummed his fingers on his M–4.

Buick was at the gate, handling the business end. He'd corralled the truck outside the inner security barrier, then checked it with the short-wavelength radar imager, the thermal infrared signature detector and the new backscatter X-ray unit. He was now insisting they fully unwrap the item for inspection.

Next, the men who had to lug the thing were relieved of weapons. The mountainous black man was intimidatingly thorough. Finally he gave the thumbs-up. 'Detail cleared to enter.'

'Got the card?'

'Yaybo.' The huge bodyguard held it up to a camera.

The control room staff opened the inner gate. The compound guards took over. They were taking no chances and still had four snipers concealed along the route.

The detail looked like a centipede. It took ten men to carry the thing.

Stick scanned the monitors again. Buick had led them around the left of the main building so that Braden couldn't see them. He had to get it arranged and get the card to Connie. And if Braden sussed something or moved, the entire operation fizzled.

But Braden remained buried in his project.

'Delivery positioned. Fuck! Where's Connie?'

A guard pointed to a monitor.

Ah, yes. She'd nipped out to Buick. It was looking good. He bent to the mike and hissed at her, 'Ready to roll, Miss Sefton? You got the card?'

She waved it at the security camera.

He flicked down the audio master-switch. 'In position and all standing by. Well done, guys. Aaaaaaand . . . we have go.' Braden chuckled. It was going to be amazing. The flight to a secret location — the entertainment, celebrity guests, cash bonus . . . The guys wouldn't know what'd hit them.

Connie tapped his shoulder.

He looked up, 'Hello, beautiful. Listen to this. I've got the photo-recon. And if I can wangle an on-the-spot video of the shot-up rig, we could . . .'

'Can you tear yourself away for a moment?'

'What's up?'

'Just something I want you to see.'

'Like what?'

'Don't fuss. Just come along.'

He stood up, scattering papers. She gripped his sleeve, led him around the colonnade and out to the terrace.

And he saw it!

She smiled at his expression. 'I don't know where we'll put it. Perhaps you could build a special room.' She handed him a card with the Presidential Seal on the front.

It read:

> How can I ever thank you? How can your country ever thank you? Because, Chuck, what you've done can never be publicly exposed. All I can think of is this.
>
> It's yours — with affection always. And my deepest gratitude.
>
> Dougie

'Oh, Christ,' he spluttered. 'Oh, Christ.'

She tenderly stroked his hair.

He looked at the resplendent oval — the wonderful rug — and sobbed.

Author's Note

Any story set in many countries becomes a spelling and terms conundrum. American spelling has 'defense' not 'defence', 'license' not 'licence' and so on. Then there is measurement. America remains imperial and US aircraft manuals perpetuate their system. Shipping and particularly aircraft now use a curious mix — knots for speed and windspeed, feet, metres, nautical miles. Runways in Australia are measured in feet but visibility in kilometres. Small boats are still measured in feet but Lloyds registers shipping in metres. Different flight zones require one system or the other. I use both, adjusting for context and the mindset of the characters, and hope this will not offend. A glossary is provided for acronyms, military or scientific terms.

Acknowledgments

My thanks to the experts who nudged this book toward credulity.

First the warriors. For C–130 gunship information I am indebted to Gerald Harris — 17th Squadron USAF (Major Rtd). Without his help, enthusiasm and encouragement key scenes could not have been written. He will, sadly, never read the gunship book he always urged me to do as he died before it could be published. My thanks to Daniel Brooks — Captain 17th Squadron USAF and now Logistics Engineer for Lockheed — for stalwart help on flight deck procedures and more. Thanks to FSGT Brian Castelijn, RAAF. And to CPOCIS4SM Colin Coke, Chief of the Boat HMAS *Dechaineux*, 2000–2002, for submarine ops fine-tuning. Acknowledgment also to the Spectre Association.

Bhutanese atmosphere came from globe-hiking mathematician, Jill Paillas. American sections were vetted by Brian Brennan, Dorothy Mead, Richard Meisel and Ann Read. Siobhan McCammon and Richard Spear checked English scenes. Professor William J. O'Sullivan honed my arabesques on chemistry, quantum physics and viruses. Nanotechnology scientist Geoffrey Baxter tweaked flights of fancy in that area. Achim Albers corrected the German, James Moore the Latin. Swissair's Peter Bolz graciously fine-tuned Cargologic details. I was helped by the Derby Visitor Centre, articles on biological warfare in *IDR* and by Rodney A. Brooks' book *Robot*. Di Morgan provided her usual penetrating refinements to the draft.

Glossary

109–B Ground surveillance radar.

AAA Anti-aircraft artillery.

AC–130A Gunship 2 Presumed designation of Braden's World War Two gunship. A gunship is basically a transport aircraft adapted to carry artillery and heavy automatic weapons. Gunships, while slow and vulnerable, have proved so effective that this apparently ramshackle concept shows no sign of being superseded. (*See*: Gunship.)

AEHF Advanced extremely high frequency satellite providing secure high-bandwidth communications — follow-on system to replenish the extensive Milstar programs.

AFB Air force base.

Air America A CIA-financed airline.

Anechoic tiles Submarines can be tiled to reduce their noise signature — the incident energy produced by enemy active sonar equipment. There are also decoupling or dampening tiles designed to reduce machinery-induced noise radiated into the water.

ANG US Air National Guard.

Antigenic drift Occurs when viral hemagglutinin changes its amino acid composition because of mutations and protection against the immune system is gradually lost.

Arcs Established fields of fire for each weapon.

Astra SPX Business jet.

ASW Anti-submarine warfare.

ATGM Anti-tank guided missile.

AWACS Airborne warning and control system (aircraft).

B–1 The bomber originally intended to replace the B–52. It developed into a low-level penetrator of startling potential and cost.

B–2 Stealth bomber with flying-wing configuration.

B61–11 A ground-penetrating nuclear warhead with great advantages over non-penetrating predecessors.

Bacteriophages An old concept, now revisited, with the potential to replace antibiotics.

Bats Freight aircraft generally fly at night.

BDA Bomb damage assessment.

Bends Decompression sickness. Breathing air in the high ambient pressure underwater causes blood and tissue to accumulate nitrogen and other inert gasses. Decreasing that pressure can be fatal without graduated decompression.

BG Bomber group.

Bhutan A mountainous land at the foot of the Himalayas — slightly larger than Switzerland but with a sixth of its population.

Bint Arabic for a 'woman of easy virtue'.

Black Crow An early gunship system that detected the ignition pulses of gasoline engines.

Black Hawk Air assault and military helicopter.

BLU–116/B Lockheed Martin advanced unitary penetrator warhead, probably on a GBU–24 laser-guided bomb with a hard-target smart fuse.

Cannons — airborne Both the Apache attack helicopter and the A10 'Warthog' anti-tank aircraft have 30mm cannons.

Chhang Local mild beer consumed in Bhutan.

China — GPS Chinese GPS satellites probably use WAAS (wide area augmentation system) technology. If so, China could continue to use Navstar GPS in wartime, even if the US tries to block access.

CIA Central Intelligence Agency, also known as 'the Company'.

CISS Centre for International and Strategic Studies.

Civpol Civilian police. Civilian security forces are now seen as a better solution than the military for peacekeeping and civil control.

Clare Valley A wine-growing area in South Australia. If interested in Blake's previous adventures, read *The Fourth Eye*.

COB Chief of the boat. Generally a chief petty officer. Interface between officers and ratings.

Code clicks Field communications sometimes use button-click signals rather than voice.

CPO Close protection officer. Bodyguard.

Cytonavigation Functional: in which devices detect variations in their environment and congregate where a defined set of preconditions exist.

DARPA Defense Advanced Research Projects Agency.

DCI Director of Central Intelligence, CIA — an unenviable office because it lacks a military, political or industrial powerbase.

Death zone Most dangerous area on Everest. Above camp six.

DEMI Defence against Enslavement through Manipulation of Information — a fictional non-aligned incursion force funded by a consortium of Western philanthropists, retired ex-judges, ministers, senior ranks in the services and other prominent concerned citizens. See the first Colin Blake adventure, *The Fourth Eye*.

DIA Defence Intelligence Agency.

Diapedesis Passage through walls of blood vessels into surrounding tissues.

DIRCM Directional infrared countermeasures system.

Ditching C–130 Few crew members have survived a deep-water ditching in C–130.

DMSP Defence meteorological satellite program.

Dong Feng Chinese missiles.

DSCS Defence satellite communications system, the backbone of US national security satellite communications, involving the largest number of satellite ground terminals around the world. Many terminals are relay stations which exclude host countries from the information. Major stations have cipher and communications rooms off limits to host nations, even though such stations may be targets during a nuclear exchange. DSCS provides secure voice and high data rates in the SHF band.

DSN Defence switching network.

DSP Defence support program. A system designed to provide strategic and tactical warning of ballistic missile attack. Also Deputy for Special Projects.

Dzong Traditional fortified castle, Bhutan.

Dzongkha A Tibetan dialect and the official language of Bhutan. The written language is identical to Tibetan.

Echelon Eavesdropping network involving the USA, Britain and other Anglo-Saxon countries. Watches for key words in phone, fax, internet and route-intercepted messages. The NSA, reputedly, ensures that most of the information is unseen by the other participating countries.

ESM Electronic support measures — intercept.

ETA Estimated time of arrival.

ETD Estimated time of departure.

Eukaryote An organism with a true nucleus. The higher form referred to is mammals. Most genes in mammals are discontinuous.

EWGTW Emergency war gross takeoff weight.

ex vivo Out of (outside) the living body. Contrast with *in vivo*, within the body, and *in vitro*, within glass (a culture dish or test tube).

FCO Fire control officer.

Fin UK parlance for submarine conning tower. American term is 'sail'.

FLR Forward-looking radar.

FLIR Forward-looking infrared.

FLTSATCOM Fleet satellite communications.

Flu virus Flu has long been considered a feasible airborne carrier for a biological weapon. Its surface antigens, the proteins visible to the immune system, constantly mutate — antigenic drift.

FMC Flight management computers.

FOAS Future offensive aircraft system.

Fort Meade The Maryland headquarters of the NSA.

Frag Fragmentation grenade. Many have scored 'chocolate bar' serrations.

Fulbright His 'impotence of power' thesis suggested that there are political complexities in far-away countries to which military power is an inappropriate and costly response.

Galileo The Galileo satellite network is designed to give European nations command over their own sat-nav system.

GB Sarin gas.

GE Genetic engineering.

Gita The Hindu holy book, the *Bhagavad Gita*, forms part of the *Mahabharata* epic.

GPS Global position system.

GPWS Ground proximity warning system, which incorporates visual coloured map displays with aural warnings.

GTC Gas turbine compressor (auxiliary power unit).

Gunship In this story, a C–130 (Hercules military transport) adapted for night barrages by sophisticated targeting devices. Gunships adopt a terrain-hugging approach and fire from the port side only, while circling. The successors to the World War Two gunship proved their formidable effectiveness in the Gulf War and Bosnia. Current versions have highly sophisticated sensing systems and devastating armament.

HE High explosive.

HEI High explosive incendiary.

Helo Helicopter.

Huey Bell 412–EP, four-bladed light medium support helicopter.

HUMINT Jargon for human intelligence — information collected by agents on the ground.

IBM Intermediate range ballistic missile.

ICBM Intercontinental ballistic missile.

IFR Instrument flight rules.

IO Illuminator operator.

IR Infrared.

IV Intravenous.

IW Information warfare.

Jackson Amendment Forbids the granting of MFN to nonmarket economy countries not permitting free immigration.

Jackhammer Combat shotgun with rotating magazine.

LAIRCM Laser-based version of DIRCM or Nemesis.

LED Light-emitting diode.

Light-set Technically, the illuminator assembly on a gunship.

LOX Liquid oxygen.

M1014 Assault shotgun.

M4 9mm Spectre sub-machine gun.

M4A1 Close-quarter battle weapon, replacement for MP5N sub-machine-gun — used by Marine expeditionary units.

M72A2 Anti-tank rocket launcher.

MAC Military Airlift Command, disparagingly called Mediocre Air Command.

MAD Mutual assured destruction.

Masked costs According to the USA General Accounting Office, in 2001, the sum of federal money unaccounted for was $17.3 billion.

MEMS Microelectromechanical systems.

MFN Most favoured nation status for trading.

MIA Missing in action.

Microsub safety Several manned microsubs and submersibles use the emergency separation system mentioned in the story. The cabin-sphere, freed of infrastructure, disengages and floats to the surface.

Milstar Extremely high frequency military, strategic and tactical relay satellites designed during the 1980s to provide anti-jam, low probability of intercept comms for vehicles, ships, submarines and aircraft. They have been significantly restructured and updated since then to provide much increased bandwidth and aggregate data capacity.

Miniguns Developed by General Electric as a smaller version of their Vulcan. Firing rate is around 4800 rounds per minute.

MIRV Multiple independently targetable re-entry vehicles.

Mk19 Automatic 40mm grenade launcher.

MO Medical officer. Also *modus operandi*.

Mongo Nickname of the Oscar — the largest and most heavily armed guided missile submarine known.

MP5 Heckler and Koch sub-machine-gun.

MP5K Shortest version of the MP5.

NASA National Aeronautics and Space Administration.

MUV Manned underwater vehicle.

natation Ability to swim.

Ngalops The Bhutia — largest of the country's three ethnic groups.

NOAA National Oceanic and Atmospheric Administration.

NOC In the CIA: nonofficial cover. Relates to specialist workers also recruited as CIA agents and generally hired through phoney front companies. NOCs are not listed as CIA staff.

NOD Night observation device. Basically an enormous starlight scope fitted to early gunships that magnified ambient light up to 38,000 times. Later replaced by low light level TV.

NORAD North American Aerospace Defense Command.

NRA National Rifle Association.

NRO National Reconnaissance Office.

NSA National Security Agency — the largest intelligence agency, and the most covert, in America. Concerned with worldwide electronic eavesdropping, code cracking and code preservation.

NSC US House of Representatives National Security Committee. Also the National Security Council — ostensibly the supreme authority in the USA for security/defence policy and coordination.

OOD Officer of the deck.

OPEC Organisation of Petroleum Exporting Countries.

Oscar-class A Russian SSGN — a guided missile craft designed to destroy carrier battle groups.

Paro Second major city in Bhutan.

PD Periscope depth.

PET Positron emission tomography.

PLF Parachute landing fall.

Plug Prefabricated section added to the hull of a vessel.

Prayer wheels A *chorten* or *stupa* with stone walls and the traditional roof. Prayer-wheel examples are generally open at the sides.

Predator An 8.2-metre UAV (unmanned air vehicle). Some are used for surveillance. Others launch precisely targeted missiles.

PTAs Palm top assistants. Some can link with cellphone networks.

Puzzle Palace A nickname for the Pentagon.

Rack Berth in a sub.

Rasit The Rasit 3190–B ground surveillance radar. Seeks movement along suspected enemy routes.

RBS70 Unpleasant laser-guided man-portable SAM.

RCV Remote controlled vehicle.

Rishis 'Seers of truth' — a name also applied to the sages who wrote the Vedas.

RN Royal Navy.

RNA Ribonucleic acid. In some viruses, RNA is the inherited material and self-replicates. It is more generally concerned with translating the structure of DNA into protein molecules.

SAM Scanning acoustic microscope. Also Surface-to-air missile.

Sans Souci Without care.

SAS Special Air Service.

SBIRS Space-based infrared system. Upgrades warning of ballistic missile launches.

Scrubbers In submarines, if efficient evaporators and enough spare power to run electrolysers exist, air can be fully recycled. Some boats use oxygen generators as backup systems.

SDI The strategic defence initiative.

SEAL Sea–air–land units of the US Navy.

SEM Scanning electron microscope.

SFM Scanning force microscope.

Shema Israel etc. Hear, Israel, the Lord our God, the Lord is One.

SIGINT Signals intelligence. Also designates the various satellites designed for this purpose.

Sitrep Situation report.

SLADS In early gunships, the side-looking aiming device that aligned the NOD with other on-board sensors and the pilot's electronic gunsight.

SLBM Submarine launched ballistic missiles.

SLEP Service life extension program.

SLR Side-looking radar.

Smerch A Russian designed MRS (multiple rocket system). Russian technology transfer to China is ongoing. China's other sources of expertise include France, Spain, Austria and Israel. China and North Korea also sell missiles and guidance systems to allies.

SMRT The US Air Force is looking at a Soldier Metabolic and Remote Telemonitor that uses lab-on-chip or nanosensors to monitor constituents in exhaled breath during combat. The US Army Research Office (ARO) is interested in carbon nanotubes for body armour with potential to increase ballistic protection 5–10 times.

SOSUS US Navy underwater sound surveillance system. Passive hydrophone detector arrays are deployed in Atlantic and Pacific oceans.

Spectre Association for crews and enthusiasts of the USAF C–130 gunship plus maintenance and support personnel.

SPM Scanning probe microscope.

SRF Russian strategic rocket forces — units that operate the country's ICBMs.

SSBN Nuclear-powered ballistic missile submarine.

SSGN Nuclear-powered guided missile submarine. The Oscar is in this class.

SSM Surface-to-surface missile.

SSN Nuclear-powered attack submarine.

Stinger Infrared man-portable air defence system. Successor to Redeye.

STM Scanning tunnelling microscope.

STOL Short takeoff and landing.

STRATCOM US Strategic Command.

Stringer Freelance journalist.

Sunyata The Buddhist doctrine of emptiness. The word is variously spelt in English.

Tallyho A code meaning 'target visually sighted'.

Taping magazines Taped opposite ways. During a firefight, the spent mag is reversed to slot the second into the gun. Three can be taped this way.

TDM Time division and frequency inversion are standard encrypting system techniques.

TMA Target motion analysis.

UFO UHF follow-on communications satellites used by the US Navy.

UGS Unmanned ground sensors.

Uzi Compact sub-machine-gun.

USAF United States Air Force.

Veep Vice President.

VLF Very low frequency.

Vulcan The M61 Vulcan, a Gatling design with six rotating barrels, delivered 20mm rounds at a variable 4000 to 7200rpm (rounds per minute). Each Vulcan, though capable of over 6000rpm, was geared down on A model gunships to 2500.

Waffen CIA Pentagon nickname for the CIA Special Operations Group's air arm.

WCSN Western commercial shipborne navigation.

Wiesel Light, mobile German tracked reconnaissance vehicle.

WSC Weapons stowage compartment.

Yak butter tea Yak milk is also used to make rock-hard cheeses such as *choogo*. In Bhutan, cubes strung like beads on a thread of black yak hair are still used as change after barter.

Zodiac Inflatable dinghy.

EXIT ALPHA
CLINTON SMITH

With heart-stopping action and suspense,
dangerous power plays and international
intrigue, EXIT ALPHA takes the thriller to
a new level.

When five superpowers — the US, Japan, Germany,
France and the UK — put their heads together in the
name of global political stability, the result is EXIT:
the most deadly and efficient intelligence agency the
world has ever known. EXIT specialises in the
removal and replacement of 'problematic' people —
be they political or religious leaders, scientists,
academics or those with extraordinary talents.

Ray Cain is EXIT's most skilled agent, a man
trained specifically for one long-term mission in
Pakistan. His task successfully completed, Cain now
faces retirement in exile.

Then he is recalled for a final assignment — a
project that should be straightforward. But
allegiances are compromised, promises are broken
and Cain finds himself at the centre of a gathering
storm on the most inhospitable continent on earth.

EXIT is about to combust, The stakes are high,
the players deadly — and there can be only one
winner.

'A fast-paced thriller containing sympathetic,
approachable characters. Highly recommended.'
— *Good Reading*